THE TRUTH OF THE MATTER

LEIGH FLEMING

The Truth of the Matter
by
Leigh Fleming

Published by Envisage Press, LLC
Copyright © 2021 Envisage Press, LLC
Cover by www.spikyshooz.com
ISBN: 978-1-7347380-2-5 Print

This is a work of fiction. All of the characters, names, incidents, organizations, and dialogue in this novel are either the products of the author's imagination or are used fictitiously.

In memory of Sally and Jonathan

CHAPTER 1

Like a ghost—floating, lingering, shadowing my every move—Father's words haunted me as I rushed down the street, breathing in the fetid, smoky air. The August morning was hot and sticky, and my dress clung to me like Father's hateful tone.

"You're just as stubborn. And your silly art...where will it get you, Laurel?"

Last night he had been on another rampage, reeking of whiskey, slurring his words as he ranted. I sat stiffly on the embroidered armchair, my gaze locked on the gas lamp's globe.

"That damned red hair and freckled face...so much like her."

Who in the world was *her*? If I'd asked, he would have slapped me. He'd done it before.

Reaching the corner, I hopped on the waiting horse-drawn streetcar and gripped the metal pole. We passed brick townhouses, one after another, all the same, until my vision blurred.

Father had never been affectionate, not like he was with Emily. He rarely complimented me, except when I played the piano at church on Christmas Eve. He saved his praise for Sampson and Elvin, and for Emily, whose pretty blue eyes and blond hair reminded us all of an angel.

When the streetcar stopped outside the mill, I barreled across the cobblestones, knocking elbows with the other workers heading to their respective positions. The mill was one of the multitudes of Philadelphia textile plants dotting the Delaware River, employing natives and immigrants alike.

Finally at my loom, surrounded by dozens of other women, young and old alike, all of us sweating in the dank mill, I forced Father's cruelty from my mind and daydreamed of the oil landscape I was creating in my art class. It needed something— perhaps a few birds frolicking above the tree lush with ripe peaches, or a touch of burnt sienna or dark umber on the trunk. I wasn't sure. Keeping the hillside, with its rambling stream and field smattered with daisies, fresh in my mind quelled the monotony of guiding newly spun yarn from a thick wooden spool onto a loom, and erased Father from my thoughts.

If only I could sit under that tree and breathe in the fresh summer breeze. The incessant rhythm of the loom—*a-click-a-clack-a-click-a-clack*—thrummed through the factory, a deafening sound that left my ears ringing. By the end of the day, it would be difficult to hear Mr. Ferretti explain a brush stroke or a shading technique.

Though work was monotonous and left my shoulders aching, my spirits were high. When the steam whistle blew, my ten-hour shift would end. I'd go to my sanctuary, the Philadelphia School of Design for Women, the place that gave me the greatest joy. Tonight was my oil painting class which was my favorite, but equally stimulating was the lithography class on Wednesday and Friday's wood carving, which was the most challenging. In seven months, I would complete my degree and take up work designing textiles. That would spell the end of my ear-ringing shifts at the factory.

Three short, shrill whistles announced our midday break and the cumbersome looms decelerated to a stop, leaving the cavernous warehouse quiet for the first time in hours. I rushed toward the outhouses, hoping to get ahead of the line so that I had more time to consume the sandwich Mother had packed for me that morning. On my way out the door, my shoulders brushed and bumped against other women with the same intention.

"Will ye be joining me today, Laurel?"

Cillian O'Brien's rich tenor voice shouted over the din. I turned to find the lanky, dark-haired Irishman forcing his way through the crowd to catch up to me.

"Would I sit with anyone else?" I replied with a laugh.

"Of course not. What was I thinking, eh?"

He wrapped his bony arm around my shoulder, pulling me through the scrum, and deposited me behind Sally O'Leary, who was waiting at the first wood-clad privy. Rancid odors from the outhouses hung heavy in the sweltering heat.

"I'll save ye a seat, eh?"

"Why don't ye save *me* a seat, ye mangy maggot?" Sally reached out and pinched his arm.

"I'll do that for ye, milady." Cillian tipped his hat, sketched a deep bow, and rushed away, narrowly escaping the spray of gravel Sally kicked up with her boot.

"That's a squirrely one, I'll tell ye. Best be leaving him alone. Not who ye want to take home to yer da."

"Cillian is my friend. There's no need to introduce him to my father."

"A pretty lass like you should be looking for a husband, am I right?"

"Please, Sally. Not again."

"You know I'm speaking the truth." She swung her blockish body around to face forward and nodded knowingly over her shoulder.

I had heard her opinions more than once as we stood at the outhouse or worked side by side at the looms. I had no intention of getting married. My sights were set on a career in design, and a husband and babies did not figure into that future. No matter how many times I argued, she insisted Cillian's interest in me extended beyond friendship. Only Cillian and I seemed to recognize the fact that our relationship was purely platonic. We were kindred spirits, with dreams beyond the humdrum of factory life.

I found Cillian sitting in the shade at the end of the bench, hunched over a slice of lamb and a bit of bread, chatting amicably with the workers across from him.

"Ah, there ye be. Sit yer bones next to mine."

"That sounded positively morbid."

"I didn't say yer dead bones, lass."

"Thank heavens." I gathered a fistful of calico and lifted my boot over the bench, sitting astride the seat before raising my other leg, as ladylike as possible, to the other side.

"So did you complete yer bonny painting?"

"How do you know it's *bonny*?"

"You showed me, don't ye recall?"

"Oh, yes." I had forgotten that I showed him the pencil sketch I'd done before transferring the scene to canvas. "Well, if you thought that was nice, you would be very impressed with the state it's in now. I have to add a few touches before I'm finished."

"And will I get to see this fine work?"

"Perhaps, if it's chosen for the art exhibit."

"And if it's not?"

"Perhaps I'll show you anyway."

I nudged my elbow into his ribs and received a blushing

smile in return. Though our gazes locked and his smile lingered, I knew Sally was wrong. Cillian and I had a kind of familial friendship—trusting, supportive, jovial. Besides, there was one thing Sally was right about—my father would never allow me to marry an Irishman "right off the boat"—as he referred to recent immigrants to the Philadelphia harbor. My father was proud of his Scots-Irish roots, mysterious as they were, and believed the best course for peace in this diverse city was for people to live among and marry their own kind. Thankfully, I didn't plan to marry—to my own kind or not. I had bigger dreams to fulfill first.

"So how is your invention coming? The...what do you call it?"

"The Brew Maker. It will cut beer production time in half." He chuckled as he ripped a hunk of bread with his teeth. "Never again will there be a shortage of beer."

"So this machine will brew a good stout, and faster?" Across from us, Billy Cramer burst forth with a hearty laugh, bringing the rest of the men nearby into his rousing guffaw. "I think you best come up with something else there, O'Brien, if you hope to get out of this place."

With a shake of his head, Cillian's shoulders curled forward and his ears burned red. He had so many ideas for contraptions and gadgets to make our lives easier. "We're on the cusp of a scientific revolution," he had said to me when he first told me of his inventions. He had come to America four years ago to make something of himself, and I for one would be the last person to squelch his dreams.

"Don't listen to him, Cillian," I whispered against his ear, picking up the scent of the oil he used to lubricate the automated handlooms. "Someday they'll buy a good stout brewed with a Brew Maker and wish they had invested in your company."

"From yer lips to God's ears, eh?"

Three quick whistles announced the end of our midday break. Knowing that in a few hours I would be on my way to school, I was anxious to get through the day.

AT FIVE O'CLOCK, MY HANDS ACHED FROM FEEDING YARN ALL DAY, and my brief break to eat a sandwich of cold meat and dry bread left me hungry. But the weariness was forgotten once I was out on the street, rushing toward the streetcar that would take me to the city center. Emily had promised to remind Father of my class and that I would return home by eight o'clock. For the past three years, he had grumbled in protest that I was wasting my time on a fool's errand.

"A lady's place is in the home, taking care of her husband and children, not scurrying after a career fit for suffragettes and old maids." This was his usual protest. Then he would point to my sister, quietly embroidering in the corner. "You don't see Emily running around the city, doing Lord knows what. She's learning a practical trade—sewing. I suggest you do the same."

I continued through the waning light and thick fumes from the factory smokestacks, working my way to the streetcar. It did no good to think of Father's hatred. There was nothing to be done about it, and it only put me in a foul mood.

"Laurel, wait up, please." Cillian jogged beside me, taking the cloth satchel holding my paints and brushes from my hand. "Did ye not hear me, lass? I've been callin' to ye like a squawkin' bird."

"That was you? I thought it was the nightingale singing to me from that tree, across the way in the square."

"So funny are ye? Maybe ye should join the troupe playin' at the theatre in town."

"Maybe I shall." I laughed at Cillian and looped my arm through his, memories of Father's rage forgotten.

"Ye know ye shouldn't walk alone at night."

"Yes, big brother, but you'll notice it's still daylight and I'm certainly not alone." We were surrounded by dozens of other mill workers rushing home. I chuckled as I tucked in tighter to Cillian. "I'm sorry, but I wanted to get ahead of the crowd."

"You're always in a rush, aren't ye now, lass?"

"I can't help it. You know how much I love my classes."

"Aye, I do."

We walked along the uneven sidewalk, the sound of several languages punctuating the throng. As we passed the glass factory, a group of Italian men sitting on the loading dock called out as we passed.

"Those buggers have no respect," Cillian mumbled as he glared at the men with their tanned skin and shiny black hair. "That's no way to speak to a lady."

"How do you know what they were saying? Do you understand Italian?"

"Well, I don't need to know Italian to understand that what they're sayin' is wrong." He stopped in the middle of the sidewalk, bumped and jostled by the people coming from behind, and pointed at the Italian men. They rattled off a string of words I was sure were obscenities while waving their arms at Cillian. I slipped my hand through his elbow and gave him a tug.

"Come now, let's not get in a fight this evening. You realize you're outnumbered."

"Well then..." He let me draw him away from the angry threats and shaking fists. "'Tisn't right, that's all I'm sayin', lass."

"Yes, Cillian, my dear, 'tis not right." Huddled against the crowd, we cackled at his bravado and hurried on our way.

The pair of horses came to a halt, stopping the streetcar a block from the school, and I leapt off amid a rush of people scrambling onboard to take my place. I was but a yard from the heavy oak door of the design school when I happened upon Mr. Ferretti.

"Good evening, Miss Whitman." His hanging jowls jiggled like a laughing walrus and his bushy eyebrows arched as if surprised.

"Good evening, Mr. Ferretti. Do you think this heat will ever let up?"

"By winter perhaps?"

"I surely hope we won't have to wait that long."

He cupped my elbow in his hand and guided me through the doors and up two flights of stairs to our classroom.

"You know, Miss Whitman, I'm quite taken with your landscape. Such lovely lines and excellent shading."

He led me across the room to my peach orchard, braced between the tension bars of the easel, awaiting my return. I was sure he could hear the beating of my heart, its rhythm not unlike the clacking of a loom. His ample chin rested between his thick fingers as he studied the colorful scene of a perfect spring day.

"Have you considered expanding your painting? Sort of a triptych? Wouldn't it be lovely to carry this further on either side, stretching the scene over two more canvases?"

"You mean paint what is happening to the left and the right of the peach tree?"

"Yes. It would make a most impressive display at the spring exhibition."

I was sure my thumping heart would explode from my chest at the mention of the spring art show. I'd had a few smaller pieces in past shows, but this canvas, over four feet wide, was already impressive in size.

"So, two more of the same width?"

"Yes, my dear. Perhaps a grist mill with a field of clover over here." He flicked his meaty hand to the left. "And a flock of sheep dotting the hillside over there." His hand tossed to the right and he turned to look at me with his bushy brows once again lifted high. "It would be the first thing our guests see as they enter the gallery space. What do you think of this idea?"

"Mr. Ferretti, I'm—I don't..."

"Surely, my dear, you wouldn't turn down this opportunity to create the central showpiece at this year's exhibition?"

"Oh, no, sir. I would be honored. I'm just not sure how I'll find the time, since I work six days a week at the mill and I have my other classes to consider."

"Good. Well, with that settled, I'm sure you will find a way." He patted my shoulder as if he had not heard anything I said and toddled off to the front of the room, where he began calling roll. I laid my hands against my burning cheeks, aware they must be assuming a strident shade of red.

Each year, a graduating student was chosen to create the piece of work displayed on the coveted central wall inside the entrance to the main gallery. This work was considered the masterpiece, the one against which all others paled, and I had just been given this incredible accolade. All I'd ever wanted was to learn and grow as an artist, never imagining such a distinction would be given to me. As I arranged my brushes on the small table beside my canvas, I conjured ways to tell my parents. My mother would be proud and beam with joy, but I would need to tread carefully with my father. The best I could hope from him, if announced at the right moment, was a lukewarm reception.

"Absolutely not. Isn't it enough you're out three nights a week, missing the family meal, not getting enough sleep? No, not one more night. Not one!" My father's baritone boomed against the plaster walls of the parlor, where my mother sat on the cane-back chair with her hands folded in her lap. Father paced a groove in the carpet. He hadn't been drinking when I arrived home but had been singing along with Emily as she played the piano. "I've been more than patient with your folly, learning to paint pretty pictures and draw horses with charcoal. For what? How, may I ask, will this help you find a husband and raise children?"

"Father—"

"And don't spout that propaganda that you can contribute to your family's coffers by earning money as a *designer*." He spat out the word as if it were poison on his tongue. "We both know you have about as much chance of being a designer as I have of becoming the police chief of Philadelphia." It hadn't seemed possible that he could shout any louder, but his voice managed to reach a volume every home along Frankford Avenue could hear.

"Please, Father—"

"You heard me, Laurel Rose. Not another word."

"Now dear, you have to admit it is quite an honor to—" He cut off my mother's meager attempt to defend me with a wave of his hand.

"Enough, Susan. I've heard enough."

"But dear..." My mother rose from her chair and took a timid step toward my father, her birdlike hand quivering in the air. "Laurel has worked very hard and this is a great achievement. Elvin escorts her home from her classes each evening. Perhaps he wouldn't mind two or three more nights. Just until she finishes the other two canvases."

"It's quite alright, Mother. I can find my way home."

"Walking the streets alone like a common harlot, mingling with the riffraff of the city? I should say not." Father's loud protest should have cracked the plaster walls.

"Calvin," my mother spoke at a soft, pleading tone. "Our

daughter—both daughters—are fine young ladies who should never be called such foul words. Please apologize to Laurel."

My father bellowed an audible breath and thumped his fist against his thigh. Mother was the only one who could calm him, if this state could be called calm. At best, his voice stepped back an octave and his language improved, but the underlying emotion—the thick, roiling rage—swirled like a dark, stormy sea around us.

"You know how I feel about this," he spouted between clenched teeth, turning toward my mother with his back to me. "She's just...so willful. Don't you see?"

"Dear," Mother said as she placed her hands on his broad shoulders and turned him around to face me. "Since Elvin brings her home on Mondays, Wednesdays, and Fridays, we will ask Sampson to do the same on the other evenings until she is finished. He is old enough now and would enjoy receiving a few coins for the errand."

Father puffed up like a bullfrog, drawing in a deep breath. "Fine. Sampson can walk you home. But—" his thick forefinger came within an inch of my nose "—you, young lady, will pay him for the courtesy, the same as you do Elvin. You may have received free admission to that God-forsaken establishment, but you will pay for the inconvenience to your brothers."

"Yes, sir."

"And you will give your mother another ten cents a week and eat all of what she saves for your dinner when you get home."

"Yes, Father."

"And you will attend worship both Sunday morning and evening. Do you understand?"

"Yes, sir."

"Fine. Get out of my sight." With a wave of his hand, I was dismissed to the bedroom I shared with Emily. As I mounted the stairs, I thought it had gone much better than I had imagined. Though it would leave me little from my meager earnings, the extra money paid to Sampson and my mother would be worth it. Father had only compared me to a prostitute and had but once mentioned finding a husband. Yes, indeed, it had gone much better than expected.

CHAPTER 2

This new schedule of working at the mill each day and painting in the evening left me exhausted by the end of the week, and all I wanted to do when I came home each night was fall on my bed and sink into a deep sleep. But one night, Father had other plans.

When Sampson and I came into the parlor, Father was sitting on the floral embroidered armchair in the corner. The only light in the room came from the oil lamp on the oak table beside him. He was smoking his pipe and held a tumbler of amber liquid in his hand. A cloud of smoke enveloped him.

"I was starting to worry about you two," he said without a speck of concern in his voice. In fact, the sarcasm in his words and the smirk on his face warned me there was far more on his mind.

"I had to wait on Laurel for a few minutes," Sampson said as he sat on the horsehair sofa. "She had to put away her paints."

"Laurel, you're not to keep your brother waiting. He's kind enough to—" He interrupted himself with a hearty belch.

"I'm sorry, Father. I—"

"Don't barge in, girl," he bellowed, rising unsteadily to his feet. He wobbled across the room, pointing his pipe at me. "When I said you were to be home by eight o'clock from this folly of yours, I meant eight o'clock. Not a minute later. Do you understand me?"

"Yes, Father." I slowly sidestepped toward the staircase, hoping to escape another one of his tirades. "I'll make sure to be ready next time."

"You're damn right, girl." He stumbled on a ripple in the carpet and landed his hip against the arm of the sofa, splashing his whiskey on the seat cushion. Sampson scrambled away and disappeared through the dining room to the kitchen as Father righted himself.

"I think I'll go to bed now. Good night, Father."

"Don't take another step. You haven't eaten the dinner your mother saved for you. Get in the kitchen."

"Yes, Father."

My stomach was in knots and I was sure I couldn't eat a bite, but I knew if I defied him, it could get much worse. With a tip of my chin, I walked toward the kitchen but was stopped when I heard him land on the sofa with a loud grunt. I turned to make sure he wasn't hurt, but found him glaring at me with pure hatred in his eyes.

"You're just like her." He slurped from his near-empty glass, never taking his eyes off me. "Same face, same high-and-mighty..." With a shake of his head, he drew on his pipe and continued to glare at me through the smoky cloud. "Doing what you please. Stubborn. Disrespectful..." The tumbler had only a drop left in it, but Father tilted his head back until it touched his shoulders, and he drained the glass before dropping it on the side table with a thump. He slowly rose to his feet, planting his beefy hand on the sofa arm. "Someday you'll get what you deserve. Someone will knock you off your pedestal and—"

"Father, I don't know what you're talking about."

His eyes bulged from their sockets and his mouth twisted, giving him the bearing of a crazed man. It was as if he were no longer talking to me, but a ghost only he could see.

"You believed him. Just a scoundrel. Should never have come. Hoarded what was mine."

Although fear made my body quiver, I was growing concerned for my father's mental state. I swiped my damp palms across my cotton skirt and took a tentative step toward him, not knowing how or if I should help. His words were slurred and he listed to the right as if he were experiencing an apoplexy. His tirade made no sense and I worried he would lose his faculties.

All at once, his spine straightened and his vision cleared. He dropped his pipe into an ashtray and smoothed his fingers over his mustache.

"Why are you standing there gawking at me, you twit? Get to your room." With that final, clearly spoken command, he walked toward the front door, lifted his coat from the tree stand, and went out into the night.

For the next two weeks, I charged ahead like a steaming locomotive, rushing to work each day for my ten-hour shift and then hurrying to school for classes and a chance to work on the two additional canvases, always making sure to be ready before Elvin or Sampson arrived to fetch me. Mr. Ferretti had moved my paintings to the back of the classroom, where three easels were aligned side by side to hold the canvases of my springtime triptych. Instead of a grist mill in the left-hand scene as he suggested, I decided to paint a lovely barn with chickens pecking in the yard. On the right-side canvas, I gave the lonely peach tree a whole orchard to keep it company, with a few sheep on the hillside. The barn was still only a pencil sketch, but the rows of peach trees were coming to life in shades of emerald, viridian, and oxide of chromium. As I added dabs of color and shading, I longed to walk among the dewy grass and smell the richness of the soil.

"Miss Whitman." Mr. Ferretti's booming voice shocked me out of my reverie, and as I turned, a drop of cerulean blue dripped off the end of my brush onto the toe of his leather boot.

"Quite a lovely—" He looked to the floor and I feared his bright red face was an indication of his displeasure with my clumsiness. I was quite wrong. A hearty guffaw burst forth from the depths of his belly and he shook his head, making his saggy jowls jiggle. "I guess it is unwise to sneak up on an artist at work."

"I'm very sorry, Mr. Ferretti. Let me—"

"Never you mind, dear. It certainly isn't the first time a dollop of paint has landed on my toe." He tipped his chin and raised his brows. "And it won't be the last. Now, let me have a good look at this masterpiece."

"It is far from a masterpiece."

"But it will be. Mark my words."

Warmth began at the base of my neck and travelled to the apples of my cheeks—I surely looked like a speckled tomato. One of the hazards of having an alabaster complexion dotted with freckles was the inability to hide my embarrassment. My cheeks were so warm I turned my back to him, pretending to study my work with great concentration.

"You've made quite a bit of progress. Have you been here every night?"

"Yes sir. Since your invitation, I've worked on the paintings each Tuesday and Thursday night and sometimes after class, only taking Sunday as a respite."

"Please don't burn the candle at both ends, my dear. You have plenty of time to complete your work."

"Yes, sir." How could I tell him I wanted to finish as quickly as possible before Father changed his mind and prohibited me from coming to the studio on my off nights? Since that awful encounter when I watched my father rant at his ghosts, I made sure to be home on time and to be especially helpful to my mother on Sundays. So far, I'd successfully avoided being alone with him. Lately, his incessant tirades had been focused on his discontent at work and not my paintings, which he considered foolish. I glanced at the regulator clock on the wall. Knowing my brother would arrive soon, I quickly closed my paints and plunged my brushes into a solution to soak overnight. Tomorrow I would escape once again to the lovely orchard to begin dotting the trees with a heavy harvest of peaches.

THE NEXT DAY, CILLIAN AND I WERE EATING OUR LUNCHES AT OUR usual table, surrounded by men from his department.

"So wouldn't ye know my rotatin' ramp is almost ready for a demonstration?"

"Your what?"

"Have ye not been listenin', lass? My rotatin' ramp. I told ye about it."

"Of course. I'm sorry, Cillian," I said around a yawn. It was all I could do to keep my eyes from slamming shut. Three weeks of nonstop work were taking their toll on my concentration. "I thought you were working on your Brew Maker."

"Aye, I was, but don't y'know I ran into a snag? The bugger kept overheatin', so I set it aside and went back to work on my ramp. This contraption holds much more promise, I'll tell ye that."

"Exactly what does this rotating ramp do?"

"It lifts and carries cargo, y'see. A leather strap turns a series o'metal rods, then—"

My face must have shown confusion. I was an artist, not an engineer.

"You think this little lass understands any of that, O'Brien?" Billy Cramer butted into our conversation with a wry grin and then turned his remarks to me. "Shouldn't you be sitting amongst your own kind? You know, the more gentler sex, if you will, where you can talk about babies and doily making and hair fripperies and such?"

"Well, if you must know Billy Cramer, I have no interest in talking about *fripperies*."

"A feisty one, aren't you?"

"You be leavin' Laurel alone, Cramer. If she wanted to talk about such frivolity, she would, wouldn't she? Just go back to mindin' yer own."

Cillian was right. The topics discussed by most of the women I worked with bored me almost as much as the monotony of yarn spinning. Their continuous gossip about the price of fabric on South Street, the most comfortable stays and corsets, and which loom operator was the most handsome nearly drove me mad. I preferred to talk with Cillian about his inventions, my artwork, and the ever-growing industry of our city.

"I guess it'd be best if you saw it for ye'self, don't ye think so?" He leaned his head toward mine, making sure Billy Cramer couldn't hear our conversation.

"Yes, I think I must, because I truly can't picture it. I'm sorry."

"No need to fret. Come with me to my workshop one evening and I'll show ye what I mean."

"Oh Cillian, I can't, not until I finish my paintings. I *must* finish them, and besides, my father won't allow me to go anywhere after work except straight to school, and certainly not alone."

"Well then, I'll call on ye Sunday afternoon and deliver ye

back home safe and sound."

Father would never allow me to go out unescorted with a man, even in the afternoon, and most especially not with an Irishman. All I knew of Fishtown, where Cillian lived, was that it was full of factories and docks and immigrants, a combination that would surely raise Father's hackles. Even if I asked Elvin or Sampson to take me, Father would forbid it.

"Sunday? No. That will never do. I have worship to attend both morning and night."

"And what of the hours in between? Are you praying to the Almighty during those hours as well?"

Cillian pressed the palms of his hands together and tipped his chin heavenward, the pumping of his shoulders and quiet laughter revealing his jest.

"You think you're quite funny, don't you?"

"Aye, I do at that."

I chuckled and took a drink of water from my tin cup. Cillian's humor faded and his face grew serious, as if he had something most important on his mind.

"Ye know, Laurel, I'm aware of yer need to finish those paintings, and wouldn't presume to compare their importance to that of my inventions..." He cleared his throat and kept his head tipped down, shielding his gaze from mine. "But it would mean a great deal to me if ye would come to my home to see what it is I've been workin' on."

When he turned his face toward me, I could see the sincerity with which he spoke and my heart burned knowing I had hurt him by refusing his invitation. His inventions were just as important to him as my paintings were to me, and he wanted to share them with me. There had to be a way to visit his workshop without Father finding out, but I had never defied him before. Frankly, I was frightened.

"Cillian, I do want to see your inventions. I do. I just don't know how it would be possible."

"Would ye be willin' to forgo a night of yer paintin'? Ye could walk with me to my home and then I'd ride with ye to the school on the streetcar so ye return safely before yer brother arrives."

"Would you? That's an awful lot of traveling on your part."

"I'd let you tramp along the waterfront without an escort, would I? What sort of lout do ye think me?"

"A very kind lout to bring me all the way back to school." While his face blushed pink, I chewed on my thumbnail, considering the chance that Father would find out I hadn't gone to the design school after work. As long as I was back by half past seven, before Sampson or Elvin arrived, he couldn't possibly know where I had been or how much effort I had put into my paintings. Neither brother stepped into the classroom when he came to walk me home. Both preferred to stand in the corridor, as if exposure to art were poisonous.

I had never been to Cillian's part of the city—the two of us living in opposite directions of the mill—and I was curious about where he lived. As long as we didn't dawdle and I returned on time, maybe I could go see his inventions without Father finding out.

"Perhaps on a Thursday?"

His head jerked back as if I'd splashed him with a bucket of cold water. An enormous smile spread across his face, making his pale blue eyes glow.

"I think a Thursday would be grand indeed, lass. Should we plan for it this Thursday, two days hence?"

"*Grand indeed.*" He laughed at my near-perfect imitation of his Irish lilt, and turned back to his meager meal. Though he looked contented, I niggled over how I could complete this journey without my father seeing the deceit on my face. Imagining his discovery and consequent anger made my insides turn sour, and I quickly lost my appetite.

CHAPTER 3

With each block we walked, the factories seemed to grow in number and size until we reached the riverfront, where large ships were berthed for repairs or unloading. The clanging of metal and pounding of wood, along with the briny smell of fish, heightened my senses to a part of the city I had only known through Cillian's stories. We turned left after passing the shipping warehouse and continued toward his home, making several more turns and passing row after row of brick townhouses. Though his neighborhood looked similar to mine, I noticed the houses here were smaller, more tightly packed like pickles in a jar, with very narrow alleyways behind.

"My house is up ahead, with the blue door." Cillian cupped my elbow as we crossed the narrow street, waving his hand at a group of men standing in a circle on the opposite corner.

"Why, who do we have here, Mr. O'Brien?" A lovely woman standing inside her doorway called to him. She had a baby perched on her hip and a toddler at her side.

"Ah, good evenin' to ye, Mrs. Murphy. Lovely time of night, wouldn't ye say?"

"'Tis indeed, Mr. O'Brien. You haven't answered my question."

"Yes, please forgive my rudeness, will ye? This..." Once again, he wrapped his large hand around my arm and led me to the bottom of her marble steps. "Mrs. Bernadette Murphy, may I introduce Miss Laurel Whitman, of the Kensington Whitmans."

"Oh, Cillian." My cheeks grew hot as burning coals when he introduced me as if my family were part of the aristocracy.

"Pleased to meet you, Miss Whitman. If you haven't already learned, Mr. O'Brien is quite a comedian."

"Yes, I have noticed."

"Laurel, Mrs. Murphy is the one I was tellin' ye about who makes the lovely drawings of flowers and trees and turns them into wallpaper."

Mrs. Murphy laughed, bouncing the baby on her hip, and waved her hand as if to brush away a puff of smoke. "Not exactly. *I* don't turn it into wallpaper, that's done at the factory. I create designs for the United Textile Company, over on Levy Street."

"Oh yes, Cillian told me. You graduated from the School of Design, am I right?"

"I was in the first graduating class."

"And you were able to start a career in textile design."

"I was. Would ye like to see my studio?"

"Could I?"

"It's in here, by the picture window."

Mrs. Murphy stepped into her house and waited as Cillian and I mounted the three steps to her threshold. We followed her through the foyer and there in the front of her parlor was a canvas perched on an easel with a scene of snowy white swans, tan reeds, and coral blooms, all on a black background. It was a beautiful design, one I pictured in my mind's eye repeated across a large wall in a very elegant dining room.

"Oh, Mrs. Murphy, this is beautiful."

"Thank ye. Please call me Bernadette, seeing as we're sisters of the same school."

"Yes. So you do this here in your home? You don't go into the factory to work?"

"No, I create my designs from home and once a month I take in several for Mr. Chalmer's consideration. He prefers I work from home because the factory is overcrowded as it is."

"And your husband doesn't mind?"

This amused her more than Cillian's earlier jest. She slapped her open palm on her knee and barked out a laugh. "Mr. Murphy knows better than to mind my work."

"Aye, Patrick knows who wears the pants in this family."

Bernadette gave Cillian's shoulder a slap as she continued to laugh. "Ye be mindin' yerself, too, Cillian O'Brien, before I box yer ears." She swiped a hand across her forehead and bent over to set the baby on the floor. When she stood back up, she captured my hand in hers. "What is it ye be wantin' to do with yer art, eh?"

"As it turns out, I want to do exactly what you do. I want to design wallpaper and carpets and drapery fabrics. It's the reason I went to the school, so I could get out of the weaving department."

"Well then, ye will. If ye want me to put in a good word for ye at United, I will be glad to do it. No matter. There are more textile mills in this town than ye can shake a stick at, so ye won't be having much trouble finding work."

"Thank you, Bernadette. I sincerely appreciate it." I gave her rough, dry hand a squeeze and then startled when a large grandfather clock chimed six loud gongs.

"We best be going, Laurel, if ye want to see my inventions."

"Ah, so that's why y'are visiting so late in the day. Cillian is going to show ye his discoveries, is he?"

"Yes, I've heard so much about them."

"Well, isn't he going to be a famous inventor one day?"

"Keep praying 'tis so, Mrs. Murphy."

With a light touch to my lower back, Cillian guided me toward the door and out into the warm evening air. The sun had sunk lower in the sky by the time we stepped off Mrs. Murphy's stoop and continued to Cillian's home three doors down.

"Would that be ye, eh, Cillian?" A woman's voice echoed from the back of the row house, presumably from the kitchen, while sounds of children laughing wafted from upstairs.

"That'd be my sister's kiddies upstairs," he said, guiding me down the hall.

A rich, beefy aroma filled the house, which was decorated with worn but comfortable-looking furniture adorned with lace doilies on the arms and backs. A stout woman in a gray print dress met us in the hallway, wiping her hands on a linen towel. Her silver-streaked hair was wound tightly in a bun and she had the same translucent blue eyes as Cillian.

"Oh, I wasn't expecting company." She stopped her trek and smoothed a few loose strands across her head. "Ye didn't tell me y'were bringin' home a friend."

"Ma, this is Laurel Whitman, from the mill. Laurel, my ma."

I extended my hand, delighted to meet Cillian's mother, who seemed embarrassed by my sudden appearance.

"It's a pleasure to meet you, Mrs. O'Brien." Her chubby hand was coarse, but its warmth and her delicate smile made me feel welcome.

"So, I'll be settin' another place?"

"Oh, no, thank you Mrs. O'Brien. Cillian just brought me to—"

"I'm showin' her my workshop, Ma. Laurel here is interested in what I've been workin' on."

"And so she should be. Y'are going to make something very necessary someday. Go ahead then. Be off with ye."

Cillian led me to a doorway tucked under the staircase, and I followed him down the narrow steps to the basement. Along one wall was a large shelf that held rows of canned vegetables and meats in blue glass jars, and bottles of what looked like beer.

"Are these from your Brew Maker?" I pointed in the direction of the dusty bottles.

"Ha! Oh no, that'd be some of my ma's elixir she makes to cure the fever or the grippe. But if I could get the bloody machine to work, it might help speed up her production."

We continued through a doorway at the back half of the basement. The dankness burned the inside of my nose as he lit a kerosene lamp. The room illuminated to a golden glow and I was taken aback by the number of *discoveries*, as Bernadette had called them, in various states of construction.

Tools of every type, screws and nails, and metal plates were scattered over the L-shaped workbench that stretched the length of two walls. I turned slowly, like a train engine in a roundhouse, and took in the magnificent machinery, the various purposes of which I couldn't begin to imagine.

"Here it is. The rotatin' ramp." Cillian scurried across the room and whipped off an old stained sheet covering his invention, like a magician revealing his trick. The machine was about three feet tall and twice as long. It was made of an intricate series of gears and pulleys, and a long strap of leather that wrapped around several metal bars in a continuous loop.

"It's lovely," I exclaimed, at a loss for another word to describe this unique contraption, like none I had ever seen.

"Lovely? You call this miracle work lovely? Do you know what it can do?"

"No—but please show me."

With that, Cillian bent over and inserted an S-shaped bar into a slot and threw his weight into cranking the bar until the leather strap started to move. His face was beet red and his lungs were heaving, but a smile lit up his face and I knew whatever this was, it brought him pure joy.

"Cillian, I'm impressed. It's so...so..."

He stopped turning the bar and stood up straight, perching his fists on his hips. "Please do not tell me it's lovely."

"It's impressive. Tell me what you can do with it? How did you think it up?"

"Well, like I told ye before, I noticed how much work went into loadin' up the ships down at the dock." He pulled an old wooden chair out of the corner, and pointed toward it as an invitation for me to sit. "The longshoremen heft the box or bale on their shoulders, and scurry one after the other up the ramp to the ship to deposit their cargo. I sit most Sundays on the wood bench there at the quay and ponder how to make that job easier, eh?"

"It makes perfect sense. Go on."

"So, I said to myself one day, what if that ramp were to move, to roll right over, so the men could put the bale on the ramp and *it* move the cargo to the deck of the ship, savin' their backs, ye see?"

"I do." As if a bright lamp had been lit inside my brain, I could finally envision what Cillian had been trying to explain to me for weeks. Most of his inventions sounded rather like a lark, but this one might have some practical uses.

"My da used to work on the docks and was stooped over like a cane before he died. That's why I never worked down there, but if I could find a way to help those men, y'know, wouldn't that be a balm to their struggles?"

"Yes, it would indeed." I scooted to the edge of my chair and ran my fingertips over the leather strap. A trace of oil coated my skin and I rubbed my thumb across my fingers, contemplating other uses for his machine. I could think of none but knew it could surely have many applications.

"Of course, my machine would need to be much larger if it

were to move heavy boxes and bales. And it would run by a steam engine, not by a crank. But I think I may have somethin' here."

"You certainly do, Cillian. Perhaps you should talk to one of the ship owners to see if he would be interested in financing a larger model?"

"Aye, I think I shall." He puffed out his chest, quite proud of himself. "Before long, you'll see Laurel, I'll be livin' in luxury like those folks there along Chestnut Street, bein' pulled in a handsome brougham, tossin' coins to beggars on street corners."

I joined in his laughter and rose to my feet, feeling a pinch from the cracked leather at my big toe. All that walking from the mill hadn't been good for my already-worn boots. "Try not to get ahead of yourself, Cillian. First you have to build an actual rotating ramp, big enough for use on the docks. Don't start spending your money before it's earned."

"Aye, ye have no worries there, lass."

"Well, it's getting late. Perhaps we should start back now and try to catch the streetcar."

"Perhaps we should. After you, milady."

As promised, Cillian delivered me to the front steps of the design school well ahead of Sampson's arrival. I bid him farewell and rushed upstairs to the classroom to find Thursday night's first-year students filing out into the hallway. I leaned into the throng, threading my way among students rushing to get home, and entered the empty classroom, hoping to appear as though I had just completed this evening's task. I applied a drop of azurite and saffron to the pallet and swirled a brush through the pigments, mixing them into the lovely shade of a ripe olive. Often, upon arriving home, I would find smudges of paint on the side of my hand or on the tip of my nose. To make

my evening's work convincing, I dipped a finger into the paint
and smeared it across my palm and cheek. After letting the
colors dry for a moment, I dampened a linen cloth with some
turpentine and attempted to remove the paint, making sure to
leave a trace of evidence.

Father could not possibly suspect I had been anywhere
other than the school when I arrived home with the tell-tale
sign of an artist who had worked hard on her craft that evening.
What I could potentially expect from him was a lecture on the
importance of keeping the paint off my clothing. *Our name isn't
Rockefeller and money doesn't grow on trees.* I had heard the
admonishment so often it haunted me in my sleep, so I was
always conscientious about wearing my artist's frock when I
worked.

As I was about to close the draperies at the large window, I
heard footsteps enter the classroom. I turned to find Sampson
scowling at me from the doorway.

"Where have you been, Laurel?"

CHAPTER 4

I released a high-pitched squeak at the sound of Sampson's voice. His knitted brow and the thin line of his lips reminded me of Father as he stepped into the room. I prayed he wouldn't notice my thumping heart through the bodice of my dress.

"Oh heavens, Sampson, you startled me. I've been right here working on my painting, see?" I swung my arm toward my triptych, keeping a sweet smile on my face. "Why do you ask?"

"I looked in the classroom a few minutes ago and you weren't here."

My hand quivered at the base of my neck as I tried to think of a plausible explanation.

"Why, I stepped outside for a few minutes to catch a breath. It was quite stifling in here earlier with all the students crowded in the room."

"But the wind's blowing something fierce."

"Yes, and it felt good to me. I was quite flush. You're here early."

"I needed to get out of the house. Father was in another one of his snits, complaining about his boss, the union, the city council. I told him you asked me to fetch you early."

"And if I wasn't ready to go and we didn't arrive home before eight o'clock? What would I tell Father then? Did you think of that?"

"I figured you would think of something. You always do."

I turned to leave the room with my satchel in hand, but Sampson didn't follow. Instead he wandered around the room, stopping at each painting, studying them closely. I waited in the doorway until he was ready to leave.

"And you say you can get a job doing this?"

"Well, not exactly this, though I might sell a painting or two. No, what I learn here will be used to design wallpapers, carpets and such."

"Huh. Father says you're wasting your time. That the duties of a wife and mother don't leave time for such foolishness."

"Well, I happen to know a wom—" Thankfully I caught myself before I blurted the fact that I had met Mrs. Murphy, who performs her wifely and motherly duties, and has a fruitful career. If I had spilled that information to Sampson, it might get back to Father. I couldn't let him know where I had been tonight.

I cleared my throat and continued. "That is to say, I happen to know many women make designs while fulfilling their duties as wives and mothers."

"And they get paid for this?" Sampson waved his arm at a painting of a magnolia tree in a city square.

"Yes, as a matter of fact they do."

"Well I'll be," he said, turning toward the door and scratching his head, as if I had told him women could sail passenger ships or sit on the Supreme Court.

We walked out into the night and silently made our way home, not knowing what might await us. Fortunately, when Sampson and I arrived, Father had spent all his energy railing against his boss and union, and had fallen asleep on the sofa with the newspaper folded across his lap. A whiskey glass stood empty on the table beside him.

A MONTH HAD PASSED BEFORE I ACCOMPANIED CILLIAN AFTER work to talk to the dock foreman about his rotating ramp. I had grown bold since successfully going to his home without Father finding out. The week prior, we had walked to the docks after work so that I could observe the longshoreman in action. Cillian's invention would relieve the men of their heavy loads and save their backs from permanent ruin.

After being dismissed by the foreman, we sat on a bench alongside the warehouse, sharing a bag of peanuts Cillian had bought for two cents outside the mill. We watched the men march one after another like an army of ants, up the ramp and back down again. Their backs became more stooped with each load.

"Don't give up. Your invention is the answer to these poor men's struggles."

"And it would speed up the process as well, ye see."

"It's pure genius, Cillian."

"Aye, I think so. If only I could convince the boss."

He may not have made any headway with the dock foreman, but I encouraged him to speak with the ship owner or the manufacturer of the goods being transported. In the meantime, he needed to look for other uses for his amazing machine.

"Don't ye worry, lass. Shippin' isn't the only use for my invention. It can be used in all sorts of factories, even at the mill. Once it catches on, I'll be dinin' with the Vanderbilts and Astors."

"And will have no time for me."

"Nah, not true. I'll always have time for ye. 'Tis you who

won't have time for me, what with yer paintin' and designin'. Before you know it, yer creations will be featured in the new art museum they built for the centennial."

"One can dream."

"Think of it, Laurel." He dropped the paper bag of nuts on the bench with a thump and turned to me, bright-eyed and eager. He gathered my hands in his as a huge smile spread across his face. "I'll sell my contraption to every shippin' company, factory, and mill along the Delaware. Create a company the likes of which folks will be clamorin' to work for. I'll pay my men well and treat them fairly."

"You'll be a wonderful boss."

"And ye'll be the talk of all Philadelphia society—maybe even New York—with yer paintin's hangin' in the great galleries, hobnobbin' with the wives of my compatriots."

"Compatriots?"

"My peers, ye know. They'll be invitin' the two of us to their high-and-mighty dinner parties."

"The two of us?"

"Why, yes. We'll be so famous and successful, everyone will want us at their fancy gatherin's."

I leaned back against the warehouse wall, laughing until tears sprouted in my eyes. "Oh, Cillian, you have the most amusing imagination."

"'Tis no joke, lass." He snatched his hands from mine and stood up. His slim face turned crimson and his blue eyes turned to dark pools. "Ye may not have faith in yer talent, but I do. And I damn sure have confidence in my inventions. I didn't bring my family to this country to work in that stinkin' mill the rest of my life. I'll make somethin' of myself, that's for sure, lass."

I really needed to stop laughing. I'd obviously hurt his feelings, but I couldn't help myself. I delighted in his Irish lilt when he was so animated. His exasperation had brought an attractive bit of color to his usually pale complexion.

"Cillian, please." I swiped the dampness from my eyes and jumped to my feet. "I'm sorry. I wasn't laughing at you, truly." When he turned his back to me, I scurried around to face him. "I believe you. You *will* be a famous captain of industry in the very near future, I know it."

"Don't mock me, lass."

"I'm not. Please believe me. I have every confidence you will go far in this world." He still wouldn't look at me, keeping his eyes locked on the riverfront. "I laughed because my dreams aren't quite as big. My paintings will not hang in great art galleries. I'll just be happy to have a job designing wallpaper, like I've set out to do."

"It doesn't hurt to dream big, Laurel."

"For you, maybe, but it's a little harder for me to dream beyond what I know is possible."

He tore his gaze away from the river's current and glanced down at me, his eyes narrowed and countenance serious. "I guess I'll have to do the dreamin' for the two of us."

THE NEXT EVENING, BACK AT THE DESIGN SCHOOL, I STOOD a good distance from my work and studied the small details. I had finished the peach orchard on the right-hand canvas and decided a bit of shading was needed on the barn on the left. Adding a wagon and a rooster to strut among the chickens made the scene come to life, and I longed to sit atop the wagon's seat and be carted away through the orchard.

"My, my, Miss Whitman. Your project is coming along quite nicely, isn't it?" Mr. Ferretti had been strolling about the room, checking on my fellow students' progress, giving advice when needed. "Why, this creation could rival that of Alden Weir or Winslow Homer."

"Mr. Ferretti, surely you can't be serious. Mr. Weir and Mr. Homer are, well, their work is—"

"Only slightly better than yours." He gave me a wink and his jowls jiggled as he walked away, quietly laughing to himself. Mr. Ferretti had always handed out compliments freely regarding my work, but in this case, he surely spoke in jest. Still, warmth flared in my chest, spreading to my cheeks, and I couldn't help but feel proud of his comparison.

Too excited to continue painting, I quickly cleared my workspace and covered the canvases with a cotton sheet. I would wait for Elvin to arrive outside on the school's steps and hope the evening's brisk air would cool my cheeks.

On the sidewalk, I drew my shawl tightly around my shoulders as the dwindling crowd hurried down Filbert Street to the streetcar waiting at the end of the block. Summer had ended and the brisk air of autumn had taken its place, clearing the humid stench that had hung so heavily in the heat. Occasionally, a gentleman passing by would tip his hat or give a curt nod acknowledging my presence, but for some strange reason, the tiny hairs at the base of my neck stood out. It had nothing to do with the cool evening. I was being watched—I knew it. Several times in the past weeks, I had felt as though I was being stalked or spied upon. Even when Cillian and I had sat along the dock, my senses had been on high alert. Perhaps it was guilt from lying to my parents or the fear of getting caught. I'd heard some of the ladies at work talk about ghosts, feeling a presence in their homes or sensing bad news was about to arrive, and I'd always laughed off their notions as foolishness. Perhaps they weren't foolish after all. Or perhaps I'd listened to their stories for too long. All I knew was tonight, as I stood outside the school, with the cool October night surrounding me, a set of eyes was indeed watching me.

I stepped toward the cobblestone street and leaned out to look one way and then the other. There were phaetons and carriages rolling toward Penn Square and several people walking along the brick sidewalk. No one was skulking about among the buildings lining the street, but the sensation stayed with me nonetheless.

With a snap of my head to clear my mind, I squared my shoulders and climbed to the top of the stairs to wait for Elvin inside the entryway of the school. The long days and little sleep were surely causing my mind to play tricks on me. I was relieved when Elvin's tall, lanky form strolled down Filbert Street.

Arriving home, we came into our parlor, warm and inviting after the long stroll. The fireplace was ablaze and the scent of roasted meat from the evening meal lingered in the air. Mother was reading one of her ladies' magazines by lamplight and Emily was writing in her journal. The soft strain of violin music filtered from upstairs—Sampson was busy practicing a recently learned sonata.

"Well, there you are." Mother put down her magazine and greeted us with a smile. Dark circles hung below her eyes and her lids drooped. She hid a long yawn behind her hand while arching her back. "How was your day, Laurel?"

"It was fine. Mother, why don't you go off to bed? You look exhausted."

"I will soon. I'm waiting for your father to return."

"Where is he?" I asked as I draped my shawl over a metal hook on the tree stand already swallowed up with coats and hats. "Surely he isn't working tonight."

"Apparently so. He's investigating some sort of goings-on at one of the factories. Of course, you know your father can't discuss the details of his work."

As a patrolman on the police force, Father was often called out at night should there be a disturbance at a factory or the docks. His days were typically spent patrolling a twelve-block area around Kensington, keeping the peace and providing a sense of security to those who feared the influx of so many recent immigrants to our city.

For me, it was a welcome relief to come home to the serenity of a warm greeting followed by a hot meal, rather than the railings of a man who condemned my decision to make a better life for myself. With any luck, he would be gone late into the night and I would be sound asleep by the time he returned.

MONDAY MORNING, AFTER A FULL DAY OF REST ON SUNDAY, LESS the two worship services I attended, I was rejuvenated and clear-headed as I worked through the monotony of feeding yarn onto the loom. My bladder was causing uncomfortable pressure in my lower abdomen and I prayed the whistle would blow a few minutes early. Not long after, my prayers were answered, and I rushed to relieve myself before meeting up with Cillian at our usual spot for the midday meal.

When I arrived at our table, Cillian wasn't there, but Billy Cramer was, and he began his needling with a wicked smile on his face.

"Looks to me like your man isn't coming today. I'm honored, though, that you chose to share your meal with me."

"Where is Cillian? Did he come to work today?"

"Haven't seen hide nor hair of him. But he said if he's ever not available, I'm to see you safely to the streetcar after work, so you've not a worry."

"I'll see myself to the car, thank you very much." I snapped my head around to see if there were any open seats with the ladies from my department, but their table was filled to bursting. I didn't believe for one minute that Cillian had asked Billy to escort me to the streetcar. He saw the way the Billy leered at me. A shiver coursed down my spine whenever he spoke directly to me. Though Billy was a married man with five children, rumors flew around the factory about his indiscretions with young, unwitting girls.

"No one will see ye to the car but me, ye hear me, lass?" All the pent-up air released from my lungs when Cillian's long legs appeared. I watched him climb over the bench and plop in his seat. "Mind yer manners, Billy."

"What could be more mannerly than to see the little lady safely on her way?"

"Aye, if it were anyone else, Billy Cramer, I'd say ye were right." Cillian glared at him but only received a hearty chuckle in return. With a final glare and a flip of his hand, Cillian dismissed Billy and turned his attention to me.

"I'm thinking we should go to the Hippodrome to see the Wild West Show. They're performing only one more evening this week and then the show moves on."

"Oh, Cillian, that would be wonderful. I've seen the posters around town and I've longed to see Annie Oakley shooting her guns." I pointed my fingers at Cillian, pretending to shoot, and then blew away the imaginary smoke. "How long do you suppose the show lasts? I would have to be back at the school in time."

"One of the men in my department went last night and said it was but ninety minutes. If we hurried, we could squeeze it in and have you back in time."

A million thoughts swirled through my mind as I looked at Cillian's broad smile and thick brows raised in anticipation. His enthusiasm, and my own desire to attend, made it hard for me to think of a reason not to go. Again, I would have to lie to my parents regarding my whereabouts, but so far my other secret adventures—the trip to Cillian's home and two evenings spent at the dock—had gone undetected. My paintings were nearly finished, though my father didn't know it, so if I took off one more night and returned on time, he would be none the wiser. How could I pass up Annie Oakley?

"I'll go. What night is it?"

Cillian's shoulders sagged in relief and his lips spread into an even bigger smile, if that were possible. "Friday evening. If we go directly, without diddling along, we can secure tickets and find a seat without a worry, eh?"

"Rest assured there will be no *diddling along* on my part."

FRIDAY COULD NOT HAVE ARRIVED SOON ENOUGH. EACH DAY, I slogged through my work and hurried to school for classes or to work on my paintings, which at this point only needed a few more details. Perhaps one more evening to apply a bit more shading or a touch of illumination, and I believed my painting would be finished. The only step left was to come up with a name for the idyllic scene I had created. Cillian was quite witty. Perhaps he could come up with a title even though he had yet to see it beyond the few sketches I had shown him.

The whistle signaling the end of my shift startled me out of my thoughts and I quickly shut down my machine, scurrying off to meet Cillian in front of the factory. He joined me outside a few minutes later, bundled in his wool coat and cap, and we ran to the streetcar waiting three blocks from the factory. As we drew near, a white cloud puffed from the horses' nostrils as they put the car in motion. We leapt aboard with mere moments to spare.

"We made it by the skin of our teeth, eh?"

"Yes, just in time." I pressed my palm to my chest, hoping to calm my heavy breathing. I wasn't used to running three blocks, let alone jumping onto a moving car, but Cillian's strong hand around my arm kept me by his side despite his long-legged pace. We held tight to the cold metal pole—we had to stand since there were no open seats remaining—pressed shoulder to shoulder with the other riders. We could have walked to the theatre but would never have made it for the start of the show, since it was well thirty blocks from the mill.

After purchasing our tickets—fifteen cents each, much more than we could afford—we found a seat in the center of the third row in the balcony. The view from above was spectacular. The theatre walls were painted garnet and adorned with gold-painted cherubs and scrolled accents. Crystal gas lamps illuminated the theatre from the orchestra level to the third balcony. From our vantage point, we watched the last of the spectators arrive at their high-priced seats below, the ladies dressed in heavy fur coats and hats adorned with feathers and ostrich plumes, and men in tailored coats and top hats.

Cillian was watching, too. His long neck stretched to its limit as he gazed about the theatre. "See there, Laurel? The man in the sack coat? I believe he's a bit underdressed, wouldn't ye say?" The man was actually wearing an elaborate military jacket adorned with medals and colorful bars signifying his heroic deeds—a general, perhaps, from Mr. Lincoln's war.

"Completely inappropriate." I giggled and pointed out a woman in a stunning velvet bonnet with a bushy white plume tucked into a bright red bow. "And what of her? A lady of the night, perhaps?" We broke into a fit of laughter and those around us turned to stare. I highly doubted she was anything but a blue blood from the Mainline, married to a captain of industry who considered tonight's performance just another distraction. For Cillian and me, it was a special event neither of us had ever experienced and wouldn't soon forget.

"Ah, I forgot to tell ye, I spoke with Mr. Helmut Schumer last evening."

"Who?"

"The owner of the shippin' line. The one with the hard-headed foreman who wouldn't give me the time of day. Went right over his head, I did."

"Oh, Cillian." I turned in my seat and gripped his arm, squirming with anticipation. "What did he say? Was he interested in your ramp?"

"He was quite curious. We're to meet later in the month after he returns from a business trip to Boston."

"That's exciting. I'm so happy for you."

He glanced down at my hands still holding his arm, and a deep blush flooded his face. I gave him a smile, tucked my hands back in my lap where they belonged, and turned as a performer on an enormous stallion galloped bareback across the stage. What an exciting night this turned out to be.

The performance lasted exactly one hour and we were able to reach the design school, only four blocks away, in plenty of time.

"There ye be, lass. I delivered ye on time."

"With a few minutes to spare. Thank you, Cillian."

"Well then..." He scuffed his toe against a pebble, sending it skittering down the brick walk. "I guess I'll mosey back home now. Good evenin', Laurel." He tipped his cap and turned to leave, but I grabbed the itchy wool of his coat sleeve.

"Wait, Cillian. Would you like to see my painting before you go?"

"Aye." He turned back round, a smile playing on his lips, and bowed deep with a wave of his arm. "Lead the way, milady."

When we reached the entryway, a wave of female bodies all chatting at a fever pitch pushed us back against the brick building, where we waited until the last of the first and second-year students were out on the sidewalk.

"I don't believe I've heard such a loud twitterin' in all my days. We were nearly stampeded by the lot."

"They're just happy to go home, I guess."

Other than the need for a meal and a good night's sleep, I was rarely pleased to leave the school. The nights Father chose me as the focus of his dissatisfaction were always the hardest. I could barely wait to graduate, start a new career, and make enough money to move into a boardinghouse, where I could make my own rules without the scrutiny of my father's discontent.

My triptych was right where I had left it, draped in faded white sheets along the back wall of the room. As we wove our way through the canvases, Cillian lifted the drapes to peek at the other creations in various stages of completion. He didn't comment, but I could see by the way he raised his brows or puckered his lips if he liked the painting. By the time he had made his way to the back of the room, I had removed the coverings and stood silently, waiting for his reaction. It had been worth the wait.

"Laurel." My name came out on a whisper and his eyes grew to the size of saucers as his mouth dropped open in amazement. After what seemed like hours, he closed his mouth and stepped closer, first to the painting of the barn, and worked his way slowly across the three canvases, his eyes roving over every inch. He still hadn't spoken and I twisted my hands into pretzels until I could wait no longer.

"Well? Are you going to keep gawking like that or are you going to say something?"

"There are no words, lass." He swiveled his head in my direction and the lamplight caught the glimmer in his eyes. "It's a bona fide jewel. A masterpiece of the highest order."

I burst out laughing at his expression of utter astonishment, folding in half and resting my hands upon my knees. Cillian's look of awe was quite comical to behold.

"That's the way of it, is it? I give ye a compliment and ye dare to laugh at me."

"I'm sorry, it's just..." I couldn't get my giggles under control. His face had gone from the paleness of amazement to the flush of embarrassment.

"Are ye makin' fun of me, lass? Just because I called yer paintin' a treasure to behold?"

"Cillian, you humor me so." I broke into another fit of laughter and he wrapped his large hands around my upper arms, pulling me so that our noses were nearly touching.

"Ye see if I give ye another ounce of praise, Laurel Whitman. Laughin' at me like a bloody hyena."

"I'm...I appreciate it." I continued laughing as he gave my body a playful shake.

"Sounds as though you're makin' fun of me, eh?"

"Never." By this time, he joined in my merriment and he dropped his hands from my arms and administered pinches to my waist, tickling my sides into another round of giggles.

"Cillian," I said between fits of laughter. "Stop."

"This is what ye get for laughin' at me."

"I wasn't—ooh—Cill— "

"Laurel Rose Whitman." Father's deep baritone voice reverberated off the walls and our hijinks stopped at once. "Get your hands off my daughter, boy!"

CHAPTER 5

"Father!"

Seeing his broad shoulders filling the door, his protruding stomach rising and falling with each heavy breath, and the furious scowl on his face made me stumble back against another student's canvas, knocking it to the floor.

"You filthy Mick. Get your hands off my daughter." He stalked across the room, bumping artwork aside with his bulk, and came within inches of Cillian.

"Sir, I—"

"What the hell are you doing manhandling my daughter?"

"Father, please. We were just laughing."

"Get the hell out of here, you dirty bogtrotter!" He shoved Cillian aside and turned his rage on me.

"And you, like a common whore, throwing yourself at this, this vermin. I knew you'd been lying to me."

"No, Father."

"Don't argue with me, girl. Get your lying ass home." He pushed me with such force I landed on my hip several feet away. An easel toppled over me, pinning me in place.

"Sir, I beg of ye."

Cillian grabbed hold of my father's arm, attempting to pull him away from me. His efforts were fruitless. My father surpassed him in size and girth, and Cillian had no weapon to defend against the billy club Father pulled from his belt.

"Get back, you mangy Mick, before I beat the pulp out of you."

"Cillian, go, please," I begged as I lifted the easel off my legs and slowly stood up. "Please."

"I can't leave ye here like this, lass." I appreciated Cillian's worried eyes and outstretched arm but knew he didn't stand a chance against my father.

"I'll be fine. Please go."

"You heard her, you slimy sluggard. Get out before I make you." Father raised his weapon and stepped closer to Cillian.

I beseeched him silently, mouthing *please* before Father threw his rage into beating the life out of him.

Cillian picked his cap off the floor, slapping it against his thigh, and rushed out of the room without another glance. My hand quivered at the base of my neck as my father turned his wrath on me once again.

"So that's the way of it. You lie to me about coming to this blasted school when it's just an excuse to carry on with the likes of that boy? You trashy slut."

Before I could defend myself, his broad hand crashed against my cheek, knocking me again to the floor.

"Throwing yourself at a man not worthy to lick your boots." He kicked my buttocks with the toe of his boot and I howled in pain. "That's right. Go ahead, scream. Scream all you want. You think I didn't hear those shouts coming from your room?"

Father stomped away and turned back to me, his eyes glazed over as if he'd forgotten where we were and who he was speaking to. "I saw you. I knew what you were up to. Whoring. Bearing that devil's child."

"Father, I don't know what you're talking about."

"Shut your mouth!" At least he hadn't forgotten I was here. After he yelled at me, he rushed back to where I still lay on the floor and grabbed my arm so brusquely I thought my shoulder would rip from its socket.

"You've been lying to me for weeks. I knew you weren't here. Been keeping my eye on you. Waiting for the right moment to catch you at it."

"You've been spying on me?"

So my feeling of being watched when I stood outside the school hadn't been my imagination. How long had he been following me? Did he know I had gone to Cillian's house and to the Wild West show, too?

"You, just like her, whoring around with the likes of which —" He interrupted his thought with two quick slaps to my face, snapping my head back between my shoulders.

"I should throw your lying, whoring self onto the streets. See how long you last."

"Father, please."

"Out where the likes of you belong. Just like her."

"Who? Who are you talking about?"

"My whoring mother, that's who." He cupped my shoulders in his large hands and shook me so hard, my teeth clattered. "If it weren't for the whore who birthed me, I'd have sworn you weren't mine. But you look exactly like her."

I had heard this complaint from him hundreds of times. Elvin and Sampson had dark hair and dark eyes like my father, and Emily looked like Mother, but my hair was red and my eyes green. Before gray streaks had taken over my mother's hair, it had been blonde and she had blue eyes. With my height nearly as tall as that of my brothers, I looked nothing like my parents. But I'd always been told I looked like *her*—and now I knew *she* was my grandmother. I should have known. Anytime one of us asked about Father's parents, we were hushed immediately.

"Father, you don't understand. Nothing was going on here

tonight with Cillian. I was just showing him my paintings. Let me show you."

"No! Not another word. You're done here."

"But Father—"

"You will not step foot through these doors another day. You hear me? You'll go to work every morning and return home directly every evening. And you'll turn all your wages over to me. I've had enough of this nonsense."

"No Father, I won't."

It did no good to stand up to him. He answered my declaration with the back of his hand and I stumbled to the floor.

"Get up!" He bellowed and wrenched my wrist, forcing me to stand. "You will not end up like her, do you hear me? No daughter of mine will whore herself with an *immigrant*." He spat out the word, and with his hand tight around my arm, dragged me down the stairs, past shocked students and instructors, and out onto the street.

By the time we arrived home, my throat burned from fighting back the tears in need of release. There was no way I'd give my father the satisfaction of watching me sob from the knowledge he hated me—all because I looked like his mother. But it wasn't only my appearance. He implied I was just like her, and I got the impression she had done something sinful with a man he did not approve of. What of her husband—his father? Where was he in all this? My father never mentioned his name and never included him in his hateful rants. In what way was I so like the mother he despised?

My mother met us inside the door, wringing her hands in her floral apron. Her face went pale when she saw me. Were there marks on my face where his hand had landed? Could she see the tears about to fall?

I draped my cloak on the hall tree and rushed up the stairs, not bothering to eat whatever meal my mother had saved me.

My appetite had been beaten out of me and all I wanted to do was fall apart in the privacy of my bedroom.

I flopped onto my bed and buried my face in my pillow to muffle the screams and sobs wracking my body. How could a man hate his daughter so? He doted on Emily and roughhoused with the boys, but never in my life had he said a kind word to me or chucked me under the chin with affection.

"Oh, you're home." Emily entered the bedroom we shared and didn't seem to notice my face hidden in the pillow. I could hear the squeak of metal springs as she sat upon her bed. "Why did Father go get you?"

I couldn't answer. I continued crying out all the sadness and frustration my father induced in me. Finally, she seemed aware I wasn't responding to her question and I felt her weight on the edge of my mattress.

"Laurel, what's wrong? What happened?"

Emily grunted as she forced me onto my side—I so wanted to be left alone. Through the blurriness of my tears, I saw my little sister gazing down on me with concern.

"Why are you crying? Your face—what did Father say?"

My father's shouts and bellows filtered up to the second floor, and I knew by my mother's tone that she was trying to defend me. It would do her no good to argue with him. Whatever he thought of me and my grandmother couldn't be changed. The slam of the front door brought the sound of footsteps running up the staircase. My mother threw open my door, shoved Emily out the way, and perched on my bed, where she gathered me in her arms.

"Laurel, darling," she said, smoothing her hand over my tangled curls while rocking me to and fro.

After a few minutes of comfort, I leaned out of her grasp and wiped the tears from my cheeks.

"Why does he hate me so, Mother?"

"He doesn't hate you, Laurel," Emily said, sitting beside our mother.

"He does, Emily. Has he ever spoken to you the way he does me?"

"Emily, dear, please go downstairs. I want to talk to Laurel alone."

"But Mother—"

"No arguments." Mother held up her finger and tapped sweetly on Emily's lips. "Do as I say now."

Emily grumbled her discontent and stomped out the door.

"Tell me. Why? Why does he hate me? Why does he think I'm like my grandmother?"

"He told you that?" Mother leaned back with surprise, her mouth dropping open.

"Yes."

"What exactly did he tell you?"

"None of it made sense. He called me a who—who—" It was difficult to say the word. But my mother had to know. "Whore. That's what he called me."

"Oh, Laurel."

"When he came into the classroom, I was there showing my friend Cillian my paintings. Father raised his billy club and threatened to beat him with it."

"Oh, my dear." She tugged me against her breast and rocked me again in her motherly love.

"He called me vile things, none of which are true. I'm not a wh—I'm not a bad person, but Father seems to think I'm nothing but trash. Why?"

"Well, Laurel..."

"He said I act like her and look like her. His mother, my grandmother. Why? Have you met her? Tell me about her, please."

I had to know about this woman who, for whatever reason, brought my father's blood to boil.

"Do I look like her?"

"Well, yes, you do. Of course, I didn't know her when she was your age, but she has the same red hair, the same freckles, and she's tall like you."

"What is she like? What did you think of her?"

"I only met her once and the occasion didn't go well."

"When did you meet her?"

"At your Aunt Sarah's wedding."

"Not at your own wedding?"

"No, dear. Your father would never have allowed her to attend."

THE NEXT MORNING AS I READIED FOR WORK, I FILLED A carpetbag with three dresses, a bonnet, and four pair of stockings and stuffed it under my bed. Emily and I were responsible for keeping our room clean, so I knew my mother wouldn't find it. Today was payday, so I had to go into work to collect it. Overnight, I had decided that until I met my grandmother, the woman who looked so like me and had wronged my father, I would never be able to earn his love and respect. Understanding why I inspired such hatred was more important to me now than my unfinished triptych. So that night, after everyone went to sleep, I would run away to find the woman who caused my father, and me, so much pain.

I told Cillian my plan over lunch.

"Ye can't be goin' off on yer own like that, lass."

"I'll be fine. I'll take the train. It's perfectly safe."

"Do ye even know where it is you're goin'?"

"Yes, my mother told me where she lives. It's in a place called Zion in Maryland, just over the state line."

"That wouldn't be enough information. Surely you have more."

"No, that's all I have. Her name is Margaret Hayward and she has a farm somewhere in Zion."

Cillian dropped the sandwich he was eating and turned to face me beside him on the bench, gathering my hands in his. His brows were knitted and his lips were pressed tightly together and his head shook back and forth. He was worried, I could see that. But I was sure if I caught the first train to Maryland in the morning, I would be able to ask the conductor which stop would bring me closest to my destination.

"I don't like it, lass. There are too many unknowns, eh?"

"It will be fine."

"Let me go with ye."

"Cillian, I can't ask you to do that. You have your work and your inventions. I'm not sure how long I'll be gone."

"Tell me yer plan again, lass."

"After everyone is asleep, I'm going to sneak out the door and walk to the train station. It shouldn't take long. And once I get there, I'll purchase a ticket."

"Do ye have enough money?"

"I've been saving up. You don't have to worry about me."

"Aye, but I do."

THAT NIGHT, WHEN THE HOUSE WAS LIKE A TOMB, I SLIPPED OUT of bed and pulled the same dress I'd worn earlier that day over my head. Though everyone was sound asleep, I tiptoed down the staircase in stocking feet, carrying the carpetbag over my shoulder, and reached the foyer, where I sank my arms into my heavy wool coat. It was the first of November and there had been a nip in the air when I had walked home from work, as though snow was threatening to fall.

I had a moment of sadness when I considered, depending on what I found, that I might never return to the house where I was raised. The acrid smell of Father's pipe lingered in the air, mingled with the rabbit stew my mother had prepared for dinner. These were smells I might never experience again, and it made my eyes sting with impending tears.

If only I could have hugged my mother goodbye and kissed my little sister. But not even the pull of their love could keep me from this errand to meet the woman who was so much like me. After buttoning my coat and slipping on my boots, I picked up my bag and reached for the doorknob. I took one last look at the darkened parlor where I had spent so much time with my family, and froze. A small red glow floated in the corner of the room. When I heard the puff of air and smelled the burning tobacco, I knew I wasn't alone. My father was sitting in the silent darkness.

CHAPTER 6

His laugh sounded crazed, sinister, as he clicked the knob of the gas lamp. Slowly the room took on a golden glow, and he turned to me with an evil smile so wide, I could see the missing molars along his top row of teeth. A fiery shiver ran down my spine.

"So, you're off to be with that Mick, huh? Whoring yourself to him."

"No, Father." I tried to control the quiver in my voice, squaring my shoulders to show him no fear. But the tingling in my spine and my body's quaking reminded me I was indeed frightened.

"No decent young lady would be going out alone this time of night. Only whores and street trash. Is that what you are?"

"No, Father. I'm leaving."

"Oh, leaving, you say? And where do you think you're going?"

"I'm going to find my grandmother. I need to understand—"

"Understand? There's nothing to understand but she was no good, like you're turning out to be, with your painting and spreading your legs for scum."

He took a menacing step toward me with his fist raised and I blanched, closing my eyes to the anticipated blow. My father had said some cruel things to me in the past, but suddenly I couldn't take another hateful word. He had falsely accused me of despicable things and insulted Cillian as well.

"I can't stay here another minute."

"Fine!" Instead of hitting me, he grabbed my arm and hauled me, like a sack of flour, to the door. "Be done with you. You'll find out what a selfish bitch she is. You're turning out just like her." He pulled open the door so hard it crashed against the wall, and when the cold early-morning air hit my face, he shoved me onto the landing and slammed the door behind me.

I stumbled down the steps and landed on my knees on the brick sidewalk, a numbing pain shot up my legs. My carpetbag landed beside me and it took a minute to absorb the fact that my father had physically thrown me from my home. Though I was planning to leave on my own, it still hurt to know he had forced me into the night.

"Laurel." I heard my name whispered from somewhere nearby. I looked down the street, both ways, and saw nothing but a row of identical townhouses on each side, all bathed in darkness. Without the full moon's illumination and the corner gas lamps, I would have been entirely blind. As I rose to my feet and slung the bag over my shoulder, I heard it again.

"Laurel."

I turned to the sound of rustling leaves. Cillian climbed out from between two sets of marble steps leading to side-by-side homes. He must have been curled up like a hedgehog between the stoops.

"Cillian!" I rushed past two houses and met up with him on the sidewalk, where I gathered his arm in my hand and dragged him around the corner, out of my father's view.

"What are you doing here?"

"I couldn't be lettin' ye go off in the night all alone. The city is not a safe place after dark, especially for a young lady like yerself, eh?"

"How long have you been hiding there?"

"Oh, I arrived maybe an hour ago. I started to think ye left without me."

"You silly man."

I looked both ways down the street—deserted, dark, and eerily quiet. I had a long walk to the train station, recently built across the Schuylkill River, and grudgingly admitted to myself I'd feel safer if Cillian was with me.

"Fine. Since you've come all this way..." I crooked my arm through his and led him down the street. "I guess I'll let you walk me to the train station."

IT WAS A LONG, FRIGID WALK FROM MY HOME ON THE EAST SIDE OF the city to the main train terminal on the west. We walked forty blocks through the darkness, past Penn Square and the new art museum and across the river, where barges loaded with goods streamed south in the sun's early rays. As we approached the station, a large crowd of men shouted in protest while armed soldiers tried to keep them contained. Men dressed in ragged coats and worn-out shoes were blocking the entrance to the station, holding signs and taunting the guards. A block away, there was a large crowd of onlookers hoping, perhaps, to see a fight break out.

"Excuse me, ma'am." I approached a woman with three small children encircling her and a baby on her hip. "What's going on?"

"You haven't heard? The railroad workers have gone on strike. They joined in the crusade of their brothers in Pittsburgh."

"A railroad strike? How long will it last? I have to catch a train to Maryland today."

"I'm sorry, miss, but you'll not be catching a train today or any time soon, I imagine."

I turned around to find Cillian talking to an animated gentleman who waved his arms like an orchestra conductor as he spoke. Crossing the crowded street, I joined Cillian as he walked away from the man.

"There's a strike," I said, feeling frantic. How would I get out of Philadelphia? I had to get to Maryland and now that Father had thrown me out of the house, I definitely couldn't stay here. I had nowhere else to go.

"Aye. The man told me it could go on for weeks."

"What am I to do? I can't walk to Maryland."

"Well, now, ye could, but I wouldn't recommend it. Hard on the feet, ye know?"

"What should I do?"

"The man told me we might find men lingerin' around the station offerin' rides in carriages or buckboards."

"I suppose that could work." Chewing the cuticle of my left thumb, I looked down the street in search of possible transportation, spotting a few carts in the distance. "I wonder how much they would charge."

"Not sure, but we could ask."

"I only have my small savings."

"This may be our only choice."

"*Our* choice?" I swung around, heat rising in my face. "Cillian, you can't come with me."

"Well ye can't be travelin' alone, now can ye?"

It was the first time Cillian had raised his voice to me. Usually so kind-hearted and jovial, the man standing in front of me with his fists on his hips and a scowl on his face looked nothing like my friend. We were standing in the middle of the street, people jostling around us for a better view of the strike, and we were in a standoff of our own, both of us glaring defiantly. His offer to take me to Maryland warmed my heart, but I had to do this on my own. I had to uncover the mysteries surrounding my grandmother. This was my life, not his, and I couldn't take him away from his family and job. I knew he would never agree to let me go it alone, and time was running out. It would take too long to convince him not to come. Seeing his determination, I decided on a plan. I only hoped Cillian would be able to forgive me.

WE WALKED A FEW BLOCKS PAST THE TRAIN STATION, WITH ITS growing crowd of protestors and strikers, and bought a warm roll from a street-side vendor, paying twice the going rate because of the strike. The extra pennies spent on breakfast dipped into my meager savings, but neither of us had eaten since the night before. An empty spot opened up on the curb, so we squeezed between other onlookers and ate our rolls and washed them down with cold cider.

"After we're finished, let's walk up the street to see if anyone is offering rides," I said, taking a large bite. "Hopefully someone won't gouge us like the roll seller."

"Aye, but would ye blame them? Under these circumstances, they stand to make more during the strike than they probably make in a month."

"I suppose. But Cillian, I don't have a lot of money. I gave most of my pay to Mother and my brothers. Though I've been saving, it still isn't much."

"No need to worry, lass. I, too, have been savin'. I'll make sure ye get to yer granny."

My last bite stopped midway to my mouth when a sharp stab of guilt plunged through my chest. I had no intention of taking Cillian along or using his money. He had been so supportive and had kept me safe on our walk through the dark streets to the train station. Would he ever forgive what I was about to do to him?

I swallowed my last bite and took a long drink before standing up. Brushing the crumbs from my coat, I drew in a deep breath, steeling my spine, and reached a hand out to Cillian.

"Come on. Let's go find a ride to Maryland."

As we turned up a side street that ran along the train yard, bumping shoulders with curiosity seekers on their way to the strike, we found dozens of potential rides. There were all types of carriages—phaetons, gigs, landaus, and even a stagecoach—as well as basic farm and delivery wagons. It seemed anyone with a horse and four wheels was taking advantage of the transportation stoppage.

"Ye see there now, lass, I knew we'd find a way for ye. Let's see what they're askin'."

Cillian grabbed my frozen fingers in his hand and for a moment the warmth of his palm provided a delightful thaw. We approached the driver of a beautiful black brougham with gilded gold trim, but one look at our plain, worn clothing and he turned his back on us. The driver knew we couldn't afford his services.

"Well now, I suppose we know where we stand with that one, eh?"

I tugged him toward the group of farm wagons, convinced we'd have no trouble finding a ride. But with each inquiry, we were told either they weren't willing to take us all the way to Maryland or they had raised their price beyond what I could afford. After several rejections, I slumped against a lamppost and blew out a heavy sigh. The wind whipped between the buildings, causing me to shiver uncontrollably and Cillian to prance in place to stay warm. He cupped his hands in front of his mouth and blew, but I knew after a night on the streets, nothing short of a hot bath and a raging fire could warm us.

"Excuse me, miss."

My head snapped back, hitting the lamppost, surprised to

find a small, older man standing before me, squeezing a brown felt hat in his bony, wrinkled fingers.

"Did I hear you say you needed a ride into Maryland? Just over the line?"

"Yes, yes, I do."

"My son and I are headed that way later this morning. We have a delivery in Elkton. Would that be close to where you are going?"

Anywhere in Maryland would be closer than I was at that moment. I wasn't exactly sure how far my grandmother's farm was from Elkton, but I'd risk it. Surely once I arrived, someone would help me.

"It is. Yes. How much will you charge me?"

"Since we're already going that way, just a few pennies, let's say five cents. How would that be?"

"Yes! I can afford that. Yes. Thank you. When are you leaving?"

"Oh, let's say..." He pulled a tarnished watch from his pocket and flipped the casing open. "It's nine o'clock now. We'll pull out at half past nine. How would that be for you?"

"Perfect. Yes, thank you."

"And will ye have room for another, sir? I'm comin' with her," Cillian said.

"Um, well, I'm not sure."

"Please sir. I'd be most obliged to ye."

"I suppose we could make room." He pointed down the street to where several wagons were clustered together. "My son and I'll be over yonder."

The old man hobbled away and I leapt into Cillian's arms. He spun me around and around, and for a moment I forgot the voices, the smell of bodies mixed with the lingering acridity of the steam engines, and the hateful things my father had spouted last night. I was on my way to find my grandmother, but now I had to hurt the one person whose kindness was more than I deserved.

"Before we go, Cillian..." He set me back on my feet and the dizziness made me list to the right. "I think you spun me round one too many times." I held my head between my hands until the spinning stopped. "How about I buy us some food for the road and a little something extra for the man and his son? With what he's charging, I can afford that."

"That would be most kind of ye. What would you like?"

"I saw a huckster around the corner selling apples and sausages." I opened my reticule, which I'd kept tucked inside my coat, and pulled out several pennies. "Get enough for you and me, and the man and his son, please." I dropped the coins in his hand and pressed my hand to his back with enough pressure to start his momentum.

"You're not coming with me, lass?"

"I think I better wait here until the man comes back to find me. I don't want to miss out on our ride."

"Will you be alright then while I'm gone, what with the crowd and all?"

The guilty pain now ran from my chest to my knees. I hated to dupe him, but I was doing the right thing.

"I'll be fine. I'll be right here when you return." I gave him a sweet, convincing smile and gave him a push into the crowd.

As soon as Cillian disappeared around the corner, I grabbed my skirts and ran down the street to where the wagons were gathered, stopping at each one, frantically searching faces for the little old man. I found the farmer leaning against a ratty-looking buckboard wagon. The wood sides were splintered and the wheels were rusted where they hinged to the axel. I hoped that rickety wagon would get us all the way to Maryland.

"Hello sir. Is your son here? I was wondering if you'd be willing to go now?"

"What's your hurry, little lady?"

"I'm anxious to get on the road. The sooner we leave, the sooner I'll get to my grandmother's house."

"What happened to your friend?"

"Oh, he, um, changed his mind."

"Well, if you're sure. I'll get my son and we'll be on our way."

Standing on my toes and weaving back and forth to have an unobstructed view of the street, I watched for Cillian, ready to dodge behind a wagon should I see him coming. In another time and under different circumstances, I might have liked to have him along. But for once, I wanted to do something without a man's influence. I'd lived my entire life by my father's rules, closely followed my boss's instructions, and traveled from school escorted by my brothers. I wanted—needed—to complete a task, make a decision, or take a risk on my own.

The farmer returned with his son, who stood only a few inches taller than me but wore a suspiciously elegant suit. His pants were fine gray wool and his black jacket and striped silk cravat didn't fit in with his father's downtrodden appearance.

"This is my son, Edgar." Edgar lifted my hand to his mouth and planted a delicate kiss on my ice-cold skin.

"Pleased to meet you..."

"Laurel. Laurel Whitman."

He looked at me with hooded eyes, trailing them slowly down my body to my worn boots. He raised his head and met my gaze with an unsettling grin.

"Pleased to meet you, Laurel. My father says it will only be the three of us on our little trip. Is that correct?"

"Yes."

"Fine. That is indeed quite fine."

A shiver rushed down my spine. It didn't feel *fine*, though I wasn't sure why. The elegantly dressed Edgar bowed properly and extended his hand to help me into the back of the wagon like a true gentleman. And instead of climbing up on the seat with his father, he sat beside me, so closely I could smell his strong, fruity cologne. He did everything right by providing appropriate protection to a young lady traveling alone. So why were warning bells clanging in my head?

CHAPTER 7

The farmer cracked his whip on the backside of the old nag and the creaking buckboard rolled slowly across the cobblestones, stopping and starting as he weaved between people and wagons crowded along the street. I kept my eyes on the train station, still engulfed in a massive gathering of people, hoping I wouldn't find Cillian racing to catch us. The early morning's promise of a bright day was thwarted by angry, black clouds that swallowed the sun. A hearty wind whipped across the wagon and I had to press my hand to my head to keep my hat from blowing away.

The bonnet was given to me by my mother for my nineteenth birthday. As was customary, she said it was from both her and Father, but I knew he had no part in the gift beyond supplying the money that paid for the materials. I drew the hat from my head and ran my fingers over the fine lace and soft ribbon attached with a pearl button. The delicate stitches on the velvet fabric could only be the work of my mother's hands. She was a talented milliner, having worked in the hat department in Mr. Wanamaker's store before marrying my father. Because Father insisted that no wife of his would toil for pennies, her talent was relegated to making gifts for her family and friends.

"So, Miss Whitman, what takes you to Maryland?"

Edgar's deep voice stirred me from my thoughts, and I glanced up to find him even closer to me than he'd been before. His eyes were a disarming shade of gray, so pale as to be almost clear. The dark whiskers on his cheeks touched his collar, and his upper lip was hidden beneath a bushy mustache. His fetching suit, fine derby hat, and strong chin and nose made an impressive display. Most women would consider him quite handsome. But there was something in his gaze, so empty, and the pull of his smile, rather insincere, that sent a shock down my spine. I scooted a few inches away and kept my eyes on the stately houses being built in the western part of the city.

"I'm going to visit my grandmother."

"Ah, your grandmother. Very nice. A surprise, is it?"

"Not at all. She's expecting me by tomorrow."

"Oh yes? And where exactly does she live?"

"Well..."

"Perhaps we can take you there directly."

Did my face give away the fact that I didn't have an address for my grandmother? Surely there was no way Edgar could surmise I didn't know exactly where I was going. I hadn't told his father anything other than I needed to get to Maryland.

"She lives in a little village called Zion, but you don't need to bother yourself. My uncle will pick me up when we get to Elkton."

"Is that so?"

"Yes, of course. It's all been arranged."

I pulled my coat tighter around my waist and settled my hat back on my head. Edgar chuckled, seemingly unconvinced. He picked up a piece of wheat from those scattered on the wagon floor and poked the stalk between his teeth. For the first time, reality set in that the buckboard was empty save the scraps of wheat, a wooden bucket, and the two of us. Didn't the farmer say they were making a delivery in Elkton?

"So, Mister...I'm sorry, I didn't catch your last name."

"Worthington. Edgar Worthington."

"Yes, Mr. Worthington, your father said something about a delivery."

"A delivery?" Edgar seemed genuinely confused. He pulled the wheat from between his teeth and shot a glance at his father driving the buckboard. "Yes, I believe that is correct."

"But what are you delivering? The wagon is empty."

His mustache stretched to a horizontal line and I could just make out his yellowed teeth.

"Why, Miss Whitman, you are quite observant. The wagon is indeed empty."

My body began to shake, not from the cold wind slicing through my coat, but from the reality that something was amiss. In my duping Cillian to do this on my own, I may, in fact, have been tricked myself, and the potential consequences of my foolishness coursed a wave of fear through my body. Frantically, I looked at our surroundings, now outside the city and away from the elegant homes a few miles back. I found nowhere to run should I survive jumping from the wagon.

"As a matter of fact, we're stopping in Wilmington to pick up the load, which we will deliver in Elkton. That is why our wagon is empty."

"Oh...of course."

Though his explanation was logical, his hooded gaze and unsettling sneer did nothing to calm the fright quivering through my limbs. If only I hadn't been so stubborn, so determined to make the trip alone, Cillian would be here to protect me. But protect me from what? A man who gave me the willies but who had done nothing untoward and had given me a logical explanation? At the very least, Cillian's presence would have reassured me that I would indeed arrive in Maryland safely.

"I think I'll catch a few winks." Edgar chuckled as he slumped down until the back of his head rested against the side of the wagon. He tipped his hat over his face and suddenly my eyelids grew heavy. It had been a cold, sleepless night rushing through the dark streets, and this trip would be long and uneventful. I curled onto my side, tucking my knees to my chest, and gathered my hands beneath my head. The smell of wood and dried grass tickled my nose, and I suddenly longed for my feather pillow with its light lavender scent. I chastised my weakness for comfort. This trip, though uncomfortable and frigid cold, would take me to my grandmother and the mysteries of my father's wrath.

SEVERAL HOURS LATER, AFTER TWO STOPS TO GIVE THE HORSE A rest, the late afternoon sun burned through my eyelids, causing me to blink away the sleep that had enveloped me. I had dozed on and off most of the trip. With so little to see but trees, small villages, and a river or two, I had given in to my exhaustion. After the first stop, Edgar rode on the bench beside his father, leaving me in peace in the back.

I brought my hand to my brow to block the sun hanging low in the sky and sat up to get my bearings. We had been traveling through a pine forest, but now the trees gave way to cattails and reeds. The strong smell of briny water and moldy grass hung in the air.

"Ah ha," Mr. Worthington said, throwing out his arms. "I'd recognize that smell anywhere."

"Where are we?"

"We're approaching Wilmington. That smell is none other than the brackish waters of the Delaware."

I stretched out my legs, straightening my skirts over my

stockings so that the hem reached the tops of my boots. My hat had fallen off and my hair had come unbound from its bun at the base of my neck.

"So, we'll be stopping soon? To pick up your load?" My limbs were numb and my back screamed out in pain, and I couldn't wait to climb from the wagon to walk off the stiffness.

"Yes, right, soon."

I followed Edgar's gaze toward billowing smokestacks and long brick warehouses in the distance. The water, which had been but a pond a mile back, had grown into a wide, endless bay, and I marveled at the small city before us. The loud blast from a ship's horn echoed across the water and a flock of seagulls squawked in reply.

"We'll be there soon, Mr. Worthington," the old man said, snapping his whip across the horse's hindquarters.

"Mr. Worthington?" My nerves had been settled from sleep, but now fear put me on edge. "Your father calls you Mr. Worthington?"

"Oh, ha!" Edgar laughed and glanced over his shoulder at me behind him in the wagon. He jabbed his elbow into the farmer's side. "It's a bit of a joke between me and my dad. Right, Dad?"

"Huh? Yes, right."

The old man seemed as startled as I was, having no knowledge of this joke. The pair had been suspicious from the beginning. Why hadn't I listened to my earlier instincts to look for another ride rather than give in to the lowest price? Better still, why hadn't I let Cillian come along? I wordlessly scolded myself for being so independent, insisting I could do it on my own. Because of my foolish pride, I had no one to rely upon but myself.

When we arrived in Wilmington, I would slip away and find other transportation for the rest of the trip. That seemed like my best bet. There was something unsettling about Edgar

Worthington, and the need to pick up a load in Wilmington didn't sit right, either. Even if Edgar and his "father" were sincere gentlemen, my instincts told me to abandon the rest of the trip and find another way.

The next few miles were spent in silence, with no other conversation among the three of us. The noise of ships' horns, clanging metal, and men's voices carried toward us from the harbor, and for the first time since boarding the wagon, I felt a glimmer of hope. I was halfway to my destination and would find a more suitable means of transportation.

The old man didn't take us into Wilmington as I expected, but instead stopped at a stone house on the outskirts of town. The two-story structure leaned a little to the right, and its windows were so covered in grime that it looked as though they'd been rubbed with wax. A wooden sign rocked to and fro on a metal rod protruding above the door, squeaking out its welcome. The Goose and Fox tavern, though shabby, at least offered the hope of a hot meal and a place to rest before we continued into the city. I hoped we'd get there before nightfall.

The old man offered his hand as I climbed out of the back of the wagon and I landed on my feet a bit unsteadily. I wasn't sure how long we had been riding, but the sun was sinking lower and my aching bones affirmed it had been quite a while.

"So, are we just taking a respite while you load the wagon?" I asked the old man, who replied with a huff and walked into the tavern.

"Don't mind him, Miss Whitman. My father can be a bit gruff."

"But are we only staying a few minutes?" I needed to decide if I'd steal away while the men were inside or make my escape when we traveled farther into Wilmington. I could see the docks less than a mile down the dirt road, and there was a cluster of buildings dotting the hill beside the water. Night would set in soon and I had no intention of staying here with them. Surely I could find an inn for the night and a hackney in the morning to take me the rest of the way.

"Yes, just a while. Stretch our legs a bit." Edgar raised his arms over his head and stretched until I heard a bone pop in his back. "Why don't you come inside here and have a bite to eat?"

"I think I'll walk around the building before coming in—to get the circulation going, you know."

"There will be plenty of time for that."

Edgar stepped close to me and wrapped his long fingers around my arm. Fear coursed through me—I had to make my move now.

"Thank you, sir, but I'd rather take a little walk."

As inconspicuously as I could, I tugged my arm and attempted to walk away, but he only increased his hold on me. His fingers dug through the wool of my coat into the flesh of my upper arm, sending a stinging pain down to my fingertips.

"No, Miss Whitman," he said through gritted teeth. "You're coming inside with me."

"Please. No."

He ignored my cries and dragged me toward the door. Dust billowed from under my skirts where my boots scraped the dirt as I fought to run away. Until this moment, Mr. Worthington had been pleasant, though strangely so, but now he was using all his strength to force me through the tavern door. Perhaps once inside, I'd get the barkeep or even the old man to help me, to let me go on my way. I'm not sure why Mr. Worthington was so insistent I come inside, but my instincts told me it was not for good reason.

The tavern was dark, musty with a hint of mildew and the strong smell of sour ale. Several men were crowded around the bar, and one man was huddled at a corner table with a tavern maid on his lap. Instead of leading me to a table, Edgar continued to drag me toward a hallway that ran along the side of the bar. My eyes briefly locked with the old man who had driven us here, but he quickly looked away and took a long draw of his ale.

"Please, sir. Help me!" My scream was met with hearty laughter from the men huddled around the bar. "Stop. Please. Let me go!"

No one moved. Not a single man came to my rescue. I caught the glance of the barkeep who was pouring a pint, but he simply shook his head and continued his work. What was the matter with these men? Didn't they see I was being dragged through the tavern against my will by a man who obviously didn't fit in with the other poorly dressed patrons? Finally, a voice rang out from across the room. The tavern maid, dressed in layers of ruffles, her cheeks smudged with rouge, called out, "Go easy now, Edgar. You don't want to damage the goods."

The goods? What in God's name did she mean? I threw every ounce of strength into getting away. I pulled and kicked and sank my teeth into his strong grip. Edgar howled from the pain. He released my arm from its vise, and back-handed me across the cheek. I stumbled into the edge of the bar and ran toward the door, bumping into the wall. A chair toppled to the floor. Edgar's heavy footsteps pounded behind me and I rushed as quickly as I could. The sound of laughter and shouts of encouragement thundered from the bar crowd. Within mere feet of the door, his strong arms encircled my waist. He lifted me off the floor. My feet continued running but only swung in the air, making contact with his legs.

"Settle yourself down, young lady, or you'll wish you had."

"No. Let me go." I kicked and clawed, but to no avail. "Help me! Someone."

"She's a live one, ain't she?" a filthy man said, grabbing my thigh through the thickness of my skirts. This time, I screamed with all the power in my lungs.

"Help!"

Edgar clamped his broad hand over my mouth and nose, cutting off my air. I rocked and bucked, trying to draw a breath into my lungs, and managed to bite into the flesh of his palm.

"Damn you, woman," he howled, shaking his hand while tightening his grip around my waist so that I thought he'd crush my ribs. "I've had enough of your outbursts. You'll pay for this."

He gathered a fistful of my hair and wrapped it around his hand until my neck snapped back, nearly touching my shoulder blades. I feared he'd pull my long locks out from their roots.

"Need some help with the girl?"

"No, thank you. I'll take care of the little bitch myself."

What a fool I had been to accept the ride from the old farmer and his unlikely *son*. Everything about this goodwill gesture to transport me to my destination was a sham.

Still trapped against his chest, my hair wrenched behind me and my ribs burning in pain, I had no choice but to surrender. Wherever he was taking me, I had to find a way to escape. He stomped up a narrow stairway. The darkness was cut by a lone window at the top of the steps. He pushed open a wooden door, crashing it against an inside wall, and I stumbled into the room. I fell to the floor, banging my hip on the wood planks.

"Christ, if I had known..." He looked at his hand to survey the damage my teeth had made, and shook it out as he loosened his cravat. "You've got a lot of spunk, I'll give you that."

"Where are we? Please..." I crawled to my knees and reached out my hand. "If you let me go, I won't be any more trouble. You and your father can keep the money I gave you." I climbed to my feet, swiping a quivering hand over my disheveled hair.

"You're not going anywhere. Take off your coat."

The room was sweltering, so I slowly worked the buttons

loose and dropped my coat on the window seat. Maybe if I obeyed his instructions, he'd leave me be. I quickly realized that was a foolish notion. He shrugged his suit jacket from his shoulders and ran his fingers down the buttons of his vest, unlatching each one as he declared his intentions.

"You, my dear..." his eyes became hooded as he spoke "are staying here with me." A grin formed on his face, spreading this thick moustache. "We're going to get to know one another." He dropped his vest on the wooden chair where his jacket had landed, and his hand reached to the waistband of his trousers.

"Get on the bed."

My throat locked up. Terror squeezed my vocal cords. I shook my head and scurried across the floor, as far from him as possible. In two steps, he was on me. I stumbled when he grabbed my legs. He dragged me across the floor toward the bed. My skirts rode up until my cotton knickers were the only garment hiding my lower body. He seemed to find my conservative dress rather humorous because he let out a cackling laugh and in one swift movement, had me in his arms. I wasn't there long. My back hit the thin mattress, sending shooting pain down my spine, and he hovered over me.

"Take them off."

"What? I...no."

"Take them off," he said, this time with a hint of threat.

"But I..."

He bent his knee on the mattress and, with both hands, ripped the knickers off my body, dropping the shredded garment to the floor. I tried to smooth my skirts down over my nakedness, but he slapped my hands away while unbuttoning his trousers. My breath came in sputters and spurts, and tears streaked over my cheeks. I pushed my skirts down again, but this time he gathered both my wrists in his hand and wrangled them over my head, pressing them into the mattress.

"Please, no." I wiggled and squirmed and tried everything to get away, but he was too strong, too large, and his free hand moved too quickly.

"I think I'm going to enjoy this. Like the man said, you're a spitfire."

He dropped his trousers and spread my thighs apart with his knees. I released a scream so loud, it echoed off the walls and pierced my eardrums.

"Save it. No one cares how much you scream."

CHAPTER 8

Shouting and curses from the tavern below mixed with my own screams. I kicked and squirmed, and my arms seared with pain as Edgar wrenched them farther over my head.

"Hold still, you little bitch." His putrid breath riffled my curls and dampened my forehead. His fist pummeled my thighs until my kicking legs surrendered. He gave me a painful slap for good measure, causing my head to thump against the wood slats beneath the too-thin mattress. I prayed for unconsciousness, a dark abyss to take me away.

He blew out a pent-up growl, wrenched my clamped legs apart, and pressed his stiff member against my privates. I let out a savage scream and he stopped. As quickly as he'd started, he stopped.

"Worthington!" A chorus of male voices rang up the stairwell, followed by a gun's blast.

Edgar let out a deep, guttural groan and flopped his full weight on top of me. But instead of ramming into me, he pushed off the mattress and climbed to his feet. I kept my lids squeezed shut, afraid to see his clear, empty eyes looking down at me. His breath was coming hard and fast, to the sound of ruffling fabric. Peering through one narrowed lid, I brushed my skirts over my naked body and lay perfectly still as he buttoned his trousers and slipped into his shirt.

"Once I get you broke in, you'll do."

His brief commentary forced me to open my eyes and I found him standing over me, buttoning his shirt. My stomach flipped and flopped and I sat up, retching and gagging. I turned my head toward the floor in time for its contents to spew onto the wood. I heaved again, but this time there was nothing but burning bile from my empty stomach.

"Christ. Clean this up and yourself, too. I'll be back."

Edgar snatched his cravat and coat from the chair and stomped from the room. I lay there staring at the yellow-green vomit splattered on the floor, mesmerized by its shape and contents. He hadn't even bothered to take off his boots when he assaulted me, yet he stripped off his coat and vest. Is that how it worked? Quick, efficient, so as not to wrinkle his shirt? Didn't want to ruin his fine, tailored suit?

A loud popping brought me to the edge of the bed, followed by the shouts of several men below in the tavern. I heard a crack of gunfire outside. Slowly, I climbed to my feet, feeling bruises forming where he'd punched my legs. I hobbled to the cloudy window and rubbed a clear circle in the glass with my elbow. Dozens of men formed a tight circle in back of the tavern, a few holding lanterns, around a man who lay prone on the ground. More shouting and pushing ensued. With everyone distracted, now would be my chance to escape. There had to be a way out of here without being seen.

I rushed to the door and turned the knob, thankful it wasn't locked, and stepped into the empty hallway. No sound came from the tavern below, only shouts from behind. As quietly as I could, I went to the window at the top of the stairs and looked out. Off in the distance, I could see the waning lights of

Wilmington harbor. If I could get outside, I could run toward the docks and find a place to shelter for the night.

Taking the stairs as silently as a mouse, I had made it to the landing when the sounds of men coming back into the tavern stopped my descent. Apparently the ruckus was settled and they were anxious to drink to the occasion. The fallen man was already forgotten. I tiptoed back to the hallway window and pushed up the sash. There was a slanted roof a few feet below, perhaps part of a side porch on the building.

"So Edgar, will the new lass be available for service soon? Will she?"

An Irishman's lilt, so similar to Cillian's, carried up the stairs. I knew it would only be a short while before Edgar put me to work. Thankfully, I wasn't damaged and wouldn't become what the men below thought I was. A previously unknown determination kindled deep inside me—I'd kill any man who tried to touch me against my will.

The voices from the tavern grew louder, their words more slurred. I had to escape *now*. I pushed the sash as high as I could and lifted my foot through the opening. Using my arms to leverage me up onto the sill, I ignored the pain burning through my thighs and was soon through the window and crouching on the roof. It wasn't very steep—just enough for me to skitter to the edge without rolling off. Below the roof was a grassy area where wagons were parked and horses were tethered to hitching posts. If only I were a talented acrobat like in the Wild West show, I could land on a horse's back and gallop away. Instead, I rolled onto my belly and hung my legs over the side, slowly sliding down until I let go.

Landing momentarily on my feet, I lost my balance and fell onto my hip. I looked around, finding no one about. A horse whinnied and stomped his hind leg mere inches from my hand, which I drew back and tucked against my chest. The cool, briny air cut through the bodice of my dress and lifted my skirts, chilling my bare legs. I'd left my wool coat in the torture chamber upstairs, but would have to make do without it. Pushing to my feet, I brushed the dirt and loose grass from my skirt and folded my arms for warmth. I ran toward the harbor before anyone could find me, dodging between hedgerows and outbuildings. My arms and legs ached, but I was determined to escape Edgar's clutches. My focus was solely on the harbor ahead and the safety of the many buildings in which I could hide. When my legs couldn't carry me another yard, I glanced over my shoulder, barely able to see the horrid tavern. Only a faint glow from its lanterns signaled its location. Slowing to a walk, I came to a warehouse a safe distance away that had an arched alcove which would make a suitable shelter for the night. Folding deep into a corner, I drew my knees to my chest, relieved that until tomorrow morning, I would be safe in my dark hiding place.

Hot, angry tears spilled down my face and my teeth clattered together from the cold. It took all my strength to silence my sobs for fear I'd be discovered, but the tears kept coming. My foolish, stubborn pride had gotten me in this mess. If I had only listened to Father, been a more obedient daughter, and given up my ridiculous notion of finding my grandmother, this nightmare wouldn't have happened. At the very least, I should have let Cillian come along. What I wouldn't give to have him here with me now.

My exhausted, aching body beckoned me to sleep—eyelids growing heavy as my tears subsided. I laid my head on my knees, drawing my skirts tight around my ankles, and closed my eyes to the deepening darkness.

THE NEXT MORNING, GULLS SWARMED OVERHEAD EARLY. THEIR cheery *he-he-he-he* announced the coming dawn. My head felt as though it was full of cotton and my eyelids were swollen from last night's tears. I arched my neck and turned it shoulder to shoulder, working out the stiffness. Shivering from the bone-chilling night, I climbed to my feet and stomped in place, hoping to thaw the numbness in my feet. The warehouse would be buzzing with activity soon, and surely I would be discovered in the narrow alcove where I stood.

I peered around the brick wall and saw no one about in the dim light but noticed a large cluster of shrubbery a few feet away that would make for a good shelter behind which to relieve myself. Rubbing my hands up and down my arms, I hurried toward the bushes, anxious to remain unseen, but discovered too late that I wasn't alone. Trickling water came from behind the shrubbery—someone had beaten me to the natural privy. I scurried behind a large woodpile a few feet away and crouched behind it, keeping an eye on the shrubbery. My hand found a thick branch lying close and I took it up as a weapon should Edgar step from behind the bushes. Fear streaked down my spine when a dark-haired man emerged, his head tilted down while affixing the buttons on his britches. I raised my truncheon, ready to strike.

He came within a foot of the wood pile and raised his face to the dawning light. My heart nearly burst from my chest. I dropped my weapon and ran around the woodpile, smacking head-on into him. Gladness washed over me like the waves in the harbor as I threw myself into Cillian's arms.

"Jesus, Mary, and Joseph," he spouted as he stumbled backward. "It's ye, Laurel. Thanks be to God."

He smothered my freezing cold body in his arms, and the tears I thought I'd completely shed returned in torrents. He smelled unwashed and of road dust, and it was a sweeter fragrance than a spring lilac. Cillian was here, safe and whole.

I shoved him away and punched his arm.

"What are you doing here? Are you out of your mind?"

"No, but I think ye've lost yers, lass. What do ye mean by sluggin' me arm?"

"How did you find me?"

"Twasn't easy, I'll tell ye that. Do you mind tellin' me why ye took off without me?"

"I...oh...I was...stupid." I fell back into his arms, so grateful he was here. Reluctantly, I pulled back. "Give me a minute. I was headed behind the shrubbery myself," I said.

Hurrying across the crunchy, frosted grass, I squatted behind the bushes and lifted my skirts. I finished my business, smoothed my curls in some semblance of order, and emerged from the shrubs.

"Come, lass. I have a horse."

He guided me behind the warehouse, where a young sturdy horse stood, eyes closed to the rising sun. We startled her from her slumber and she lowered her head to nibble at the frosty grass below.

"Where in the world did you get that?"

"Well, when I couldn't find ye, not knowin' if ye'd been kidnapped or were wicked enough to run from me, I decided to follow and find out."

"But where—"

"The strike was quite advantageous to some ambitious lads. Hucksters weren't just sellin' overpriced breakfast rolls, were they? This particular beauty whinnied at me as I walked by as if she'd be wantin' me to take her on a long ride."

"How much did she cost?"

"Now, ye wouldn't want me to divulge the details of my contract with one Mr. Alexander McBride, would ye? If his other customers knew what a deal he'd offered me, it might jeopardize future sales."

"But I didn't think you had much money with you?"

"Let's just say we worked out a little proposition between us, eh?"

It didn't matter how much it cost or what kind of deal he had made—Cillian was here, with a horse, and for the first time since Father threw me into the street, I knew I would make it to my grandmother's house without further harm. I threw my arms around his broad shoulders again and squeezed him with all my strength.

"Shame on me, lass. I didn't notice you were without yer cloak." He pulled off his jacket and draped it over my shoulders. "What happened to it?"

"I, um, left it."

"Let's go back and find it."

"No." I answered too quickly, too loudly, and Cillian's brows arched with concern. He stepped back and looked me over, noticing my dirt-covered boots and rumpled appearance.

"Did somethin' happen to ye, Laurel? Ye look a bit worse for wear."

His head was tipped down and his blue eyes locked with mine. I couldn't lie to Cillian, he would see right through me. But I couldn't tell him the truth either.

"What's this here?" He reached toward my cheek and I stepped back, dipping my chin to my chest. "It looks as though a bruise is forming. What happened?"

"Nothing. It's fine…nothing."

"Are ye hurt, lass? Did someone do this to ye?" He lifted my chin with his finger and gazed deep into my eyes. A streak of guilt rushed through me.

"No. No, I bumped my face against the wagon when we went over a deep rut. That's all."

"Are ye tellin' me the truth?" After I nodded, he let his hand drop to my shoulder. "And what about yer cloak?"

"Yesterday when the farmer stopped to rest the horse, I went for a little walk and grew a bit warm in the sun. I laid my coat on the ground and took a nap on top of it. When the farmer rode up in his wagon, ready to leave, I didn't think. I jumped on and left it behind."

His eyes bore into mine, and I was sure he didn't believe me. Who would believe an absurd story such as that? It was the only thing I could come up with at the moment. I couldn't possibly admit that I'd accepted a ride from a dishonest man and his lecherous "son" and had almost been violated in a most personal way—a way that no decent woman would ever speak of aloud.

"If that's so, I guess we'll be goin'."

"Please. I'd like to go to Wilmington to see about another ride to Maryland."

"We'll find another cloak for you there." Cillian cupped his hands to give me a leg up on the horse. "Here you go, lass." A sharp pain coursed between my legs when I settled into the saddle. "Ye ride and I'll walk beside. I rode this young girl hard yesterday—she could use the break."

With my frozen fingers under the pommel, Cillian led the mare around to the front of the warehouse and onto the dirt road that led to the harbor. We had made it only a few yards when the pounding of a horse's hooves and squeaking wagon wheels interrupted the morning quiet. I turned to find Edgar perched on the bench of the buckboard, and the farmer whipping the old nag into an uneven canter.

"You! Come back here, you little bitch," Edgar shouted. The farmer whipped the old horse again. They were gaining on us, but it didn't appear their horse would make it.

"Who would that be, bellowin' like a—"

"Get up here. We've got to go."

I slid back in the saddle, making room for Cillian to ride in front. My distress must have shown on my face because in a flash, without a word of argument, he pulled the reins over the horse's head and threw his leg over its back like a circus performer.

"Please, Cillian. We must hurry."

He kicked his heels into the horse's sides. "Ya!" And we were off like a cannonball, leaving the men and the old nag in the dust.

WE LOST EDGAR AND THE FARMER AFTER WE REACHED THE CITY center, turning and weaving between buildings and onto side streets. Our horse, who had responded nobly to our commands, was huffing out great white clouds. Foamy lather lined her lips, and Cillian slowed her pace. We were walking through the marketplace where vendors' booths occupied both sides of the street. Cillian hopped down off the horse and wrapped the reins around a post, raising his hands to lift me down. I ran my fingers through my tangled locks, combing out the snarls as best I could. I surely looked a fright after two nights in the elements with no bath or change of clothing. My carpetbag was probably still in the farmer's wagon, but at least I'd had the clarity of mind to keep my reticule with me with its meager collection of coins inside.

We crossed the dusty, dirt-packed street to a market stall where a plainly dressed woman was selling bread. Cillian paid the lady two cents for a crusty loaf, and my stomach growled as he tore it in half. I ripped into the bread, tearing a large hunk with my teeth, my heart pounding with delight. How long had it been since I'd last eaten? The warm, yeasty bread was the best thing I'd ever tasted, having never known such hunger. Tears burned behind my eyelids, accompanied by thoughts that if I hadn't been so foolish, I'd be warm and clean and sitting at our dining room table, eating my mother's freshly made porridge with cold, creamy milk. What if I never found my grandmother? What if I ran out of money or froze to death before I reached her? What would become of me?

"Laurel, there's a vendor just ahead. I think I see woolens

for sale. Let's walk that way and get something to warm ye up, eh?"

"Yes," I mumbled, swiping at an errant tear. "You need your coat back. You must be freezing."

"Just a bit, lass." Cillian's laugh couldn't hide the pallor of his cheeks or the shivers coursing through his body. He had so generously given up his coat to help keep me warm, and now he was quaking from the cold.

"Let's hurry, Cillian. You'll catch your death."

After a bit of haggling, Cillian paid the woman for two pairs of wool mittens and a long, thick shawl which I draped over my head and shoulders after returning his coat. Nibbling on the last bits of bread, we strolled back toward the horse, admiring the colorful booths along the way. Just shy of where our horse was tied, I grabbed Cillian's coat sleeve and dragged him behind a basket seller.

"What the world are ye doin', lass?" he sputtered, trying to stay on his feet. I tugged him down beside me and pointed across the road.

"It's Edgar. That horrible man who was chasing us."

"The farmer's son, is he?"

"Shh, we can't let him see us." I crept on bended knees behind a stack of baskets, pulling Cillian behind me, where I could still watch Edgar's movements without being seen.

"Why are you hidin' from him, lass? Did he hurt you? Did somethin' go wrong on yer trip?"

"There's the farmer." I pointed across the street where the farmer and Edgar were talking, glancing over their shoulders and seeming to compare notes. My gaze traveled a few booths away to where the farmer's wagon was parked between two market stalls. My dark floral carpetbag was perched on the buckboard's bench.

"Cillian, my bag. Look."

"Well, so it is."

"We could go between those stalls and snatch it off the wagon," I said, knowing how risky a mission it would be.

"Best not. They might see us."

"We have to try. Come on."

Still crouching low, Cillian and I hurried along the backs of the booths and peered around a fish vendor before crossing the dusty road to the other side. We stopped at the corner of a booth whose tables were piled high with orange and yellow pumpkins and squash, to make sure Edgar and his father were still occupied. They were gone. I scanned the market for any sight of them, but they seemed to have evaporated.

We slipped behind the fruit vendor and scaled along the rear of the booths, keeping an eye out for Edgar and his father, but they were nowhere around. The wagon stood between two stalls, its horse asleep on its feet.

"I'll get the bag, lass. You wait here." Cillian pulled the collar of his coat around his ears, tucked his chin to his chest, and casually walked toward the wagon. He planted his foot on the step and in two shakes had my carpetbag in hand. Leaping back to the ground, he turned and started my way but came to a dead stop, his eyes large as moons. Tiny ants seemed to crawl up my spine, putting my nerve endings on alert as I rotated behind me.

"Why, Miss Whitman, we meet again."

CHAPTER 9

"Cillian!" I turned back around and within two steps, I realized he was gone. Edgar's thick, strong fingers gripped my shoulders, spinning me around to face him and stopping my escape.

"Let me go. Help!"

My screams were muffled when Edgar covered my mouth with his dirty hand. It smelled of leather and tobacco, and my stomach roiled, remembering those filthy hands on my body yesterday.

"Don't even think of biting me."

Forcing my back against his chest, Edgar dragged me behind a stall. My feet were unable to get purchase on the cold, frozen dirt. He pulled me into an alley away from the marketplace, between two brick buildings, and slammed my face against the wall. His elbow pressed into my back as he dragged his hand from my mouth. My cheek scraped on the cold, rough brick.

"Thought you could get away from me, did you? I don't give up that easily, Miss Whitman."

"Let me go!" I snarled.

His dark, bitter laughter echoed through the alley. I sagged against the brick wall, feeling hopeless, defeated. What had happened to Cillian? Had the farmer dragged him away from the market?

"Shut up. You're coming with me."

I swung my fists behind me, hoping to make contact with some part of his body and fight my way out of this mess, but it was no use. Trapped against the building, my fists waved uselessly behind me. My heartbeat tripled, knowing I'd never get away. Edgar leaned his face close to mine, his sour breath smelled of onions and stale coffee.

"Now, we're going back to the wagon and—"

His demands were cut off with a loud *whoof* and his body slammed into mine before falling at my feet. I turned from the wall and found Cillian hovering over Edgar's motionless body and waving a brick over his head, daring him to get up.

"Cillian!" I leapt over Edgar's prone body and threw myself into his arms. "I thought they had taken you."

Still holding the brick in one hand, he encircled my waist with his other and pulled me close.

"I'm fine, lass. What about ye? Did the beast hurt ye?"

"No, he didn't hurt me. Just scared the devil out of me."

When Edgar failed to move, Cillian dropped the brick and looked me over, brushing his fingers over my raw cheek.

"He did more than that. Ye'll have a mighty bruise on yer cheek by sundown."

"It's fine. Hurry. Let's get out of here before he wakes up."

We rushed out of the alleyway, checking for signs of the farmer, and ran back toward our horse. Cillian picked up my carpetbag, which he'd left with a vegetable vendor, and we found our horse still tied up, her head and eyes drooped. She perked up as we approached, flicking her ears in interest. With help from Cillian, I settled toward the back of the saddle while he climbed on and secured my bag. I pressed close behind him as he led the horse into the crowded street. We wove between pedestrians and mules, carts and carriages, and soon reached the outskirts of the city where Cillian broke the mare into a trot. We were on our way to safety.

HOURS LATER, THE SUN SAT HIGH IN THE SKY, BURNING THE BACKS of our necks and sending a trickle of sweat down my spine. Cillian guided the horse under a leafy oak tree along the bank of a rolling creek. My legs nearly gave out as he set me on my feet. We'd been riding for so long, my limbs had gone numb. The mare drank greedily, the foam slathering her lips washed away with the creek's current. The blood began to flow into my limbs as I walked over to the bank and cupped a handful of cool, clear water, bringing it to my parched lips. Cillian knelt beside me, slurping the fresh water and splashing it over his sunburned face.

"Ah, 'tis what we've been needin', lass."

"How far did we ride?" I rubbed my wet hand over the back of my neck, bringing cool relief from the midday sun.

"Two hours, I suppose. Long enough to break me bum." Cillian snorted and rubbed the palm of his hand over his backside. "Though Nellie is the one who should be complainin', carryin' the two of us." He nodded at the horse, who shook her head and stomped her front hoof into the muddy bank in agreement. "Perhaps we should take turns ridin' and walkin' now that we're away from the city. To give the horse a break."

I drank another handful of water and sat back on my heels, glancing at Cillian as he washed his face with the handkerchief he'd pulled from his pocket. Because of me, he'd left his home, missed his shift at the mill, and could've been killed by Edgar or the farmer. He'd done too much for me, with no reward.

"I'd like to continue the rest of the way by train, if we could find a station." I stood up and brushed the dirt from the hem of my skirt.

"There's a strike on. Don't ye remember? No, I'll take ye to find yer granny. Even if we could find a train runnin', tickets cost money and Nellie here won't cost us another dime."

"You don't need to do that."

"Aye, I do." Cillian swiped his wet hands across the seat of his pants and shook out his water-soaked handkerchief. "We've come this far. I'm goin' to see ye to the end."

"But you don't need to do that. I'll be fine."

"Ye'll be fine, will ye?" Cillian's cheeks burned with rarely shown anger. "Were ye fine back there with yer face pressed against the brick wall?"

"But I'll be safe once I'm on the train."

"If there is one. And then what? Do you know how ye'll get to yer granny's from the depot?" He took a step toward me, determination and fury in his gaze. "Do ye even know where she lives, Laurel?"

"No, but I'm sure someone will help me." I fought to keep the quiver from my voice, knowing full well I couldn't guarantee help once I arrived in Elkton.

"Like they helped ye get to Wilmington? Or are ye expectin' only God-fearing saints to be waitin' for ye at the train station? Just because ye'll find country folk doesn't mean they'll be any better than the rascals ye met up with in the city." Cillian hovered over me with a fierce gaze, knitted brow, and narrowed lids. His sun-kissed skin deepened to scarlet.

A shiver coursed through me, less from the possible threat of being abducted by unsavory characters but because Cillian was angry. He was worried for my safety and hurt that I refused his protection.

"Cillian, you've done enough already. I—"

"Do ye not trust me to get ye to yer granny's in one piece?"

"Of course I trust you. But you've missed work and you have

that appointment with Mr. Schumer to show him your invention, and your mother and sister need you."

"And ye don't?" His voice softened along with his gaze and my heart broke as he turned away, snapping the wet handkerchief against his leg. "Aye, I guess ye don't." He turned his back to me and looked across the creek to the thick pine forest along the opposite bank. "Y'are a strong, self-reliant woman, Laurel Whitman, and ye don't need anyone."

"That's not true." I rushed to his side and gathered his thick, sinewy forearm in my hands. "I don't want you to miss your next shift—you need the money for your family and your inventions. You've done too much for me already. You don't need to do this."

His gaze traveled to my hands still clasped around his arm and then slowly returned to my face. His throat bobbed with a deep swallow. "Aye, I do."

He laid his free hand over mine and turned to face me, a small smile playing on his lips. My heartbeat picked up speed and a sudden heat coursed through my body that had nothing to do with the sun's warmth. Breathing was difficult, my throat tightened, and my pulse thumped in my ears. I was afraid, but not like back in the tavern where I was pressed into the mattress and forced to spread my legs. His closeness and the intensity of his gaze made me nervous.

"Why?" The question came out on a whisper as I looked at his soft lips, curled at the corners.

"I need to watch over ye." He cleared his throat, never taking his blue eyes off mine. "Ye need me too, lass."

"I do?"

"Somethin' grave happened to ye back at the tavern, somethin' y'are not willin' to share. I should've been there to stop it."

"It was nothing."

"And back in the city, with yer face smashed against the bricks. If I hadn't been there, then what?"

"I would've gotten away."

He brushed his fingertips along my temple and gathered my curls in his hand.

"Ye need me. Y'are just too stubborn to admit it."

My blood turned cold and I threw his arms out of my hands, turning my back to him. I shook with fury. Was he implying I was weak? I couldn't survive the trip on my own? I might have made a terrible mistake accepting a ride from the farmer and Edgar, but I'd gotten away from them on my own and would've been on a train by now if it weren't for Cillian's interference.

"So," I screeched as I turned back to face him, "you think I'm incapable of taking care of myself. Is that it?"

"I didn't say that, lass." He took a step back as I stalked toward him.

"I'm just a weak female who needs a man to get what she needs?"

"I have no doubt y'are more than capable of—"

"Maybe I am stubborn, but I'm also determined. This is my quest and I can do it on my own. Without your help."

Cillian's back thumped against the trunk of the oak tree and his breath came out with a *whoof*. He held his hands up in surrender and his lips twisted into a wry grin.

"And don't mock me."

"Believe me, lassie, I'm not mockin' ye."

"Then why the smirk?"

"Because you're damned lovely when ye've got yer feathers ruffled."

"You!" I stormed away, fists clenched at my sides, and marched to the horse, gathering her reins in my hands. I lifted my skirts and attempted to slip my boot in the stirrup, but landed squarely on my bottom.

"Here now, lass, let me help ye."

"I can do it myself." Wrenching my elbow from his grasp, I brushed off my dress with as much dignity as I could muster and once again raised my leg while holding onto the saddle. Bouncing three times against the ground, I finally lifted myself and swung my other leg over the saddle, settling comfortably into the seat. I adjusted my skirt, gathered the reins in my hands, and glanced down at Cillian, who was staring at me with his mouth agape.

"Aye, y'are determined, that's for sure."

"You can ride with me if you like," I said, tipping my chin out proudly.

"No, I believe it best I walk alongside for awhile—to give ye time to cool down a bit."

"Suit yourself." With a nudge of my heels and click of my tongue, the horse began walking toward the dirt road with Cillian strolling beside. Once we reached the next town, I'd find transportation to Elkton and send Cillian back to the city and prove to him, and myself, that I could and would find my grandmother on my own.

Several minutes later, still traveling in uneasy silence, we rounded a bend and passed a sign announcing the entrance to the town of Newark. Over the next rise, a cluster of buildings stood in the distance, with parallel tracks running down the middle of town. Would there be any trains running? Maybe a half mile outside town, we found the train station with a drowsy attendant sitting in the window and no sign of protestors. I woke him from his nap.

"Excuse me sir, but are the trains running yet? Has the strike ended?"

"No, miss."

"So there are no trains available?" Disappointment weighted me down. I'd have to find another way.

"There's an independent train that stills comes through

here though. Heading south to Baltimore, expected any minute." The man pointed in a northerly direction, and I glanced over my shoulder, finding a black speck with a billow of smoke on the horizon. He told me the train stopped in Elkton, but also in North East, which would be closer to my destination.

"From there, you could walk the five miles, or there about, to Zion, or find a ride," the attendant said. "You might make it by suppertime."

I'd learned a thing or two about accepting rides from strangers. It would be best if I walked the five miles to my grandmother's house.

"Thank you, sir. I appreciate your help."

I gathered up my carpetbag, which Cillian had left by my side when he led the horse to a watering trough at the corner of the depot. He hadn't spoken a word to me since we left the creek, so I was startled when he walked up beside me, leaving the horse tied to a hitching post.

"Are ye all set, lass?"

"Yes. I think so."

"Aye, ye'll be fine then." He leaned over the tracks and glanced in the direction of the approaching train, which blasted out a piercing whistle.

"You mean you aren't going to follow me? You're not going to insist on coming along?"

"No. This is yer quest, aye? And I must respect yer need for independence in the matter."

My chest deflated like a damaged hot air balloon as disappointment coursed through me. None of it made sense. My quest to find my grandmother was something I needed to do on my own, but now when I was about to say goodbye, I suddenly wanted him to come along with me. Maybe I wasn't as brave as I liked to think.

"Cillian." I laid my hand on his shoulder, urging him to face me. When he turned toward me, his eyes narrowed and his lips pressed into a thin line.

"Ye'll be fine, Laurel. I'm sure of it."

"But—"

"I have no doubt ye can make it there on yer own strong will."

The train's shrill whistle made me jump, causing my already thumping heart to pound against my rib cage. What more could I say? He seemed to have more confidence in me than I had at that moment. When he pulled me into his arms and squeezed me tight, I drew strength from his assurance.

"Thank you, Cillian, for everything you've done for me."

"My pleasure, milady." He stepped back and bowed deeply for effect.

"I'm sorry for the way I acted back at the creek. I know you've only been trying to help me, and I appreciate it, truly I do."

"Aye, I know ye do."

His words were nearly lost in the deafening scream of the train's whistle. A plume of sooty, black smoke disrupted our goodbye as the mighty machine rolled to a stop. All at once, I was afraid, hollow inside, unsure I was ready to leave Cillian behind. I had been determined to do this on my own, but now that the moment was here, my knees were weak, as if the blood had drained from my veins. Images of Edgar and the filthy tavern bed flashed through my mind. I dropped the carpetbag and leapt into his open arms, wrapping my own around his neck in a fierce hug.

"Cillian!"

"Ye can do this, lass. I have faith ye'll make it to yer granny's just fine."

His reassuring words brought back my confidence, but they didn't quell the sadness.

"I'll miss you."

"And I ye. Send me a letter once ye get settled. Ye know where I live." His warm breath tickled the side of my neck and I wanted to stay locked in his strong, comforting arms.

"I will. I promise."

I squeezed my arms tight around his neck and breathed in his familiar scent one last time.

"All aboard!" the conductor shouted, and I eased out of Cillian's embrace.

"Have a safe trip home."

I picked up my carpetbag while taking a deep, fortifying breath, and smiled more brightly than I felt inside. "Thanks again for everything. I'll write soon."

I had taken only a few steps toward the awaiting train when Cillian's hand on my shoulder stopped me. I turned around and he cupped my face in his work-worn hands. His closeness was like a gust of sun-warmed air on a chill day—sudden and unexpected and entirely, surprisingly welcome.

"Y'are a fine young woman, Laurel Whitman, and I'm impressed with yer pluck. Aye, ye may not think ye need a man, but someday maybe ye will. And when that day comes, I'd like to think it could be me."

CHAPTER 10

I dozed off, but awoke with a start when the train whistle announced we had arrived in Maryland. A crick in my neck made it difficult to lift my head from the foggy glass window. Spittle dampened my cheek and my eyes were gummy, but I was rested and anxious to complete my journey. I rubbed a circle in the dirty window and looked out at a small, wood-clad building with a lone ticket window covered in iron bars. It reminded me more of a shed for storing tools and wheelbarrows than a transportation hub. There wasn't much else around the building. I was disheartened to find only three houses and a large barn on the opposite side of the tracks. Surely this wasn't where I was to get off.

"North East," the conductor bellowed as he strolled through the packed car.

Several people rose and reached for satchels and boxes or grabbed children's hands and scurried out of the train. Bewildered, I gathered my carpetbag and followed the other passengers down the metal stairs, assisted by the conductor as I stepped onto the wood platform. Most folks were met with hugs and kisses from loved ones, and others walked away fully aware of their destination. I stood in the middle of the increasingly empty platform and watched the black iron train pull away toward Baltimore. What was I to do now? There were no liveries standing by as there were in the city, and no signs pointing toward Zion. The blood drained to my feet and suddenly I wished Cillian was there to give me guidance.

"May I help you, miss?"

An older gentleman no taller than me with snowy white hair and a long, bushy beard appeared at my side, causing me to drop the carpetbag.

"I'm sorry to have startled you, but you look a little lost," he said. He wore black trousers, a matching coat, and a pillbox cap. "Was someone to meet you here, miss?"

"No, I'm—"

What was I to say? *I'm on my way to find a grandmother whom I've never met and have no idea where she lives exactly. All I have is a name and a general location. I'm not sure she'll receive me or even if she's still alive.* What I thought was a brilliant idea a few days ago seemed like folly now.

"I'm sorry." Brushing the dust from my wrinkled skirt and adjusting my bonnet, which had gone askew during my nap, I gathered my thoughts with a deep breath. "I'm on my way to my grandmother's house in Zion. She doesn't know I'm coming —it's a surprise—but I've never traveled there on my own, so I'm not sure of the way."

"Zion's a good ways from here—about five miles or so. As you can see, there's not much activity around here this time of day."

"That's fine. Point me in the right direction and I'll walk."

My heart sank to my knees when I thought of the long walk ahead of me. Even after the nap, I was still exhausted, having slept so little for the past three days. The sun would sink low in the sky before I got there, and the breeze had picked up, so it would be a chilly trek to my grandmother's.

"That's some distance. If you go across the tracks to the lumberyard there..." He pointed his spotted, wrinkled hand toward the gray, wood-sided barn. A saw's loud whizzing sound pierced the quiet. "Ask for Mr. Schmidt—Karl Schmidt. He lives in Zion. Perhaps he can give you a lift there on his way home."

Hope swelled in my chest and just as quickly deflated as I remembered the last time I had accepted a ride from a stranger.

"He's got a farm there but works a few days a week at the mill. Tell him I sent you."

"I'm not...maybe it would be best if I walked."

As if reading my mind, the man said, "I assure you, Mr. Schmidt is trustworthy."

"Oh, I'm sure he is." I turned full circle, taking in the desolate surroundings, and shook off my fear. My back ached and my head pounded and I dreaded the long walk, so I placed my faith in the little man. "Yes, I think I will talk to Mr. Schmidt. Thank you." I grabbed the ticket seller's hand, pumping it with gratitude. "I'm sorry, but you didn't give me your name."

"So sorry, miss. It's George Blake. And you are?"

"Laurel Whitman, from Philadelphia."

"Pleased to make your acquaintance, Miss Whitman. And who might your grandmother be? Perhaps I know her."

"My grandmother is Margaret Hayward."

His complexion turned gray, as if a dark cloud had descended over his face, and his mouth turned down.

"Do you know her?" I asked, confused by his reaction.

"I know of her. So, John Hayward was your grandfather?"

His question came out like an accusation, prickling my nerves yet piquing my curiosity even more. I had assumed with a different last name that my grandmother had remarried, but I didn't know why or to whom. There was so much I didn't know about Father's side of the family.

"No, sir, my grandfather was Gray Whitman. Did you know him, by chance?"

"No, I can't say I did." Mr. Blake took off his cap and scratched the bald spot hidden among his thinning white hair. The color returned to his cheeks and a brief smile pricked his lips. "Well, I shouldn't keep you." He pointed across the tracks once more. "Find Mr. Schmidt and if you have any problems, you can find me here until six o'clock."

"Thank you, Mr. Blake." I gave his hand a final shake and stepped gingerly between the iron rails, arms extended to provide balance, as I crossed the wood planking and lose gravel. The buzzing wood saw came to life again, drowning out my farewell. "Goodbye, Mr. Blake, and thank you again," I called over my shoulder.

After climbing down the steep embankment from the railroad tracks, I followed along the fence that surrounded the lumberyard where men in shirtsleeves, oblivious to the autumn chill, pushed rough timber past sharp blades resulting in clean, flat lumber. The smell of sawdust and oil filled the air as I rounded the corner and headed toward the storefront.

The doorbell jangled as I entered a warm, cozy store—a mercantile with shelves lined with paint cans and turpentine. There were shovels, hoes, and rakes hanging from wooden pegs, and a black potbelly stove standing in one corner. It was flanked by chairs on either side, occupied by two old men who rocked in synchronized rhythm. The store had been abuzz with conversation and activity until I walked in. All the patrons, who happened to be men, and the store clerk turned as one and stared at me. My throat went dry and my legs ceased to move. Visions of the farmer and Edgar swarmed my mind, but I deliberately pushed them away.

"H-hello," I sputtered, taking a quivering step toward the counter, where two men leaned on bended elbows. They watched with curiosity as I came closer. "Is Mr. Schmidt here, by any chance?"

"What ya want with 'im?" One of the men who had been leaning against the counter rose up and took a step toward me. He had a toothpick in his mouth, which he deftly switched to the opposite side, in the process revealing pink gums where several teeth were missing.

"I'm, um, Mr. Blake across the—"

"That old geezer?" The gap-toothed man took the toothpick from his mouth and snorted. His thin, cracked lips grew into an unnatural smile as he came closer. "What's a pretty thing like you doing out on your own?"

"I'm, um—" I took a giant step backward, ready to run. There wouldn't be a repeat of what had happened in Wilmington.

"What's going on in here?"

A buxom woman, taller than most of the men in the store, came through a doorway behind the counter. She wore a pink calico dress that looked as though it had been washed too many times and a pair of thin wire-rimmed spectacles on the end of her nose.

"What are you doing, Rutherford?" She lifted the hinged counter, letting it bang behind her, and stepped between the toothless man and myself. Her cross expression seemed to quell his menacing bravado. "You giving this girl a hard time?"

"No, ma'am." Rutherford tipped his chin to his chest and shuffled toward the stove.

Satisfied he no longer posed a threat, the woman turned her attention back to me. She had a manly face with a broad nose, thin lips, and a ruddy complexion. But her smile exuded warmth and all at once my fears were gone. She perched her beefy hands on her hips, leaned toward me, and spoke with a hint of a German accent.

"Now, who were you looking for?"

"Mr. Blake over at the train depot suggested I find Mr. Schmidt. I need a ride to Zion and he thought—"

"I'll give you a ride." Rutherford snickered from across the room, but stopped abruptly with one stern glare from my female protector.

"I'm his daughter-in-law, Berta. Come with me. He's out back at the planing mill."

She cast one more threatening glare at Rutherford, who quickly folded into himself, and led the way back outside toward a long shed that sat alongside the tracks.

"So, what brings you to Zion? You don't look like you're from around here."

I glanced down at my dusty, wrinkled dress and wondered where she thought I was from.

"You speak as though you're from up north," she said as I tried to keep up with her long strides.

"Yes, I'm from Philadelphia. I'm on my way to see my grandmother. I'm surprising her. She doesn't know I'm coming."

"And who is your grandmother?"

"Margaret Hayward." I nearly bumped into Berta as she stumbled and stopped her trek. She shook her head without a word and continued on her way.

"*Vater?*" She called out as we entered the building, which smelled of wood shavings, smoke, and oil.

"In zee back, Berta." A baritone voice echoed from the doorway at the back corner of the dark building. Crossing the room, weaving between stacks of finished wood, I followed Berta into a bright, sunlit room where a man was hunched over a plank of wood, applying a sticky, pungent substance with a bristle brush.

"Vater, this is..." Berta turned toward me with brows knitted in confusion. "I don't believe you told me your name."

"I'm sorry. I'm Laurel Whitman."

Satisfied, she turned back to her father-in-law. "Mr. Blake sent Miss Whitman over here to see if she can get a ride home with us this evening."

"Yah, notta problem," he replied, never lifting his gaze from his work. Berta turned, her hands again perched on her hips. "We leave at three-thirty so we're home before dark. Meet us here and we'll give you a ride."

"Thank you very much, Mrs. Schmidt."

"Pff, call me Berta." She waved her hand as if swatting a fly and set off toward the store. Remembering something, she turned around quickly. "Have you had anything to eat today? You look a bit peaked."

"Nothing since breakfast." Actually I hadn't had anything since we were in Wilmington, and my groaning stomach confirmed it.

"Come then. I've got some bread in the office. That will tide you over until you get supper at your *oma's*."

Berta's kindness brought a well of tears to my eyes. It had been a long, arduous three days since I left Philadelphia, with few people willing to lend a hand. Her no-nonsense personality only endeared me more to her generosity. I hoped to do something nice for her once I settled in at my grandmother's house.

I spent an hour in Berta's office, sharing a mug of homemade beer and munching on thick, crusty rye bread she had made herself. While she worked on the ledgers, calculating daily sales with rapid speed and scratching out the totals with a pencil, she kept up a steady stream of conversation. She and her husband, Hans, lived with his parents, Karl and Gretchen, along with Hans' four younger brothers and sisters, who were unmarried. They hoped to build their own house on the farm very soon, having only been married six months. Berta worked three days a week at the lumberyard, riding in to work with Karl, where she took care of the bookkeeping. Expecting her first child in the summer, she would stay home and tend house once the baby arrived.

During our chat, I asked a few questions about my grandmother, but Berta only gave terse answers and returned to the story of the Schmidts. At exactly three-thirty, a tall, young man, who looked about my age, poked his head through her office door.

"Berta? Are you ready to go?"

"Yes, Garin. Did *Vater* tell you we're giving someone a ride?"

"No." Garin stepped into the office holding a brown felt hat in his hands. He blinked a few times as his gaze locked on mine, his eyes as big as moons.

"Garin Schmidt, please make your acquaintance with Miss Laurel Whitman." Garin nodded politely and took a step toward me. As I stood and dipped into a simple curtsy, Berta said, "She's Mrs. Haywards' granddaughter." That brought Garin's steps to a halt. He spun his hat in his hands a few rotations and then forced a smile onto his face.

"It's a pleasure to meet you, Miss Whitman." His grin didn't match the wariness in his eyes.

"Thank you, Mr. Schmidt. Will you be driving us?"

"Yes, miss. I needed the wagon today to make deliveries."

I ignored the hesitant reaction I got at the mention of my grandmother's name and stepped closer to Garin. His eyes were brightest blue, reminding me a bit of Cillian's, and his hair was dark blond like ripe winter wheat. He was at least a head taller than me and had an earthy, musty, but not unpleasant, smell about him.

"Deliveries?"

"Yes, we raise chickens and sell eggs to local merchants and patrons. I had a stall at the market today in Calvert."

"Calvert?"

"It's not far from Zion. I can take you there sometime if you'd like." He seemed to have forgotten about my lineage and relaxed his shoulders, letting his natural smile return.

"Well, I'm not sure. I mean..."

"She's surprising her *oma*. Let her get settled before you go carting her off," Berta scolded her brother-in-law as she wrapped a blue shawl around her ample shoulders. "Now let's get *Vater* and be on our way. We wouldn't want Laurel arriving in the dark."

THE LAST OF THE SUN'S ORANGE RAYS FLICKERED THROUGH THE stand of trees along the hillside as Garin guided the wagon down a rutted gravel lane toward a pale gray farmhouse. My backside was numb from sitting on the hard wooden bed, and I was convinced my bottom was full of splinters. The wagon, pulled by an impressively large mule, was small but sturdy. Karl rode up front on the bench alongside his son, while Berta and I rode in back, where she kept up a steady stream of mill and farm gossip.

"Ah, here we are," Berta said, throwing out a thick arm in the direction of the farmhouse. "This would be your *oma's* place."

Fearing the reaction I would receive from my grandmother, I fought to keep my nerves under control.

"It's lovely." My words quivered as I took in the idyllic farm, so much like my painting.

"True. Mr. Smith keeps a fine farm. Good head of cattle."

"Who's Mr. Smith?" Up until this moment, no one had mentioned a Mr. Smith. A streak of fear ran through me that I'd been duped once again. Was this group handing me off not to my grandmother, but to an unsavory lot? What had happened back at the tavern was still fresh in my mind.

"Why that would be your uncle..." Berta scratched her head

in thought. "No, he would be your uncle-in-law." She chuckled, making her ample bust shake.

"My what?"

"Your grandmother's daughter, Helen, is married to Charles Smith. Did you not know you had an Aunt Helen?"

"No."

Father had never mentioned his sister, Helen. Glancing off in the distance toward a fenced-in field where black and white cows grazed in the waning light, a thin, bearded man, dressed in dark pants held up with green suspenders walked toward the lane and gave a hearty wave.

"There he is." Berta lifted onto her knees and raised her arms, waving them like a windmill. "Hello, Mr. Smith," she shouted.

Mr. Smith waved back and climbed over the wooden fence, meeting the wagon midway to the house.

"Goot evenin', Charles," Karl said with a tip of his hat.

"Good evening, Karl. Stopping by for a visit?"

Like Berta, I rose up on my knees to get a better look at my newly discovered uncle-in-law. He pulled the felt hat from his head and raked his fingers through his dark hair. His lower face was covered in a beard reaching to his chest, but even through the thatch, a warm, friendly smile showed through.

"Not tis evenin', I'm afraid," Karl continued. He turned and pointed to me. "We've brought your niece for a visit."

"My niece?"

Confusion filled Charles' gaze. Not wanting Mr. Schmidt to go through a long explanation, I scrambled out of the wagon and hurried around to greet him.

"Hello." I curtsied and then clasped my quivering hands together. "I'm Laurel Whitman. I've come to visit my grandmother."

"Whitman?" His brows furrowed and his shoulders drew back. "Would you be—"

"I'm Calvin Whitman's daughter. His oldest daughter. From Philadelphia."

"Is that right?" Charles scratched his head, which seemed to help his memory. "We heard he had a daughter."

"Two actually. My sister Emily is two years younger than me. And I have two brothers— Elvin, who's one year older than me, and Sampson, the baby. Actually, he's seventeen, but my mother always refers to him as the baby. None of them look like me. The boys have brown hair and Emily has blond, but I got red somehow." My nerves were flushing out with every word. I couldn't stop my mouth from moving, but it did help to calm me. Charles's worried gaze turned to amusement as I chattered on.

"I can guess where that came from," he said. "Well, better get you down to the house and introduce you to everyone."

"Is my grandmother here?"

"She lives with us."

"I thought this was her farm."

"It was, until I bought it last year. We'll explain everything."

Charles sidestepped around me and extended his hand to Karl, who was still sitting on the buckboard. Garin had climbed down and retrieved my carpetbag from the back of the wagon.

"Here you are, Miss Whitman." Garin placed the handle in my hand and gave it a squeeze. "I hope things go well for you here." His warm smile, meant for encouragement, only made my hackles rise. Why did I get the feeling I was about to step into a maelstrom?

"Thank you, Mr. Schmidt."

"Please call me Garin." He took a step back and glanced toward the farmhouse, where a thin ribbon of smoke curled out of a chimney. "May I stop by and check on you in a day or two?"

"That would be fine, Garin." Charles had already stepped in as my guardian, allowing male visitors to call on me.

"Yes, thank you, Garin." With a final quick curtsy, I waved

goodbye to Mr. Schmidt, Garin, and Berta, and followed my uncle-in-law down the lane.

We had only gone a short way before Charles finally said, "You came just in time."

"Oh?"

"I'm not sure you'll get a chance to talk to your grandmother."

"Why?"

Charles shook his head and the look he gave me—worrisome yet sympathetic—made my heart skip a beat. "She probably won't make it through the night."

CHAPTER 11

A slow, painful burn flared in the pit of my stomach and tears threatened to fall. I'd had questions my whole life. Why was I so different from my siblings? Where did I get my artistic talent? Why did my father hate me so? I was sure if I met my grandmother, she could fill in the gaps. Long afternoons chatting with her, getting to know the woman who had always been a mystery, might not happen. She was on her deathbed. *You got here just in time.* If only I had set out earlier, maybe my curiosity would be quelled. At best, I'd get a chance to say goodbye.

"Helen, my wife, your aunt, has been doing all she can to provide comfort to Gramma. That's what the children call her. You'll meet them. We have two daughters—Cora, who's six, and Belle, who's three. To look at them, you'd think they were twins."

"I'm excited to meet everyone."

"They'll be surprised, most definitely."

"I'm sorry I didn't send a letter telling you of my arrival. I left Philadelphia rather suddenly."

"Is that so?"

There was something in Charles's warm countenance and strong spirit that made me trust him.

"My father and I had an argument and he threw me out. It was a blessing, really. I planned to visit. I'd always wanted to know more about my grandmother and my father's family. I only wish my leaving hadn't been so fraught with anger. My father said some hateful things."

"I can imagine."

"Do you know him?" I laid my hand on his arm and pulled him to a stop. "Have you met him?"

"Only once, before Helen and I were married."

"Was it here? When was this?"

"Calvin came to see your grandmother about her will. She'd let him know, along with your Uncle Jeremy and Aunt Sarah—surely you know your father's siblings?"

"I do. What did Gramma tell them?"

"She was leaving the farm to Helen and her brother, Robert. Cut the Whitman children out of her will."

"But why?"

"That, my dear, is not my story to tell."

We continued down the lane, gravel crunching under our boots, without another word. My grandmother was dying, so would I ever learn the secrets my father had been keeping all these years? Would Helen tell me? Did she know? Maybe I was expecting too much too soon from my newly discovered family. Maybe with time—and trust—they would tell me all I wanted to know.

We stepped up onto the wooden front porch and I thought for sure my knees would give out. Exhaustion, hunger, and fear made the blood drain from my limbs and I worried I might not make it through the door. Charles must have sensed my frailty, for he wrapped a supportive hand around my arm and opened the door. The smell of onions and beef cooking over a hot fire wafted from inside as two redheaded bookends met us inside the door.

"Daddy!" the smaller girl said.

"Who is this, Daddy?" said the other child, whose red curly hair and freckles matched her sister's identically. In fact, they looked like small replicas of me.

"Where's your mother?" Charles asked, guiding me to a wooden chair at the kitchen table. "Go get her, girls, please." The little girls cast a quick glance over their shoulders and scurried out of the room calling, "Mother!"

"Can I get you a glass of water, Laurel?" He pulled a clear goblet from the shelf without waiting for my reply and filled it from a large pitcher. "Here you are. Drink it slowly."

I sipped the cool, fresh water and was instantly better. Although I was tired from the long trip, my faintness was more from the emotional toll of meeting my new family and the knowledge that my grandmother was dying.

"Charles, dear..." A tall woman, dressed in a deep blue print dress, entered the kitchen, concern etched on her freckled face. Her hair was pulled back in a tight bun, but tendrils wisped around her face, confirming the same red curls as mine. This must be Helen. We could've been twins.

"Hello," she said, coming closer to me. Her brows were arched in surprise. Perhaps she, too, had noticed the resemblance between us. "I'm Helen. And you are?"

"This is Calvin's daughter, Laurel. She's come to see Gramma." Charles had stepped in to answer, perhaps sensing my inability to speak. Seeing my reflection in the flesh took my breath away.

"Calvin's?" Helen drew up short, even took a step back with the shock, and then pulled back her shoulders. She forced a kind smile on her lips and nodded slightly. "Laurel, it's so nice to meet you."

"I'm pleased to meet you, as well, Helen," I croaked,

overcome with emotion from seeing people who actually looked like me. Before I could stop them, I broke down in tears and dropped my head to the table. My sobs came out in great, uncontrollable hiccups. An arm wrapped around my shoulders and I could tell from the scent of lavender that it was Helen, trying to calm my outburst.

"There, there. It will be okay. Take your time, Laurel."

She pulled my shoulders around to face her and held me in a strong embrace as I cried into the shirtwaist of her dress. Her kind hands rubbed circles on my back as if I were a child, and the gesture calmed my emotions. Slowly, my sobs subsided and I eased out of Helen's arms. She pressed a handkerchief into my hand and I blew like a geyser. The tears slowed to a trickle and with a gulp of water, my throat opened enough for me to talk.

"I'm so embarrassed," I said between sips. "I didn't mean to break down like that. It's just—"

"You've come a long way," she said, handing me a fresh handkerchief.

"Yes, I've been on the road three days. It hasn't been easy finding you."

"Your cheek is bruised. Did you run into trouble?"

"It-it was an accident," I sniffed, feeling momentarily guilty for the lie. "Thankfully, the Schmidts knew where you live."

"Your father didn't tell you where we were?"

"He's told me nothing about you." Though it wasn't my fault, I was embarrassed to tell these kind people that they hadn't existed to me until a few minutes ago. "I'm sorry."

"You have nothing to be sorry about. We know very little about you either." She took the glass from my hand and refilled it with water. Giving it back, she said, "If you'd like to stay, we'll make up for that, get to know one another better, hmm?"

"If it wouldn't be too much bother."

"None at all. You can sleep in with the girls, if you don't mind. They would love having a guest in their bed."

"Thank you, Helen. Or would you rather I call you Aunt Helen?"

"Since we're closer in age than most aunts and nieces, you can call me Helen, how's that?"

"That suits me fine."

"Good. Now, supper will be ready in a few minutes. Would you like to freshen up?"

"Yes, but could I first see my grandmother?"

Clouds formed in her gaze and she glanced down at her folded hands. "That might be best. We don't know how much longer she has."

"What's wrong with her?"

"Consumption. She's been battling it for nearly a month."

"Oh my."

"Maybe if she knows you're here, it will give her peace so she can let go and cross over. It's like she's been waiting for something." Helen smoothed the front of her skirt and shrugged. "Maybe she's been waiting for you."

I followed Helen through the large kitchen with its table big enough to seat ten, a wall of shelves which held lovely blue and white dishes, and a cast iron stove with an oven beneath. We entered a dark hallway with a door at the end that led outside, and a door to the left from which the sound of heavy, raspy breathing came. Gramma's struggle to breathe filtered out into the hall. I knew she didn't have long.

She was propped up on a pile of pillows, most covered in hand-embroidered cases, and tucked under a colorful quilt. I wondered if she had made the beautiful blanket with its intricate double-ring pattern in shades of blue, pink, and cream. Her long gray hair, greasy and unwashed, lay loosely on her shoulders, and her pallor was almost as dull. Her chest rose and fell with shallow, irregular breaths, and I heard a distinct rattle. Though I'd never witnessed a person's death, I sensed her end was near.

"Go ahead and talk to her. She may hear you." Helen propelled me toward the bed with a light touch to my back. "Let her know you're here."

It didn't look as though my grandmother could hear me. She appeared unconscious, just a breath away from heaven.

"Grandmother?" My voice shook as I tiptoed slowly to the bed. "Gramma?" I wasn't sure what to call the woman who I'd imagined so differently. I had pictured a tall, elegant woman with red hair and animated green eyes, not a shriveled, failing, gray-haired woman so close to death.

"Gramma, it's Laurel. Laurel." I picked up her hand, relieved its wrinkled form was still warm. "Laurel. Calvin's daughter."

My grandmother's eyes flew open. They were pale green with a cloudy film and red rims, but they bore into me like she'd seen a ghost. She collapsed into a coughing fit, her body racking against the pillows. Helen gently shoved me out of the way and slipped her arm around her mother, lifting her into a more comfortable sitting position as she expelled the mucus from her lungs.

I retreated to the corner of the room, next to a mahogany dresser covered in a tatted scarf. A framed daguerreotype of a handsome man, unsmiling but with amusement in his eyes, sat on her dresser and seemed to stare back at me. He had a long, thin face, sharp nose, and wavy hair that brushed the back of his collar. His face was shaven, yet he had a bushy mustache that framed his upper lip. He looked to be around thirty years of age, and I wondered if this could be John Hayward.

"Laurel?" my grandmother whispered.

Helen drew in a deep breath of surprise and lowered Gramma to the pillows. She used a cool, damp rag to wipe her face, but my grandmother shooed her away.

"Laurel," she said again, this time with a bit more volume.

I rushed to her bedside and gathered her soft hand in mine. Her head rested against the pillows and she locked her cloudy gaze on me, drawing deep, rattling breaths into her lungs.

"Yes, Gramma, I'm here."

"Laurel?"

It seemed to be the only thing she could say. Her lips were moving, but no sound escaped. Still, she continued to look at me as if she were seeing an aberration.

"Mother, you need to rest now." Helen smoothed Gramma's hair away from her face with one hand as she held one of her wrists. "Her pulse is stronger." She lowered her head to my grandmother's chest and listened. "And her lungs sound clearer."

Helen stood back up and looked down at me kneeling beside the bed.

"I don't understand it." She leaned over her mother, adjusting the blankets under her chin, and laid her hand against her wrinkled cheek. "Are you feeling better, Mother?"

Gramma nodded slightly and closed her eyes. She squeezed my hand with light pressure—most likely all the strength she had—and fell into a deep sleep. Helen and I stood beside the bed, looking down at my grandmother's dozing form. Were we both expecting her to take her last breath? I'd heard the dying often perk up right before the end. But after several minutes watching her chest rise and fall in a steady rhythm, Helen turned down the kerosene lamp and gestured for me to follow her out of the room.

When we returned to the kitchen, the girls were sitting at the table, heads bowed over steaming bowls of stew, spooning the savory-smelling meal into their mouths.

"Is it over?" Charles crossed the room and gathered Helen's shoulders in his hands. "Did she pass?"

"No." Helen shook her head with bewilderment. "In fact, I believe she's...better."

"Did she know Laurel was here?"

Helen nodded and turned toward me. "Maybe it *was* you she was waiting for."

I'm not sure how my grandmother could have known I was coming, but if my appearance somehow kept her from leaving this earth, I was glad of it. Perhaps she'd get better—at least long enough for me to get to know her.

"Children," Helen said, turning her attention to the girls. "This is your cousin Laurel, and she'll be staying with us for a while."

The girls nodded their greetings, mouths too full to speak.

"Thank you, dear, for feeding Belle and Cora," Helen said as she turned toward the stove.

Never once had my father fed us or helped my mother with any of her duties. It was a refreshing sight to see a man help his wife. Charles slipped his arm around Helen's waist and led her to the table. After pulling out her chair and making sure she was settled, he gave an affectionate squeeze to her shoulders and returned to the stove himself.

"Have a seat, Laurel. I'll get you ladies something to eat. It's been a long, hard day for both of you."

My stomach growled loudly in agreement and I giggled with embarrassment as I pressed my palm to my abdomen. Cora, who was sitting to my right, burst out a laugh, spewing stew across the table.

"Cora!" Helen blurted. "Where are your manners?"

"I'm sorry Mother, but Laurel's tummy made a funny sound." She wiped first her mouth and then the table with a pale blue linen napkin.

"I'm sure it's not the first time you've heard hunger pangs,"

Helen said, trying to keep a smile from stretching across her face.

"It sounded like a lion," Cora said shyly.

"Like a bear," Belle added to the description.

"Like a mountain lion."

"No, a tiger."

"A freight train."

The girls continued their game of name-that-stomach-rumble, much to their parents' chagrin. I laughed at their clever descriptions, delighting in the relaxed, loving atmosphere so unlike meals in my home, where Father demanded quiet and perfect manners.

"That's enough, children. Eat your stew," Charles said, chuckling silently as he joined us at the table. "It isn't polite to poke fun at our guest."

"Oh, no, it's fine," I said. "I'm enjoying myself immensely."

In fact, all my jitters were gone and my weariness no longer dragged me down. Everything I'd been through for the past three days was worth it to be sitting now with this kind family —my family—who had graciously opened their home to me without question.

An unexpected emptiness coursed through me. Despite the food warming my body and the smiling faces warming my soul, a hollowness remained. I wasn't as surprised as I ought to have been to find the sure knowledge of what—or who—would have filled that void. *If only Cillian were here.*

CHAPTER 12

I woke the next morning with something hard and round pressed against my tailbone. The dull morning light peeked between the heavy drapes, softly billowing in and out in rhythm with the howling winds outside. Loud raindrops, like pellets, pinged against the glass.

It took a moment to remember where I was. After blinking away the fog, Belle's face came into focus. Her cheek rested against the pillow we were sharing and her long lashes feathered against her creamy skin. Sleeping between the two little girls—they had insisted we make a "Laurel sandwich"—it didn't take long to figure out the round, hard object jabbing into my back was Cora's bony little knee. Desperate to relieve the pain, I rolled over and came face-to-face with a pair of emerald green eyes. Cora smiled sweetly and wrapped her arms around my neck, whispering in my ear, "I wondered when you would wake up."

I enveloped her into my shoulder and breathed in her sweet, sleepy smell. Her red curly hair had sprung out of its plait, creating a fluffy halo around her angelic face. Cupping her freckled cheeks in my hands, I marveled at her resemblance to my younger self.

"I would've slept longer if a knobby knee hadn't poked into my back." My feigned scolding didn't fool Cora.

"I did that on purpose." She giggled, quite proud her plan had worked. I was now wide awake.

I held my finger to my lips. "Shh, we shouldn't wake Belle."

"No matter. She can sleep through a herd of buffalo." Cora dismissed her sister's sleeping form with a wave of her hand and climbed out of bed. "Come on. Mother's making porridge. Can you smell it?"

"I can." Scooting to the edge of the bed, an earthy combination of grains, cinnamon, and molasses wafted from the kitchen below. "I'm starved. Aren't you?"

"Yes. Come on, Laurel. Maybe if we hurry, there won't be any left for Belle."

She threw open the bedroom door, tugging me by the hand into the short hallway and down the staircase. Helen was at the stove in a periwinkle blue muslin dress, stirring the porridge. Tapping the wooden spoon against the iron pot, she turned around with a broad smile.

"Good news girls. Gramma made it through the night and is asking for breakfast."

"That *is* good news," I said as I sat on the bench with Cora glued to my side.

"And she asked about you, Laurel. Maybe after she's had breakfast, you can go sit with her."

"I'd like that."

As it turned out, it wasn't the greeting I had imagined. Two hours after we'd had breakfast—saving plenty for Belle, who had slept nearly an hour longer than Cora and me— Gramma asked Helen to send me in. Her breathing was much better this morning and color had returned to her cheeks. It was a miracle she was still alive, let alone looking as well as she did.

The teapot, cup, and saucer I carried into her room rattled on the lace-covered tray. She was propped against the pile of pillows with her eyes closed, though the curtains were parted to add a bit of natural light to the room. The early morning storm had subsided and faint sun rays were streaming through the windows. I tried to enter her room silently so as not to disrupt her nap, but the clattering china awakened her. I set the tea tray on her bedside table, feeling her gaze sear into me, and carefully poured the steaming tea into the cup. "Helen thought you'd like some tea," I said, trying to hide my nerves. There were so many questions to which I wanted answers, but I didn't want to rush her. She'd been on death's door last night and I didn't want to cause a setback, but I was so anxious to learn everything. This woman was a stranger to me and I desperately needed her to fill in the blanks.

She didn't reach out for the cup and saucer when I offered it to her. Instead she continued staring at me with her cloudy, green eyes.

"Would you like me to hold the cup while you drink?"

Gramma didn't answer. Her gaze turned icy as her eyes narrowed. She pursed her lips and huffed out a breath.

"Gramma, would you like some tea?"

"Why are you here?"

Her question startled me. Tea slopped over the rim and onto the saucer. Last night, I had thought she was happy to see me, that my visit had brought her back to life. Even Helen thought the timing of my arrival was some sort of miracle. Now she glared at me as her sallow cheeks flushed red.

"I don't understand." I set the cup and saucer back on the tea tray where they'd be safe from my quivering hands.

"You heard me. Why are you here?"

My stomach took a tumble and my knees gave out. I dropped into the ladder-back chair alongside her bed, feeling the blood drain from my face.

"I, uh, wanted...to see you...to meet you." I barely got the words out before she barked at me.

"Why? Did he send you?"

"Who? Did who—"

"Did Calvin send you?"

"No, Gramma, I came on my own. I've always wanted—"

"What kind of game are you playing?"

As though a strong wind had blown into me, I fell against the back of the chair, shocked at her questions. It was worse than I had imagined. Father's hatred for his mother seemed to be reciprocated. How was it possible for a mother to have such ill feelings toward her son?

It took a moment to find my voice again. I'd come so far to meet her and get the answers I sought. Swallowing the lump in my throat, I sat up straighter and squared my shoulders, fisting my quivering hands in my lap.

"I assure you, Gramma, I'm not playing a game. I came here to meet you, to get to know you. Father didn't send me."

"Why did you want to meet me?"

"Because I know nothing about you."

"So?"

My eyes burned. I was growing frustrated by this mean old woman. Maybe I'd made a mistake coming here.

"Haven't you wondered about me, and my brothers and sister?"

"It wouldn't have mattered if I had."

"What does that mean?"

Instead of answering, she folded her bony, wrinkled arms across her sagging breasts and huffed out a breath. Closing her eyes, she declared our visit over. Perhaps her near-death experience and the shock of seeing me had put her in a foul mood. Or perhaps Father was justified in keeping us away from his mother. I picked up the tea tray and left the room. Perhaps later this afternoon I could quiz Helen on the history of my father's relationship with his mother. For now, it was best I let her sleep.

November 7, 1877

Dear Cillian,

I pray this letter finds you safe and sound back home, toiling away on your rotating ramp. Once perfected, the contraption is sure to make you millions and you'll soon be hobnobbing with the Vanderbilts. You must tell me how your interview with Mr. Schumer went.

Please forgive me for the lateness of this letter, it being six days since we parted at the train station in Delaware. I should have written you right away to let you know I made it safely to my grandmother's home. I had an uneventful trip on the train, but was blessed with a bit of luck once I arrived. It was my great fortune to meet the Schmidt family, who live on the neighboring farm. They gave me a ride in the back of their wooden cart pulled by the most enormous mule, delivering me in time for supper.

One of the mysteries of my being has been solved! I now know from where my red hair, green eyes, and speckled complexion come. As soon as I walked into my grandmother's house, I was met by a gaggle of smiling, redheaded, freckle-faced women. My half-aunt, Helen, and I could be full sisters, and her two daughters are miniatures of me. In fact, six year-old Cora is my spitting image. She even has green eyes. Though hers are cloudy with age, I believe my grandmother is the source of that unique color.

As far as the rest of it—why my father has kept my grandmother from us and why he won't speak of her—that remains a mystery. When I arrived, my grandmother was near death, but miraculously recovered, enough to accuse me of an evil intent. Her angry countenance has not improved much where I'm concerned. *For nearly a week now, I've avoided her so as not to hamper her recovery.*

Helen and her husband, Charles, have been most welcoming. I repay their hospitality by reading to Belle and Cora, helping fix meals, and assisting Charles on the farm. Today he taught me how to milk the cows! Can you imagine? Me, milking a cow? They have two dozen black and white Holsteins (dairy cows, so Charles tells me) who must be milked morning and evening. They produce enough milk to supply the family for drinking, churning into butter, and making into cheese. Cheese-making is quite an interesting process that I'll have to save for another letter. Charles shares any extra milk with the Schmidts who, though they have cows of their own, have such a large brood to feed, they always welcome his offerings. In return, they keep him supplied with the amber beer they brew. (I have even acquired a taste for the rich, malted drink.) Perhaps I'll tell them about your Brew Maker!

Cillian, you have always been such a dear friend to me, and I can't thank you enough for your assistance in getting me here. Your encouragement and understanding of my independent nature are most appreciated. Even though I know little more than I did when I arrived, I feel sure I made the right decision in coming. Country life is slower and more physically demanding. I didn't appreciate how easy I had it in Philadelphia, but the crisp, clean air and bright sunshine, unhindered behind buildings and smokestacks, refreshes my soul.

I wish you could be here to experience it with me, dear friend. I believe you'd love riding on Charles's big black horse, Titan, across the now fallow cornfield at breakneck speed with the wind in your hair and the sun at your back. Even though it is November, and quite cool most mornings, the clear blue sky warms my heart. If only you could see it.

Say hello to everyone at the mill, and give my regards to your mother and sister. Most especially, be well dear Cillian. I pray for your health and happiness each day.

Sincerely yours,
Laurel

The pen tumbled from my hand, splattering a blotch of ink on the wood desk as I dropped my head onto my folded arms. Everything I had written was true. Helen and Charles had been most accommodating and the children were a delight, but my grandmother was still hostile and untrusting of me. The few times I'd delivered her lunch to her or tried to visit with a cup of tea, she glared at me with her frosty gaze, refusing to speak to me. I hadn't had the nerve to ask any more questions for fear she'd unleash her wrath upon me again.

Helen had shared very little, stating my grandmother would come around, which only fueled my impatience. Though kind and encouraging, Helen wouldn't be my source of information. Only my grandmother could reveal the truth behind the hatred between her and my father.

I swiped the errant tears from my cheeks and quickly slipped Cillian's letter inside an envelope. I scribbled the address on the front—*Mr. Cillian O'Brien, Richmond Street, Philadelphia, Pennsylvania.* Charles was taking his cheese to the market in Calvert this morning, and had invited me to ride along. We would pass a small post office where I could mail my letter. Smoothing my hand across the now dry ink, Cillian's handsome face appeared in my mind. His dark hair, crystal blue eyes, and wide grin summoned a smile to my face.

He'd been so kind at the train station, wishing me luck, even hinting at marriage should I need it. What a gentleman. Though Cillian was in full support of my aspirations, he couldn't help himself in suggesting we marry someday, knowing how hard it was for a woman to be on her own. But marriage couldn't simply be based on a deep friendship. What about affection, admiration, even desire? Didn't he want those things? If he extended the offer again, I'd tell him he deserved more than a companion. The woman he married someday should want him above everything else. Me? I had too many goals and dreams—marriage would just get in the way.

THE RIDE INTO CALVERT WAS NOT LONG—ONLY A FEW MILES down a well-tended dirt road, past dormant fields where, in the spring, corn and wheat would be planted. Fenced-in meadows where horses and cows grazed dotted the landscape as we rode. I sat up on the bench seat next to Charles, while Belle and Cora kept a close eye on four large wheels of cheese surrounding them in the back of the wagon.

"Have you lived here your whole life, Charles?"

"Not my whole life, no." He snapped the reins, instructing the mule to pick up speed. "I grew up in a little town up the road there in Pennsylvania. Oxford, it's called."

"How far is it?"

"Eight or ten miles."

"Then how did you meet Helen?"

A sweet grin stretched across his face and his eyes softened. I could only imagine the depths to which those memories brought him happiness. He chuckled and shook off his thoughts.

"I met Helen at my cousin's wedding. My cousin, Nathaniel Smith, married Helen's cousin, Emmeline Lynch. Actually, she's Helen's second cousin—her grandfather and Emmeline's grandfather were brothers."

"What a lovely occasion to meet."

"Well, one would think. The two Lynch brothers had a long-running feud over a land dispute, and even though they've both since passed, that feud continues through both sides of the Lynch family. A few of Helen's cousins almost came to blows before Emmeline and Nathaniel could say 'I do.'" He snorted a laugh and rubbed his forehead with his rough, work-worn hand. "The bride's side of the church cleared out, anxious to watch the fight, leaving only Emmeline's mother and sisters, Helen, Robert—Helen's brother who you'll meet today—and Margaret to watch the rest of the ceremony."

"Why were all those cousins invited if Emmeline knew of the feud?"

He shrugged his bony shoulders and shook his head. "I never figured that one out myself. But it was advantageous for me. As soon as the ceremony ended, I made a point to introduce myself to Helen, who I had noticed the moment she walked into the sanctuary."

"She caught your eye, did she?" I joined in his gaiety and nudged my elbow into his ribs. "Tell me about it."

"Oh, she was lovely, as you can imagine. Her red hair was like flames when the sun hit it, and she was wearing a fetching blue gown that set off her eyes."

"How old were you when you met?"

"Helen was twenty and I was twenty-three. She was shy, if you can imagine that, and I was forced to do all the talking. We sat under a tree and shared our picnic lunch while we got to know one another. Margaret—your Gramma—wouldn't leave us alone, even though we were surrounded by friends and family, but I guess that was only right. They had been through a lot and Gramma was overprotective."

"What do you mean?"

"She kept Helen and Robert close to her."

"And what about their father? John, isn't it? Gramma's second husband?"

"Yes. John Hayward."

"What about him?"

"He died when Helen and Robert were young. Their mother had a tough time of it."

"Raising her children alone?"

"It wasn't the aloneness that bothered them. They were used to that. It was the looks and the comments."

"I'm not sure what you mean."

"No?"

A deep crease formed between Charles's brows and his lips pressed tight when he turned to look at me.

"Well..." His concentration returned to driving the cart up a long, gradual slope, and he snapped the reins against the mule's back. "I guess you wouldn't, what with you being from Margaret's first family. I'm sure Calvin wouldn't have mentioned it."

"No, Father has told me so little of his family. That's why I came. I want to know everything."

"I'm not sure you want to hear about *everything*."

"Why? I want to know everything about my grandmother, even about John. All I know is her first husband, Gray, my grandfather, died from the ague when Father was eight. That's all I know. Father refuses to tell me anything else."

"I'm sure he doesn't want to relive it."

"But why?" I wrapped my hands around his arm and tugged so hard, the reins dropped from Charles's hand. "Why won't Father or Gramma tell me? How terrible can it be?"

"Bad enough that the name Hayward is still scorned around here. Your Uncle Robert hasn't had it easy."

"Tell me, please. What could possibly have happened that no one will speak of it?"

"Well..." Charles lifted the brim of his brown felt derby and repositioned it low over his brows, sucking air through his teeth. He cast a quick glance over his shoulder at the girls, who had dozed off, and then leaned close to me, keeping is voice low. "Helen's father...he..."

"Please, tell me."

He then glanced around as if expecting a crowd around us. He flicked the reins and cleared his throat. "He went to prison."

CHAPTER 13

It was as though a herd of horses had trampled across my chest. Our mule's hooves *clop, clop, clopped* up the road at a steady pace and I tried to match my shallow breaths to the rhythm. Of all the things I had imagined, my step-grandfather going to prison wasn't one of them. Myriad questions swirled through my mind. I didn't even know where to begin.

"Prison? What on earth for?"

"It's a long, sad tale. Helen was quite young. Doesn't remember most of it. He died not long after."

"When did he die?"

"It's been...well, he died in 1860. Helen was ten."

"That means I was three when he died. Father never said a word about it, not in all these years."

"Yes, well, I suppose he wouldn't." Charles's grin wasn't one of humor, but reluctance, even sadness. I fidgeted on the buckboard's bench, grinding my bottom against the rough wood. It took all my patience not to shake the whole story out of him. My interrogation had to be slowly measured if I wanted him to open up.

"Ah, here we are." Charles turned the wagon into a dried-up grassy field. "Belle. Cora. Wake up."

The girls rose to their knees as Charles pulled the wagon behind a row of stalls.

"Look, Father. That's Gertie's wagon." Cora was on her feet, pointing at a yellow wagon across the way.

Charles brought the mule to a complete stop and Cora jumped out of the wagon but drew up short when her father said, "Whoa there, little miss. Before you go speeding off, let me get these wheels of cheese to the booth."

"Yes, sir." Cora wiggled and pranced, anxious to see her little friend.

The area around the farm was so sparsely populated, we couldn't even see the neighboring farmhouses, so it was surprising to find such a large gathering at the market. Though smaller in size, it reminded me of the market on Arch Street where Emily, Mother, and I would go on Saturdays to purchase beef and freshly plucked chickens, apple cider in the fall, and leafy greens in the spring. The little community of Calvert wasn't as small as I'd first thought.

It took only a few minutes for Charles and me to carry the cheese to a table, which we shared with Robert, who was selling lard and jars of pickled pig feet.

"Robert, may I introduce Laurel Whitman? Calvin's daughter."

The block of lard that Robert had been holding landed on the wooden table with a thud. "Calvin's?" There was little resemblance between Robert and Helen. Near-black hair peeked from beneath his hat and he had dark eyes, but he was tall and slim like her. He wiped his greasy hands on his pants and cleared his throat, dipping his chin. "Please to meet you, Laurel."

He leaned toward Charles, speaking quietly, hoping I wouldn't hear. "Does Mother know she's here?"

"Yes, and as matter of fact, her health has improved since Laurel arrived."

"Is that so?" Robert turned back to me, pushing the brim of his hat high on his forehead, and smiled for the first time. "Will wonders never cease?"

"She may have recovered, but she hasn't warmed up to me at all," I said.

"Give her time. Our mother can be a bit stubborn."

"You can say that again," Charles said, nudging Robert into laughter.

"Daddy!" Cora tugged on the hem of Charles' coat, bouncing on her toes. "Can I go see Gertie?"

"Run along, and take Belle with you. Stay where I can see you."

"Yes, sir. Come on, Belle." Cora dragged her little sister across the grassy space to a booth where four children were playing.

"Laurel, would you mind searching for a ripe pumpkin or two?" Charles dropped a few pennies in my hand. "Helen wants to make pies for Thanksgiving dinner."

"Gladly." Charles must have noticed how anxious I was to stroll around and meet some more people. I had only met the Schmidts, and now Robert. I longed to spend more time with Berta or perhaps meet another girl my age, but as I walked around, I received a few smiles and nods, but no one actually spoke to me. Instead, they clustered in groups of three or four, catching up on the local news, too pleased to reunite with friends.

There were two farmers selling fall produce—smooth butternut squash, dried corn, fat, round pumpkins, and among them, smaller sugar pumpkins the likes of which Mother used for her pies. It was surprising to find such generous quantities of the fruit so late in the season. I fitted a small, plump pumpkin in the crook of each arm and turned toward the farmer to pay him when two pairs of hands snatched away my pickings, causing me to stumble.

"Let me help you with that, miss."

"Easy there."

I snapped around, angry, but was shocked to find a young man, not much older than me, and his identical twin standing beside him. Each held a pumpkin and a satisfied smile. They had white-blonde hair, clear blue eyes, and matching buck-toothed grins. My gaze pivoted from one to the other, and it took a moment to comprehend how utterly identical their faces were.

"Hello, Miss. I'm Samuel Moffitt and this is my brother, Solomon."

"Oh, I'm—"

"We thought you might need some help with those gourds," Samuel said. Or was it Solomon?

"We're at your service." The twins bobbed their heads in unison and I still wasn't sure which was which. I'd seen twins before, but not as perfectly mirror-like as the Moffitt brothers.

"Thank you. I'm Laurel Whit—"

"We know who you are. Garin told us. He's over there." Samuel or Solomon turned and pointed toward a stall selling dark glass bottles of beer.

"We've come to introduce ourselves," said one.

"And help you with your pumpkins," said the other, barely allowing the first brother to complete his thought.

"Shall we carry them to your wagon?"

"Or should we deliver them to your uncle?"

"Either way, we'll be happy to help."

Their exuberance made me a bit light-headed, but I laughed at their toothy grins and found myself uplifted by their energy.

"Thank you. If you could take them to the wagon, I'd be most obliged."

"Very fine. Lead the way." Samuel, I think, tipped his head toward the field of parked wagons, but I had to restrain his enthusiasm long enough to have the pumpkins weighed. Once the farmer was paid his three cents, I escorted my heroes to the wagon, laughing along with their quick-fire assessment of the people we passed.

"That's the widow Martin." One of the twins discretely pointed at an old woman selling skeins of lambswool. The other twin followed up with, "They say she's not really a widow. That she's got her husband locked away in her attic." They burst out laughing.

"Those men are the elders of the new Methodist Episcopal church. Very pious and saintly."

"But on Saturday night, you'll find them deep into a card game, soused on ale, and cursing like sailors."

As if on cue, Samuel and Solomon threw back their heads and blew out identical guffaws that caused me to burst out laughing. They reminded me of the comedy act Cillian and I had seen at the Wild West show.

"Oh, look there, Laurel. That's the mayor of Calvert."

"He's not really the mayor," a twin whispered in my ear. "He just acts like he is."

"That's Jacob Simpers. The richest man in the county."

"He has a thousand or more acres up toward Rising Sun."

"It's a few miles west of here."

As we passed the "mayor," the twins' faces became stoic and respectful. They bowed slightly as the mayor glared at them, and I wondered if Mr. Simpers could see through their feigned deference. Once we rounded the last stall, the three of us burst out laughing. Samuel or Solomon nearly dropped his pumpkin as he bent over laughing. When we got the hilarity under control, we continued toward our wagon and I glanced at the smiling brothers, realizing I'd met some potentially very good friends. In some ways, they reminded me of Cillian, who, like the twins, had a perpetual smile and quick wit. After the pumpkins were securely installed in the back of our wagon, I laid a hand on an arm of each twin.

"Before you two get away, you have to help me discern which one of you is Samuel and which one is Solomon. There must be something that distinguishes you."

"I'm Samuel and I'm better looking."

"And I'm Solomon, smarter than my brother."

The twins snorted out a laugh, one patting the other on the back.

"Very funny." I perched my fists on my hips and feigned anger. "You have to do better than that. Does one of you have a scar or a mole?" I looked them over as if I was examining a bug, but for the life of me, I didn't see any distinguishing marks.

"I'm afraid not, Laurel. Even our mother can't tell us apart."

"I don't believe you."

"It's true," one said as his eyes bugged out indignantly. "The only way she can tell us apart is by our clothes."

"Samuel only wears blue shirts and I only wear brown."

Indeed, one twin was dressed in blue and one in brown, but how would I remember that?

As if reading my mind, Solomon continued.

"Just remember both the word blue and Samuel have a *u* in them, and brown and Solomon have *o*'s."

"That's how our mother picked the colors."

The twins tipped up their chins and wore identical smiles, proud of their mother's cleverly devised plan to tell her sons apart. I silently memorized the code and had to admit it was quite brilliant.

"Okay then." I reached out my hand to the one wearing the blue shirt. "I'm very pleased to meet you, Samuel." And then I turned toward the one in brown. "And equally as pleased to meet you, Solomon."

As if we were lifelong friends, I looped my hands through

the crooks of their arms and the three of us returned to the market. Samuel stepped out with his right leg and we soon fell into a perfectly synchronized skip across the parking area. We rounded the first stall and nearly collided with Garin Schmidt, halting our giggles. Garin looked none too pleased at our antics —his black slouch hat, which sat low on his brow, couldn't hide the anger simmering in his gaze. His lips were twisted in a grimace.

"What are you clowns up to?" He turned his anger first on Solomon. "What were you doing among the wagons, Samuel?"

"No, that's not Samuel." I pointed to Solomon, hoping to correct Garin's mistake.

"What about you, Solomon? Aren't you supposed to be helping load bales of hay for Mr. McHenry?"

Obviously, Garin hadn't learned the secret code for identifying each twin. He had them confused, which, I had to admit, was easy to do.

"Relax, Schmidt. We were helping Miss Whitman," Samuel said.

"Don't blame us if you're too preoccupied to help a damsel in distress." Solomon snorted a laugh, which only made Garin's face turn a deeper red.

"Some of us have to work around here, Samuel." When the twin and Garin stepped nose to nose, I squeezed between them.

"Garin, the twins were nice enough to carry my pumpkins to the wagon." I placed my hands on his chest and applied enough pressure to make him step back. "Besides, you've got the twins mixed up. This is Solomon. See his brown shirt?"

"What are you talking about, Laurel?"

"Solomon always wears brown and Samuel always wears blue. That's how you tell them apart."

"Who told you that preposterous story?" Garin glared down at me, and then his gaze traveled to his chest, where my hands still lay. I pulled them away and clutched them to my stomach as if they'd been burned.

"Why, Samuel and Solomon told me. That's how their mother..." My explanation faded to silence while Garin continued to stare at me as if I'd told him men could walk on the moon.

"I think you've been duped by these two buffoons."

Garin nudged each twin with such force, they stumbled backward. I turned my own anger on them, creasing my brow and pursing my lips, ready to give them a piece of my mind. But they dispelled my fury with duplicate shrugs and cheesy grins, and I burst out laughing. I may have fallen for their tall tale, but they had made me laugh like I hadn't in a week. I would have to figure out another way to tell them apart.

"Why don't you troublemakers find someone else to trick and leave Laurel alone?" Garin laid a gentle hand against the small of my back and fear quivered down my spine. Uncomfortable with his possessiveness, I took a modest step to my left, enough to dislodge his hand from my body. The harrowing experience at the inn flashed before my eyes.

"Aw, settle down, Garin. Where's your sense of humor?" The one who I thought was Samuel poked Garin in the chest, but it didn't help his mood.

"I apologize, Laurel, for our prank." The twin dressed in brown dipped his chin to his chest.

"There is a way to tell us apart." The other twin rolled up his blue sleeve and showed me a deep, red scar running the length of his forearm. "I ripped open my arm on some barbed wire when I was ten."

"Until that time, our mother did dress us only in blue and brown." The one in brown glared at Garin before continuing. "So when Soloman tore open his arm, my mother was happy we could wear some of our older brother's hand-me-downs."

"So, you are Soloman?" I pointed to the blue-clad twin. "And you're Samuel?" I said, nodding toward the one in brown.

"Yes," they both replied together.

"All I have to do is ask you to roll up your sleeve if you happened to be dressed in stripes or plaids?"

"And I'll be glad to show you," Soloman said.

"That seems simple enough." I turned toward Garin, who was still in a foul mood, and smiled sweetly at him. "See that, Garin? No harm done."

"It was rude of them to mock you." Garin's gaze softened and a smile played at his lips.

"They made me laugh, so all is forgiven."

"Thank you, Miss Laurel." Samuel bowed deeply, extending his leg and waving his arm as if he were addressing a duchess. Solomon followed suit and the three of us once again succumbed to laughter, much to Garin's frustration.

"Come on, Laurel. Berta wants to see you." Before I could say goodbye to the twins, Garin wrapped his hand around my elbow and dragged me away. Though his manhandling set my teeth on edge, I refused to make a scene.

"You have to admit, Samuel and Solomon are quite funny," I said as I withdrew my elbow from his grasp.

"Not as funny as they think they are. They're annoying."

"I got the impression when I first met them that they were friends of yours."

"Hardly." Garin ripped the hat from his head and slapped it against this leg as he raked his fingers through his thick blond hair. He clamped his mouth closed and his jaw pulsated with tension. I held my tongue as we walked past the stalls to his family's beer stand, surmising nothing I could say in the twins' defense would put Garin in a better mood.

"Laurel!" Berta shouted to me from across the market, holding her arms out wide.

"Hello, Berta." She drew me into a hug that briefly stopped

my breath. Once released from her strong embrace, I readjusted my bonnet and gathered her large, masculine hands in my own. "I was hoping I'd see you today. It's been so long."

"Ya, it has. I worked three days at the lumberyard last week, hoping to get the books in order before the little one arrives." She splayed her hands over her growing belly. "So Garin found you, did he?" Berta glanced over at her brother-in-law who, along with her husband, Hans, was talking with a gentleman about their brew. Taking the opportunity, she slipped her arm through mine and tugged me behind a leafless tree.

"Tell me everything." She dipped her head and whispered conspiratorially.

"Tell you everything about what?"

"You and Garin."

"What about us?"

Berta huffed in frustration and rested her hands over her swell. "Why are you being so secretive?"

"Berta, I don't know what you're asking."

"Did he invite you to the church social tomorrow evening?"

"No. Why?"

"Auck, that boy." Berta stomped her foot, shook her head, and spewed out several German words I couldn't understand. "That's why he went looking for you."

I'd never been invited to a church social or any outing with a young man, save the Wild West show with Cillian. My cheeks flared as if they were on fire. I glanced over my shoulder, where Garin was still deep in conversation with a customer, but he lifted his gaze and caught mine. Instead of a smile or a nod, his mouth twisted into his now-familiar scowl and he returned to his business. I wasn't sure I wanted to go with him.

"I don't know why he would invite me. He doesn't seem to even like me."

"Ha, that's what you think." Berta's beefy hand landed on my shoulder with a slap and she hugged me against her ample bosom. "You're all he's talked about since the day we drove you home from the mill. Hans has tried to advise him on the ways of courting, but obviously his lessons were for naught."

"I...I'm not sure, Berta. Garin is—"

"Shh, here he comes. I better leave you alone."

"Berta," I whispered, reaching out to stop her from leaving. "Wait."

My heart thumped in my chest as Berta scurried past Garin. I had trouble swallowing, my throat had gone dry, and my palms became as sweaty as if it were a summer day.

"Laurel?" Garin slowed his approach, taking long, tentative steps toward me. "Are you not well?"

I wasn't sure why he asked that question. Yes, my heart was drumming, my ears were ringing, and I thought I could possibly faint, but surely he couldn't see that.

"Fine, yes, of course." I cleared my throat as my fingers fumbled across my bonnet.

"I hope you weren't vexed with me over the twins. They're a good lot—a bit rambunctious, but they aren't so bad."

"No, of course not."

"I was wondering..." His knuckles turned white as he gripped his hat in his hands. Seeing him as nervous as I was seemed to loosen up the lump in my throat and slow my heart rate. "Our church is having a social tomorrow evening. A harvest celebration. I thought perhaps you might like to attend with me. That is, if your grandmother will allow it."

His voice quivered and his forehead was damp with a light sheen, even though the sun was hidden behind a cloud. I should be flattered to have a tall, striking young man labor to extend an invitation to me. Garin was quite handsome upon closer inspection. Much taller than me, he had broad shoulders and a sizable chest for one so young. His face was cleanly shaven, his hair was cut closely around his ears, and he had a prominent nose that together made a fetching appearance. The thought of being alone with a man was terrifying, but we wouldn't be alone. We would be among plenty of others. I had nothing to fear, and I really wanted to meet more people.

"Maybe. I'll speak to my grandmother and send word tomorrow morning." Perhaps by tomorrow, my nerves would be settled. Garin seemed to be a fine young man—nothing like that brute Edgar.

"That would be fine, Laurel."

As quick as a hummingbird, Garin buzzed away, but then seemed to remember he had left me standing there. He returned just as quickly and tipped his chin. "Yes, that would be fine." Turning away and then back around, coming full circle back to me, he lifted my hand and kissed it. "Yes, perfect. I'll wait for your reply tomorrow. Goodbye, Laurel."

I stifled a laugh behind my hand as I watched Garin stumble away, weaving at top speed through the crowd. To think I could befuddle such a big, strong young man with a simple *maybe*. It was quite flattering, indeed. Hopefully, I could attend the social with him and dispel my fears of being close to an unfamiliar man. I refused to let Edgar and that horrible incident control my life.

CHAPTER 14

"Garin Schmidt?" Gramma unfolded her arms from over her chest and raked her cloudy, green gaze down the length of my body and back again. A hint of a smile crossed her lips as her eyes settled on mine. "Karl's boy?"

I was standing a few feet from the side of her bed, where she was once again propped up against a mountain of pillows. The old woman scared me, but I had just enough courage to ask about going to the social with Garin. Charles had said it was best that I ask permission from my grandmother, seeing as we were only related through marriage. I'd been here for over a week now, and it was the first time Gramma's mood had softened toward me.

"Karl's mother, Ethel, was a fine lady. She helped me stitch this quilt, did you know that?" Her bony, blue-veined hands swept over the colorful quilt that had replaced the one that had been on her bed when I first arrived. It was a crazy quilt with oddly sized geometric shapes in blues, yellows, and greens on a white muslin background. "I used some leftover dress fabric—ones I wore when I was much younger."

For once, her sallow, wrinkled face was bright with healthy

color, and her usually stringy gray hair was knotted neatly at the base of her neck. There was still a slight rattle with each breath, but her voice was strong and she was more alert. Helen continued to declare my arrival as the miracle that brought Gramma back to life. Until now, my grandmother had glared at me with contempt and grumbled whenever I asked her a question. Today, she seemed ready to have a friendly chat.

Taking a brave chance, I perched my hip on the side of her bed and ran my fingers over a blue gingham hexagon, tracing the stitching.

"This one is pretty. It must have made a lovely gown."

Gramma leaned over to get a closer look at the piece. "Yes, I remember that one. It was the first dress I made completely on my own. My mother was an expert seamstress and wasn't too keen on giving up control of my wardrobe." She snickered, exposing yellowed teeth interspersed with smooth, pink gums. "It had several tucks stitched down through the bodice with a white lace collar and cherry red bow. The skirt was full and I wore a lace petticoat that peeked out the bottom when I walked." Sighing deeply, she fell back against the pillows with a sweet smile on her face. For the first time, I could imagine what she must have looked like as a girl. She closed her eyes, seeming to retreat into her memories.

"Can you remember where you first wore it?"

Startled, her eyes snapped open and turned dark. Gone was the sweet old lady who relished her memories. Instead, the crotchety shrew I'd come to know returned.

"Of course I remember where I wore it. I'm not senile. It was on a buggy ride." She folded her arms over her chest and turned her gaze toward the window. "Shouldn't have gone."

"Why, Gramma?"

Turning her attention back to me, the crease between her eyes deepened and her lips drew down.

"Don't you have something to do? Feed the chickens or something?"

Obviously, our brief, pleasant conversation was over. Hope had swelled my spirit and I thought for sure we had made a breakthrough. But now my shoulders sagged as I headed for the door. She stopped me with another cutting question.

"How long are you staying?"

"How long?"

"You heard me. This isn't your home and never will be. I hope your good-for-nothing father told you that."

I stumbled back from her sharp words as if I'd been slapped. What a cruel, nasty woman she was. But Gramma was right. Even though Helen and Charles, and the children, had welcomed me with open arms and made me feel part of the family, it wasn't my home. Originally, I had intended to stay long enough to get answers, but it was clear my grandmother wasn't interested in getting to know me, let alone answer my questions. Maybe it was time to leave. But where would I go?

"Why do you hate him so?" I asked, stepping closer to her bed.

"Tit for tat."

"What?"

"The better question is, why does your father hate me?"

"That's why I'm here." I rushed back to her bedside and took her birdlike hand in mine. "I want to understand. All my life I've never understood why—"

"Why what?"

"Why Father is cruel to me. Why he treats me much more harshly than Emily or Elvin or Sampson. Why I look like none of them. Why—"

"You've got a lot of questions."

"I do, Gramma. Won't you help me fill in the blanks?"

"No good will come of retracing history. Some things are best left unspoken."

"But Gramma—"

"Go, girl. Find something to do. I'm tired."

For a moment, I thought we'd made a connection. Her angry glare had softened and I sensed a bit of sympathy from her. Why was she so determined to lock me out?

Gramma rolled onto her side and tugged the quilt over her shoulder, signaling our talk was over. I had pelted Helen with questions to no avail, and Charles was reluctant to say much. What could have happened to cause such hatred between a mother and son, and why was she taking it out on me?

I SAT DOWN AT THE LITTLE MAHOGANY DESK TUCKED INTO THE window alcove in the bedroom I shared with Cora and Belle, and carefully tore a sheet of bleached paper in half. Garin was waiting for a reply to his invitation, and I felt I must decline. My grandmother had not given her permission and Charles was remiss to do so. Besides, there was no point in starting a friendship with Garin if I would soon be leaving Zion. If he did care for me as Berta said, it would be unfair of me to inflate his hopes.

> Dear Garin,
> I apologize for the lateness of my reply to your very kind
> invitation. My grandmother, as you know, has not been well,
> and was unable to grant permission for me to attend the
> social. So, I'm afraid I will have to decline. It's just as well as
> I've concluded it is best I return to my family in Philadelphia.

"Laurel?" I set down my pen when Helen shouted to me from the bottom of the staircase. "You have a letter. Should I bring it up?"

"No, thank you. I'll be right down."

It was my first bit of mail since I arrived and I was excited to learn who had written. Rushing down the stairs, I nearly missed the last two steps in my haste, and stumbled into the kitchen. Helen was waving the letter like a flag and humming merrily. As I reached for the envelope, she snatched it behind her back and arched her thick, red brows.

"And who exactly is Cillian O'Brien? Hmm?"

I hadn't spoken of Cillian to Helen or anyone, and had kept my recent letter to him tucked inside my coat pocket until I mailed it on market day. Reaching around her back, she spun away and held the envelope over her head. She was acting more like a schoolgirl than a mother of two.

"No. You won't get it until you tell me all about him."

"He's only a friend." I leapt up and swiped my hand through the air, unable to grab the letter from her vise-like clutches.

"You are quite the charmer, dear Laurel." She tucked her hand behind her back and leaned toward me. "First Garin Schmidt and now Cillian O'Brien. Or is it the other way around?"

"I'm no such thing. Now give me my letter." I threw my arms around her, pinning her arms to her side, and clumsily poked and prodded all her ticklish spots until she fell against me in a fit of laughter. She still held tight to the letter. "I'll tickle you until you let go."

"Never!" Helen giggled and struggled to get out of my clutches, but my assault on her ribs finally won the day. "Fine. I give!" She dropped the letter on the floor and I snatched it before she could renege on her deal.

"Goodness," I said, fingering some stray locks back into my bun. "Rather childish, don't you think?" Poking Helen once more in the ribs, I smiled sweetly and tucked Cillian's letter in my pocket.

"Maybe so, but things can be rather dull around here." Helen fell to the bench with a heavy breath and gathered one of the girls' skirts in her hand. She had been folding laundry and the arrival of Cillian's letter had pulled her away from the monotonous job. "It's none of my business."

Her cheery voice didn't hide the disappointment on her face. Helen and I had formed a friendship since I had arrived, so the least I could do was read Cillian's letter to her.

"Very well. You win." I sat on the bench across the table from her and unfolded his letter, starting with a little background. "Cillian is a very good friend of mine—probably my best friend."

"Just friends?"

"Yes, friends. We met at the mill where I work."

"Fine. Tell me more."

I pulled a pair of Charles' pants from the basket and smoothed them out on the table as I told her about Cillian.

"Cillian came to America from Ireland with his mother and sister about four years ago, after his father died. They felt they could make a better life here. His sister and her husband and their three children live with Cillian and his mother. We met about two years ago. He's so funny, keeps me laughing with his stories, and he truly appreciates my art."

"Your art?"

"Yes, I'm an artist. In fact, I'm scheduled to graduate from the Design School for Women in May."

"Laurel." Helen dropped the thin cotton nightgown she was folding into her lap and blinked rapidly. "You never told me you were an artist."

"I guess..." I shrugged, surprised at myself for not telling her. "We've had so much to talk about, getting to know each other and all that I never got around to telling you."

"Are you a painter? Sculptor?"

"Painter. I do oil painting on canvas."

"Are you good?"

A blush warmed my cheeks, remembering the praise I had

received from Mr. Ferretti. "Yes, I'm very good." I owed him a letter to explain my sudden disappearance.

Helen stared at me as if I were a stranger and shook her head. Slowly, a smile formed on her lips and she snorted. "Well, I'll be. Not only do you look like us, but you've inherited Mother's talent."

"Her talent?"

"Yes. She has a keen artistic bone as well."

"Really? Show me."

My feet tangled as I climbed from the bench and I stumbled against the table. Helen chuckled and waved at me to follow her into the parlor.

"There." She pointed to a lovely landscape I had admired, which hung over the fireplace. Its surface had become hazy with smoke and dirt over the years, but there was no denying the artist had a fine eye for detail. "Mother painted that when she was first married to my father."

"It's beautiful." I crept closer, feeling the slackness in my jaw as I stared in amazement at the lovely brush strokes and clever shading depicting the familiar vista outside the farmhouse. "Has she painted others?"

"Every painting hanging in our house and in Robert's as well. She painted all of them. There are even some unframed canvases and half-finished paintings in her closet. Mother painted up until a year or two ago, when her eyesight began to fail."

My chest tightened and my eyes prickled with unshed tears. It all made sense. My hair color, my eyes, my stature...and my artistry. The revelation that Gramma was an exceptional artist was the final clue that clicked the puzzle piece into place. I spun around to face Helen, who was standing behind me.

"Another reason why my father hates me. Not just my looks, but my love of art. All of it reminds him of Gramma."

CHAPTER 15

Garin arrived in a shiny new gig, complete with tan leather seats and bright yellow wheels, pulled by a handsome tan and white paint horse. He was dressed in a clean but outdated suit by Philadelphia standards. Perhaps it had belonged to his father. A maroon-striped cravat peeked from beneath his gray sack coat and a sharp crease ran the length of his pressed black trousers. He took off his black derby hat, revealing blond hair combed smooth across his scalp. I let the heavy drapes fall as I stepped away from the window and glanced down at my dress. Apparently, a Sunday evening social at his church was rather formal.

"He's here," Cora announced, out of breath with excitement. "Come on, Laurel." She reached out her hand and latched on, dragging me into the foyer to await my handsome escort. His knock seemed to rattle the door on its hinges. Cora squeezed my hand while Belle plastered her little body to the back of mine, shaking with anticipation. The little girls had never experienced a gentleman caller, and neither had I. They were much more excited about this adventure than I.

"Good evening, Garin." Charles extended his hand in

greeting after he opened the door. Cora, Belle, and I stood inside, looking like three birds on a tree limb, huddled against the cold.

"Evening, Charles." The men clasped hands as I dried mine against the overskirt of my dress.

"Looks like you'll have good weather for the social," Charles said, inviting Garin in.

Helen rushed in from the kitchen, wiping her hands on a tea towel and smiling as though her cheeks would burst. Not wanting me to miss an opportunity, she had granted permission for me to attend the social by proxy. Charles had delivered the message this morning while Gramma remained in a disagreeable mood the rest of the day when she wasn't sleeping.

I had spent the day with Cora and Belle, who advised me on which dress to wear and how to style my hair while they dabbed several cologne options on my wrist. I smelled like I'd stumbled into a bawdy house by the time they were finished with me. Fortunately, the aroma faded from my skin after a long soak in the tub.

I wore the dress of their choice—a lovely one Mother had made for me right before I left home. It had a navy and green tartan bodice with a fluffy, white lace cravat and pearl buttons running down the center. The navy broadcloth overskirt split at the knee to reveal the ruffled tartan underskirt. Helen had pulled my hair tight along the sides, tucking it in place with dozens of pins, letting my curls cascade down my back. After I was dressed to their satisfaction, the girls had left me alone. I sat down at the little desk and found Cillian's letter, yet unopened. The hours had flown by since it was delivered.

My hands shook as I unfolded the crisp paper.

November 15, 1877
Dearest Laurel,

It was a bonny day when I received your letter, so curious I had been about your adventure. Though I worried for your safety, I had no doubt you would make it to your granny's unscathed. For how could any man risk the wrath of the great Lady Laurel Whitman? All jesting aside, I am most glad you made the trip safely and you've found some of the answers you seek.

So, does this mean you have given up painting for cow milking? Perhaps your dexterity with a paintbrush helps with your milking technique? I'd pay a week's wages to see that performance.

Thank you for asking about my progress with my rotating ramp. I did indeed meet with Mr. Schumer and he's very interested in my building a similar contraption on a larger scale for his shipping business. Next week, we are having dinner with Cornelius Vanderbilt to inquire as to his interest in our new venture. Ha! From my lips to God's ears. But I am most encouraged by Mr. Schumer's enthusiasm and hope that from our partnership, I can perhaps begin to manufacture several more for other shipyards.

What I wouldn't give to see the miniature version of you in little Cora. You must have had quite a shock when you met three red heads like your own. A most unique shade of red not easily replicated. I pray that by the time you read this, your granny has come around and welcomed you. 'Tis a blessing her health has improved and with it perhaps she will give you the clarity you need. I'll pray for your questions to be answered.

Until then, I continue to toil away at the mill and count the days until your return. Philadelphia is a cold, cloudy place without your bright smile.

Most fondly,

Cillian Aengus O'Brien

P.S. I have sent you a package which you should expect any day now.

A STREAK OF GUILT CREPT DOWN MY SPINE AS GARIN SHOOK hands with Helen. It made no sense to have such a feeling since Cillian was but a friend and nothing more. And this outing with Garin was just an evening of fun with a new acquaintance. Surely my nervous jag wasn't guilt, but anticipation.

After he completed his greetings to Charles, Helen, and the girls, Garin's gaze landed on me and his smile faded. His eyes trailed down the length of my dress and settled at my boots, which only served to amplify my nerves. He cleared his throat while he clenched his hat between his hands. Finally raising his head, he had a warm smile on his face and I was reassured when he said, "You look mighty fine this evening, Laurel."

Relief swept away the tension in my chest. The girls had made a fine choice. "Thank you, Garin."

"You two should get going, before the evening light fades." Charles wrapped his hand around my elbow and tugged me from the cement holding my feet to the floor. Garin extended his arm in invitation and I looped my hand through it.

"I'll have her home by nine." With a nod from Charles and a beaming smile from Helen, Garin led me onto the porch and down the steps to his waiting gig. The carriage was as fine as any I'd seen along Chestnut Street.

"The church isn't far from here. Maybe two miles."

"That's fine." My throat had dried up from the reality that I was on my first outing with a young man—a tall, handsome young man—who had made every effort to impress me. We were only inches apart on the smooth leather bench and his shoulder brushed mine as he clucked at the horse until it led us down the long gravel lane to the main road. He smelled of rose water and hair tonic, and I noticed a streak of dried blood along his jaw where he had nicked himself shaving. Though our closeness unsettled me, I was somewhat flattered.

"So, um," Garin coughed nervously and glanced over his

shoulder away from me. "I was happy to get your message this morning. Glad your grandmother allowed you to come."

"My grandmother didn't exactly say yes. It was my aunt, Helen. My grandmother has been rather perturbed with me since I arrived."

"What do you mean?" His head snapped around and his bright blue eyes locked with mine. My stomach took a tumble.

"Yes, my grandmother hasn't been..." How much should I tell him? Would he even be interested in the grouchy old woman? "Have you ever met my grandmother?"

"I have. I remember her spending time at our house, quilting in the parlor with Oma—my grandmother."

"She told me. Your grandmother helped her make the quilt that's on her bed." I glanced down at my hands wringing restlessly in my lap. "It's the only time she's spoken to me with even a hint of kindness. She must have been very fond of your grandmother."

"Suppose so. I'm surprised to hear you say she is unkind to you, what with you being her granddaughter. She was always friendly to us children. I remember she used to bring us cookies with walnuts from the tree outside her house."

"Is that true?" Realizing Garin may have some information about my grandmother that could lend insight, I turned slightly, inadvertently knocking my knee against his. He glanced down and I noticed a bright red flush fill his cheeks. I scooted over an inch or so until I was pressed against the seat rail.

"Tell me more about her."

"I know you said your visit was a surprise, but had you not met your *oma* before?"

"No, I had never met her until two weeks ago, when I landed on her doorstep. She and my father had a falling out some time ago. We were forbidden to talk about her at home."

"I wonder if..." Garin scratched his head through his black

derby hat and then flicked the reins. "I remember when I was a boy, maybe five or six, when Oma went to stay with Helen and Robert while your grandmother went to Baltimore. Something about Mr. Hayward."

"You knew John Hayward?"

"Oh, no, I never met him. He wasn't around. But I remember another time, a few years back, after he died, there was quite a ruckus. And I..." Again, he scratched his head and I quickly learned that gesture was used to drum up deeply buried memories. "It seemed like Opa—my grandfather—was involved."

"Involved? How so?"

"I don't know, but I remember him and my Uncle Gunther —he lives in Pennsylvania with his family—grabbing the muskets and tearing off across the field on their horses, heading for your grandmother's house."

"Oh my. Why? What happened?"

"I'm sorry, Laurel." He pulled back on the reins, slowing the horse to a walk, and turned to face me. "I wish I knew more. Whatever happened that night, well...it went on for a while. Opa and Uncle Gunther didn't return until the next morning, and when they did, they refused to speak of it in front of us younger children. It had something to do with your grandmother's oldest son, Calvin."

I sucked in my breath to the point of light-headedness and pressed my fist to my mouth.

"Would that be one of your uncles?"

"No." I blew out the breath I was holding and twisted my skirt in my fists. "Calvin is my father."

WE RODE THE REST OF THE WAY TO THE CHURCH WITH GARIN carrying on a one-sided conversation about the history of the land, this season's crops, and other minutiae to fill my silence. I was deep in thought, wondering what could have happened, why Gramma had gone to Baltimore, and what was the ruckus to which he referred? The mystery of my family's past seemed to grow.

Garin guided the gig onto a grassy lawn outside a small brick building with colorful stained glass windows glowing from the light inside. Several carts, wagons, and carriages were parked on the grass, and families entered the building carrying baskets of food. I drew in a deep breath, taking in the smell of horse, leather, and wood smoke billowing from the church chimney. The earthy aromas seemed to settle my nerves.

"Are you ready?" Garin gathered my hand in his, and from the softness in his eyes, I realized he had been concerned for me. Even with his empathy, I wasn't comfortable with his grip on my hand. With a tip of my chin and a shake of my shoulders, I brushed away the swirling questions in my mind, determined to forget everything Garin had told me. I discretely pulled my hand from his and turned to climb down.

"Yes, I am."

"Well, then."

He climbed out of the carriage and rushed around to my side to help me down. Reaching up with both arms, he lifted me out of the carriage, and when my feet hit the ground, I found myself inches away from him. His crystalline eyes were on me, causing a quiver in my belly—a quiver of fear.

"You really are a pretty girl, Laurel." He stated his assessment without a hint of nerves and it brought heat to my cheeks. Though somewhat flattered, I didn't like the churning in my stomach caused by our standing so close. Surely it was inappropriate to be alone with him in the waning sunlight. I pushed out of his arms and straightened my hat.

"Thank you, Garin," I murmured and circled the carriage. He followed behind me and lifted a basket, which had been tied on the tail board. "What have you there?" I peeked under the cloth napkin, hoping to relieve the awkwardness.

"It's apple strudel. Mutter made them this morning."

"Oh, I adore strudel."

"You've heard of it?"

"Of course. Cillian and I walk down to the market on Second Street on Wednesdays during our break. It's run by the German Methodist church."

"Cillian?"

"My friend, from the mill." Heat rose in my cheeks and I dropped my chin to hide the blush. Again that nagging, guilty feeling burned through my chest. It didn't help that Garin's gaze had turned cold. I wasn't exactly sure why I had mentioned Cillian.

"From the mill?"

"Yes, it's where I work." I dipped my nose into the basket, hoping my flushed cheeks would fade, and took a deep whiff. "Strudel! I cannot wait to taste your mother's. I'm sure hers is just as delicious, if not more so. The ladies at the Methodist church sell apple, walnut, and cherry, when they're in season. They also make sausage. Sometimes I buy sausages when I have extra money and take them home to Mother. She cooks them with onions and serves them with mashed potatoes. Such a treat."

"It sounds like what my *mutter* makes."

"Maybe I've got a bit of German in me." I nudged my elbow into his ribs, hoping to ease my nervousness. He gave me a small grin and nudged me back.

"If you don't now, maybe you will."

The heat drained from my face, dragging the blood along with it. His innuendo froze me at the entrance to the church and I stared at him longer than I should have. He pulled open the heavy oak door with a smile and pressed his hand to my lower back, guiding me through.

Was this how courting was done? The man sets his sights on a woman and immediately assumes their future together before they even get to know one another? Most women would be flattered, but instead I panicked. I found it hard to breathe. What was wrong with me that I wasn't blushing with pride? Instead, a chill ran through my veins. I should have a say in whether or not I wanted a future with a man. A vision of Edgar shot through my mind like a lightning bolt. The stuffy tavern room, his weight pinning me down, and my utter loss of control. That was the last time any man would take away my freedom to choose.

CHAPTER 16

"So you're Maggie Hayward's granddaughter?" the inquisitive old woman asked as she reached out her hand to me. Regardless of the fact that she had several teeth missing in front, she smiled broadly while her eyes narrowed behind her scratched lenses. "You're not at all what I would have expected."

"What were you expecting, Mrs. Hoffman?" Garin spoke the question before I could ask it.

"Well, she's quite lovely, looks a lot like her grandma. Charming with a pleasing demeanor…"

Mrs. Hoffman's assessment was peppered with skepticism. We had met a moment ago while surveying the delectable assortment of pies, cakes, and pastries arranged on the dessert table. Garin had been in a playfully heated discussion with some other young men about whose horse could beat whose in a race, and I wandered away to survey the sweets. Mrs. Hoffman and I had been debating whether or not our waistlines could accommodate more than one treat when she asked my name. It was at that moment that Garin had joined us and now the two of them were carrying on a conversation as if I weren't there.

"You're right about that, Mrs. Hoffman. Laurel is everything you said she is." Garin smiled at me, acknowledging my presence before returning to the two-way conversation.

"I'm surprised, that's all. We've had a most delightful conversation about the baked goods."

"Why surprised? Talking about dessert can bring a smile to anyone's face," he said.

"Yes, but with what the family has been through. The trial and all."

I cleared my throat to remind them I was still present.

"Please tell me what you mean, Mrs. Hoffman. I'm new here and—"

"Come along, Laurel. I see Samuel and Solomon over there." Garin's large hand engulfed my arm and as he dragged me away, I noticed Mrs. Hoffman shake her head and flick her hand as if dismissing the two of us.

"I'm sorry, dear," she called to me as I was forcibly hauled away.

"What did she mean by a trial?"

Garin didn't reply, but continued to pull me across the room. I had had just about enough of everyone skirting around the facts of my family's history. It was apparent Garin knew something or he wouldn't have manhandled me in such a fashion.

"Stop, Garin." I locked my knees and planted my feet on the wood floor, refusing to move another inch. "Let go."

"I wanted to—"

"You wanted to get me as far away from Mrs. Hoffman as possible." Finally breaking free from my captor, I smoothed my hands across the front of my dress and tucked a stray curl behind my ear. "Now, what did she mean by a trial? All evening, people have watched me with wary eyes, acting a bit standoffish. Mrs. Hoffman was the first person to actually speak to me, and then you cut her off. What was that all about?"

Garin released my arm and ran his hand through his hair while heaving a heavy sigh. He tipped his head toward the door and I followed him. Outside, we stood under a leafless oak tree, the moon our only source of light. It had grown colder since we arrived and I wished I had thought to get my coat before we came out.

"Well?" I said, rubbing some warmth into my upper arms.

"I'm sorry, Laurel, but I'm not the one to tell you about your grandmother's last husband. In fact, mostly what I know, I've heard through gossip. My family doesn't talk about it. I told you as much as I know on our way here."

"But why does everyone stare at me so? What happened at the trial? What horrible thing did my step-grandfather do to have been sent to prison?"

"Only your grandmother can answer your questions."

"But she hardly speaks to me."

"Maybe it's best you forget about it."

Noticing my chill, Garin took my hands, slipped them inside his jacket and around his waist, and then pulled me close. His strong, thick arms enveloped me. I should've savored the warmth, but his gesture made me uncomfortable, afraid. He was being far too familiar, taking liberties I had not granted. Besides the fact that I shouldn't be alone with him, nor closely pressed together, I didn't like his assumptions about us. I barely knew him and had no intention of carrying this *relationship* beyond friendship.

"It doesn't matter what went on at your grandmother's. It had nothing to do with you."

"But Garin, I need to know." I wiggled my way out of his clutches and took a step back, thankful he wasn't forcing me back into his arms.

"Ignore their looks and comments. As long as you're with me, no one will dare say anything to upset you. Besides, it's water under the bridge."

"Apparently not. Everyone I've met since arriving here has reacted the same way. Don't you see? I need to know what they haven't forgotten."

"It's not important. I'll keep them from upsetting you."

Now he had designated himself as my personal protector. What right did he have to insert his authority? He was offering to shield me from gossip, but instead of feeling grateful for his support, it was stifling and restrictive. He wanted me to forget the stares and whispers and give up my quest to unravel my family's past.

"I think it's time I went home."

"But you didn't get any dessert. Let's go back inside where it's warm."

"I've lost my appetite. Would you please get my coat?"

"You want me to take you home?"

"Yes, please."

Garin's nostrils flared as he turned and stomped up the church steps like a child who had not gotten his way. When he returned, he clumsily placed my coat over my shoulders and stalked through the dark night to the carriage, where his paint horse stood with its head drooped.

"Surely you understand my need to know." His shoulders were rigid and he refused to look at me. "It's why I came here." After handing me onto the seat, he stalked around the carriage and climbed in, flicking the reins before he was even settled. "Garin—"

"Why can't you leave it be?" Finally, he looked at me. Even by the light of the moon, I could see his eyes were smoldering with anger. "Every family has secrets and things they would rather forget. Have you ever thought maybe your grandmother doesn't want to dredge it all up again?"

"But I—"

"It's her choice, isn't it? And if your aunt and uncle don't want to talk about it, you should let it lie."

"Then my trip has been for naught."

"It appears so."

He snapped the reins down hard against the horse's rump, and I fell against the seat back as the buggy shot forward. We traveled along the dirt road at double the speed it had taken to get to the social, but the silence between us seemed to last a lifetime. Finally, Garin pulled the gig close to the front porch and without speaking a word, helped me climb down.

"Thank you for taking me to the church social. I'm sorry—"

"You're welcome." He tipped his hat and circled around to take his place on the carriage. "Evening," he said with a quick nod, keeping his gaze pointed away from me. My heart was heavy as I watched the gig rattle and clang down the lane. Was he angry that I had cut our evening short, or was he frustrated that I wasn't willing to give up my quest? Or, more likely, was he upset that I didn't yield to his protection?

I wrapped my coat tightly around my body and stood outside the house in the cold evening breeze, drawing in the fresh smell of dried leaves, manure, and chimney smoke. There was no question I had come to love the easy pace, clear air, and natural beauty of the countryside, but if my grandmother's scorn continued, I wasn't sure I could stay.

THAT NIGHT, I TOSSED AND TURNED AS MUCH AS I WAS ABLE between Cora and Belle, and decided if I was to get to know my grandmother, I would have to resort to old-fashioned snooping. In the morning, while she slept, I would investigate her closet, where Helen said she kept her unfinished artwork. Maybe we could find common ground in our love for art, and eventually Gramma would warm up to me.

At breakfast, nervous excitement coiled through my belly as I ate my porridge. I prayed the thick cereal would stay down. The children were playing with their dolls in the parlor and

Helen would soon join Charles in the cheese shed, leaving me alone with Gramma. I hadn't even begun my sneaky detective work and already I felt guilty.

"Do you mind checking in on Gramma from time to time?" Helen asked as she slipped her arms into an old, worn coat she wore when collecting eggs or milking cows.

"Can we help with the cows, Mother?" Cora asked, slipping her arms clumsily into her coat.

"It's quite chilly outside, girls."

"Play outside!" Belle jumped at her coat hooked on the peg.

"Okay, you can come outside with me. Maybe Daddy has a job for you." Helen helped the girls with their coats, hats, and mittens, and then turned to me. "I just checked on Gramma and she's still asleep. She probably won't wake for another half hour."

"I don't mind. I'll work on the mending while I wait for her to wake up."

"Thank you, Laurel. I'll be in the shed if you need me."

As soon as the back door snapped shut, I scurried down the hall to Gramma's room and hesitantly peeked around the doorframe. She was lying flat on her back with her hands folded on her chest, still and ghostly, as if she was laid out for a funeral.

To test if she was sound asleep, I rattled the door knob and then coughed. She didn't budge. I tiptoed across the room and opened the closet door, not making a sound. Four dresses hung in the small closet, and a pair of shoes sat beneath. It was small, so I couldn't imagine it would hold many canvases. I knelt down on my hands and knees and reached into the left side of the closet, immediately discovering that it was much larger than originally expected. The space extended several feet behind the wall, far enough that I crawled in and was engulfed in darkness. If it weren't for the sliver of light from the bedroom window, I wouldn't have seen the half-dozen paintings stacked against the back wall. I wished I had a lamp so I could see her work. I patted my hand on the floor around the paintings, being careful not to make a sound, and landed on a pile of books. Unable to see their titles in the dark, I slipped one into my skirt pocket to examine later. I heard the springs squeak in my grandmother's bed as I was backing out of the closet. My heart rose to my throat.

"What are you doing in there, young lady?"

"I, um..."

"Don't you know better than to snoop around someone's things?"

I crawled backward, fearing my grandmother's wrath. Once outside the closet, I turned around, still on bended knees, and looked up at her fury. Catching me in the act must have given her the strength to sit up in bed.

"What gives you the right to crawl in my closet when I'm sleeping?"

"I'm sorry, Gramma. I was—"

"Trying to steal something?" For a weak old woman, Gramma sure had plenty of angry energy coursing through her veins this morning. Her hands were fisted on her lap and she glared down at me, still squatting on the floor. "Well, speak up."

I rose to my feet, brushing the dust off my hands, and mimicked her threatening countenance, setting my fists on my hips and glaring right back at her. The room smelled of stale coffee and unwashed old lady, and despite the coolness of the room, sweat beaded on the back of my neck. I had taken all the abuse I was willing to take from this old goat.

"If you must know, I was looking for your paintings. Helen told me you had some unfinished ones in the closet."

"And what were you planning to do with them?"

"I was planning to ask your permission to look at them and talk to you about your art, but frankly, I'm no longer interested."

Indignantly, I spun around, chin held high, and marched toward the door.

"What do you want to know about it?" Though she snapped out the question, her angry sneer softened. Her eyes grew large with interest as I glanced over my shoulder at her. "You know anything about art?"

"Well," I said, drying my damp palms on my skirt. I let go of the doorknob and tentatively stepped back into the room. "As a matter of fact, I do. I'm an artist myself. I will graduate from the Design School for Women this spring—or at least I *was* scheduled to graduate."

"What do you mean?"

"I should still be in school, but since Father threw me out and I came here, now—"

"What do you mean your father threw you out?" Her shoulders dropped and her arms folded over her belly. For the first time since I had arrived, true concern showed on my grandmother's face.

"That's why I'm here. We had an argument because I wanted to know more about you. He said some terrible things and threw me out."

"Hmm." She swung her legs over the side of the bed and eased off the mattress. She hesitated then, seeming to war with herself over her next move. After a few moments, something inside her must have relented, and she looked up at me with more softness than I'd thought her capable of. Responding to her beckoning gesture, I held her elbow as she trudged over to the armchair and settled into it. "I bet he did. Sit, child." Waving her hand at another chair tucked in the corner of her room, her eyes crinkled at the corners and she gave me a sweet smile. "It's time you tell me everything."

CHAPTER 17

April 9, 1860
I buried my second husband today on the rise behind the
house. Thomas and Rolfe dug the hole the day John passed,
never questioning my decision to keep him with me. There
wasn't a graveyard that would've welcomed him anyway.
I'm happy knowing I can look out my bedroom window and
see the hillside where he's laid. Maybe I'll catch a glimpse of
him from time to time, coming from the back pasture, leading
Ruby to the barn or carrying a load of firewood. He was
always busy doing something around the farm that I'm sure
he's already hard at work in heaven. He is in heaven, no
matter what others may think. And I hope it won't be long
before I'm there with him.

I slammed shut my grandmother's journal as tears
threatened and a clog paralyzed my throat. Who were
Thomas and Rolfe? After telling Gramma about my row with
Father, she had grown weary, so I tucked her into bed and I

retreated to the bedroom upstairs. I opened the little leather-bound book I had tucked in my pocket to a random page and was immediately sucked into her words. She was so sad, even hoping her death would come soon. I would love to know more about her husband and the reasons no church would have allowed him to be buried in its graveyard. How could I broach the subject with her? I feared if I asked her about it, the door that had just been tentatively cracked open might close with a resounding slam.

I tucked the little book back in my pocket, determined to return it to its hiding place. If I wanted my grandmother's love, I first needed her trust. The only way to earn that trust was to put the book back and wait for her to open up to me.

Helen called to me and I rushed down the stairs for what I thought was supper. Instead, she pointed to a large wooden box sitting by the back door.

"Look what Charles brought back from town."

"What is it?"

"It's addressed to you." I instantly thought of the package Cillian had mentioned. I inched toward the crate as if I expected it to suddenly explode, and jumped when Charles burst through the door.

"Here you go, Laurel." He handed me a metal crowbar. "I think you might need this."

"What could be inside?"

"There's only one way to find out." Charles laid the crowbar in my hand and wrapped his arm around Helen's shoulder, smiling broadly. He was as thrilled about the package as Helen.

"Go on. Don't keep us in suspense," she said.

I slid the narrow point of the crowbar under the edge of the lid and, using both hands, pushed down until a corner popped open. Bits of straw spilled from inside onto my feet and suddenly I was just as excited.

"Hurry up, slowpoke," Helen chided with a chuckle.

Not wasting a moment, I pried the lid at each corner until the flat wooden top landed on the floor. Together, Helen and I rooted through the straw, searching for the crate's contents. I was the first to discover something.

"Paint brushes." I held up the bundle as if it were a golden torch, and laid them on the wood floor to resume digging until I pulled a paint tube from under the packing. "Burnt sienna."

"And look, here's cerulean blue and oxide of chromium." Helen held out two tubes and gazed at me in amazement. "Who could have sent this? There were no markings on the outside of the box."

"It's from Cillian. Help me pull out the rest of the straw."

Charles watched in amusement as Helen and I reached deep into the crate, scattering straw all over her polished floor. My fingers grazed across tightly pulled fabric and I knew at once it was a canvas—a small stretched canvas—and under it were five more. As I lifted the stack of canvases from the box, a piece of paper fluttered to the floor.

"Wait. Here's a note," Helen said, retrieving the folded paper.

Brushing a strand of straw from my hair, I unfolded the note and immediately recognized Cillian's handwriting. "It *is* from Cillian."

"Is it now?" Charles winked at Helen and the two of them shared a knowing glance.

"He's my *friend*, remember?"

"Does Garin know that?" Charles's teasing hit a nerve. He didn't know how upset Garin had been with me for ending our evening early. Needing to escape from Charles and Helen's nosy glances, I took my note outside to the back porch. The late afternoon was cool and breezy, but there was just enough sunlight left to read by.

November 15, 1877

Dear Laurel,

I thought by now you would be going mad without your paints and canvases, so I stopped by the school and talked to Mr. Ferretti. I wove a tall tale about you being called to your granny's bedside and how she begged you to paint a portrait of her before she met her maker. He was relieved to hear you hadn't dropped out of the class, but had only been called away on a family matter. I hope you don't mind my interfering. I assured him you would indeed return to complete your painting and was greatly looking forward to the spring art show. (Please do not make a liar out of me, Miss Laurel Rose Whitman.)

I was pleased to receive your last letter and enjoyed your stories of the children. It seems as though your granny's house is a bustling place. Keep the news coming.

I think it only fair that you know your sister Emily stopped by the mill last week. She was waiting outside by the gate after my shift was over. She told me your mother was distraught over your leaving and had taken to her bed. You didn't exactly make me promise to keep your whereabouts a secret, so I reassured Emily you were safe and sound in Maryland. I let her know we had corresponded and all was well with you. Emily asked me to tell you she would like a letter from you and that you can mail it in care of me if you don't want your father to intercept it. From what she tells me, he has been on a tear ever since you left home, I'm sorry to say.

So, Laurel, after you have painted a portrait of your granny, paint one of yourself and send it to me. I miss seeing your freckled face. Be well.

Yours,

Cillian

P.S. Mr. Schumer has installed the rotating ramp and is so impressed with its efficiency, he's going to pay me to build two more. It won't be long before I am dining with the Vanderbilts.

I smiled through the tears that blurred my vision as I struggled to reread his letter. Dear Cillian, I missed him so. Last night, I had rebuffed Garin's attentions, smothered by his assumptions. Earlier in the evening, he'd been kind and flattered me with compliments, but I could never return his affection. Even if I wanted a husband, Garin could never fit the bill. My husband would need to see me as his equal, support my goals and dreams, and make me laugh.

Like Cillian.

I fell back against the porch post and glanced out across the field as memories of the past few years exploded in my mind like fireworks. No one made me laugh or warmed my spirit the way Cillian did. The day we'd met, he noticed me carrying an armload of heavy, wooden spools to the spinning department. Instead of automatically taking them from me in a show of chivalry, he'd made a joke about spindles and where my boss could stick them. I'd spilled them onto the floor in a fit of laughter. We'd become fast friends from that day on.

When he had caught me sketching in my notebook during our lunch break, he had marveled over my work as if it were a masterpiece. We'd spent our midday break together every day since.

And when my father had attacked me, the night he'd caught Cillian and me alone in the classroom, I'd seen the pain and fear in Cillian's eyes, and his deep need to protect me. But instead of charging forth and creating a bigger spectacle, he'd yielded to my request for him to leave. Even in his concern, he'd respected me.

At that moment, I realized that Cillian and I weren't meant to be just friends, and I was equally sure he had come to that understanding well before me. Hadn't he said as much at the train station? *And when that day comes, I'd like to think it could be me.*

I needed to get the truth about my father from Gramma

soon, because suddenly my heart was homesick for Philadelphia.

I folded the letter and tucked it inside the pocket of my skirt. Charles met me at the back door, holding another letter in his hand.

"I almost forgot to give this to you."

The letter was from Mother. My hand shook as I carried it into the parlor and carefully unfolded it. It was the first time I'd heard from her since I arrived.

November 14, 1877

Dear Laurel,

I apologize for the delay in writing you, but frankly, until yesterday, I didn't know where you were. I had an inkling you had gone in search of your father's mother, but couldn't imagine how you made it that far on your own. Calling on all your friends, stopping by the mill, even making inquiries at the police station, I finally accepted that you had indeed left the city in search of your grandmother. Emily confirmed to me this morning that she learned you have been living with her and Helen's family. Thank God you made it there safely. Though I don't approve of your traveling alone with a young man, I am grateful to your friend Cillian for delivering you safely to Maryland. (Emily conveyed this information, grudgingly, to your father and me this morning.) At least I can sleep at night knowing you have a roof over your head and place to sleep.

When are you coming home? Christmas is a month away and it wouldn't be the same without you here to play carols on the piano and lead in our Christmas Eve sing-along. You must put away this silly anger directed at your father and come home where you belong. Proper young ladies don't run off willy-nilly. You should be home, working at the mill and completing your art courses. Emily learned from your friend that your painting is still to be displayed at the spring art show. You must come home to finish it. Though it wasn't our first choice for your future, you should at least complete the journey you've begun and finish your studies.

Please write and tell me how you are faring. Father worries for you so.

With love,
Mother

"Father worries for me? Hardly!" I stuffed the letter back in the envelope and slapped it on the table.

"Bad news?" Helen had entered the living room as quiet as a breeze.

"Oh, not really. Just that Mother thinks I'm being foolhardy and should come home right away. She says my father worries about me."

"Maybe they're both worried." Helen settled on the tufted sofa.

"If my father was worried about me, he wouldn't have thrown me out of the house on a dark night."

"Why didn't your mother stop him?"

"She was hiding in her bedroom. She often makes herself scarce when Father is in a rage. No one argues with or defies my father."

"Except you."

"Except me." I dropped into the upholstered armchair and released a heavy sigh. "I figured I didn't have as much to lose as the rest of them."

"You lost your home...but it sounds like they would welcome you back."

"Mother might, but I doubt Father would. He's never made a secret of the fact that he despises me. Obviously, it's because I remind him of his own mother, but he would never tell me why. It can't simply be because of my hair color and our love of art. I wish Gramma would explain it."

"Have you actually asked her?"

"Yes."

"I heard the two of you carrying on a pleasant conversation yesterday. Maybe now that she's stronger, you could broach the subject again."

"Maybe so."

THE NEXT MORNING, AFTER THE BREAKFAST DISHES WERE cleared, Helen took the girls outside to help Charles in the cheese shed, leaving me alone with Gramma. Thinking she was still asleep, I nearly leapt out of my skin when she slowly shuffled into the kitchen, where I was scrubbing potatoes for the midday meal. Water slopped over the side of the washtub, soaking the front of my dress, when I dropped the fat potato.

"Gramma, what are you doing out of bed?" I reached for a tea towel, quickly drying my hands as I met her at the table.

"It was about time I got out of that stuffy room," she grumbled as she leaned on her cane and gripped the handle of the wooden armchair usually reserved for Charles at the head of the table. "I can't look at the same four walls without going mad." Once her bottom hit the seat of the chair, she blew out a heavy breath. She leaned her cane against the table and smoothed her bony hands across her wrinkled nightdress.

"What can I get you? Coffee? Porridge?" I rushed to the stove and poured a cup of coffee from the tin pot. "I was just about to fix your breakfast."

"Slow down, girl. No need to rush. You'll spill hot coffee down the front of you the way you're hustling around."

Though her tone held its usual gruffness, she smiled a gummy grin and I realized her chastisement was in jest. I placed the coffee cup in front of her and, with shaking hands, she lifted the cup to her lips, taking a loud slurp.

"Thank you."

I dropped to the bench beside her, thrilled to see her so much stronger and more alert than she had been. She still had a cough, which some nights woke the house, but her coloring was better and she appeared to have put on some weight.

"So, breakfast. What can I get you?" I patted her hand, which now lay on the table beside the coffee cup. I expected her to snatch it away, but instead, she laid her other hand on top of mine. My heart swelled to bursting at her unusual kindness.

"In a few minutes. I'll drink the coffee for now."

"Okay, I'll finish the potatoes while you—"

"No, stay here. Sit with me." Her hand still engulfed mine—in fact, now her hand was rubbing across the back of my hand as if she were petting a kitten. "Would you like to get some coffee while we talk?"

The bench teetered as I jumped up and rushed to the stove to fill a cup. She wanted to talk. I had to move fast before her mercurial mood reverted to grumpy.

"You are quite a spry thing, aren't you?"

"Oh, not really." Warmth spread across my cheeks. "I'm happy you want to talk." I set the coffee cup on the table and climbed over the bench, lifting my skirt and placing one leg over, then the next, rather unladylike. "Where should we begin?" Folding my hands on the wooden surface, I leaned toward Gramma, excited and ready to listen.

"Where would you like to start?"

"From the beginning. Tell me everything about you. From the time you were born. Everything."

Her lips rolled over her snaggled teeth as she let out a chuckle. "I don't know if I'll live long enough to start that far back."

"That's fine. You start when—"

"I've kept journals most of my life. That's where you'll find the tales of my childhood."

"Oh?" I picked up the coffee cup and hid my guilt behind the rim. The earlier warmth in my cheeks was now a raging inferno.

"Did you get a chance to read that part?" She rested her elbows on the table and paralyzed me with her hazy, green gaze.

"I, oh, I—I..."

"Did you think I didn't see you take one of my journals?"

"Gramma, let me explain." The coffee cup rattled to the table as my hands went numb. "I wanted—"

She stopped me with a stern glare, but slowly her face softened and her eyes crinkled at the corners. Her back pressed against the chair and she sucked in a wheezy breath. Closing her eyes, she raked her fingers through her stringy gray hair and blew out the breath she was holding.

"You came here to get answers."

"Yes," I whispered, afraid to say more.

"Your father treats you unfairly, does he? He's hard on you?"

"He's not like that with my brothers or sister."

"I guess not." She took another sip of coffee and then gave me a brief smile. "I'll need something to eat if you want to learn why."

Finally, my grandmother was about to open up. I was delighted to discover the history between my father and Gramma that I nearly burst with excitement. I jumped from the bench, once again sending it teetering on two legs, and hurried to the stove, where Helen had left porridge warming.

"Would you like porridge? How about toasted bread?"

"Yes, please. And a bit of that apple butter Helen made last week."

"Yes, ma'am."

As quickly as my hands and feet could move, I fixed Gramma's breakfast while dozens of questions swirled in my mind. Where should I ask her to begin? Should I ask her to go all the way back to her childhood, or just focus on my father's life? What happened to Father's father? And how did John die? Where did our love of art come from? Why had Father kept us from knowing her? I hoped I wouldn't overwhelm her with all my questions. The last thing I wanted was for her to have a relapse.

Setting the warm bowl of porridge, silver-plated spoon, and buttered toast with apple butter in front of her, I once again took a seat on the bench and rested my chin in my hand. I tingled in anticipation.

"Well, to understand why your father is the way he is..." She sunk her sparsely spaced teeth into the toast and chewed deliberately as her gaze stared through the window. After an audible swallow, she continued. "...I better start with when I met *his* father."

She dipped the spoon into the porridge and continued to glance toward the window, as if seeing her life unfolding there before her. With a shake of her head, her throat bobbed with a deep swallow, and she wiped the cloth napkin across her lips.

Then, she began.

CHAPTER 18

April, 1833

"Hello, Mr. Edwards. Quite a fine day, isn't it?" Gray's deep voice carried up the staircase to my room, where Mother was pinning her cameo to the neck of my new blue gown. "Is Maggie at home?"

"She is indeed. Please come in, Mr. Whitman." Father enthusiastically welcomed Gray into our home, as he'd done the past three weeks each time he'd come to call. And why wouldn't he? His only daughter was being courted by Gray Whitman, son of one of the wealthiest landowners in the county. Obviously he was pleased.

Mother closed the bedroom door, making their conversation muffled and indecipherable. "Mother!"

"Hush now. Let your father speak with the young man. They don't need us busybodies listening."

"Says you."

I hopped from the wooden bench and slowly, so as not to make a sound, opened the door enough to hear their conversation.

"With your permission, I'd like to take Maggie for a ride this afternoon."

"I believe you've asked this before."

"Yes sir. It's just that I think she would enjoy seeing the dogwoods beginning to bloom along the river."

"Of course. That's fine. I guess it would be alright, as long as you don't keep her out too long."

"No sir."

"Let me get her."

I rushed back to my perch in front of the mirror as Father's heavy boots galloped up the treads, sounding an awful lot like a horse. He threw open the door, breathing heavily, with a broad grin on his face. Mother stood behind me, tucking an imaginary strand behind my ear.

"My heavens, dear, you're out of breath," she said, appearing unaware of the visitor waiting in our parlor. She was quite a good actress.

"Afraid so." Father pressed his hand to his heaving chest. "Gray Whitman is here to take Margaret for a ride in that fancy gig of his."

"Oh, how delightful." Mother's cheeks flushed rosy red as she pressed her entwined hands to her chest. "He wants to take you for a ride."

"Alone?" Suddenly, a rather large stone lodged in my throat. I couldn't swallow.

"Yes, darling. Your father has given his permission."

"But I've never been alone with him—any boy—before."

"He must be quite smitten with you." Beaming with pride, Mother smoothed her hands down the length of my sleeves, barely able to contain her excitement.

"But what will we talk about? What should I say?"

"Let him lead the conversation. Men like that. Agree with him, compliment him, and make him feel admired."

"But what if I don't agree with him?"

Mother dropped her hands and stomped her foot in frustration. "Margaret Edwards! The most sought-after young man in the county is waiting for you downstairs. Your father has given his permission. For once, could you hold your opinionated tongue and let him take you for a pleasant ride?"

"But Mother—"

"Do as she says, Margaret." Father crossed his arms over his broad chest and I knew I'd lost the battle.

"You will not have a better prospect than Gray Whitman," Mother said.

A husband? I'd only known Gray for a little over a month. Then again, I was now twenty-five, almost twenty-six—quite old to be unmarried. Most of my friends had long since wed and started families. I should count myself lucky that such an eligible gentleman was still available.

I leaned into the mirror for a final look at my curly red hair, arranged quite nicely, pulled away from my face and tumbling down my back. Unfortunately, there was nothing I could do to hide the freckles that dotted my face. Mother was right—Gray Whitman was my best prospect. I placed my bonnet on my head and turned toward Mother and Father.

"How do I look?"

"Lovely, dear," Father said.

"Gray is quite a handsome young man, don't you think?" Mother's eyes glistened.

"From a fine family," Father added.

"I'll do as you say, Mother. I'll let him do the talking and I'll hold my tongue if I should disagree with him."

"That's my girl."

With each step down the staircase, my nerves intensified. Until today, we had sat in the parlor along with Mother and Father, Gray carrying on a conversation with them about the weather and the early corn crop. Mostly I had sat with my hands folded in my lap with a granite smile on my face. We were about to be alone, forced to chat about God knew what. Did we have anything in common? I barely knew the man. My hands twisted against my midriff until I reached the bottom of the stairs. Gray's face lit up with admiration, and a soothing calm washed over me.

Mother was right. He was quite handsome—tall, thick-shouldered, with a powerful presence. A thin scar ran from the corner of his right eye toward his ear, which only made his appearance more beguiling. The most noticeable thing about him was his dark brown eyes—almost dark enough to mask his black pupils. Those eyes against his sooty black hair made quite a picture.

"How fine you look today, Maggie." Gray held out his elbow. "Are you ready to go for a ride?"

"Yes, thank you."

"I'll have her home before dark, sir."

I almost didn't notice Father and Mother had followed me into the parlor.

"You two run along and have a wonderful time." Father patted Gray on the back as we stepped onto the porch. They watched us through the window as Gray helped me into the carriage. He snapped the whip against the horses' backs and we rolled down the lane and out of my parents' sight.

ALL SUMMER LONG, GRAY CONTINUED TO COURT ME, TAKING ME on long carriage rides, escorting me to the county fair, and having me to Sunday dinner at his parents' home. It was only a matter of time before he proposed. He never spoke of love, but he showed his feelings with affection, giving me long, passionate kisses whenever we were alone. In fact, most of our time was spent kissing rather than talking.

That was fine with me. Gray could be a bit of a braggart, often proving his knowledge of most subjects, and at times he was quite overly confident, bordering on conceited. Generally though, I enjoyed his company. He was a masterful storyteller, and I admired his big dreams of running his own farm. We shared an interest in horses. He was kind to me, and doting, and about as handsome as a man could be. Gray was worldly and intelligent, and I couldn't help but be enthralled. Occasionally he was condescending and patronizing, but I chose to ignore those shortcomings. He was, after all, a man accustomed to getting his way.

One warm October afternoon, Gray pulled up in his carriage, dressed in a fine gray cutaway suit and top hat, looking as though he were dressed for a day at the races. He bowed deeply when I came to the door.

"Miss Edwards, it would give me the greatest pleasure if you'd ride with me this afternoon."

I giggled at his theatrics. "What are you doing, Gray?"

He rose tall and extended his open hand to me. "I'm asking my sweetheart to ride with me. Will you?"

His sweetheart. A warm blush rose in my cheeks as I placed my hand in his, letting him whisk me away through the thick, colorful trees. He led his carriage through the woods and we stopped alongside the creek. Before I could say a word, he gathered me in his arms and drew me in for a long, passionate kiss. Forceful and insistent—so unlike him—he shoved his tongue into my mouth. I pushed him away.

"Gray, what are you doing?"

"I'm kissing you."

"But you've never...I—"

"It's the way lovers do. Didn't you know?"

"No, I—"

"I have so much to teach you."

Once again, he smothered my mouth under his and pried my lips open with his tongue. Such a strange, new experience. Slowly, I began to relax and enjoy this new way of kissing. I liked it. Emboldened, Gray ran his hands over the bodice of my dress, and I let him. He cupped my breasts, squeezed and teased, running his thumbs over my nipples until they were hard as stones. A strange, delightful sensation tingled between my legs. Confusion swirled in my mind, but I didn't dare make him stop.

He dragged his lips down the side of my neck and murmured, "Do you want me, Maggie?"

"Do I want you?" I wasn't sure what he was asking, but I turned my head to allow him better access to the curve of my neck. My mind warred with the pleasure of his hands and the impropriety of what he was doing.

"Do you want to make love with me? Because I surely want you."

Gray swept his lips across my chest and settled his mouth between my breasts. His hand skimmed down my arm and gripped my hand, placing it over the hard bulge in his trousers.

"See that? I want you, Maggie."

"But Gray..." The spell he'd cast over me disappeared and I snatched my hand back.

"Tell me you feel the same for me."

"Gray...no...yes..." I wriggled my hands between us and pushed him away, breathless. "We shouldn't."

Gray fell against the back of the seat and ran his hands through his thick, black hair, blowing out a frustrated breath. With his back against the seat, he turned to me, his eyes dark with desire. "But if we were married, would you want me? Would you like me to make love to you?"

I adjusted my bonnet, which had gone askew, feeling quite warm and embarrassed at this topic, and tucked a loose strand of hair behind my ear. "Well, yes, I suppose, if we were married."

Gray perked up and a sparkle lit up his eyes. "Well then, that's what I wanted to hear." He gathered my hands in his and looked deeply into my eyes. "Margaret Edwards, would you do me the honor of becoming my wife?"

"Just so we can make love?"

"No, damn it."

"But that's how it sounds to me."

"I don't want to marry you just to make love." Gray hopped down out of the carriage and kicked up a pile of leaves. "I can do that without getting married."

"With whom?" Anger burned through my limbs. What was he saying, exactly? I scurried out of the carriage and stood behind Gray, who was gazing off toward the creek.

"Christ, Maggie, you can be so dense sometimes."

He had never spoken to me in that way, and before I knew it, tears stung my eyes.

"There are plenty of women in this county who would gladly spread their legs without receiving a marriage proposal."

I sucked in a deep breath, shocked at the coarse words spewing from Gray's mouth. How dare he speak of wanton women in my presence? I refused to climb back into the carriage with such a vile man, so I began to walk home. Having only gone a few yards, Gray caught up to me and pulled me around to face him.

"I'm sorry, Maggie. That was very rude of me."

"If you're so fired in need, why don't you find one of those women to *spread their legs?*"

I ripped my arm from his grip and continued my march up the hill. Gray ran around and stopped me. "Please, forgive me. I've made a mess of things."

Still angry and hurt, I folded my arms across my chest and looked over my shoulder toward the creek.

"Please, my dear, let me start again."

He unfolded my arms and tenderly held my hands in his. "What I was trying to say to you earlier is that I want to marry you, not only to make love, but to spend my life with you."

"By why did you—"

"The feelings between a man and a woman, the desires they have for one another, are very important in a marriage. That's all I meant, and somehow my words got twisted around."

Gray lifted my hands to his lips and touched them with a soft kiss. "Forgive me?"

My anger melted away. "Of course." I shouldn't have flown off the handle. He was only trying to gauge my feelings for him before proposing. "Ask me again."

This time, Gray went down on one knee and gazed up at me —a gesture I'd only read about in books. It was quite dashing and romantic. "Will you bring me the greatest pleasure and be my wife?"

"I will."

He gathered me to his chest and kissed me deeply, and this time I gave in to his ardent caresses. We were engaged, after all. A few breathless moments later, as Gray nibbled at my ear, he said, "I promise you, our life together will not be boring."

"I never thought it would."

CHAPTER 19

November 19, 1833

Who would've thought Margaret Edwards would someday marry Gray Whitman? A simple farmer's daughter and the son of a wealthy landowner? Improbable, but it was happening, and I wasn't sure how I felt about it. Gray was handsome and charming, and he could certainly provide for us and our future family. I'd always imagined myself married to a teacher or a reverend, someone of a higher intellect. He certainly wasn't dumb, just uninterested in my thoughts and opinions. I guess at twenty-six, I should be glad to marry at all.

Standing in the parlor of the Methodist Church where we were about to be married, I smiled at my reflection in the looking glass—my red hair falling softly down my back. A matching blue bonnet with the most intricate lace sat atop my head. Though it was November, it was as warm as a summer day, making the church stuffy. Mother lifted the window sash and immediately the musty smell was replaced by that of dried leaves. A film of sweat dampened my back, but I still felt pretty in the blue muslin dress Mother had made for the occasion.

"Don't you look lovely, dear?" My mother dabbed at the tears trickling down her cheeks. How in the world would she make it through the ceremony? "Such a beautiful bride."

"Thank you, Mother. It's because of the dress. You did a fine job on it."

"Only the best for my only daughter. I hope Gray finds you as beautiful as I do."

"Of course he will." Father came into the church parlor, dressed in a fine gray cutaway and blue cravat, smiling from ear to ear. "Are you ready to go down the aisle? The church is packed with guests and your groom is anxiously waiting."

"Yes, I'm ready."

Father held out his elbow and, looping my hand through it, we followed Mother into the church, my knees shaking and threatening to give out. Gray stood nervously at the front of the church next to his brother, Norville, and the reverend. His cheeks were as pale as a bedsheet. A quivering smile played on his lips as I drew closer. He seemed quite pleased with my dress. His eyes grazed the length of my body as Father placed my hand in his sweaty palm. Rolling my lips inward and dropping my chin, I fought back an anxious giggle. I was getting married! Though he wasn't the cerebral man of my dreams, I'd grown quite fond of him over the course of our courting and knew he would indeed make a fine husband. He was more than a woman of my background could ask for.

After the I do's, cake and punch was served in the churchyard because of the pleasant weather. While Mother flitted around to the guests, gushing over my good fortune, well-wishers rained praise and congratulations upon me.

"You're a lucky young lady, Maggie."

"You've got yourself quite a catch."

"You're a Whitman now. You should be honored."

Though I didn't hear the same accolades expressed to Gray, I knew that was the way of it. Women were lucky to land a strong, desirable husband, and men were...well, men hoped for an obedient, fertile wife.

After an hour of *congratulations* and *best wishes*, Gray helped me into his carriage, snapping the reins against the horse's neck as we waved goodbye. He drove us to a rustic cabin along the Susquehanna for our honeymoon night. Though the cabin sat atop a cliff with a magnificent view of the river, it was a small, dilapidated log house in desperate need of repair. There was a chunk of roof missing from the corner eaves and the chinking between the logs needed repointing. A shiver of dread streaked down my spine, but I reminded myself it would be fine for one night. I forced a smile as he lifted me in his arms and gallantly carried me over the threshold.

"What a sweet little cabin," I said, hiding the dread churning in my stomach. As I expected, it was rather dark and musty, but Gray was smiling proudly, and I didn't want to hurt his feelings. He obviously thought it was a fine place to spend our first night.

"It's ours."

"What?" I jumped from his arms, stumbling when my feet hit the dirt floor. There were cobwebs in the corners, only a few pieces of dust-laden furniture, and oil cloths covering the few windows. My eyes felt as though they'd pop from their sockets. This had to be a joke. "Ours? But I thought we were going to live with your parents."

"Not at all. I just let you believe that." He took my hand and twirled me around as if we were waltzing. "This cabin has been sitting empty for years on our land, so I took it over. It'll give us much more privacy."

"But I don't see a stove or a wash tub. How will I fix meals?" Panic started to set in.

"You'll get all those things," he said as he lit a few candles.

"What about a bedroom?" A narrow, lumpy bed was tucked

in a corner, and my mouth went dry imagining the filth hidden beneath the quilt.

"Did you think you would move into a palace once you married me?"

"No, I—"

"We have to start somewhere, and I didn't want it to be under my father's roof."

Gray's angry tone crackled like a burning flame and I regretted complaining. I'd hurt his feelings, and that was no way to start a marriage. I had promised myself since that first carriage ride that I'd keep my opinions to myself and let him be in charge, even though protests were perched on the tip of my tongue. It would be best to keep a positive attitude.

"At least there's a lovely stone fireplace." I walked over and rested my hands on the mantel, happy at least that we wouldn't freeze this winter. "It's quite cozy in here."

Gray didn't respond. His dark eyes flamed with a candle's reflection and I knew I had to do something to bring back his jovial mood. Our marriage had to begin on a pleasant note.

"It's a wonderful place to spend our first night." I walked slowly toward Gray and noticed his eyes soften. "Our first night as Mr. and Mrs. Whitman."

"A night," he said, his face softening just enough to suggest his anger would soon thaw, "you'll never forget."

UNLIKE WHAT I'D EXPECTED AND HOPED FOR, GRAY TOOK MY virginity none too gently. Mother had warned me the first time might be a bit uncomfortable, but it would get better the second time. It didn't. He continued to satisfy himself several times throughout the night until I was raw and miserable. The burning sensation between my legs drew my knees to my chest to ease the pain. It was as though saying "I do" had turned Gray into someone else. Gone were the sweet, tender kisses of our courtship. Gray was no longer the kind gentleman I had come to know, instead transformed into someone demanding, impatient, and brutal. My gut roiled as I realized I might have made a mistake in marrying him.

After a week of living in the rustic cabin, unable to prepare a proper meal or keep the spiders from crawling on our bed, neither Gray nor I felt we could make a home in such a dank place. He complained to his father, who in turn purchased a little house for us on the edge of his vast property, overlooking the river. I was sure that idyllic place would be the domestic haven I'd dreamed of.

Once more, I was wrong.

"Where the hell's my dinner?" Gray stumbled through the back door, bouncing off the walls as he made his way to the kitchen. He fell into the closest chair and hung his head between his knees.

My heartbeat tripled as I gave him the bad news. "It'll be at least another hour. I have a roast in the pot."

He slammed his big hand on the wooden table and shouted, "I want my dinner when I get home."

"It's only four o'clock. I didn't expect you this soon."

Somehow, Gray regained his balance and rushed across the room, pulling my hair until I thought my neck would break. We'd been married only a month, but already I'd lost count of the number of times he had come home drunk and looking for a fight. Whiskey fumes nearly knocked me out as he murmured against my cheek, "Find something for me to eat." He punched me in the ribs and I doubled over in pain. Shoving me into the sideboard, he stomped out of the room and slammed our bedroom door.

I wiped the back of my hand across my damp forehead while pressing my other into my side. If my ribs weren't broken,

I'd at least have a nasty bruise. Gray often spent his day in a tavern rather than learning how to run his father's farm—a farm he was promised to inherit. If it wasn't his dinner he complained about, it was some other mundane thing that would end with a slap or a punch. Usually he followed up his punishment with a reminder that I was lucky he had married me. He could have had any girl in the county, but I was fortunate he had chosen me.

I wished he hadn't.

I did my best to hide the bruises, embarrassed by the deplorable life I was leading. No one would have believed me anyway.

ONE AFTERNOON, JUST SHY OF OUR FIRST WEDDING ANNIVERSARY, Father dropped by to deliver an apple pie Mother had made. I enjoyed his weekly visits, but found it harder and harder to hide the evidence of Gray's anger.

"Everything going alright for the two of you?" he asked as he settled into a kitchen chair.

I placed a cup of coffee in front of him and returned to the trousers I was mending. "Everything's fine."

"Did you have a fall?"

I shook my head, letting my long locks shield my face. "What do you mean?"

"The bruise there." He reached out and touched my swollen cheek. "How did that happen?"

"Oh, that. You know how clumsy I can be." I laid down the mending and smiled sweetly. It took all my strength not to burst into tears and crawl onto my father's lap, like I did when I was a little girl. "I tripped over a log on my way to the clothesline. I hit my face on the post."

"Are you sure that's all it was?" My heart dropped to my stomach as Father's gaze seared into me, urging me to confess.

Gray had threatened to kill me if I told anyone about the beatings, and I had no doubt he would follow through.

I forced a giggle and patted his hand. "Of course. What else could it be? What? Do you think Gray did this? How silly."

"Is it?"

"Of course. Gray is a wonderful husband."

"I hear he's supposed to take over the farm but rarely goes to work."

"Where did you hear that? You can't believe hateful gossip."

"You'd tell me if something was wrong, wouldn't you?"

"Father." I straightened my spine and looked him square in the eyes. I'd been faking it so long, it had become second nature to lie. "You have nothing to worry about. I'm fine." I cleared my throat, pulling back my shoulders, but this time, I dug deep in my soul and found my truth. "I'm a strong woman."

As soon as Father climbed on his horse and rode away, I collapsed on the floor, sobbing pent-up tears.

A month later, I discovered I was pregnant with my first child. I convinced myself that once the baby came, everything would be perfect like it was when we courted. Less optimistic, my father set aside forty acres of his own land and put only my name on the deed without Gray's knowledge. Father had a roomy farm house built for us, and shortly after Calvin was born, we moved in. I had always dreamed of having my own farm where I could raise cattle and chickens and sheep and horses—most especially horses. Gray was all too happy to move into a larger, more impressive home than the little cottage we had lived in. By this time, Gray's daddy had washed his hands of him.

I was right, things became much happier once the baby arrived—at least for a while. Gray was thrilled to have a son and he proudly boasted to all his friends. He loved showing off his little family at Sunday worship, and the whole community thought we were the most contented couple. After a few months, his demons returned and he went back to spending time at the tavern, leaving me to raise the baby and run the farm on my own.

Gray knew I was a horse lover, so one day, after a particularly bad night, he brought home three thoroughbreds as a peace offering. Horse racing was a burgeoning industry, and Gray believed we could get rich with them.

"Where in the world did you get them?" I ran one hand down the forelock of the most beautiful of the three while my other hand pressed into the pain in my back.

"I won them. A guy owed me money, but gave me the horses instead."

"Thoroughbreds? They must be worth a fortune."

"Are you saying I stole them?" Gray's face turned ugly, his eyes narrowed, and his lips curled into a sneer. I stepped away from the horse and twisted my hands into my gut.

"No, of course not. You would never do such a thing. I'm just surprised, that's all."

"Do you like them?"

"They're beautiful, especially the chestnut. I think I'll name her Ruby. Do you like that?"

"Name 'em whatever you want. Now get inside and get my dinner."

CHAPTER 20

Gramma's porridge had grown cold and half her toast was still uneaten. The whole time she spoke, I sat quietly, doing my best to sit still rather than give in to the nervous energy coursing through my veins. Her gaze had been locked on the kitchen window, and from time to time, I'd glance in its direction to make sure Gray Whitman wasn't standing outside.

"I need the chamber pot. Will you help me, child?"

I scurried around behind her and slipped my hands around her fragile ribs, helping to lift her from the chair. She gripped my offered elbow and I escorted her back to her room, where the chamber pot sat on a chair in the corner. Once she finished, I helped her settle back in her bed, where she reclined against the pile of pillows with her eyes closed. She was exhausted not only from walking to and from the kitchen, but from the emotional toll her memories had taken on her body. While she dozed, I carried the chamber pot to the outhouse and rinsed it out with a scoop of water from the rain barrel. By the time I returned to her room, she was once again awake and ready to talk. I pulled up the ladder-back chair to listen.

"One evening, back in forty-two, Gray came in the house,

ignoring the children's greetings, and announced, 'I'm going to Havre de Grace to see someone about that horse we've got out there. It's sure to be a winner. I'll be back.' He rushed into the bedroom and tossed a few items in his knapsack, yelling, 'Just imagine the money we can make.'

"The children were crazy about their father. He spoiled them something awful. Calvin, your daddy, who was eight at the time—his eyes got as big as saucers. 'How much money, Father? How will you get the money?'

"'I'm going to meet with the men in charge of the track and enroll Ghost in an upcoming race. A filly as fast as she will surely win. That's how I'll get the money, son.'

"Little Sarah, four years old at that time, jumped up on our bed and bounced on her knees, shouting 'Can we go? We want to watch Ghost run.' Even two-year-old Jeremy got caught up in the excitement.

"That horse, Ghost, was a beautiful gray filly, progeny of the original thoroughbreds he had brought home years ago. I told him the horse wasn't ready to race. She'd only done a few practice runs and wouldn't be ready to race for a while."

"What did he say to that?" I had scooted to the edge of my chair, my heart thumping in anticipation of Gray's reaction. Gramma had made it clear he didn't tolerate her contradicting him.

"He raised his fist at me and said 'Shut up, woman!' I thought those brown eyes of his would pop right out of their sockets. He stalked toward me and the children scattered." Gramma raised her fist, mimicking Gray, and her eyes glazed over. "'I didn't ask your opinion!'"

"Did he, did he—" I was too frightened to ask what happened next.

"He didn't hit me that time. I dropped to the floor and covered my head, ready for the first blow, but he backed off. You'd think I would've learned long ago to keep quiet."

I reached for her hand and gathered it to my bosom, telling myself she needed comfort, when in reality it was me who needed her touch. How horrible to live each day in uncertainty. My own father had a frightful temper, but I'd never seen him raise a hand to my mother. What would I have done if he had?

"Satisfied he'd shut me up, he said, 'That's more like it. I don't want to hear another word out of you until I'm gone. As soon as I make the arrangements, I'll be back to get the horse and will enter her in the race.'

"I knew darn well he would go and lose a lot of money—money we needed to run the farm. He loved the races and lost more than he won. He'd done it a few times before and always came home angry and full of excuses. Usually he found a way to make it my fault. He had it in his head that entering Ghost in a race would bring in hundreds of dollars. That fool."

Gramma pulled her hand from my chest and coughed into her fist. "Would you mind getting me a glass of water, child?" Her throat must have gone bone dry, so scratchy was her request. I should have thought of that earlier, but had been so enthralled with her story.

"Of course, Gramma. I'll be right back."

As I went into the kitchen, I pressed my hand to my stomach to quell its roiling. How frightened she must have been living with such a brute as Gray Whitman. Was that how it was with Mother? Did she live in fear of Father's unpredictable moods? Though I'd never seen him raise a hand to Mother, he certainly was hard on her, demanding perfection from her and us children. From what Gramma told me, it seemed my father was cut from the same cloth as his own.

When I returned to Gramma's room, she was softly snoring, so I set the glass on the bedside table and tucked her quilt up under her chin. She needed rest and I needed time to absorb everything she had told me thus far.

. . .

THE REST OF THE DAY WAS SPENT HELPING HELEN PREPARE DINNER and reading to the girls. Gramma had slept into the afternoon, and I didn't have the heart to press her for more information. Surely tomorrow morning she'd continue her saga once we were alone.

Late in the afternoon, there was a knock on the front door. Helen and I were cutting up root vegetables for the stew when Cora came into the kitchen.

"Mother, Garin is here to see Laurel."

The knife I was using to peel a potato dropped from my hand and clattered on the wood floor. I hadn't expected him to visit after the chilly way our evening had ended.

"Go ahead, Laurel." Helen nodded toward Garin. "I'll finish this up." Then, she glanced at Cora. "Cora, you and Belle go outside please. We need some more kindling for the stove. Pick the smallest pieces from the woodpile and stack them on the back porch."

Helen had efficiently arranged for Garin and me to be alone, so I had no choice but to lead him into the parlor, where I offered the tufted sofa to him while I sat on the armchair across the room. With my hands tightly folded in my lap, I held my gaze on the floral carpet while I waited for him to begin.

Garin cleared his throat and said, "Laurel, I want to apologize for my behavior last evening. After speaking with Vater, I realized I was unkind. He said I should have been more sensitive to your plight."

"Thank you, Garin." I glanced up at him and smiled at his contrite expression. He was spinning his brown felt hat in his quivering hands.

"You wanted to know more about your grandmother. I understand."

"I'm glad." I crossed the room and perched on the edge of the sofa beside him. "It's been a bit difficult since I arrived."

"Vater reminded me how emotional women can be. Being the fairer sex, you're easily prone to hysterics and vapors."

The tiny hairs on the back of my neck stood at attention. "I'll admit I've been on pins and needles since I've arrived, but—"

"All I'm saying is if we're going to continue courting, I need to be more aware of your fragile emotional state."

"Fragile?" I stood up, seething, and glared down at the top of his wavy blond head.

"Yes. Your grandmother can be—well, she's scared me a time or two. I should've been more understanding of what it was like to live with her."

My spine went rigid. It was one thing to accuse me of being a *weak* woman, but Garin was on the verge of saying some nasty things about my grandmother and I wouldn't stand for it. Since she had opened up to me and made me her confidante, no one could say a derogatory thing about her. "She's an old woman."

"I know."

"She's had a very hard life. She's been through more than anyone can imagine."

"I thought you said she wouldn't talk to you."

"She has, finally, opened up to me." Tears burned behind my eyelids as I defended the woman who trusted me enough to share the darkest secrets of her life. The last thing I wanted was for Garin to see me cry. He might accuse me of being hysterical when my tears were caused by fury.

"I can see I've upset you again." He stood up and gently touched my arm. I snatched it back as if he'd laid a hot pan against my skin.

"Yes, you have."

"I'm sorry. See, I still haven't figured out how to read your feminine emotions yet. You'll just have to be patient with me."

"No, you certainly haven't learned." I poked my finger into Garin's chest, forcing him to take a step back. "For your information, I'm not fragile." This statement was followed by another jab to his chest. "Nor do I get hysterical." Garin's eyes grew large as he fell against the doorframe. "Nor do I have to be patient with you." This time, I placed my hands on his shoulders and turned him around to face the door.

"I'm sure you only meant well, Garin, but you will never understand me. It's time you went home." I applied enough pressure to propel him toward the door and he stumbled forward, glancing over his shoulder in confusion.

As he reached for the doorknob, he asked, "May I call on you another time, Laurel, when you're feeling more like yourself?"

My blood fairly boiled through my veins and I fought to keep the Whitman temper under control. "I feel perfectly fine, thank you."

His jaw dropped open and his brows knitted together. He stared at me so long, I was tempted to press my fingers under his jaw and snap his mouth shut. Finally, he plopped his hat on his head and opened the door. As he crossed the threshold with a shake of his head, I heard him mutter to himself, "Women!"

"THEY FOUND HIM DEAD OUTSIDE THE PADDOCK. HIS THROAT slashed and his pockets emptied." Gramma took a sip of coffee, picking up the story where she had left off yesterday. She spoke in a monotone, with no emotion, as if she were recalling yesterday's weather.

"That's terrible." I set my elbows on the table and leaned toward her. We were sitting at the kitchen table—she having breakfast and I enraptured by her story—like we had the day before.

She shrugged her shoulders and spooned a dollop of porridge in her mouth. I waited patiently, sipping my coffee while she ate the cereal and a freshly baked biscuit Helen had made earlier. This morning, Gramma didn't leave a single crumb on her plate, and I marveled at her appetite. She ate in silence and my curiosity was killing me. I couldn't wait to hear more about my grandfather's death.

Once breakfast was over and her morning toilette complete, she asked that I help change her nightdress and twist her long, gray strands into a bun.

"I need a change of scenery this morning," she said as I settled her on the parlor sofa. Her strength and energy were so much stronger than the night I first arrived. I sent up a silent prayer of gratitude as I sat beside her.

"So where did I leave off?" She tapped her index finger, crooked with age, against her knee while looking toward the lacy curtains that covered the parlor window.

"You were telling me about my grandfather's death."

"Oh, yes, the news came in a telegram. You'd think I would have been relieved, but all I could think was *now what?* Three days later, we buried him in the church graveyard and the next day, I got back to work running the farm."

"Just like that? It was business as usual?"

"Not for long."

Her eyes returned to that hypnotic gaze as she stared through the gossamer curtains to a world only she could remember.

CHAPTER 21

September, 1843

S ummer refused to loosen its grip. A strong, hot breeze blew in from the south as I fought to pin the wash on the line. Sweat ran down my back, soaking my cotton dress, and long red strands covered my eyes, having escaped my tightly wound bun. Jeremy contented himself at my feet by pouring the clothespins on the ground and dropping them one by one back into the metal can. As hot as it was, I'd take this weather to the cold of winter any day. Sarah and Calvin were down in the pasture, feeding and watering the horses—mostly the work fell to Calvin, but Sarah often took credit. We had settled into a nice routine since Gray had been gone, and though running the farm was hard work, I was at ease for the first time in years.

A bump and clang startled me from my work. *Please let it not be Norville—again.* Gray's brother had taken it upon himself to act as surrogate father to the children, even attempting to take his place as my husband.

"Maggie," he'd said last week after we'd finished eating, "I'm quite fond of you. Always have been." He'd invited me and the children to Sunday dinner at the lavish family home he'd taken over since his father's passing. My mother-in-law had passed ten years prior. Since Norville was the only remaining son, the responsibility—and wealth—had fallen to him. Calvin, Sarah, and Jeremy had gone outside with the groom to look at Norville's vast collection of horses. He took my hand in his. "Gray would want me to look after you and the children. Don't you think it makes sense for us to marry?"

He'd been skirting around this idea for months, ever since Gray's death. Norville was just as handsome as Gray, but where my husband had been a sluggard, Norville was stalwart. He'd always been responsible, stepping in to fill his father's shoes, continuing to make their farm a successful enterprise. Even with all his admirable traits, I had no intention of marrying him. I sensed a bit of simmering anger beneath Norville's polished façade, and I wasn't about to take a risk on another Whitman.

"Norville, I truly appreciate the offer, but the children and I are fine on our own. Besides..." I laid my hand over his. "I think of you as a brother. It wouldn't be fair to you."

"The children need a father."

"No, they need a doting uncle—that's you. Please know you will always be welcome in our home and may spend as much time with the children as you like."

Somehow he'd misunderstood the message and had called upon me every day since.

I took a deep breath, turned, and found Father's buckboard rolling into the yard as I clipped a corner of a bedsheet to the line. Relief washed over me. Since Gray had passed, Father frequently stopped by to check on us. Some days, he would help with the chores or take us to get supplies. Today, I didn't need anything in town, but could use some help harvesting the corn.

After tacking up a pillowcase—the last of the laundry—I

turned around to greet my father and was surprised to find a young man sitting beside him on the bench. He hadn't said anything about bringing over a visitor, so I was quite surprised when he jumped down from the wagon and told me that the man sitting with him was my new help.

"Margaret," he said, "meet John Hayward, your new farmhand."

John climbed down from the wagon and bowed his head in greeting. I nearly fell over. Even before Gray was gone, the children and I had taken care of the farm, with the occasional help from Father or my brother, Thomas. Norville even sent one of his men to pitch in from time to time. I didn't need any help, nor could I afford it. But my strange reaction to John Hayward had little to do with the lack of need and more to do with the man himself.

He had thick, dark hair that curled at the nape of his neck and a sharp, distinguished nose. A red scar lined his jaw and he had crystal blue eyes—the kind of eyes that seem to look right into your soul. I looked away, pressing my hand over my thrumming heart, taking a moment to collect myself. John Hayward wasn't a handsome man by society's standards, but my body awakened to him in a way I'd never experienced before. Perhaps the time alone and the harrowing years of my marriage were the cause of the warmth tingling through my body. I brushed a stray hair behind my ear and took a deep breath before turning back around to face my father.

"Forgive me, Mr. Hayward, but I don't need a farmhand."

"Grandpa!" Calvin shouted as he and Sarah ran up the hill from the barn.

Sarah slammed into her grandfather and wrapped her skinny arms around his legs. "Grandpa, you're here."

"Yes, children. I've stopped by to introduce your mother to Mr. Hayward."

"Father, I don't—"

"Margaret, you do. You need help around here and I found just the man for you." Father gripped my shoulders between his big hands and gave me a gentle shake. "He came all the way from England to work with you and your horses. He'll do chores and can even help with the training."

I stole another look at the young man as he stepped forward with a courtly bow. In a most proper English accent, he said, "Good morning, Mrs. Whitman. If you will give me a chance, ma'am, I believe you will find my work quite satisfactory."

I suddenly grew light-headed and stumbled against the clothesline pole. Jeremy toddled over and reached his arms up for me to hold him. I studied Mr. Hayward through my lowered lids as I picked up my son. John was dressed in worn, dark trousers and a black sack coat faded to gray, but he spoke like an aristocrat. He sounded more like a duke than a farmhand.

"Mr. Hayward arrived earlier this morning from New York City, where he arrived four days ago. I've been corresponding with him for the past two months after he answered my advertisement, and I'm quite satisfied I've found the right man for the job." Father wrapped his arm around my shoulder, perhaps noticing my knees had gone weak, and tweaked Jeremy's cheek.

"But Father..."

"Now, Margaret, give the man a chance. I believe he'll be a great help to you and the children."

"But Father..." I turned and whispered to him, "I can't afford to pay him."

"That's quite alright, ma'am." John Hayward stepped closer and it was then I saw his perfectly straight, white teeth. His smile took my breath away. "I'll be happy to work for food and lodging. With time, you'll see I can help you make the farm profitable, and perhaps then we can revisit a talk of wages."

I didn't have the strength or inclination to argue any longer.

. . .

WE SET UP A ROOM FOR JOHN IN THE BARN. THERE WERE TWO large rooms inside the stables—one used for storing harnesses, saddles and such, and the other for tools and farm equipment. With Calvin's help, we moved the tools into the tack room and turned the storeroom into John's sleeping quarters. Father brought over an old bed from his house, and a dresser and mirror. I had an extra washbowl and pitcher, which I arranged on the dresser. The well was right outside his door and the outhouse was only a few yards away, so he had all he needed. The first few days, I brought his meals to him in the stable, but in no time, he took his meals inside the house with me and the children. It didn't seem right for him to eat outside alone and, besides, I enjoyed having another adult to talk to.

It wasn't long before John and I dropped the formalities between us. From the first day, he insisted I call him John, and after a week of calling me Mrs. Whitman, he started calling me Lady Margaret, as if I was of royal lineage. I believe he was teasing me, but I liked it.

"And should I call you Sir John or his royal highness or my lord?" I asked with a giggle.

He smiled sweetly and said, "Simply call me John."

He had such a beautiful accent, I found myself asking several questions just to hear him speak. He didn't sound like any of the men I heard in town who had recently arrived in America. He spoke like a fine English gentleman, not that I'd ever met one, and had a dignified air about him. The children seemed to enjoy his accent as well, giggling the first few times he spoke. He called them master and mistress, and they found their new titles rather silly.

One night during dinner, Sarah asked him, "Mr. Hayward, why do you talk funny?"

He got a sly grin on his face and a gleam in his eye.

"Mistress Sarah, where I come from, everyone talks as I do. I was raised to address all beautiful ladies with their deserved titles. You, my dear, are a pretty little girl. Therefore, I shall always call you mistress."

Sarah's face turned red when he said she was pretty and then she said, "You call Mother Lady Margaret. Does that mean you think she's pretty, too?"

My fork clattered against the plate as it spilled from my hand. John turned his piercing gaze on me. "I think your mother is most lovely of all." His persistent stare made me squirm and heat rise in my cheeks. I dropped my gaze to my half-eaten stew and took a painfully dry swallow. Inappropriate thoughts swirled through my mind. John was twelve years my junior and my employee. I slowly raised my chin to meet his gaze and my stomach took a tumble. For a moment, I forgot my age or his youth and the fact that my three young children were sitting with us at the table. We held our gazes until the kettle whistled, breaking up the awkward moment. I jumped up from the table, grateful for the distraction. We finished the rest of our meal in silence and John quietly excused himself to his sleeping quarters.

The next morning, after the breakfast dishes had been cleared and the children were settled at the kitchen table to read from their books, I walked out to the pasture to feed and water the horses. The air was cool and the leaves had begun to turn golden, red, and brown. I tugged my shawl around my shoulders and opened the fence gate. It was obvious John had already been up for hours because the water troughs and feed bins were full. I found him raking out the stalls and spreading fresh straw.

"Good morning, John."

He startled and spun quickly around. "Ah, good morning, Lady Margaret. You're out quite early this morning."

"I could say the same for you."

"Yes, 'tis true. I rose early this morning. So much to be done. I plan to repair the fence on the other side of the pasture. I noticed some rotting wood the other day. And I need to trim back the trees that are too close to the house."

"You act as though you're running a race."

"The weather is changing and I want to get it all finished before frost sets in."

I wanted to argue with him, tell him he shouldn't work so hard, but the truth was, in the short time John had been there, the farm was in the best shape it had ever been. Long ignored repairs were getting done, the crops had been harvested in record time, and the fields were ripe with recently spread manure. He had promised to make the farm more profitable, and I was beginning to believe him. In a matter of months, John had made himself indispensable.

Norville didn't like it.

CHAPTER 22

The front door burst open with a gust of wind and Helen, skirts billowing and hair scattered around her face, rushed in.

"My goodness, it feels like a nor'easter out there." She planted both hands on the back of the door and shoved it closed. When she turned, she stopped dead, looked at the two of us, and her eyes grew wide with surprise. "Well, what do we have here? Mother, you're in the parlor."

"So it seems." Gramma's cloudy eyes had lost that hypnotic glow and now twinkled with delight. "Laurel fixed my hair and helped me walk to the parlor. I didn't feel like crawling back into that bed again."

"That's wonderful." Helen plopped down on the armchair as she unbuttoned her coat. "You've had breakfast? Feeling well this morning? Any coughing?"

"Yes. Yes. And no." Gramma snorted, rolling her lips over snaggled teeth. "I'm beginning to think it wasn't consumption, but maybe the ague. When Hildie Moffitt came down with consumption, she never got back up again."

"Perhaps Dr. Huber was mistaken."

"I never did think that man was very smart." Gramma's chin tipped upward as she smoothed her wrinkled hands across her lap.

"Well, it's nice to see you up and about. You and Laurel are having a nice visit." Helen gave me a covert wink as Gramma fiddled with a button on her dress.

"Yes. Gramma was telling me about the first time she met your father."

"Were you?"

"Yes, well, I'm feeling a bit tired now." My grandmother placed her hand on the sofa arm for leverage and rose to her feet. "I'd like to lie down."

Her joyous mood suddenly turned somber as she shuffled toward the doorway. Helen rushed to her side and offered her arm for support. By the expression on Helen's face, I got the notion she had not heard much about her father's first few days on the farm. Would it be traitorous of me to tell her what I'd learned from Gramma? As freely as her words had flowed, I wasn't under the impression she was telling me any secrets.

I was washing the last porcelain plate as Helen returned to the kitchen. Her arms were crossed and her teeth worried her bottom lip. Without speaking, she picked up a towel and methodically dried and stacked each dish. After returning the dishes to their rightful places on the shelf, Helen sat at the table with her hands folded in front of her. Her head rose slowly and her gaze locked with mine.

"What did she tell you about my father?"

"Oh, well..." My mind warred between loyalties to the two women whose home I presently shared. Helen and Charles had been so kind and welcoming to me, I owed it to her to reveal everything I'd learned. But then again, I couldn't risk compromising my budding friendship with my grandmother. When I sat across from Helen at the table, she saw my struggles.

"I don't want to put you in a precarious position. It's just, I was so young when all the trouble started, and Mother has spoken very little of it."

"What kind of trouble?" I slid my hand across the table's smooth wooden surface and grasped her wrist. "I know he went to prison."

She snatched her arm back as if she'd been scorched. "What have you heard? Who told you?"

"Helen, I—"

"It's probably not true. You have no idea the rumors and falsehoods passed around this community." Helen rose up and planted her hands on the table, leaning close to me. "My father was falsely accused of something he didn't do and he didn't deserve to go to prison."

"I didn't mean to upset you." I rushed behind her and placed my hands on her shoulders, noticing they were shaking with anger. Applying gentle pressure, I eased Helen back into her chair. "Let me warm your coffee." As I reached for her cup, her hand encircled my arm and she gave it a squeeze.

"Thanks, Laurel. I have plenty." She patted my hand and gestured toward my chair. "Sit down please."

I slipped back into my chair and gave Helen a side-glance. She sat with her back poker straight, her breaths coming quick and shallow. The house was so quiet I could hear the muted sound of Gramma's breathing from her room. Feeling guilty for upsetting Helen, I decided to share some of what Gramma had told me about John Hayward.

"Gramma told me how her father hired John to help on the farm. Apparently, he was good with horses."

"He had a way with them."

"She said he was very polite and proper. He even called her Lady Margaret. He spoke like an aristocrat."

"Yes, he did. He had a very proper British accent." With this, the lines on Helen's face softened and her lips curled into a smile. "Sometimes I hear his deep voice in my dreams calling me *princess*. He called me that and then would bow deeply, as if I were royalty." Her gaze locked with mine and I saw the faint glisten of unshed tears. "He was very funny, always making Robert and me laugh."

"So he was a good man."

"We thought so." Her smile faded as her eyes trailed to her coffee mug. "The judge didn't see it that way."

"What was he convicted of?"

Helen abruptly left the table and commenced fixing the midday meal, keeping her back toward me. She picked up a fat, round potato and spun it in her hand as she peeled it in record time. She laid the potato on the wood board and wacked it as if the knife were a hatchet chopping through a tree. It pained my heart to see her so upset at the injustice her father had received.

"Helen." When I laid my hand on her shoulder, she jumped and a large chunk of potato rolled onto the floor. "Sorry. I didn't mean to startle you."

Her chin sank to her chest with a heavy breath and she dropped the knife onto the board. "I guess I understand why Mother never talks about him." When she turned around, I noticed all the color had drained from her face. Her cheeks sagged, and she looked much older than her twenty-seven years. "It's too painful, the unfairness of it all."

I gathered her damp hands in my own. "Maybe it's best to focus on the good memories, on what you know to be true."

When she lifted her gaze to meet mine, her lips formed into a gentle smile.

"Here's what I now know about your father," I said. "He was a very hard worker, he was dedicated to your mother from the first day he arrived, and he was a good father."

Helen burst forth a hearty chuckle, rolling her eyes with a huge smile. "He always made me laugh." Her hands twisted around mine and held them in her grasp. "Robert looks exactly like him."

"Ah, your brother inherited his looks?"

"He's the spitting image."

And Helen was the spitting image of Gramma. Helen had her mother's hair where Robert's was dark brown, but they both had pale blue eyes that must have come from their father. The other thing she and her brother shared was the tall, slender build—the same as mine—which came from Gramma.

"Thank you, Laurel. I'm glad Mother recalled my father in happy terms. He was good to me, which I will always remember. You're right of course—I should only focus on his goodness."

She returned to the task of preparing dinner, but now had a sweet smile on her face. I had learned a bit about John Hayward, where my father's anger came from, and why I had bright red hair. But I realized there was much more yet to discover.

LATER, AFTER EVERYONE HAD GONE DOWN FOR THE NIGHT, I squirmed in my bed, sandwiched between Cora and Belle, who were sleeping soundly, needing desperately to use the chamber pot. I searched around in the moonlight for the porcelain bowl, but didn't see it. Perhaps Helen had forgotten to return it to our room. I would have to go to the outhouse. The wind howled outside our tiny gable window and I dreaded facing the cold, dark outdoors. After a few more minutes of squeezing my stomach muscles and crossing my legs, I gave up fighting nature. I padded on bare feet downstairs and through the kitchen, where I sunk my feet into a pair of Helen's boots and wrapped myself in Charles's coat. As I opened the back door, I heard Gramma's raspy cough.

The first flakes of early winter dotted my cheeks and dried

leaves crackled underfoot as I crossed the backyard. Quick and efficient, I finished my business and ran back to the house, fighting the whipping north wind. Shrugging out of the coat and boots, I scurried past Gramma's room and once again heard a dry cough. When I tipped my head through her open doorway, I found her sitting up and curled over, with her fist pressed to her mouth.

"Gramma? Are you not well?"

"It's my throat." She tapped a bony finger against her neck and croaked, "Could you get me a glass of water, please?"

"Of course." Taking the empty water glass from her bedside table, I filled it from the pitcher and quickly returned. She drank half of it in one long gulp.

"Feeling poorly?" Like a mother to a child, I laid my hand on her forehead as I took the water glass in my other hand. She didn't have a fever. "Trouble breathing?"

"No, child. Just a dry tickle in my throat, that's all." She piled an extra pillow behind her back and reclined against the headboard. "Would you mind turning up the lamp?"

I turned the knob on the kerosene lamp Helen kept glowing softly on her bureau, and the flame brightened the darkness, casting long shadows as I pulled up the chair beside her bed.

"What are you doing skulking around in the dark? Ghost hunting?" Parallel wrinkles curved in her cheeks as her lips curled into a wry grin.

"Hardly. I had to visit the privy." I smiled when she chuckled, noticing she was wide awake. "What about you? You should be asleep."

"Should be, but I'm not. I guess I napped too long today."

"Would you like some company?"

"Yes." Gramma reached out to me and I cupped her hand possessively, savoring its frail, soft warmth. "Where did I leave off today?"

"Oh, that, yes. Are you sure you want to talk now? It's quite late."

She turned her gaze to the window across the room, its heavy drapes blocking the moonlight and swirling wind, and expressed a soft sigh.

"I dreamed about him. Right before I woke up coughing."

"John?"

"He called to me—'Lady Margaret'—so clear, I was sure he was standing in the room."

"Maybe because you were telling me about him earlier."

"No, he comes to me from time to time." She turned toward me, a small smile playing on her lips, and pulled her hand from between mine. "You think I'm crazy."

"No."

"I would if I were you, but I remember my grandmother telling me when I was a little girl that the dead never leave us. If we listen real hard, they'll talk to us and give us guidance."

"Does John do that for you? Give you guidance?"

"He's comforted me when I've needed it."

"What about Gray?"

"Umph." She thumped her fist down on the quilt and crossed her arms over her belly. "I wouldn't listen even if he tried to contact me."

I sagged against the back of the chair and looked down at my hands clasped on my lap. It was certainly understandable with the way he had treated her. Though it wasn't the same, I'd built a wall of resistance around me when Garin tried to explain the emotions of women. Even though he had infuriated me, he wasn't as malicious as my grandfather had been. I couldn't imagine what it was like to be married to such a controlling, hateful man.

"I'm sorry, child. I wish I could tell you your grandfather was a kind, decent, Christian man, but I can't. Your goodness must've come from your mother's side of the family."

"Or yours?"

This brought a big smile to her face. "Or mine." She chuckled softly, folding and smoothing the quilt across her lap. "No, you get it from your mother. She's a sweet girl."

"My mother is a weakling."

"Don't confuse kindheartedness for weakness. She's making the most of what God has given her. That's no task for the faint of heart—believe me. I only wish she had it easier with Calvin."

"She hid like a coward the night Father threw me out. She often does when he's on a rampage. Slinks into her room and pretends it doesn't happen."

"Your mother never defends you?"

I felt guilty describing Mother in such derogatory terms. The truth was she often stood up to Father. "Well, she does have a way of calming Father down. But lately, she stays in their room when he's in one of his rages."

"And you would never do that."

"No."

"Never let a man treat you like that?"

"Positively not. Garin Schmidt dared to tell me I was being irrational when we were at the church social simply because I wanted to know why people treated me as if I were a pariah. Then the next day, he had the nerve to say it was because I was a woman who became easily emotional. 'Hysterical,' in fact."

Gramma threw back her head and burst out a hearty laugh.

"It was infuriating. He had no idea what he was talking about." With my dander fully up and tingling, I leapt to my feet and perched my fists on my hips at the foot of her bed. "We met a couple of weeks ago, had one pleasant conversation and an evening out, and he talks as if we're intended. He acts like it's all up to him, that it's his decision whether or not I marry him."

"He asked you to marry him?" Gramma had stopped laughing and now had a cross look on her face, brows knitted and lips pursed.

"No, but the way he spoke...I read between the lines. He has his sights on me, but I seem to have no say in the matter."

"I take it you wouldn't even consider it."

"Absolutely not. I would never marry a man who doesn't respect me or consider me his intellectual equal, no matter how handsome he is."

"Garin has grown into quite a fetching young man."

"A fetching young beast, maybe."

With that, we both broke into a fit of laughter. I circled back to her bedside and sat in the chair. Gramma looked twenty years younger with her eyes wet with tears and her chest heaving as she laughed. Her laugh was coarse and deep, but it was the best sound I'd ever heard. She was happy and healthy, and I thanked God she'd finally accepted me. What we had at that moment was exactly what I had hoped for.

"I wish I had been as sure of myself at your age. Looking back, there were things about Gray that I should have noticed." She swiped at her cheeks and blew out a sigh. "If I hadn't been so impressed with his fancy gig and his dapper suit and his charm and good looks, I would have detected his mean, angry streak. I wouldn't have married him." Her eyelids squeezed shut and she sucked in an audible breath, then reached toward me. "But if I hadn't, I wouldn't have you, would I?"

It was the dearest thing she had ever said—maybe the dearest thing anyone had ever said to me. Tears burned behind my eyelids as I leaned over her outstretched hand and pressed it to my cheek.

"Thank you, Gramma." I held her birdlike hand against my lips and placed a soft kiss on her silky skin. "I'm very glad I came."

"My prayers were answered."

I popped my head up and lowered her hand to the bed. "You prayed about me?"

"Every day. I say a prayer for all my children and

grandchildren, even your father. I pray that someday he'll come around, come to terms with what he's done and ask forgiveness."

"What he's done?" My spine locked and my nerve endings tingled in anticipation. Gramma was about to reveal the mysteries I'd been seeking.

"Yes, it's quite a story. But first, maybe I should take up where I left off earlier."

CHAPTER 23

October, 1846

The old mule brayed and the horses stomped their hooves as I entered the stable. The sturdy wood structure provided shelter from the blustering winds that tossed and twirled dried leaves in the crisp autumn morning. I tucked a few loose curls back into my bun, wrapping my shawl tighter around my shoulders.

I'd had a restless night. Norville had stopped by earlier to bring the children some books and toys, and me a lovely dress made of satin and lace—much too fancy for a farm woman. John was in the barn milking the cows, and after the children settled at the kitchen table with their new treasures, Norville pulled me into the parlor.

"Maggie, I've something to tell you."

"What is it, Norville?" I settled on the armchair across the room from him, not wanting to get within reaching distance of him.

"There are rumors going around about you and the farmhand."

"John? What kind of rumors?"

"They say you're living in sin under the same roof."

Anger seared through me. How vicious small-town folks could be. John and I had been nothing but the epitome of decorum. The poor man still lived in the barn.

"That's absolutely untrue." I stood up, grinding my fist into my palm. "John stays in the barn. You know that. The children and I are the only ones who live in this house."

"Maggie, Maggie," he cooed, coming to his feet and resting his hands on my shoulders. "I know that, my dear. You are and always have been nothing but a fine, upstanding lady. But I don't think the rumors will stop. If anything, they will get worse."

"What am I to do?"

"Marry me. It's the only way to silence the gossipers."

"But what about John?"

"We'll find a place for him on my farm."

"What about my farm?"

"We'll sell it."

Though Norville's suggestion made sense on the surface, I couldn't possibly marry him just to stop the rumors. This was my farm, my home, mine. My children's inheritance. I'd worked hard and wasn't about to give it up because of some hateful gossip. Not to mention I had no desire to marry Norville, knowing all that marriage entailed, I wouldn't bind myself to a man again—at least not one I couldn't trust.

"Norville, thank you, but I can't marry you. I've told you before, several times, you're like a brother to me. It wouldn't be fair to you. Please, find a nice lady to marry and have a family of your own. You deserve that."

He drew in a deep breath until his chest barreled and his eyes grew dark. He glared at me as his mouth drew to a straight, angry line. "That's it then." He slapped his cap against his thigh and stalked to the door, pulling it nearly off its hinges. Before he left, he turned and pointed at me. "That's the last time I'll ask you, Margaret Whitman. I'm through. Don't come crying to me when your reputation is in tatters."

My body shook the next morning at the memory of Norville's visit as I strolled toward the beautiful thoroughbred. "Good morning, Ghost." I climbed on the bottom plank of the horse stall and reached up, scratching her behind the ears. Her gray coat glistened from the brushing John had obviously given her that morning. The barn smelled slightly of manure, but more of freshly spread straw. He took pride in keeping the horses well fed and housed.

After a final pat to the horse's neck, I walked through the stable and into the pasture where John was breaking in a young horse, training it for riding. He had promised Sarah a horse of her own. As he pulled on the lead, the feisty filly reared up on her hind legs and kicked at him. He responded with a stern warning and she settled back on all four hooves. He had broken several other horses since he'd arrived three years ago, and I had no doubt he would break this one. He seemed to have a mystic connection to the animals. Several times I'd noticed him whispering in a horse's ear, as if they had a little secret between them, and afterward, the horse would simply obey. It was quite remarkable how the animals acquiesced to his patient, softly spoken commands.

"Looks like you could use a hand," I offered as I stepped out of the stable and into the pasture.

"No thank you, Lady Margaret. You should stay back. She's in a bit of snit this morning." Despite the cool temperature, sweat glistened on John's forehead. He had removed his coat and rolled up his shirtsleeves.

"Really, I can help." I walked toward the back of the horse a bit too quickly, spooking the filly. The horse's hind leg shot out and landed a kick to my midriff. I fell to the ground and curled into a ball, fighting to get air back into my lungs.

"Margaret, are you alright?" John released the horse and ran over, lifting me upright. He kept his arm securely around my shoulders as I wheezed air back into my lungs.

"There, there now. Take it slow." He gently brushed a strand of hair away from my face and cupped my cheek in his leathery hand. "Can you breathe? Is it getting better?"

I nodded, though I was unsure if I could actually breathe. His strong arm around me and his forehead wrinkled with concern made my lungs lock up all over again.

"Let me take you in the house." He slid his arms around my back and under my knees and hoisted me into his arms, lifting me as easily as he would a child. Throughout the trek toward the house, he whispered reassurances and I fell under his spell just like the horses he trained. "You'll be fine, milady. I'll take care of you. You can rest all afternoon."

I'd never known such tender care from a man. His masculine smell, mixed with sweat and earth, was pleasantly intoxicating, and I soon forgot the throbbing ache in my side. I laid my head on his shoulder and gave in to his care.

John kicked open the back door and lumbered toward my bedroom behind the kitchen, gently placing me on the bed. He ran his hands down each side of my body and tenderly probed my ribs. "Do you think anything is broken?"

I gazed at his face, so near to mine, and got lost in his crystal blue eyes until I cried out. He had touched a sore spot on my upper ribs.

"I'm sorry." John placed his large hand across the painful spot, checking to see if the rib was broken. His hand lightly brushed beneath my breast and I sucked in a breath. He glanced down at me with a bashful smile. "I don't think it's broken," he whispered as he let his hand slide down to rest on my hip. I should've pushed him away, removed his hand from my body. But our gazes locked and before I could stop him, he leaned down and placed a tender kiss on my lips.

"John, we—"

The front door closed with a loud bang and the children came running into the house. John jumped away from the bed and met them at the bedroom door. "Your mother had a little accident and she needs to rest."

Calvin, who had recently turned thirteen and considered himself officially a man, looked at John suspiciously, as if he thought there had been more going on in the bedroom than simply tending to an injury. Or was it my imagination? "What happened?"

"She was kicked by that filly I'm breaking in, but I don't think anything is broken. We need to let her rest awhile." John walked away from Calvin's accusing stare.

"Mother, are you okay?" Sarah ran in the room and gathered my hand in hers. "Where does it hurt?"

"I'm fine, Sarah, just a little banged up. Let me lie here for a few minutes and then I'll get dinner ready."

John turned around quickly, filling the doorway. "Lady Margaret, I will be happy to prepare the afternoon meal. I think you should stay in bed the rest of the day."

I laughed at him. "You're going to cook?" I laughed even louder but stopped suddenly when gripped by a stabbing pain to my ribs.

"I believe I can handle putting a meal together for the five of us." John's huge grin and playful nature were infectious and I found myself giving in to him.

"And how do you propose to do that?" I challenged him with a big-eyed stare and, despite the pain, was having more fun than I'd had in years.

John crossed his arms over his thick chest and leaned against the doorframe. "Oh Lady Margaret, I have talents you have yet to discover."

My grin faded as I absorbed his veiled meaning. A warm quiver tickled deep in my belly as I held his gaze and his face took on a serious expression. We were paddling in unsafe waters—a widowed woman and her employee—but we continued to stare at each other. We couldn't let the hateful rumors become true.

I finally turned toward Calvin and Sarah, who had been all but forgotten, and said, "Sarah, see what you can do to help John with dinner."

He let out a husky laugh and walked out of my bedroom.

MY BRUISED RIB HEALED QUICKLY AND SOON I WAS BACK TO MY daily routine. I saw to the household chores while John took on most of the responsibilities of running the farm, just as we had for the past three years. The children pitched in with harvesting and tending to the animals, especially Calvin, being the oldest. Most days, there was so much to be done, it left little time for me to ride my horse—something I dearly loved to do. One of the only things Gray had done right was to bring Ruby home, my beautiful chestnut horse with a distinctive white star on her brow. I loved that horse. Now that my ribs were healed, I was itching to take her for a gallop.

"I believe she's somehow your offspring. She has your red hair." John teased me about the horse's coat, so similar to my coloring. I chuckled as I ran my hand down the length of Ruby's back.

"Minus the curls," I said.

"True, but just as lovely all the same."

Since the accident, John had become more flirtatious, seeming to ignore our age difference and the fact that I was his employer. I enjoyed the attention and encouraged his toying, convincing myself it was all quite innocent—Lord help me.

"Why don't you take her for a ride?" John said, setting aside the shovel he was repairing.

"Oh, I have too much to do. I need to put the bread in the oven. It should be finished rising by now."

"Another hour of rising shouldn't hurt it."

"I really shouldn't even be out here, what with the mending and such I need to do."

John came behind me and reached out his hand, running his fingers through Ruby's long mane. "I'm glad you came out." I shivered when his warm breath tickled my ear. "It gets lonely out here by myself."

"Doesn't Calvin keep you company?"

He snorted and a wry grin formed on his lips. "He doesn't say much around me, you know. I suppose he's going through the surly teen years."

"Well, then..." I was at a loss for what to say. Calvin had indeed grown into a grumpy young man, but I was sure it would pass as he grew older. But what should I do about the pleasant thrum running through my veins? John was so near—too near to be appropriate—and yet I had no desire to ask him to move. "I guess I..." I turned my back to Ruby and froze when I came face to face with John.

"You deserve to enjoy yourself, Lady Margaret. You work too hard around here."

"Enjoy myself?"

"Do what you want. Whatever makes you happy."

He leaned his elbow on Ruby's back, bringing his face within inches of mine. Did he notice the creases at the corners of my eyes? The lines that had formed on my forehead and the wrinkles in my cheeks? Was he bothered by the wisps of gray in my hair? He was still a young, virile man. So why hadn't he stepped out with some nice young lady from the county?

"I'll saddle up Ruby for you." He walked away and I fell against the horse for support. I let out the breath I'd been holding and shook the silly notions from my mind. John wasn't attracted to me. How could he be? Twelve years his elder, widowed with three children? Silly.

In no time, John saddled Ruby and I was trotting across the backyard. As soon as we were in open pasture, I nudged the horse's ribs with my heel and we ran across the fields and through the woods to the creek. John had promised to watch over the children while I was gone and I used the time to clear my head. Whatever heat I had for John needed to be doused before I did something I'd regret. I pulled my long, curly hair from its bun and let it fly free in the cool November breeze. The creek's earthy smell tickled my nose as I watched the current drag a leaf through the rocks, reminding me of how it was with John. Since the day he came, the pull was so strong whenever we were near one another, but since the accident, it had only intensified. It—we—couldn't be. With a deep breath and a squaring of my shoulders, I resolved to reinstate our employer-employee relationship and forget my silly attraction. I tugged Ruby's reins around and kicked her into a canter.

When I returned, John greeted me at the gate. Before I could stop him, he lifted me down off Ruby and encircled me in his strong arms. He touched a light kiss to my lips and looked down at me, our mouths a breath apart. We were alone near the stable with only the sound of the rustling leaves to keep us company, and I longed for another kiss. My strong resolve was forgotten. Ruby stomped her front leg, knocking me into John's chest, nickering as if she'd done it on purpose, and he took the opportunity to kiss me again. This time it was much longer, much deeper.

When the kiss ended, he ran his fingers through my curls and said in his deep, aristocratic voice, "You're a beautiful woman, Margaret. Be warned, I plan to kiss you again very soon...and very often."

He picked up Ruby's reins and walked the horse into the stable, leaving me so weak, my knees buckled.

Winter set in early that year, with snow on the ground by
Thanksgiving. I had successfully avoided being alone with
John, knowing what would happen if we were, until one early
December evening when a frightful nor'easter blew through.
The wind howled, snow mounded up on the windowsills, and
the temperature dipped to well below freezing. The children
had gone to my brother's house earlier that afternoon and
hadn't returned due to the weather. I placed two extra logs in
the fireplace, sat in my rocking chair, and picked up a pair of
pants to mend. The fire was bright and the kerosene lamp
beside me illuminated the room enough to see the small
stitches. A pounding on the door brought me out of my chair
and soon I heard John calling. I rushed to the door and the
blast of wind nearly ripped it from my hand.

"I'm sorry to bother you, Lady Margaret, but I don't think I
can last the night in my room. The wind is blowing through the
walls. Would it be possible to stay here with you and the
children tonight?"

John already appeared frozen to the bone. His body shook
violently from the cold. There had been other cold winters
since he had arrived, but none like this. It would be inhumane
to force him to stay in the barn.

"Of course. Come in. I saved you some supper, if you're
hungry."

I slammed the door shut and locked it against the wind.
John huddled in the rocking chair close to the fire as I wrapped
a quilt around him.

"I'll fix you a cup of tea." He shivered and quaked. I should
have invited him in sooner and considered his welfare before
my need to keep a safe distance.

After a time, his shaking settled down and he dozed off in
the chair, giving me time to figure out where he should sleep.
There was a small alcove opposite my bedroom which had a
single bed in it. Sometimes Gray had slept there when he came

home too drunk to stand. There wasn't enough space for him in the room the boys shared, and he couldn't sleep in Sarah's room. The alcove seemed the only place for him.

While John rested in the chair, I made up the bed, piling it with extra quilts from the blanket chest, then woke him long enough to show him where to sleep. His eyes closed as soon as he was prone, and deep, steady breaths came from his chest. He would be fine there until morning.

The next day, when Calvin, Sarah, and Jeremy arrived back home, I told them John had spent the night in the alcove.

"It was terribly cold last night, Mother," Sarah said as she hooked her coat on the tree stand.

"Uncle Thomas said we had a *north eater.*" Jeremy's naïve words caused Sarah and me to burst forth a chuckle.

"It's a nor'easter, dummy." Calvin chucked Jeremy on the shoulder before unbuttoning his coat.

"Calvin, please don't make fun of your brother." I scolded my eldest son before turning to Jeremy, whose head hung with embarrassment. "It's called a nor'easter, dear." I tickled Jeremy under the chin until he smiled up at me. "It means a storm that comes out of the northeast. It usually brings terrible winds and often snow."

"Like last night!" Jeremy hopped like a rabbit and threw his arms around me.

"Like last night. It was bitterly cold, and that is why John had to spend the night in the alcove."

"Where is he now?" Calvin asked, still scowling.

"He's out milking the cows. Perhaps you could give him a hand."

Calvin glared at me as Sarah reached for her coat. "I'll help him." Sarah shoved her arms in the coat sleeves. "John should sleep inside with us, especially in the winter."

"He's not an animal. He's a man," Jeremy said, tugging on his mittens. "Only cows and horses sleep in barns."

Sarah and Jeremy went outside, happy to help John with the milking.

"So he'll sleep in the alcove? Across from your room?" Calvin's question had a hint of accusation that sent a shiver of guilt down my spine.

"Just until spring."

Calvin's eyes still burned with skepticism, but he nodded as he went out the door.

The younger children agreed John should sleep there until spring because his room inside the barn wasn't warm enough for a man to get a decent night's sleep. I should have considered the concern etched on Calvin's face, but I was too distracted by the idea of John's sleeping mere steps away from my own bed each night.

Had I heeded my eldest son's furrowed brow—the set of it so like his father's—I might have done everything differently.

CHAPTER 24

Gramma slumped deeper under the quilt and closed her eyes. I was speechless. She had all but admitted she had had lascivious thoughts about John—thoughts I didn't realize a woman her age would have had, let alone talk about. In my house, Mother and Father never spoke of intimacy or physical desires. In fact, when I started my monthly cycle, Mother handed me a pamphlet that explained what I was to expect. It was full of frightening warnings about cramping and bleeding and painful breasts. I was fortunate in that I only experienced the bleeding. No need for laxatives and hot water bottles as the pamphlet suggested. I knew that my monthly affliction was related to my ability to become a mother, but the pamphlet said nothing about desires.

Accepting my grandmother was down for the night, I lowered the lamp's flame to a hazy glow and returned to my cocoon between Cora and Belle. Sleep came slowly as my mind absorbed everything I had heard from Gramma. Maybe tomorrow she'd tell me more.

. . .

THE NEXT MORNING, GRAMMA AND I WERE AT THE KITCHEN TABLE
—the place where she seemed to start her history lessons.
Helen had gone to visit her friend, Ida Simcoe, who had just
had a baby. The girls had gone with her, and Charles was
somewhere on the farm. Helen had left me to care for Gramma.
Little did she know how much I relished this time.

"Is there any more cornbread?" Gramma asked, wiping
golden crumbs from her lips. Her appetite had returned with a
vengeance, resulting in several much-needed pounds added to
her body. She was growing stronger each day and had even
walked into the kitchen without the aid of her cane.

I quickly placed another square of cornbread on her plate
and topped it with a dollop of butter. After refilling our coffee
cups, I returned to the bench and perched my elbows on the
table.

"So, John moved into the alcove."

"He did."

"And did the children ever catch you?"

"Catch me doing what?"

"Did Father and Aunt Sarah and Uncle Jeremy catch you
kissing?"

"Eventually they figured it out. And your father was none
too happy."

The rattle and clang of wagon wheels disrupted Gramma's
story. I went to the kitchen window and pulled the white eyelet
curtains aside to find Helen tugging on the reins to stop the
mule. The hairy brown beast snorted a white cloud from his
nose and stomped his foot. Charles came from inside the
cheese shed and gathered the reins in his hands as he planted a
soft kiss on Helen's cheek. She rushed up the back stairs,
guiding the girls along, and stumbled through the door.

"Gracious. It's downright frigid out there." Winded from the
blustery morning, Helen hung their coats on the pegboard and

hurried across the kitchen to the stove, where she warmed her hands in front of the grate. "I thought it would warm up today."

Cora and Belle scrambled onto the bench beside me and tucked themselves under each arm.

"It's cold, Laurel," Belle said, burrowing into my ribs.

"It was terribly cold last night." I wrapped my arms tightly around the little girls.

Helen poured the last of the hot coffee into a mug and joined us at the table.

"How is Mrs. Simcoe's baby?" I asked.

"She's a dear, sweet thing with a head of long, dark hair. I swear she needs a trim already."

"Lord, I hope she takes after her mother," Gramma said as she took another bite of cornbread.

"Now, Mother, what did you mean by that?"

"The Simcoes aren't exactly a handsome bunch—especially Roderick. That boy could stop a train."

I folded over with laughter and Gramma joined in, the two of us cackling like hens. Helen tried to feign anger, but soon joined in the merriment. Cora and Belle laughed along, though I wasn't sure they understood the joke. Charles came in from the shed and found the five of us laughing like hyenas.

"What's this all about?" he asked, confusion furrowing his brow.

"Mother is being ornery," Helen said while holding her ribs. "She's afraid the Simcoe baby will look like Roderick."

"God help her if she does. She'll never find a husband."

With that, all of us burst out laughing—Charles slapping his knee, Gramma rubbing her eyes, and Helen pressing a hand to her ribs. I had never met the Simcoes, but it didn't matter. Joining in on the laughter brought me joy. I was finally part of the fabric of the family, and for that I was enormously grateful.

. . .

ONCE OUR GUFFAWS HAD SUBSIDED, ALL OF US CARRIED ON WITH the afternoon. Helen put a lamb shank on to roast, Gramma and the girls napped, and Charles went out to the barn. After helping Helen bake some rye bread, I went up to the bedroom I shared with the girls and pulled out the art supplies Cillian had sent me. I wanted to give a painting to Helen and Charles for Christmas and needed to start it before the girls rose from their naps. It would be a picture of the farm with its pale gray house, big red barn, and rolling fields, so like my triptych.

I had finished sketching the scene when two pairs of feet clomped up the staircase.

"Laurel, are you up here?" Cora called among the stampede.

"Up here. I'm painting."

"Can we paint, too?" Belle asked as the girls poked their heads through the door.

"How about you get a piece of butcher paper from your mother? I'm saving these canvases."

"What for?" Belle asked, placing her foot on the bed frame.

"I'm planning to make Christmas presents with them— something for you to remember me by."

"What do you mean?" Cora lifted Belle onto the bed and looked at me suspiciously.

"Well, I can't stay here forever. My home is in Philadelphia." I dabbed on a bit of burnt sienna to the tree trunk, avoiding the bewildered look on the girls' faces.

"But we don't want you to go," Cora said.

"Stay here," Belle chimed in.

"Who will read to us?" The paintbrush fumbled in my hand, so startled by the sadness in Cora's question. Each evening, the three of us would lie in bed and I'd read to them until they fell asleep. I cherished our nighttime routine, but I couldn't stay. What about the art show? I had to graduate. I couldn't possibly begin a career in design in such a rural place.

The children were offering a permanent home where I knew I'd be happy. But would I be satisfied not fulfilling my dreams?

LATER THAT EVENING, AFTER I'D READ TO THE GIRLS, I SAT BEHIND Gramma and pulled the horsehair brush through her long, brittle, gray strands until her thin hair gleamed. Every so often, she'd sigh with pleasure from the gentle scalp massage. Helen and I had helped her into the bathtub earlier that evening—the first full bath she'd had since she'd fallen ill—and she luxuriated in the steamy, sudsy water. Her recovery was miraculous and I prayed it continued. She seemed alert and energized after her bath, and I was itching to hear more of her story.

"So, where were you in your story?" I prodded as I raked the brush through her hair.

"Let me see. I think it was..."

"You fixed up a bed for John in the alcove."

"Ah, yes. That's right."

She laid her hand on mine, urging me to stop brushing. I helped tuck her legs between the sheets, fluffed the pillows, and pulled the quilt over her lap. This time, instead of gazing toward the window, her eyes locked on mine, becoming as unfocused as before.

CHAPTER 25

December, 1846

About a week after John moved into the alcove, the children asked to spend the night at Norville's house. His bird dog was heavy with pups and was expected to whelp any day. They wanted to be there when the puppies arrived and took to spending more and more time at his farm in anticipation of the new litter. I was tempted to keep them home because their leaving meant John and I would be alone. But how could I deny them the excitement of new puppies?

The first evening the children were gone, I took a hot bath while John was outside checking on the animals one last time. I slipped on a clean cotton nightgown and went to bed early, closing my door as a signal that I did not want to be disturbed. John didn't heed the message. After he, too, had taken a bath, he came into my room, where I was reading by lamplight, and reported on the condition of the horses.

"I think we should call for the blacksmith. Ghost and Ruby need shoeing."

"Fine. We'll send for him in the morning." I picked up my

book and flipped a page, as if absorbed by the story. Rather than leave, John stood inside the doorway, undeterred.

"Did you have a good soak?"

My heart raced at such intimate talk. John moved closer to the bed and fiddled with the oil lamp's chimney, turning it in its cradle.

"Yes, thank you. A very pleasant bath."

"You smell fine, Margaret." He reached out and curled a strand of my hair around his finger. "Is it lavender?"

"John...I don't—"

"The children are away for the night."

I snapped the book closed and laid it on my lap. I took a deep breath and looked up at John. His blue eyes sparkled in the lamplight and his soft lips parted. He ran a calloused finger down my cheek and my resolve melted at his touch.

"May I stay with you tonight, Margaret?" He pressed a tender kiss to my brow, and without hesitation, I folded back the quilts, inviting him to my bed.

No longer was I the older lady and he the young employee. We were two needful lovers, consumed with each other, unable to stop the tidal wave that had been building for three years. John kissed me sweetly and when he slowly pulled the ribbons of my nightgown, I wasn't ashamed of my naked, aged body. He inflicted no violence or pain, only pleasure. He stayed with me all night, wrapping his strong body around mine, and I slept more restfully than I'd ever known.

But the next morning, when I awoke to find John already at his chores, I came to my senses and cringed. What kind of a woman had I turned into? The kind of woman who'd made the hateful rumors true. I sat up in bed and prayed for God's forgiveness for my shameful lust. A woman my age shouldn't partake of pleasures with a younger man *and* outside marriage. It couldn't continue. What if the children found out?

The rest of the morning, in between prayers and chores, I

avoided John as best I could. But after the midday meal, where we mostly ate in silence, he wanted to talk about last night.

"We have nothing to be ashamed of, Margaret."

I dumped the supper dishes in the tub of sudsy water and tugged my arm from his hand. "The children will be home soon."

"All the more reason we should talk about what happened."

"I can't talk about it." Tears of frustration and shame welled in my eyes and I swiped my wet hand across my brow.

"Well, I can." John cupped my shoulders in his large hands and turned me to face him. My sudsy hands dripped onto my apron and I locked my gaze on the wet circle forming on the cotton. "Look at me." He placed his finger under my chin and forced me to look at him.

"We are adults who work hard and deserve happiness. I think we've behaved ourselves long enough."

"John, you're—"

"Yes, I'm under your employ."

"Twelve years younger than me. I have children and wrinkles and my middle has gone soft."

"None of that matters to me."

"You should find a nice young lady your own age. Get married and have a family."

"I want you, Margaret."

"Then you're a fool." I swiped my hands across my apron and rushed to my bedroom, slamming the door behind me.

LATER THAT EVENING, AS THE SUN WAS SETTING, ONE OF Norville's farmhands rapped on the door. When I opened it, he told me the children planned to stay another night.

"The wee pups are about to be born," he said. "The kiddies don't want to miss it. Mr. Whitman said for me to tell ye they'd be fine stayin' with him."

I nodded my consent and fell against the door after closing it. What else was I to do? It would be another night alone with John and I wasn't sure I had the willpower to turn him away. It couldn't continue. I knew it was wrong, but God help me, I was weak in his presence.

"Who was that at the door, Margaret?" John had come through the back door for supper, his cheeks flushed red from the cold and his dark hair tousled.

"It was Norville's man. He said the puppies were about to be born and the children wanted to stay the night."

"What did you tell him?"

"What do you think I told him?" I kicked the door with the heel of my boot and charged toward the kitchen. "I wouldn't deny my children the joy of seeing puppies born."

John grabbed my arm and held fast. "Just as you shouldn't deny your own joy."

"This has to stop."

"Why?"

"It's sinful. The age difference, unmarried..."

"Then marry me."

I snatched my arm from his grasp like his words had burned and I glared at him, heat rising in my cheeks. "Don't joke about such a thing."

"I'm not joking. Marry me. Be my wife."

"John, don't be ridiculous. You don't want to marry me. I'm too old. I'm—"

"Stop saying you're too old."

"But you'll want children of your own someday and I can't give them to you."

"Are you done with your monthly courses?"

"John Hayward! That is none of your business." I marched into the kitchen, picked up a cast iron skillet, and slammed it onto the stove. The sound of iron against iron echoed off the walls.

"It doesn't matter if you can't give me children, Margaret. I'm not wanting to marry you just to have children."

"Please, John, stop."

"I won't stop. I want you, Margaret, and you want me. Don't try to deny it."

"Last night was a mistake."

"It was no mistake."

I opened my mouth to spout all the reasons why we shouldn't be together, but John silenced me with a deep, needful kiss. He pulled me firmly against his chest and bent my head back, kissing me until I could no longer deny the longing between us.

THE CHILDREN FINALLY RETURNED TWO DAYS LATER AND BY THEN, John and I had admitted to one another that we wanted to be together. We decided it was best not to let the children know, so he continued to go to bed each night in the alcove until he was sure the children were asleep upstairs. Then, he would slide in bed beside me and hold me until the sun came up.

A YEAR PASSED OF JOHN'S NIGHTLY VISITS TO MY BED. THE SPRING of 1848 came early, with March coming in not as a lion as the saying goes, but rather warm and dry. I worried over the lack of rain as I did laundry on the side porch. Calvin was helping John plant wheat and corn in the lower field and the younger children were at school. I washed my undergarments in the steamy hot tub and suddenly stopped, realizing my monthly bleeding was overdue. I laid my hand against one of my breasts and flinched at the tenderness. *Please Lord, don't let this be what I think it is.*

What would I do if I was with child? It was risky having a child at forty-one. I had heard there was a local woman who could take care of it. But could I possibly get rid of my own flesh and blood—John's only child? Then again, how could I possibly have a child? I would be the scorn of everyone around —a widowed woman carrying the child of a much younger man. The rumors about us were bad enough, but would become far worse. I wouldn't be able to hold my head up in public.

The night before, John had spoken again of marriage, but I had brushed it off as the ravings of a man delirious from lovemaking. Why would a virile young man want to be strapped to a widow with three children? I had given him dozens of reasons why we shouldn't marry, but he wouldn't listen. Determined he would eventually come to his senses, I held off marriage—but if I was indeed with child, we might not have a choice.

CHAPTER 26

"So, was he happy about the baby?" I crawled up on the bed and sat at the end of it, arms wrapped around my knees and eyes wide from the thrilling story.

"He was. The fool," she muttered, seeming disgusted.

"Why a fool? Weren't you relieved?"

"He was only twenty-nine years old!" Her eyes bulged at her proclamation and her arms tightened around her middle. "He should've been courting a number of young ladies half my age. Don't you see?"

"But he loved you."

"No."

"Fine. He cared deeply for you."

"He was trapped. He just wouldn't admit it to himself."

"Gramma..." I leaned over and placed my hands around her bony wrists. "From what I've heard from you and Helen, John was a good man who loved his family. It doesn't sound like he was trapped."

"Well, I for one wasn't going to keep him locked in a marriage he couldn't get out of. I knew one day he'd wake up and realize what a mess he'd gotten himself into."

"I thought you *were* married." My mind whirled until I was dizzy. Were they married or weren't they?

"Eventually, yes, but not until a whole lot of trouble came our way."

CHAPTER 27

July, 1848

One evening I was serving up supper to the children while John put the horses in the barn. It looked like we were in for a fierce storm, with thick clouds forming and the trees bending in the wind. I pressed my hand to my back where it ached down low, a sure sign the baby would come soon. It couldn't be tonight. With the pending storm, we'd never get the midwife here.

John came through the back door, dusty and smelling of manure, straw, and other farm-life aromas. He pecked a kiss to my cheek and greeted Calvin, Sarah, and Jeremy with a wave of his hand as they shoveled stew into their mouths. Stripping off his filthy shirt, he leaned over the sink and scrubbed his hands and arms with lye soap.

"Will there be any left for me?" he teased the children. "You're gobbling it in a mighty hurry."

The boys kept their heads bent and ate as if their plates were to be taken away from them, but Sarah answered with her mouth full to bulging. "Delicious."

"Your mother is a fine cook." He rinsed off and dried his arms with a linen towel, and went into our room for a fresh shirt. When he returned to the kitchen, he sat down at the table as the children scurried away.

"Was it something I said?"

I snickered as I placed the plate of venison and potatoes in front of him. "No, dear. They're just anxious to read their books before going off to bed."

"Well, we can't exactly fault them for that."

I sat down beside him with my own plate even though I didn't have much appetite. The pains were growing stronger by the minute. We had only taken a bite when a loud knocking rattled the front door. I patted John on the shoulder and struggled to my feet.

"I'll get it, dear. Finish your dinner." I waddled to the door, surprised to find the sheriff and Norville on our porch. It had been months since I'd last seen Gray's younger brother. In that time, he'd aged, his hair speckled with gray, and there were deep creases across his brow.

"Ma'am, may I speak to your husband please?" the sheriff asked, pulling his cap from his head.

"He's not her husband," Norville grumbled under his breath.

"What's this about?" I heard John push back his chair, its legs scraping across the wood floor, before he joined me at the door.

"Can I help you, Sheriff?" he asked.

"Yes, sir. Mr. Hayward, may we have a word outside, please?"

John squeezed my shoulders gently before he stepped onto the porch. I wasn't about to miss anything, so I stood inside with the door cracked and listened to their conversation.

"It appears one of Mr. Whitman's horses has gone missing. A bay gelding with a snip on its nose. Do you know anything about it?" Norville glared hate at John as the sheriff asked his questions. They'd hardly spoken a word to each other in the past so I didn't understand his countenance.

"I know the horse, yes. It's the one he stole out from under me at the auction three months ago."

"Goddamn bastard." Norville charged at John, grabbing a fistful of shirt in his hand.

I shrieked and rushed onto the porch. "Norville, what's come over you?"

"Stop it, Whitman. Let go of him." The sheriff stepped between them and shoved Norville back until he stumbled off the porch. "Fighting won't get us the answers we're looking for." Tucking his shirt into his pants, the sheriff continued his interrogation. "So you know the horse?"

"Sheriff, here's what I know. Mr. Whitman has it in for me, causing trouble for us—"

"John," I shrieked.

"He was in cahoots with the auctioneer, making sure I wouldn't win."

"That's a lie, Hayward." The sheriff held out his arm, blocking Norville from getting back on the porch.

"You deny you're associated with Mr. Cramer, the auctioneer?" John shouted.

"Who I conduct business with is none of yours."

"Gentlemen, please." The sheriff turned to Norville. "Go wait over there, by the tree. Let me talk to Mr. Hayward myself."

"Sheriff DeMond, I'm not some scalawag you can boss around."

"Go!"

Norville stomped away, running his hand through his long, thick beard.

"Now, Mr. Hayward. I understand you were over at Mr. Whitman's place yesterday and you had words. He said you threatened to steal his horse."

"That's a lie."

"John!" I tugged John around to face me. "You went to Norville's? I asked you to let it go. Stay away from him."

"I was tired of the trouble he's been causing. Acting all high and mighty, a pillar of the community—it's a farce. He started rumors about us, but pulling that stunt at the auction was the last straw."

"But John—"

"Mrs. Hayward, would you please go back inside?"

"It's Whitman. Mrs. Whitman, you buffoon," Norville shouted, hopping up and down like an angry jackrabbit.

"Keep quiet, Norville." Losing control of the situation, the sheriff slapped his cap against his leg and glared at me. "Please Mrs.—er, go back inside."

"Go on, Margaret. It will be alright." Wrapping his arm around my shoulders, John escorted me to the door and made sure I was inside before he returned to the sheriff. I kept my ear pressed to the door.

"Yes, I was there and we had words, but I never threatened to take the horse."

"Would you happen to know where it might be?"

"I do not."

"Are you sure?"

"Maybe he did something to the horse." John pointed at Norville, who in turn rushed back to the porch.

"Gentlemen." The sheriff stood between them with his arms outstretched.

"What have you done with my horse, Hayward?"

"I have no knowledge of its whereabouts." John crossed his arms over his chest and glared at Norville. "Perhaps you should question some of your servants. Maybe one of them stole it, sold it for the money. I hear they're overworked and underpaid."

"That's a lie."

"Buy yourself another horse, Whitman. You've got plenty of gold coins to spare."

"Sheriff, are you going to do anything about this?"

The sheriff dropped his arms with a heavy sigh. "Mr. Hayward, for the last time, did you take Mr. Whitman's horse?"

"I did not."

I pulled the curtain aside and watched John spread his legs and cross his arms over his chest, looking down his nose at the befuddled sheriff.

"Liar!" Norville charged up the porch steps but was stopped by the sheriff.

"Settle down, Mr. Whitman." The sheriff's words were more like a threat. Norville stomped down the steps and back to the tree.

"Would you mind if I looked around your farm a bit?" the sheriff asked. "Search the barn and outbuildings?"

"Be my guest. I was about to have my supper. Mind if I finish?"

The sheriff looked at John as if he were crazy.

"I'll let you know if I find anything." The sheriff positioned his hat back on his head and stalked off toward the main barn with Norville squawking in his ear. John came back into the house, brushing past me as he returned to the table and his meal that had grown cold.

"Let me warm your plate."

"It's fine, Margaret."

He shoveled the meat into his mouth, keeping his eyes downcast. This was all my fault. Because of my refusal to marry him, Norville and the rest of the community had made life hard for John. He couldn't go to town without a snide comment or a judgmental glare. It had gotten so bad, it was affecting our ability to sell crops and trade goods. I couldn't stand the silence any longer.

"John." I placed my hand on his arm. "Why did you go to Norville's? I asked you to let it go."

"Damn it, Margaret." He threw his spoon on the table and it bounced and clattered to the floor. "I've had enough of him. He stole that horse out from under me."

"You can't be sure."

"I saw the signals between him and Cramer. I had the highest bid at the auction. That horse was mine. Then all of the sudden the horse was pulled, no longer available for sale."

"I know, but—"

"So explain to me how it ended up in Norville's pasture, eh?"

"There are other horses, John. You have to let this go and stay away from him."

He lurched to his feet, knocking the chair to the floor. "He tosses around his money, getting everyone to do his bidding. Acting the courtly gentleman when he's nothing but a scoundrel."

"Oh, John." My head dropped into my hands, heavy with worry. I couldn't help but feel this was all my fault.

"I see the way he looks at you, Margaret. He wants you for his own."

"I certainly never wanted him," I said wearily.

"Maybe you'd be better off."

"John."

"You'd be the lady of the manor, wearing fine silks and satins, with hands as soft as a baby. Not toiling away from sunup to sundown."

"And I'd be perfectly miserable."

Another knock came at the door and this time, he answered it. I rushed across the room and stood behind him.

"I've found something in your barn I'd like to ask you about," the sheriff said, waving us outside. He led the way around the side of the house as the rain started to fall.

"I knew it, Sheriff. I knew you'd find my horse here." Norville pushed off from the tree and stood behind the sheriff. "I told you he stole it."

"Hush up, Whitman, and stay where you are."

We followed the sheriff into the barn and were welcomed by a friendly whinny. As we passed four horses secured in their stalls, John stopped to scratch one on her forelock. The sheriff waved him over to the last empty stall where feed and extra hay bales were stored.

"You mind telling me why there's a halter laying here on the ground?"

John scratched his head, obviously confused at why the sheriff would be so interested in a halter that had fallen from its hook.

"I'd say either one of us dropped it there or it fell off the wall. Why?"

"Because…" The sheriff bent over and picked up the halter, flipping over the leather strap and holding it out for John to see. "It says Whitman right here, etched inside the leather."

"Let me see that," I said, rushing into the stall. John didn't respond, just kept a straight face as the sheriff continued his investigation.

"Mind telling me how it got here?"

"John?" I tried to catch his gaze, but he turned to the sheriff instead.

"Was this the halter Whitman's horse was wearing yesterday when you stopped by his farm?"

"I can't say which halter the horse was wearing yesterday."

"Was the horse wearing a halter?"

"I don't recall."

The sheriff didn't like John's lack of information and stepped within inches of him. "I'm going to keep looking around your property and if I find that horse, I'm hauling you in."

"You won't."

"I could arrest you for obstruction of justice. You know what that is?"

"I'm not a stupid man."

"Then I'd suggest, if you took Norville Whitman's horse, you either return it before I find it or save us all a lot of time and tell me where it is."

Horse stealing was a serious crime, no matter what the circumstances. The sheriff was talking like John had actually taken the horse. He'd never do that. He was a good, honest man. It was impossible. I glanced over at John, seeking reassurance, but his shoulders were squared and his back straight, and he had a defiant gleam in his eye that turned my blood cold.

He'd stolen that horse. I was sure of it.

CHAPTER 28

"John, you have to return that horse. What were you thinking?"

I followed John into the parlor after the sheriff and Norville had left. The children had retired to their bedrooms upstairs and we were alone. He sat down hard in the armchair and dropped his head into his hands.

"Norville Whitman is a bloody scoundrel who's cruel to his help, eyes you while thinking unspeakable thoughts, stole the bay right out from under me, and has made our lives a living hell." His head snapped back and his angry glare burned into my soul. "The vile words he's used against you...I'm not returning the horse. It's safe and well fed. Nothing to worry about."

"But John, dear, what about the ba—" A stabbing pain, like a pitchfork, jabbed into my lower back, doubling me over with a mighty groan.

"Margaret!" John leapt to his feet and rushed to my side. "Is it time? Should I get the midwife?" He helped me to the sofa where I sat, panting like a thirsty dog, clutching my back.

"Yes, the baby is coming."

"I'll be back soon." I reached out, stopping him from leaving, holding tight to his arm.

"Send Calvin. I don't want you to leave me."

"Fine." He lifted my ankles off the floor and eased me onto my back, tucking an embroidered pillow behind my head. "Rest here a minute."

He stormed up the steps to the children's bedrooms and soon returned with Calvin at his heels who ran from the house, slamming the door behind him. Within minutes, I heard the heavy beat of a horse's hooves trotting away from the house. The midwife lived at the next farm over, so it wouldn't be long before she'd be here. I'd been through childbirth three times before, but I had been much younger then. Giving birth at the age of forty-one had another set of challenges, and I was afraid.

"Calvin's on his way." John returned to the parlor and knelt down, taking my hand in his. "What can I do for you, milady?"

I chuckled at the endearment and gripped my back as another pain seared through me. Sarah skidded around the corner, out of breath as if she'd run a mile, with Jeremy close behind.

"Mother, is the baby coming? I saw Calvin flying down the lane," she said.

"Yes, dear. It's—" Another pain scorched my back, this time curling my knees into my chest. This baby wasn't going to slip quietly into the world, but come out fighting. The birthing pains were strong and only centered in my back, which was so unlike my other deliveries. I prayed the baby would be born safe and healthy.

"What can I do, Mother?"

I reached out to Sarah, whose face was stricken with worry. There was plenty she could do to help, but right now I wanted her near me.

"I'll be fine, Sarah. Sit with me a while, until the midwife comes."

"Let me move you to the bedroom, Margaret. You'll be more comfortable."

"I can walk."

John wouldn't hear of it. He scooped me into his arms and carried me to our bedroom behind the kitchen, depositing me on the mattress. He and Sarah helped me out of my muslin gown, leaving me dressed in my slip, and covered me with a sheet.

Sarah ran from the room and returned a few seconds later with her favorite dolly. She climbed up on the bed, placing the doll in my arms, and laid down beside me. I tucked my arm around Sarah and drew her closer. As long as the baby didn't come in the next few minutes, I could comfort my daughter and reassure her the pain of childbirth was worth the reward of a healthy, happy baby.

THE RAIN HAD STOPPED, THE SUN LONG SET, AND THE NIGHT WAS moonless. I panted and moaned as another contraction stabbed into my lower back.

Ethel Schmidt laid a cold, wet cloth on my forehead and patted my hand. "It won't be long now, Maggie."

"Errrrr!" The pressure overtook me and I knew the baby was ready to come. I had expected my labor to be quick, with this being my fourth child, but the baby hadn't been in a hurry. It was well past midnight, hours since John had sent for Ethel. Rolfe and Ethel Schmidt were some of the few people who still socialized with us, which was fortunate, since Ethel was the only midwife around. Another strong contraction ripped through my body, and it was time to push.

"The babe is ready, he is." Ethel helped me roll to my back and spread my knees out wide.

"Why do you...think...errrr...it's a boy?" I curled my chin to my chest and bore down with the next contraction.

"You were carrying low."

John pounded his fist against the bedroom door so hard I thought it would come unhinged. "What's going on in there?" he shouted.

Ethel, who had been kneeling at the foot of the bed, climbed to her feet and cracked open the door. "Now Mr. Hayward, you wouldn't want the first sound your baby hears to be you shouting your fool head off, would you?"

"How much longer?"

"That's up to God and the baby. Now go back out to the kitchen and I'll call you when the babe is born."

"It's coming." I gritted my teeth and released an unearthly growl. Ethel rushed across the room in time to catch the slippery baby in her arms.

"*Ja.* Like I said. It's a boy."

Robert Thomas Hayward was born at three in the morning, coming into the world kicking and screaming. He was a big baby, with a shock of dark hair just like his daddy's. We named him after John's father.

John wasn't shy about grabbing up his boy and holding him close while I dozed between feedings. The older children had gone to my brother Thomas's house at John's request. John took charge, refusing to accept help. "I want it to just be the three of us for a day or so."

"You'll spoil him if you don't put him down," I said, fading toward sleep.

"That's my intention." John chuckled as he looked down at his son, swaddled tightly in a blanket. He rocked him slowly in the rocking chair. "Don't worry, Mama, I'll put him in his cradle in a bit."

In a few days, I was back on my feet, having rested longer with Robert than I had with my other children. John had doted on me so much that I'd gained back my strength in record time. He had taken care of the baby and only did minimal farm chores while I recovered. Now that I was up and about my daily business, it was time we dealt with the stolen horse.

I wrapped little Robert in an extra blanket and carried him to the barn, where John was mucking stalls. The fresh air and smell of horsehide, leather, and hay was a welcome balm to the lingering aroma of childbirth.

"Busy at it, I see." I'd startled John, who spun around quickly, pointing the pitchfork at me.

"Bloody hell, you scared the bejesus out of me." He swiped the sweat from his brow with the back of his arm and leaned the pitchfork against the wall. Tickling Robert's soft cheek with the tip of his finger, John then tapped a light kiss to his son's head. "He looks content."

"He is. He has a full belly and a clean diaper. I figure he'll sleep for a while."

"Let's go outside then. I could use some fresh air."

We strolled out of the barn and stood under the oak tree, its leaves creating a canopy against the hot July sky. John couldn't take his eyes off his sleeping son. Gray never had that look of love when he observed his newborn children. John would be a good father, there was no doubt. He'd tried to be a good father figure to Calvin, Sarah, and Jeremy. The younger two were receptive to his affections, having been so young when Gray died, but Calvin had always been standoffish. Anger and resentment seemed to burn in his belly, and no matter how hard John had tried to win his love, it was rejected.

Now with this horse business hanging over our heads, I had a terrible fear that I'd be the only one to raise this child. How could John have taken such a risk? He had to return that horse. Robert needed his father.

"John, I want to talk to you about the horse. Norville's horse. I want you to—"

"Don't worry, Margaret. I've already returned it. I took it back the morning after the babe was born."

"You did?" Holding Robert in one arm, I encircled the other around John's back, resting my head against his sweat-soaked chest. "Thank you, dear. I appreciate it."

"It pained me to do it, but I apologized to Norville."

"Oh, John, that was kind of you. I understand why you did it, but you did the right thing in returning the horse. I couldn't bear it if you were to go to prison because of Norville's trickery."

"It took seeing my boy to make me realize I'd made a mistake. I plan on watching this little man grow up." This time when he tickled Robert's cheek, the baby let out a high-pitched squeal, as if protesting his interrupted sleep. "He's going to be a feisty one, don't you think?"

"Like his daddy."

"You may be right."

Cupping my elbow and resting his hand against my back, John walked us back inside the house. He took Robert from my arms and pressed a soft kiss to his head before laying him in his cradle. He raised the sash on a few more windows, allowing the summer breeze to flow through the house. I handed him a glass of water and he drank greedily, swiping the back of his hand across his wet lips.

"Thank you, Margaret. I better get back to work." He kissed me with his cold, damp lips and patted my bottom. "I'll be back for supper."

As he turned to leave, giving me a sweet smile, I noticed someone standing on our porch, looking at us through the screen door. The sheriff had returned.

"Mr. Hayward. May I speak with you please?"

The happiness drained from my heart and settled like a heavy stone in the pit of my stomach. What could have brought the sheriff here again?

John stepped out onto the porch and extended his hand in greeting. "What can I do for you, Sheriff?"

"Norville Whitman contacted me this morning. Apparently, he found his horse tied up on your property a little while ago."

"That's impossible." John's face swelled red with anger. "I returned the bay to him three days ago. He accepted my apology. We even shook hands. That horse can't be on our land."

"Well, it is. I just found it."

"Where?"

"Follow me."

I ran to the door and watched as John followed the sheriff across the front yard toward the woods. "John," I yelled, but he didn't reply. He stomped along behind the sheriff and they disappeared into the shelter of the forest. Confusion and disbelief surged through me as I waited on the porch. Calvin came running from around the back of the house and leapt up beside me.

"Was that the sheriff?" he asked, huffing and puffing.

"Yes."

"What does he want?"

"Apparently, Norville's horse is tied up somewhere on our property."

When Calvin didn't respond, I looked at my son, fourteen years old and as tall as me, as a wry grin formed on his lips. He gazed off toward the woods with a satisfied look in his eyes.

"Do you know anything about this, Calvin?"

Instead of answering, he continued to stare off across the yard, his eyes narrowed and his mouth curled in a sneer. I grabbed his upper arm and pulled him around to face me.

"You know something about his. What is it?"

"I don't know anything." He shook his arm out of my grasp. His satisfaction was replaced with anger. "John stole Norville's horse. That's all I know."

"But he returned it to him."

"And you believe him?"

"Of course, I believe him."

"Were there any witnesses?"

"Calvin Whitman, how dare you."

"What?" He wouldn't look at me, but instead concentrated on brushing his shirt sleeve where I had grabbed him, as if I'd dirtied it. I cupped his chin in my hand, forcing his gaze to fix on me.

"Are you calling John a liar?"

"Not exactly."

"Then what exactly?"

"I'm saying..." He knocked my hand off his chin. "It's his word against Norville's, that's all."

"And you would side with Norville?"

"I'm not saying that."

Our discussion was interrupted when the sheriff and John returned, leading the horse behind them. John looped the horse's lead shank around the hitching post and followed the sheriff onto the porch.

"Mrs. Hayward, I'm taking your husband with me. He's being charged with horse stealing."

"No." I lunged at the sheriff, grabbing hold of his shirt collar. "He didn't steal that horse."

"Margaret." John stepped between us. "Let go now. It will be fine."

"No, John. He can't take you in."

"I have no other choice, ma'am. That horse was tied to a tree down by the creek on your property. Unless you know who put it there, I'm taking Mr. Hayward in and charging him with the crime."

"But Sheriff, I just had a baby."

"I have no choice. If he can make bail, he'll be back in a day or so."

"John!"

With a quick kiss to my cheek, John followed the sheriff to

his wagon, where he allowed him to lock him in shackles. Tears fell unchecked down my cheeks while Calvin stood beside me, seeming thoroughly entertained by the spectacle. It wasn't fair. John had taken the horse, that was true, but he had returned it. I believed him. He'd never lied to me before, and he hadn't lied now.

"Well, do you think he can make bail?" Calvin asked with humor in his voice.

"We'll get him out." Taking my teenage son's shoulders in my hands, my angry glare washed the smirk off his face. "As much as you'd like to see him rot in jail, he won't. He's done nothing wrong."

Calvin let out a throaty grunt of protest.

"And when he returns, you, young man, are going to apologize for the way you've been behaving."

"Me?"

"Yes, I'm sure he saw the disrespect on your face as he left here. He's tried to be a good father to you and this is the thanks he gets?"

"He's not my father."

"He could be if you'd let him."

"I'm fourteen years old. I don't need a father anymore."

"Oh, a grown man, are you? Well, if you're not careful, I'll send you out into the world. See how long you'd make it without us."

Calvin stepped back, anger darkening his face. "I could make it just fine. Uncle Norville would take me in."

"You'd go to that conniving, hateful man? He did this...he put that horse on our property to implicate John." Calvin looked down, kicking the toe of his boot against the rocking chair. "Or was it you?"

"Me? I didn't take that horse."

"You better be telling me the truth."

"You think I'm lying? I won't stay here where I'm not respected or welcome."

The screen door banged against the house as Calvin stormed inside. My head dropped in my hands and I wept, unable to comprehend what had happened. John was taken off to jail and now Calvin was leaving. Pressure filled my breasts and then released when I heard baby Robert's loud wail from inside. He was hungry and most likely wet. As I entered the house, Calvin knocked me aside, stomping across the porch and down the steps carrying a knapsack. He was making good on his threats to leave, and I didn't have the energy to stop him.

CALVIN RETURNED HOME THE NEXT DAY AND JOHN THE DAY AFTER. We had just enough in our savings to make the bail to bring him home. We hired Mr. Creswell, a respected lawyer, to represent him.

"Go home, go about your business, and stay out of trouble," Mr. Creswell advised. "I'll contact you as soon as the trial date is set."

John did as the lawyer said. He returned home and resumed his work on the farm. Tensions still ran high whenever he and Calvin were in the same room. Calvin was angry and disrespectful, and whenever possible, I would send him to stay with my brother Thomas, even though he had little room to spare. I loved my son, but it certainly was peaceful when he wasn't around.

Early in September, Sarah and Jeremy rode along with us and the baby to the market in Calvert to sell tomatoes and corn. It was the first time I had been out in public since giving birth and I worried about the reaction we'd receive. John assured me we would be welcomed because no one could resist seeing a newborn baby.

John pulled the wagon alongside the Schmidts'. Rolfe and

his son, Hans, were selling home-brewed beer and eggs. John set out baskets of tomatoes and corn for purchase while I sat on the tail of the wagon and held a sleeping Robert in my arms. Sarah and Jeremy ran off with their friends. Several people purchased beer from Rolfe, but walked right by John without speaking. So much for a hearty welcome. Usually his crops sold out in short time, but today, no one was buying.

"Mr. Janney, good morning to you, sir." John called out to the elderly man who was always the first to scoop up our crop. He had an infectious smile and jowls that wiggled when he laughed, but today Mr. Janney pretended not to hear John's greeting.

"Good morning, Mrs. Benjamin." Again, he called out to one of our best customers and this time received a disgusted "Hrumph!" as she walked by.

"John." I slipped off the edge of the wagon and joined him beside the baskets. "No one is buying."

"I see that, Margaret."

"It's because I'm here, with the baby."

"No, Margaret. It's because of me. Word is out about my arrest. Norville didn't waste any time spreading the news."

I followed John's gaze to where Mr. Janney and Mrs. Benjamin had joined a tight circle of other folks, and Norville was in the center. He was running his mouth, waving his arms, and the group stood slack-jawed, listening to him. I could only imagine the lies he was spouting. The entire cluster turned as one and glared at John.

"Maybe you should take us home," I said.

"Perhaps you're right." He turned and shouted at the group. "I don't want to sell our goods to you people anyway. If you're too bloody high and mighty to speak to us, let alone buy from us, I'll have nothing to do with you." He loaded the baskets into the back of the wagon, waved Sarah and Jeremy over, and we trudged away from the market, never to return.

.   .   .

LATER THAT NIGHT, AFTER ROBERT HAD BEEN FED, AND THE other children were asleep, John climbed in bed. He'd had something on his mind all evening, so quiet and introspective, and seemed ready to share his thoughts.

"Margaret, this is plain silly. We have a son and we should be married. This notion of yours that I will wake up one day and realize I've made a grave mistake sharing your bed is absurd. You're my wife in every sense of the word. The only difference is we don't have a piece of paper to prove it."

"But John—"

"What will it take to get you to the altar? Will I have to hog-tie you to get you to the church?"

"John, don't you see—"

"All I see is a stubborn woman who refuses to face the fact that I've made my choice and will not change it."

I cupped his bristled cheeks in my hands, my heart warm and full, and pressed a soft kiss to his lips. "You're a wonderful man, John."

He turned his face and kissed the palm of my hand. "There's something else you should consider."

"What's that?" I settled down beside him and laid my head on his chest.

"Mr. Creswell told me you could be called as a witness, since you saw the sheriff bring the horse up out of the woods."

"Oh, dear." I rose up on my elbow and looked down at the worry lines on his brow.

"But if we're married, you won't be forced to testify."

These past two months, I'd done my best to forget the trial would ever take place. I had prayed the charges would be dropped, that Norville would somehow come to his senses, and life would go on as we'd known it. For the first time in my adult life, I was content, but harsh realities kept warring with my happiness.

"I know you returned the horse to Norville. No one could convince me otherwise." I ran my hand over the soft downy hair on John's chest. "And I would never testify against you." I kissed his brow and the tip of his nose. "So I guess that means we're getting married."

CHAPTER 29

September, 1850

Helen was born and still we hadn't married. I had agreed to marry him two years ago, but we'd had trouble making it to the altar. Between running the farm, raising the children, and being scorned by every preacher in the region, we'd accepted the fact that we would continue to live as we'd been. John was smitten with his little red-headed baby girl and his young son, who was walking and talking like a champ. He struggled with the nasty looks and snooty comments when he went to town, but chose to ignore them. Since he no longer had customers in Calvert for his fresh vegetables, he drove the wagon six miles into Oxford, Pennsylvania, each week. There he formed new friendships among the other farmers and customers who pretended to know nothing of his marital status or impending trial.

One day, when Helen was only two months old, a man, dressed in a tweed suit and dusty old boots, rode up the lane on his horse. He looked like he'd been tramping through mud for days. I was raking the leaves from beneath the oak tree while the children napped inside. John came out of the barn where he'd been putting up hay and greeted the man with a firm handshake.

"Hello, sir. I'm Josiah Bennett with the United States Census."

"Good afternoon. I'm John Hayward." Mr. Bennett pulled a thick ledger out of his saddle bag and glanced at the house. "Would you like to come inside? Margaret can fix you something to drink."

"Much obliged, Mr. Hayward."

John settled the census worker in the parlor while I hurried into the kitchen to light the kettle. Sarah and Jeremy were still at school, and Calvin had gone to the Schmidts' to deliver a pie I'd made that morning. I checked in on Robert, who was now awake and playing on the floor with a wooden horse John had whittled for him, while baby Helen slept in the cradle.

"Margaret, that man in our parlor—" John had followed me into the bedroom, his eyes wide with worry.

"The census worker. What of him?"

"Margaret." He gripped my arms, forcing me aside as he shut the door. "We're not married. What should we tell him?"

"The truth, I suppose."

"The truth? Christ, woman, we already have enough trouble."

I folded my arms over my belly and held back a laugh. To my knowledge, it wasn't a crime to live unmarried—or was it? Worry washed away my mirth as I patted Robert on the head and checked on a still-sleeping Helen. "Robbie, we'll be in the parlor. Watch your sister for me, please." I held John's hand in my own as I opened the door and whispered. "It'll be fine, dear." After gathering up the tea tray, I followed John into the parlor and joined our guest.

"Here we are, Mr. Bennett. Care for a cup of tea?" I handed

him the steaming cup and offered another to John. "We weren't introduced outside. My name is Margaret—"

"Hayward. Margaret Hayward." John's cup shook in his hands as he took a seat beside me.

The census worker set his cup on the side table, glanced over his ledger, and poised his pencil over the book. "So, Mr. Hayward, I assume you're the owner of this farm."

"Actually, it belongs to me. It's my farm." I corrected the man, much to John's frustration. It had slipped out before I considered the consequences.

"It's in her name—the deed that is. The farm is in her name." John squeezed my hand and glared at me through the corner of his eye. "It once belonged to her father."

Just then, the front door blew open and Calvin came in, stomping his feet. "Mother, I'm back. Mrs. Schmidt asked that I tell you—" He stopped when he noticed our guest in the parlor.

"Calvin, this is Mr. Bennett." I led Calvin into the room. "He's with the United States Census."

"Hello, sir." Just as John had taught him, Calvin reached out his hand to Mr. Bennett in greeting.

"Calvin, there's some warm bread in the kitchen. And fresh pressed cider. Why don't you help yourself to some?" I laid my hands on his shoulders and fairly shoved him out of the room. "Mr. Bennett, would you care for some cider or bread?" I asked, glancing over my shoulder toward the kitchen.

"That's mighty gracious of you, Mrs. Hayward, but I'll pass, thank you." Mr. Bennett tapped his pencil against the tip of his tongue as I resumed my seat.

"So, the farm. I suppose I will put Mrs. Hayward as head of household then, hmm? Margaret Hayward?" The census worker's eyes narrowed as he glanced at me suspiciously. "How old are you, Mrs. Hayward?"

"I'm forty-three, sir."

"And how old are you, Mr. Hayward?"

"I'm, uh, I'm thirty-one."

His gaze hopped from his ledger to John to the kitchen, obviously surprised at our age difference—and confused at my teenage son. "Eh-hem, thirty-one," he said, scratching the information in his book. "Married, I presume?"

John dropped my hand and we looked at each other, silently wondering how we should respond. "Yes," we answered in unison and gave him matching smiles.

Mr. Bennett checked another little box in his ledger, satisfied with our ruse. "Any children, eh, besides...?"

"Well, my son Calvin, you just met him, he's sixteen, my daughter, Sarah, is twelve, and Jeremy is ten. Their last name is Whitman. Their father died a few years back," I said.

"Sorry to hear that."

"Yes, well, and we have two others."

"And their names?"

"Robert is almost two and Helen is only two months."

"And Hayward is their last name?"

He asked a few more questions about our place of birth, occupation, and the value of my land. "I believe that will do it." Mr. Bennett slammed the ledger closed and rose to his feet, arching a kink from his back. "Only three more households to visit before I stop for the day."

"That's fine. Only another hour or so, I suppose." John helped Mr. Bennett with his coat and guided him toward the door.

"Daddy!" Robert toddled through the kitchen and into the foyer, holding his arms in the air. John scooped him up and planted a kiss on his rosy cheek.

"Who might this young man be?" Mr. Bennett asked as he plopped his hat on his head.

"This is our son, Robert."

"Quite a fine boy you have." He tickled Robert under the

chin and reached for the door. "Well, I'm off. Good to meet you folks."

As soon as the census worker stepped off the porch, I sagged against the door, almost too weak to stand. John blew out a heavy sigh.

"You lied to him. I heard you. To a federal man at that." Calvin stalked into the foyer, his cheeks red and his hands fisted in fury.

"I know." I reached out to pat his shoulder, but Calvin slapped my hand away.

"My mother, a liar. How does that make you feel?" Calvin got in my face, spitting the words like venom. John shifted Robert to his opposite hip and got between the two of us.

"Don't ever speak to your mother in that tone again, young man."

"You can't tell me what to do. You're not my father."

"Boy, you better watch your tone." As John's anger rose, he handed Robert to me and laid his hands on Calvin's shoulders. Calvin might be sixteen now—a young man—but John would not allow him to disrespect his mother.

"Take your hands off me. I can speak to her any way I want. She's my mother. I don't have to answer to you."

"Calvin!" I pushed away from the door and got between him and John. Calvin was slightly taller than me, but it didn't stop me from putting him in his place. "You may think you don't have to obey John, but you do need to answer to me. You apologize right now."

"I won't."

"You will or you'll not have any supper."

"You'll starve me, your legitimate son, but you'll make sure your bastard children get fed, huh?"

John shoved me out of the way and grabbed a hold of Calvin's shirt, lifting him onto the tips of his toes. They were nose to nose and John shook with anger. "You will respect your mother. Do you hear me?"

"How can I respect a mother who has a man half her age sleeping in her bed each night?"

John's hand cracked across Calvin's cheek so loud it echoed off the walls. Sarah and Jeremy had come through the back door, witnessed the altercation, and burst out crying. Robert wailed and Helen chose that moment to burst forth a cry. In the chaos, only Calvin stayed quiet, stone-faced as he glared at John, who still had his collar gripped in his hand. He lowered the boy to the ground, his face pale with regret, and smoothed his hand down Calvin's rumpled shirt.

"I'm sorry, Calvin. I went too far." John's voice was about to break. "Apologize to your mother, please."

"Never!" Calvin rushed past me, grabbed his coat off the peg, and went out the door. He was gone for three days.

CHAPTER 30

"Where did he go?" My hands twisted and tangled in my lap, and my stomach turned into a burning pit. Father was a hateful person even back then. No wonder there were hard feelings between him and Gramma. "What happened when he came back?"

"He had gone to my brother's house, only a few miles from here. The farm's been sold since Thomas died."

"Did you know he was there?"

"Yes. Thomas sent word. He told us Calvin needed time to cool off."

"So what made him finally come home?"

"John."

"What?"

Gramma's mouth spread into a wide, cracking yawn, and her eyes drooped. I had kept her up far too long. Swinging my legs over the side of her bed, I leapt down to the cold wood floor.

"You can finish the story tomorrow," I said, tucking the quilt up to Gramma's chin. "We'll have plenty of time." I turned down the oil lamp and picked up the handkerchief she'd dropped beside her bed. When I laid it on her bedside table, she reached over and encircled my wrist with her bony fingers.

"In fairness to your father, John and I were living in sin, and it had to have been hard on him."

"Why weren't you married, if you don't mind my asking?"

"We had tried several times, but no preacher would marry us. Between us living together unmarried and John's arrest, we were turned away at each church."

"Still, Father shouldn't have spoken to you that way. It wasn't right."

"It wasn't. But after we had lied to the census worker, we were determined to get married at last."

WE AWOKE THE NEXT MORNING TO AT LEAST SIX INCHES OF SNOW covering the barn, the fields, and everything in sight. Cora, Belle, and I pressed our noses to the bedroom window and watched as the fat, white flakes came down. The sky was a smoky gray and it reminded me of home, where there always seemed to be a haze hanging overhead as I walked to the mill each morning.

"Play outside." Belle slapped her little hand against the glass.

"Mother won't let us," Cora said, sounding defeated. "She makes us stay inside until it stops snowing."

"We'll have to find something else to do today then," I said, hugging the little girls against my belly.

"Paint!"

"Fine, Belle, yes, we'll paint today. But first, we eat breakfast. Let's go."

I chased the girls down the staircase to the kitchen, where the smell of ham, eggs, and coffee filled the room. Cora and Belle scrambled onto the bench and waited patiently as Helen spooned fluffy eggs onto their plates.

Although I loved spending time with the girls, I had hoped to hear the rest of Gramma's story. Thankfully, she was strong and healthy, so I reminded myself to be patient. We would have plenty of time to talk tomorrow once things got back to normal.

Hope quickly faded as more and more snow dumped on the farm throughout the day—and the next day and the next. Charles said it was the most snow he could remember so early in December. The horses were shut up in the stable and the cows huddled close to the barn. Though the snow was nearly two feet deep, Charles still had to milk the cows each morning and night and feed all the animals from the dried corn they had stored away for the winter. Even with the cold, blustery weather outside, the rest of us were warm and dry inside the house. I kept the girls from underfoot by giving them proper painting lessons, sacrificing the precious canvases Cillian had sent. I gave a brush to Cora, but Belle was relegated to using her fingers only. We set up side by side in the parlor, laying an old horse blanket over the carpet to protect it from paint droplets. Gramma sat on the sofa, giving guidance to the girls as they worked.

"See how the trees look small in the distance?" Gramma asked, pointing through the window. "You know trees are very tall, but since they're far away, you wouldn't want to paint them big in your picture."

"Yes," Cora said, her tongue sticking out the corner of her mouth and her brows knitted in concentration as she dabbed light gray paint on her canvas. "Laurel calls that 'spective."

"She's correct. You must paint all the objects as you see them, in *perspective* with one another."

"Look." Belle held up her painting of a large blob of brown covering almost half of her canvas, and tiny dots of gray beside it. "This is the barn and this is cows."

"Very nice." Gramma chuckled quietly and patted Belle on the back.

"Did you know Gramma was an artist?" I asked the girls as I looked over Cora's shoulder. Her painting was shaping up nicely and I wondered if she hadn't inherited an artistic proclivity.

"You are?" When Cora turned, she forgot to lift her brush from the canvas and ended up adding a long black streak to her scene. Her chin quivered and her eyes welled with tears as she discovered her mistake.

"Don't cry, child." Gramma leaned over Cora's shoulder and pointed at the picture. "That can be the fence."

"But the fence is brown."

"The fence looks black when it's in the shadows. You can paint the sky gray like it is today."

Gramma's idea seemed to satisfy Cora, who cleaned her brush and commenced covering the top of the canvas with gray paint. She then asked, "Can we see your paintings, Gramma?"

"There's one there, over the piano." Gramma pointed to the large landscape of the farm in autumn. "I painted that a few years after I moved here."

"Where did you live before?" Cora asked, still smearing gray on her sky.

"In a little house down by the river. I moved here after my daddy gave me this land. It had been part of his farm."

"When Mother was a little girl?" Cora abandoned her painting and sat cross-legged on the floor at Gramma's feet.

"No, it was long before your mother was born. It was right before Laurel's daddy was born."

This bit of news seemed to penetrate Belle's concentration. She whipped her head around, messy fingers waving in the air, and stared at Gramma in confusion.

"Who?"

"My father and your mother are brother and sister," I said, sitting beside Gramma on the sofa.

Belle and Cora both had blank, confused expressions on

their faces. They apparently had never considered how I was related to Helen. It hadn't been important to them, until now.

"What is your daddy's name?" Cora asked.

"His name is Calvin Whitman."

"But Mother's name is Helen Smith."

"Yes, but before I was Helen Smith, I was Helen Hayward." Helen entered the parlor, wiping her hands on a linen tea towel. She glanced down at her mother and Gramma closed her eyes, giving permission with a nod of her head. "My daddy's name was John Hayward. He was Gramma's second husband."

"What happened to her first husband?" Cora seemed to understand, but Belle's mouth hung open, still confused.

"He passed away, child. Then I married John Hayward."

"Is he Uncle Robert's daddy, too?" Cora asked, now seeming to understand a bit more.

"Yes, he was."

"Where is he now?" Cora scooted closer to Gramma. Belle joined her on the floor.

"He's passed on, too, child. I've outlived both my husbands."

"I wish I could have met him," Cora said, dropping her chin to her chest.

"I do, too. He would have loved you girls and your cousins," Helen said.

"You want to see some of my other paintings?" Gramma stood up slowly. "I'll show you a painting of your granddaddy."

"Mother, you never told me you had a painting of Daddy." Surprise lit up Helen's face as she offered a steadying hand to Gramma.

"Well, I do. Laurel, if you wouldn't mind?"

I scurried out of the parlor and crawled on hands and knees into the back of her closet, where several paintings were standing on end. Gathering them in a pile, careful not to scratch them, I headed out of the room but turned around quickly and snatched the daguerreotype off her bureau. Back in the parlor, I leaned the paintings against the table leg beside Gramma and handed her the photograph.

"Ah yes." She ran her shaking fingers over the image of the dark-haired man. I knew by the softness of her gaze that she was looking at John Hayward.

"It's the photograph of Daddy," Helen said as she leaned over Gramma's shoulder.

"A photographer was traveling through and I insisted John sit for the man."

"What about you? Why didn't you have your photograph taken?" I asked, lifting the daguerreotype from her hand for a better look.

"I was as big as a whale. Carrying Helen. I couldn't pose for a picture in that condition." Gramma chuckled and reached for the canvases. "Let's see what we have here." She lifted the first painting and held it out in front of her as far as her arms could reach. Through squinted eyes, she examined her work. "Yes, this one I painted when I was carrying Robert. Hmm. Never liked it though." She handed it to Belle, whose smile lit up her face.

"It's Bessie."

"It might have been Bessie's grandmother," Gramma said, referring to the brown and white cow in the painting.

Belle passed the painting to Cora and Gramma picked up another one. Discarding that one as amateur, she passed it on to the girls. She showed us two more unfinished paintings and waited until all had made the rounds to each of us. Finally, Gramma unwrapped a small, ovular, unframed painting covered in a soft black cloth. She held it out and studied it at arm's length. The room fell silent, each of us growing still, waiting while emotions played across Gramma's face. Her cloudy eyes glistened, her mouth tightened, then relaxed, only to tighten again, and her cheeks sagged. Helen laid her hand on her mother's back and leaned over her shoulder to get a good look at the painting.

"I've never seen this before." Helen sucked in a shallow breath as a tender smile spread on her face. "He looks like Robert, doesn't he?"

"One and the same."

"When did you paint this, Mother?"

"Right before he went away. I was afraid I'd forget his face. I was sure I'd never see him again." Gramma swiped an errant tear from her cheek. "I wish I hadn't."

CHAPTER 31

November, 1852

"So if you take your blade and run it right down the middle, like this..." John sliced through the thick layer of skin, pulling it away from the fatty sheath beneath. He was teaching Calvin how to butcher the hog that had been fatted for the past year. I'd come in to ask about breakfast, but didn't want to interrupt the lesson.

Though the morning was cool, the shed was warm from the fire burning beneath the cauldron where they rendered the fat. It wouldn't be long before Calvin set out on his own and he needed to know how to do such things. He had a sour expression on his face and I feared things wouldn't go well. I was right.

Instead of accepting John's teachings, Calvin snatched the knife from his hand and elbowed him aside. "I can do it. I've done it before. Norville's man taught me."

"Did he now?"

"It's like gutting a deer." Calvin stabbed into the hog, hitting bone, and dropped the knife in frustration.

"Here, let me—" John said.

"I don't want your help. I don't need to know how to butcher a hog."

"Calvin, please—" I reached toward my son.

"Let me handle this, Margaret."

"Forget it." Calvin stomped out of the shed, slamming the door behind him, leaving us openmouthed. We had hoped Calvin would have outgrown his anger by the time he turned eighteen, but it didn't appear to be so. He was still rude to me, ignored Robert and Helen, and was combative with John. As a young boy, he seemed to enjoy John's attention, but once I became pregnant with Robert, everything changed.

I could hardly blame the boy. Gossip and judgment ran rampant, and Calvin had surely borne the brunt of it. We'd been living as husband and wife for nearly five years and still weren't legally married. It wasn't from a lack of trying. We had met with the reverend at the Methodist Church, but he refused to marry us because of John's impending trial and the fact that Robert and Helen were born out of wedlock. He had his church's reputation to consider. We received the same refusals from the Methodist, Presbyterian, and Anglican pastors. Raising the children and running the farm took up so much of our time, we had put our quest aside until winter.

Father passed away after a stroke in the winter of 1851, laid to rest beside Mother, who had died the winter before. Mr. Creswell paid a visit in March of that year to prepare John for the trial set for May. We made plans for the possibility he'd be sent to prison, but were given a reprieve when the trial was set aside and its location changed to the next county over. With all there was to do around the farm during the summer and fall, finding a minister to marry us hadn't been a high priority.

For the next few hours, John finished the butchering alone, carefully packing the meat in salt and boiling the fat into lard.

He was sweaty and stunk of pig fat when he finally came in for the midday meal, his belly growling from missing breakfast.

"Why don't you rest a bit after you've finished eating, John."

"I might at that."

"After I wash the dishes, I'll clean the stalls." I had been pinned in the house of late, putting up vegetables for winter. It would be good to get outside and spend time around the animals. Helen climbed onto our bed for her afternoon nap, and Robert curled beside her, quickly falling asleep. John was rocking on the front porch, his eyes mere slits from exhaustion.

Crossing the yard, leaves crunching under my feet, I heard Ruby's friendly nicker as she stood with her head over the fence. "Hello there, girl." I took a moment to rub the soft fuzz between her nostrils and pat down her neck. "Maybe tomorrow we can go for a ride. Would you like that?" Ruby replied with a snort. "It's a date, then." With a final tickle to her ear, I continued toward the cows huddled outside the barn. As I pulled open the door, I heard a loud grunt and found Calvin weaving and stumbling into a post.

"Calvin? What in God's name?"

"Well, if it isn't my dear mother." His words slurred as he leaned against the wooden beam.

"Are you drunk?"

"Maybe." He pinched his fingers together and let out a gruff laugh.

"I don't like you drinking, Calvin. Your daddy couldn't handle his liquor and it looks like you can't either." Fire burned through my belly as I fisted my hands on my hips.

"Don't you talk about my daddy. He's a better man than that whoreson you got in there."

"Don't you dare." I rushed across the barn and dug my fingers into his bony shoulders, forcing him to straighten up.

"Get your whoring hands off me."

I stumbled back, shocked at the foulness coming from his

mouth. This wasn't my son—it was Gray Whitman reincarnated. A streak of fear rushed through me, followed by a steely determination. I'd been beaten down by his father, but I wouldn't let him do it to me."What's going on in here?" John ran into the barn, kicking up straw on his way to my side. He wrapped his arm around my shoulder as Calvin wobbled away from the pole that had kept him upright. He stumbled within inches of my face. The liquor on his breath was so strong, it snuffed out the smell of manure and animal hide. His anger was deadly.

"Where have you been?" I pulled out of John's embrace and gathered Calvin's coat in my fist. "You're acting just like your daddy."

"He was an honorable man. Better than the likes of you." He pointed his finger in my face.

"Calvin!" John reached out and grabbed his shoulder.

"Pff. Honorable." I spat, shoving against his chest. "You don't know what you're talking about. Darned if I'll be badgered by you—I had enough of that from your father. You should thank your lucky stars John Hayward came along."

"What, so he could warm your bed?"

John stepped between Calvin and me and cracked his open palm across the boy's face, knocking him to the floor. "Show some respect to your mother."

"Don't you ever talk to me like that again. Do you hear me?" I stood over him, rage simmering through me. I was no longer talking to my son, but to Gray. Finally defending myself after all these years. "I won't stand for it another minute."

Calvin crawled on hands and knees to the post and slowly stood up, stumbling until he got his footing under him. He glared hatred at John as if he was looking for a fight. This time, John wouldn't back off.

"I'll talk to you any way I damn well please." Calvin reached out and gripped the pitchfork that was leaning against the wall.

"You think I like living here with a whore of a mother and her bastard children? With a horse thief scoundrel, not man enough to marry her?"

He jabbed that pitchfork at me and John stepped between us, holding his hands out to calm the angry boy.

"Calvin, put down the fork. You don't know what you're doing. It's the liquor talking."

"Shut up, John. Stay out of this."

He stabbed the pitchfork at John and fell into a stall, landing on the floor beside one of the horses. John pulled Calvin by the ankles back into the middle of the barn.

"Get up. We need to get you sober." He slid his hands under Calvin's arms and lifted him to his feet. "You need to stay away from those boys you've been running with. They're not a good influence."

Calvin threw a punch but whiffed through the air without hitting his target. "And you are, huh? Stole Norville's horse and lied about it. You should be in jail."

"Calvin, I've had enough. You'll stay the night in the barn with the other animals," I said, shoving my hands into his chest, knocking him onto a stack of hay bales.

"While you curl up in a warm bed with that bastard like a common slut?" Calvin grabbed a hoe off the wall behind him and jabbed it at my midriff, making me stumble against a stack of wooden boxes. John's face darkened with rage—I'd never seen him so angry. He grabbed the heavy scoop shovel used for cleaning stalls and swung it against Calvin's back. The metal against flesh made a cracking *whomp* and Calvin's head hit a post before he landed flat on his face. Blood oozed from his forehead as he struggled to his feet. Again, he grabbed the hoe and this time swung it at John, missing his knees by a mere inch.

"You better apologize to your mother, and fast, boy." John

threatened to hit him again with the shovel, but Calvin refused to surrender.

"Hell no. I won't apologize for the truth. She's a whore, you're a thief, and those are your bastard children."

John aimed the shovel at Calvin's legs, knocking them out from under him, and he hit the ground with a *thump*. Rather than climb to his feet, he writhed and rolled, moaning like an animal. After a few minutes, he settled down, passing out into a steady snore.

I stooped beside him and checked his cut. "It's not bleeding too bad. He'll be fine here until morning."

"What about you?" John helped me to my feet and gathered me to his chest. "Did he hurt you?"

"No, I'm fine."

John cupped my face in his hands. "Are you sure?"

"I'm fine, John. He didn't hurt me."

"You plan to leave him here?"

"I won't have him back in my house. Throw a blanket over him. It will do him good to sleep out here tonight." Maybe it wasn't fair to take out my years of abuse from Gray on Calvin, but he'd done enough to earn a place on the floor of the barn. He'd been out of control and I couldn't risk the other children's safety by letting him inside. After a cold night and a raging headache in the morning, I'd hoped he would come to his senses. But it wasn't to be.

The next morning, Calvin was gone. He soon returned with the sheriff.

CHAPTER 32

I dropped my head into my hands as if my neck had lost all strength to hold it. Gramma and I were back at our usual spot, sitting at the kitchen table, sipping coffee. The sun was back for one last gasp of autumn, and the snow outside had melted to a white film over the ground. The children were helping Helen feed the chickens and Charles was chopping wood. Gramma and I hadn't had any time alone for over a week, though I'd been itching to hear more.

"I can't believe Father would get the sheriff after John like that." Popping my head up like a jack-in-the-box, anger streaked through me like a lightning rod. "He deserved that beating. He should never have spoken that way to you."

"The apple didn't fall far from the tree. It wasn't much worse than the way his daddy talked to me when he was alive." She stared into her coffee cup as if searching for an explanation. "His anger and hatred, well, he came by it honestly."

"It's no excuse. You can't help where you came from, but you certainly can control your actions. Now it all makes sense."

"What does?"

"The way he treats me." I was boiling with fury, I pulled off the wool cardigan I was wearing and leapt off the bench. "My hair, my eyes. I inherited my looks from you. And my art. He never wanted me to take classes. When I was a little girl, if he caught me doodling with pencil and paper, he'd snatch it away from me. He'd find chores for me to do to keep me from being idle because when I had nothing to do, I drew pictures."

Stomping back and forth like a caged lion, I pounded my fist into my hand, growing angrier with each step. How dare he put me through a life of misery just because he had a beef with his mother? I wasn't his mother! I was his daughter, who he was supposed to love and encourage, not tear down at every opportunity. Sampson and Elvin had dark brown hair like Father's, and Emily's coloring was light, like Mother. None of them had green eyes or red hair like me. But was that a reason to hate me?

"I'm sorry you've had it so rough, child. Come now, sit with me." Gramma patted my usual spot on the wooden bench. "Maybe you should thank your daddy."

"Thank him?" Was she trying to make me explode? I dropped to the bench. "For what? For talking down to me, making me feel stupid and ugly?"

"There, there. Settle yourself." Her soothing hand rubbed against my knee, calming me down. "I meant, maybe because he's been hard on you, you've grown stronger. You've got just enough of that Whitman stubbornness in you that instead of allowing yourself to be beaten down, it made you the strong woman you are today."

"I don't know ab—"

"I do. I know what it's like to live with a man who makes you feel worthless. You start to believe it."

"I did believe it, until I met people who made me believe in myself, like Mr. Ferretti and Cillian."

"There you go again, mentioning your friend Cillian. Are you sure there's not something more there between you?"

"No. He's just my friend." The words left a sour taste in my mouth. Who was I trying to fool—Gramma or myself?

"Friends make the best husbands."

It was such a silly notion—Cillian and me married—that I burst out laughing. No matter the warm feelings I had for him, I had no intention of getting married. Husbands expected you to cook and clean and have their babies. They didn't encourage you to pursue your passions or work outside the home.

"No, marriage is not for me. I plan to support myself with my art. When I go back to Philadelphia, I'm going to work as a textile designer."

"Well now, this is the first time you've mentioned your plans."

"Yes, I'm going to finish art school in the spring and get a job designing wallpaper and fabric. Wallpaper is all the rage in the city."

"Well, isn't that wonderful." My heart swelled with pride as Gramma beamed at me. Her mouth was stretched wide in a smile, showing her gums and smattering of teeth, and her eyes glistened. "Don't get such big britches that you won't come to visit your Gramma every once in a while."

"Never," I said, reaching across the table to squeeze her hand in mine. So much had changed since my first few days here, and I relished the time we spent together. It warmed my heart to know she trusted me with her story.

"So, what happened when the sheriff arrived?"

"He took John to jail, but the charges were dropped. The sheriff had more than enough on his plate with John's upcoming trial."

CHAPTER 33

June, 1855

"Hear ye, hear ye. The case of the State of Maryland versus John Hayward. The honorable Judge Henry Mackall presiding. Please be seated."

The courtroom was filled to capacity with family, friends, and the usual courtroom busybodies who spent their time watching trials as if they were stage shows. Ethel Schmidt sat on the pew beside me, holding my quivering hand. Robert, now seven years old, sat on my other side, while I held five-year-old Helen on my lap. Ethel's daughter had offered to keep the children at home, but I feared it might be the last time they saw their father if he were to be found guilty.

John sat beside his lawyer, Mr. Creswell. The trial had been delayed several times and now that it was happening, I wasn't sure if I had the courage to sit through it. Thomas, sitting to the left of Ethel and sensing my worry, reached across and patted me on the knee. My dear brother, Thomas, had been a constant source of support and love through it all.

He'd been there when John and I were finally married by a

circuit minister at the Methodist Episcopal Church in Oxford. It was a lovely little ceremony on a warm day in May, 1853. Thomas, Ethel and Rolfe, Robert and Helen, and Sarah and Jeremy had attended. Calvin had refused to "bear witness to the sham of a wedding." It had been years in coming, but we were finally man and wife, according to the authorities.

I twisted the gold band on my left ring finger, remembering the day, wishing I had married him sooner. Maybe all of this could have been avoided.

The courtroom hummed with chatter as more people crowded in. Across the aisle, in the first pew, sat Calvin, Sarah, and Jeremy, staring straight ahead at the judge's bench. The children hadn't looked at me when they'd entered, keeping their gazes down as they walked up the aisle of the courtroom. They had grown distant in the past month, but denied there was a problem. They still went about their chores and were mostly polite, but something had changed in their demeanor. I was convinced Calvin and Norville had poisoned Sarah and Jeremy against John. Otherwise, they'd be sitting beside me.

Norville made a spectacle as he entered the courtroom at the last minute, smiling to the crowd and shaking hands as if he were running for political office. He even had the gall to smile and wave at me before he sat down beside my children.

Judge Mackall settled his considerable girth into his throne-like chair, causing the wood to creak so loudly that it echoed through the room. He wore a heavy black robe too warm for this June day and surveyed the scene before him. His dark hair was brushed back from his forehead and his heavy beard lay on his chest.

"Call your first witness, Mr. Grason," the judge said to the prosecutor, dabbing at the sweat drops rolling down his temples.

"I call Mr. Norville Whitman, your honor."

Norville strutted through the gate toward the witness stand

as if he were a prized peacock on display. He'd trimmed his hair and beard and wore an impressive suit—a knee-length coat with a velvet collar, a plaid double-breasted vest, and a crisp bow tie. The epitome of a fine gentleman—if only the judge knew what a scoundrel he truly was. I was sure his hand would scorch against the Bible as he swore to tell the truth.

"Mr. Whitman, state for the court how you know Mr. John Hayward."

"Mr. Hayward is living with, *eh-hem*, now married to my former sister-in-law. My late brother's wife."

"Where do Mr. Hayward and your former sister-in-law live?"

"On my brother's farm."

"How far is your late brother's farm from where you live, sir?"

"It's about four miles from my place."

My cheeks turned so warm, surely they were the color of a tomato. That farm had never belonged to Gray, and he knew it. What other lies was he about to tell?

"In your own words, Mr. Whitman, please tell us what happened on the afternoon of July 18, 1848."

"I was out in the paddock checking on one of my horses who'd gone lame when John Hayward came riding up. He was shouting and kicking up a fuss, accused me of stealing a horse from him at auction—rather ironic, wouldn't you say? He said he would steal it back from me."

"He threatened to steal the horse, you say?"

"Yes, sir. He accused me of somehow rigging the auction. He was mad I got the horse. So, he threatened to steal it from me."

"Objection, your honor." John's lawyer jumped to his feet. "Calls for speculation."

"Overruled."

Norville crossed his arms and nodded his head as if his testimony was the God's honest truth. Or was he so confident because he had the judge in his pocket? I wanted to climb over the railing, pull him off that witness stand, and beat him to a pulp. He continued on with this testimony, saying he'd never seen the horse again after the morning it went missing. John had returned the horse to him, but Norville didn't acknowledge it. Even when Mr. Creswell cross-examined him, Norville stuck to his story that he'd never seen the horse again until it was found on my property in the woods.

"One last question, Mr. Whitman. Why do you suppose Mr. Hayward stole your horse?"

"He's a sore loser. He didn't win the horse at auction. And to get back at me for being a Whitman. He hates anything to do with his wife's former husband."

"Your honor, I object again. Speculation."

"Overruled."

"Thank you, Mr. Whitman. Your honor, I'd like to now call Calvin Whitman to the stand."

Shocked to hear his name called, I drew in a tight breath as my eldest son opened the wooden gate and walked toward the witness stand. His back was straight and his chin held high. A surge of anger blew out with my sigh. How could he do this to me?

Calvin had been living the last three years with Norville, since the charges were dropped against John for the shovel incident. He rarely came by to visit us, but when he did, he'd been cordial toward me, even polite to John. I had hoped most of the hard feelings had dissipated, but seeing him on the stand confirmed that the resentment had merely been dormant, simmering all this time.

"Mr. Whitman, would you please tell the court how you know Mr. Hayward?"

"He's married to my mother."

"So he's your step-father."

"I don't think of him as my step-father. He's my mother's husband."

"Do you live with your mother and her husband?"

"No, sir. I moved out three years ago."

Calvin's gaze shifted to me. His eyes narrowed and his lips drew in a tight, straight line. His hatred burned a hole in my heart.

"Why did you move out?"

"My mother was living a sordid life, having given birth to two bastard children, and with a horse thief. In all good conscience, I couldn't allow myself to live there any longer."

Tears burned behind my eyelids, but I wouldn't give him the satisfaction of seeing me cry. How could my son, my first-born child, say such cruel things about me in public? We'd had difficulties in the past, but one would think respect for his mother and family would keep him from spewing such hate. I had underestimated the depth of his anger toward me.

The prosecutor continued his questioning, establishing that Calvin had been present, though I had my doubts.

"Tell the court what you saw the afternoon of July 19, 1848."

"I was down by the creek when I heard someone coming. It was John Hayward and he was leading Uncle Norville's horse through the woods. He didn't see me. He walked on a ways further, disappearing through the woods."

"How did you know it was your Uncle Norville's horse?"

"I'd ridden him a couple of times. I was sure it was his."

"Did you say anything to Mr. Hayward?"

"No sir. I went back to fishing and later on, when I got home, I saw the sheriff and Uncle Norville there."

"Did you tell either of them what you saw?"

"No, sir. I didn't want to get involved."

He was lying. My son was lying and there was no way to prove otherwise. Norville and Calvin had cooked up their stories to convict John of horse stealing. And they had done it to hurt me.

Calvin continued his testimony, portraying himself as the upstanding son who didn't want to cause any trouble by reporting what he had supposedly seen that day. He even made a point to slip in the shovel-beating incident, even though those charges had been dropped. How could I ever forgive what my son had done?

"Your honor, I'd like to call Sarah Whitman to the stand."

My heart dropped to my knees. What in the world would Sarah have to say about the case? She was only ten years old at the time.

Sarah settled into the witness chair and fiddled with the bonnet she was wearing. The prosecutor started his questioning and she answered quietly, keeping her eyes downcast.

"Miss Whitman, tell the court what you remember from that day."

"I was in the backyard, feeding the chickens, when I saw my step-father, John, coming out of the woods, carrying a halter."

"And what happened next?"

"He went in the barn and came back out a few minutes later."

"Was he still carrying the halter?"

"No, sir."

"No more questions for this witness, your honor."

When Sarah stepped off the dais, she gave me a side-glance before taking her seat on the pew beside Calvin. She was white as a sheet and I noticed a tear roll down her cheek as Calvin wrapped a comforting arm around her. Jeremy was the next one to be called to the stand and he had a similar story.

"I was in the barn petting the horses and I saw John drop a halter in one of the stalls."

"What did you think when you saw him?"

"Didn't give it much thought."

Mr. Creswell did a fine job cross-examining both children, establishing that they were only ten and eight at the time of the occurrence, even getting Jeremy to admit his memories were sketchy. Why would they testify to something they had not witnessed?

"I'd like to call my next witness, your honor. Sheriff Eb DeMond."

Sheriff DeMond had aged in the past seven years. He'd grown larger around the middle and his hair had turned gray, but his mind seemed as sharp as ever. He had no problem testifying to the details of the case.

"The first indication that something wasn't right was when I found the halter with *Whitman* etched into the leather in the empty stall. My gut told me I was looking at a horse thief."

The gallery let out a collective gasp, including me. The sheriff's testimony had sealed John's fate.

Mr. Creswell had no witnesses to dispute the prosecution's claims except John, who had insisted he take the stand. He stuck to the same story he'd told me again and again over the past seven years. I believed every word, but could see John was defeated. He spoke quietly while on the stand, keeping his gaze on the judge. I willed him to look at me, to look at his children, who were so young. He needed to fight for himself, show some indignation, and accuse Calvin and Norville of lying on the stand. Instead, John seemed to accept his fate and replied to the defense attorney's questions with abbreviated answers.

The jury of twelve men took only a half hour to deliberate. It happened too fast. With a crack of his gavel, the judge dismissed the court, having accepted the jury's guilty verdict. John was sentenced to eight years in the Maryland Penitentiary in Baltimore City.

CHAPTER 34

Telling the story had taken the last bit of Gramma's energy. She'd been strong and hearty lately, but the reminiscing took an emotional toll. Her cheeks were sallow, her eyes dull, and her breathing labored.

"Come on, Gramma. Let me help you to bed. You should rest a while."

"For some reason, I'm drawn to bad men," Gramma said as we walked toward her bedroom. "Gray Whitman was a drunkard, a womanizer, and would have gambled away his children if I didn't keep a close eye on them. His mother and daddy spoiled him something fierce and he never did an honest day's work in his life. He got by, for a while, on his charm and his daddy's good name. Neither came in handy in the end. Mr. Whitman had cut him off and the bookies weren't impressed with his silver tongue. He wasn't able to talk his way out of the mess he was in, not with a knife at his throat."

"But John wasn't a bad man." I helped her climb in the bed and laid an extra quilt across her lap. I sat in the ladder-back chair as she continued.

"Everyone thought he was, though—and in a place like this,

what people believe often becomes the truth. Maybe he was. He had a bit of a temper and he made some poor decisions, but he was a good father to Robert and Helen, and an even better husband to me. He hadn't been given much of a chance in this life."

"What do you mean?"

"He left England to get away from working the mines, hoping to find a good life here in America. He would've, too, if it weren't for Norville. If only he could've left us alone and not started the hateful rumors, maybe John wouldn't have done the things he'd done. He wouldn't have landed in jail. If only they had left us alone..."

Before I could respond, Gramma's eyes closed and she fell into a soft, steady snore. Sharing her story had exhausted her and I hoped she'd wake rested and refreshed.

"He had a hard time in prison."

Those were Gramma's first words when she woke from her nap. I was sitting by her bed, embroidering Cillian's monogram with dark blue thread on a cotton handkerchief. Helen had shown me how to make my stitches smaller and tighter, giving the scrolled letters a professional look. It would be a Christmas gift.

"Gramma, you're awake. Would you like the chamber pot?"

"In a minute. I have some letters I want you to see."

"Letters?"

"From John. I've never shown Helen or Robert. I didn't want them to know the suffering their father went through in that awful place."

Gramma leaned up on her elbow and pointed toward her bureau. "There, in the top drawer. Bring me that leather portfolio." Her voice was strong, insistent.

I set my embroidery on the bedside table and opened the

bureau. Under her nightgowns and stockings, I found the portfolio. Its brown leather was cracked with age and the ribbon tying it closed was frayed on the ends.

"Open it. John's letters are inside. I only received three in all the time he was incarcerated."

"In eight years, he only sent three letters?"

"He said he'd sent more, but this is all I got."

I returned to my chair beside her bed and carefully removed the letters from the pouch. The paper on which they were written had yellowed from age. Opening the first one, I realized they were in rather good shape for being nearly twenty years old.

"Find the one from 1858. That's the first one. Three years into his sentence."

I found the letter and carefully unfolded it. John's handwriting was clear and readable, quite lovely in the way his letters dipped and curled.

"Read it to me, Laurel." Gramma settled back against the pillows and closed her eyes.

I tucked the quilt under her chin, patted her hand, and settled into the chair, tilting the letter toward the waning sunlight.

Dear Margaret,

They give me but one sheet of paper and three minutes to write. Forgive my haste.

Conditions are deplorable here and I'm not sure I can bear it much longer. Knowing you and the children are left to run the farm on your own brings my blood to boil all because of my idiocy in taking that horse. I spoke with Mr. Creswell last week and he tells me my request for an appeal has been denied. If I don't get out of here soon, I shall go mad.

Besides my desire to escape, I am healthy, though a bit leaner. I think of you and Robert and Helen often, and pray for your well-being.

> *Your devoted husband,*
> *John*

"He got caught trying to escape a week later." Gramma was staring off toward the window, as was her custom when her mind returned to the past. "The story made the papers before I was officially notified. Apparently he had managed to remove several bricks from below his bed, creating a hole big enough to climb through. A watchman, making his nightly rounds, thought his bed looked suspicious. When he came into the room, he found pillows and blankets lined up to create a figure of a man sleeping. The watchman found John down in the hole, digging his way out. He was put in a solitary cell while his room was searched. A saw, two knives, and a piece of iron were found. He was kept in solitary for a month and then lost his yard privileges for two months. Four months after this happened, Thomas took me to see him."

This must have been the time Garin had mentioned—when his grandmother had come to stay with Robert and Helen while Gramma went to Baltimore.

Gramma's lips curled in and her eyes squeezed shut. The memories she saw brought a sickly pallor to her cheeks. I rested my hand in hers and she squeezed until I thought my bones would break.

"I never went back after that. He was all but a skeleton. Eyes sunken in his skull, his lips so dry they bled through the cracks. Thomas spoke with the warden, but we were assured John was being well cared for. There was nothing I could do."

"Were you able to bring him food or blankets or anything at all?"

"Yes, I brought him a new pillow—one Helen had embroidered with a cluster of flowers. Robert had fashioned a toy for him—whittled it himself. It had a wooden handle and ring on the end of a string. John was to toss it in the air and land the ring on the end of the handle. Robert said it would help pass the time. I brought him some apples from the tree out back, and some cheese."

"Did he eat them right away? He must've been starving."

"No. He stared at the food and the gifts as if he couldn't comprehend what they were. I tried to get him to talk to me, but he wouldn't. He just sat there, like he was deaf and dumb. The starvation was taking a toll on him. Either that or they had drugged him with opium. I'd heard sometimes they gave opium to the prisoners to keep them quiet."

Gramma reached up with her quivering hand and rubbed her forehead between her gnarled fingers.

"Read the next letter. The one from June, 1859."

I found the letter she requested next in the pile and carefully unfolded the brittle paper.

This time, John's handwriting was difficult to read. The beautiful curls and elegantly slanted letters were now crooked and jagged.

Dear Margaret,

Today marks the fourth year of my confinement. I've been moved to a smaller room with only three other mates. Though our quarters are small, it is quieter with only the four of us. I've been assigned to a work detail outside the prison walls. Each morning the watchman comes and shackles a dozen of us, loads us onto a wagon, and drives us a mile outside town. We're clearing a path through a field which will become a road leading into the city. The work is hard. Though my back and arms ache until I fear they will fall off, I relish the fresh air and sunshine which reminds me so much of home. Don't worry for my health. The prison doctor gives us a heavy dose each night to help curb the pain so we can sleep.

Give Robert and Helen my love. How I wish I could be there to help you with the farm.
> *Your loving husband,*
> *John*

"He sounded better in this letter. Being outdoors each day must have lifted his spirits." I gently folding the letter along its deep creases and put it beneath the pile. Only one letter remained. "Would you like me to read the next one?"

"He wasn't better. I think he was just trying to reassure me. I called on Mr. Creswell after I received the next letter, so sure John was being drugged or was dying. Something had to be done about that place."

"Was he able to help?"

"No, he wasn't. Go ahead. Read the last one." This time, when I unfolded the yellowed paper, I could barely decipher the scrawl. It was evident John had grown weaker, so scribbled were the words. As best I could, I read the letter aloud.

November 1, 1859
Dearest Margaret,
Taken off the work. Trouble sleeping. We have a new doctor.
Won't give us what we need. Please do not visit any more. I
pray I make it home to you someday.
John

"Gramma, what does this mean the doctor won't give them what they need? Was he sick?"

"I'm convinced he was addicted to opium. Mr. Creswell made a visit to the prison on John's behalf, but he wasn't able to see him. The warden assured him John was fine, but he was taken off the work detail because he had strained his back. He was resting comfortably and shouldn't be disturbed."

"But you didn't believe it?"

"No, I didn't. The very next week, John landed up in the newspaper again. He was accused of assaulting the prison doctor. They put him in solitary confinement for three months. That was the beginning of the end."

"The end?"

"John died five months later, right here in this bed."

CHAPTER 35

April 19, 1860

My knees creaked as I squatted, lifted the wooden bucket with both hands, and toddled through the barn to the trough, paying close attention not to spill the water. The morning was cold and the wind was brisk as the horses huddled together, waiting patiently for a fresh drink. I'd gotten a late start with the daily chores this morning. It had been so cloudy and gloomy, everyone had slept in, which made Robert and Helen late getting off to school. As I lifted the heavy bucket and poured its contents in the trough, a sharp pain seared into my back. I was too old for this hard labor. Thankfully, Robert finished school in another month and would be able to help. Helen had two more years before she completed her lessons. It was important that both children complete their schooling.

I tramped back through the barn to refill the bucket at the pump when a stranger pulled into the yard. He appeared to have driven a long way—his black coat was covered in dust and his eyes drooped with exhaustion. It looked as though he had a load of straw in the back of his wagon.

"Hello, sir. May I help you?" I called out, setting the bucket on the frost-covered grass.

"Mrs. Hayward, I presume?" The driver climbed down off the wagon and pulled his slouch hat from his head. "I'm Cyrus McVey, here to make a delivery."

"Oh? A delivery for me?" I followed the man to the back of the wagon, where he dropped the gate. Among the loosely tossed straw was what appeared to be a brown sack, but when Mr. McVey lifted it, I realized it was a body—a human body—wrapped in a dirty, old blanket. It was John.

"He doesn't have long, ma'am."

"What?" My legs nearly gave out. I slumped against the wagon and rubbed my quivering hand over my eyes. Surely this was a trick. "John?"

"Yes ma'am. He got an early release due to his condition."

"John?" I was so bewildered I couldn't seem to form a coherent thought.

"Ma'am? Where would you like me to put him?"

Still unable to form a single syllable, I pointed to the back door and led Mr. McVey inside. I showed him to my bedroom and quickly pulled back the quilt and sheet beneath. He laid John gently on the bed and unwrapped the blanket, exposing his frail, skeletal body. He looked like he was already dead—nothing but bones and skin, and that skin an ugly shade of gray. Without another word, Mr. McVey tipped his chin and departed, leaving behind a document stating John had completed his sentence.

I set to work, doing all I could to bring some life back into his body. I filled a basin with warm water and, using a freshly laundered cloth, scrubbed the filth from his arms and legs, praying he'd live while thanking the Lord the children weren't home to see him like this. He didn't wake during his bath, nor when I slipped a fresh nightshirt over his head. After I tucked him under a heavy quilt, I rushed to the kitchen to get a cool cup of water.

When I returned, John's eyes were open, but his gaze was trance-like, staring blindly at the ceiling. His once-beautiful blue eyes were sunken into his head and his jowls sagged below hollow cheeks. He was forty-one years old, but looked years older. He was weightless, and I had no trouble slipping my arm under his shoulders and lifting him to offer a few sips of water from the cup. Some of the water trickled down his chin, but most of it he took with greedy swallows. Successfully getting water into him, I then tried a few spoonfuls of broth which he took, but soon raised his hand to signal he'd had enough. He fell into a deep sleep and didn't awaken again until the next morning.

As THE SUN CAME UP, I CLIMBED OUT OF THE ALCOVE WHERE I'D spent the night and went to check on John. He was awake, but not moving. But instead of his gaze locked on the ceiling, he turned his head when I entered the room and a faint smile formed on his lips.

"John, you're awake."

He didn't answer, but reached out his shaky hand to me. His lips moved without a sound.

"I'm here, darling." I sat on the edge of the bed and gathered his hand to my breast. "You're home and I'll take good care of you."

Appearing to comprehend, John nodded and closed his eyes, falling back into a deep sleep. I tucked his arm back under the quilt and ran my fingertips across his bony forehead and over his sunken cheeks. Even emaciated and with a long, straggly beard, I recognized the man I'd married.

"Have no worries, dear. I'll nurse you back to health," I said, placing a tender kiss over his brow. The sound of footsteps, like a herd of cattle, came from up above. The children were awake. I hadn't told Robert or Helen their father had returned, keeping my bedroom door closed. I wanted to wait until he was stronger, so as not to frighten them. I hurried through the kitchen, where I met them at the bottom of the stairs.

"My heavens, I thought some of the horses had gotten inside the house. Could the two of you be any louder?"

"It wasn't me, it was Robert's big feet," Helen said, giving me a brief hug.

"You were the one running down the stairs," Robert said as he slipped on his boots. "What's for breakfast?"

I perched my hands on my hips and shook my head, silently chuckling at my growing boy whose appetite continued to amaze me. He'd eat us out of house and home if I let him.

"I've got some biscuits and bacon."

I fed the children, helped them gather their books, and kissed them on the way out the door to school. With them gone for the rest of the day, I planned to dedicate my time to making my husband well.

The next day, after a bit more food and rest, John's healthy color had returned to his face and he was able to sit up in bed. When Robert and Helen returned from school, I told them their father was home. They refused to leave his bedside, so pleased to have him home, awake and alert. They both took a role in nursing John back to health. Helen fluffed his pillows and curled up beside him while Robert read to him. John was now able to eat a bit of porridge and some bread soaked in broth and applesauce for supper. The food did him good.

That evening, after the children had gone to bed, John was wide awake and able to talk. I climbed up on the bed and lay beside him. Suddenly, the lonely years melted away.

"John, darling, how did you get in this state? Surely they starved you."

"I don't want to talk about prison, Margaret. It's behind me now."

"Thank the Lord." I wrapped my arm across his scrawny chest, so different from the strong, virile man I'd once lived with. It was like holding a stranger.

"Tell me about the children," he said, laying his bony hand over mine.

"Well, you can see Robert and Helen have grown so. They are smart as whips and have more energy than young foals. I can hardly keep up with them."

"Yes, I see. You've done a fine job raising them, my dear."

I knew it to be true, but it warmed my heart to hear it from their father. I snuggled closer to him and rested my head against his shoulder.

"And what of Calvin, Sarah, and Jeremy? How are they faring?"

Anger shot through me like a lightning bolt. Would I ever get over their betrayal? I sat up so quickly, John bounced against the mattress. "John Hayward, why in the world would you ask about them after what they put you through?"

"Now Margaret—"

"If it weren't for them—especially Calvin—you wouldn't have gone to prison. I'll never forgive them for making up those lies about you, for letting Norville talk them into falsely testifying against you."

"Margaret—"

"I mean it, John. After you went off to prison, Calvin stayed at Norville's, and I'm glad of it. He has disappointed me so." My dander was up and I couldn't sit on the bed another minute. As soon as my feet hit the floor, I paced around the room, wringing my hands against my belly. "He got married two years ago to Susan Bolten. Do you remember her? Heaven help her. Sarah and Jeremy are both married now, too. Sarah moved to Baltimore with her husband, and Jeremy lives with his new wife in Calvert. Even though they live close, I don't see much of them. It's just as well." I took another lap around the bedroom and finally noticed John leaning on his elbow, reaching out his hand to me.

"Please, Margaret." He lay back against the pillows and patted his hand on the mattress. "Sit, my dear. There's much I need to say before I..."

"I'm sorry, John. I've been going on and on. What it is? What do you want to tell me?" I sat on the edge of the bed and gathered John's hand in my lap.

"Listen to me now." John's plea came out on a whisper. His voice was raw and breathy. "You must forgive the children. They did what the court expected of them. They gave their testimony."

"But they lied."

"I deserved to go to prison. I stole the horse."

"You returned the horse. It was Norville who set you up, and Calvin conspired right along with him."

"No, dear. I took the horse. You must not blame them."

"John Hayward." I tossed his hand off my lap and stood up abruptly. "Stop it now. You don't have to defend them. You told me you returned the horse and I believed you."

"It wasn't true."

"Stop it, John. You wouldn't lie to me."

Heat rose in my cheeks and anger surged through my veins. It was just like John to be so noble as to take the blame for Norville's actions and my children's false witness. He had never lied to me and never would, so why was he saying these untruths now?

"Please, Margaret."

"No. You are a good and honest man, John, and you don't have to do this. You don't have to tell me you stole the horse just to heal the rift between me and the older children. Stop it at once."

"I took the horse."

"I won't hear another word." I turned down the oil lamp, leaving the room in darkness, tucked the quilt under John's chin, and tapped a kiss to his forehead. "Sleep now. I won't hear another word."

The next morning, I found John lying in the bed, staring at the ceiling. He was dead.

CHAPTER 36

Gramma finished her story of John's demise, dabbing her lace handkerchief to the corner of her eye. My heart had fallen to my feet. What a sad, tragic ending.

"I'm sorry, Gramma. It sounded as though he was getting better."

"He was. At least, I thought so. If only I'd had a few more days. There was so much I wanted to say to him."

"He should've been released sooner, then you could've helped him."

"I guess I should be thankful he didn't die alone in prison."

Helen and Charles came through the back door, letting in a blast of cool, pleasant air. Helen was as pale as a ghost. "There's someone here to see you, Laurel," she said, dropping her chin to her chest.

Father and Mother stood behind her.

WE SAT IN THE PARLOR—GRAMMA, FATHER, MOTHER, HELEN, Charles, and me—talking about the strange weather we'd encountered recently and their bustling life in Philadelphia.

My nerves prickled and poked, causing me to squirm and my stomach to spin like a whirlpool. It was all so polite, very cordial, everyone speaking in controlled tones, but our rigid spines couldn't hide the emotions roiling inside. After several minutes of innocuous talk, we fell silent. Leave it to Gramma to get to the point.

"So, Calvin, I guess you've come to take the girl home?"

"Well, Mother, I think that's obvious. You've made it clear in the past that we aren't welcome here."

My mother laid her hand on Father's knee, preemptively calming him before his temper got the best of him.

"I never said you weren't welcome here."

"You made that quite clear the last time I was here."

"As I recall, you tried to strong arm this property out of my grip. You made such a scene, the neighbors had to intervene. Since then, you've chosen to stay away."

"Excuse me for my mistake." Father's retort dripped with sarcasm.

"Maybe guilt has kept you away."

"I didn't steal the horse!" Father jumped to his feet and glared at Gramma, who was sitting stoically on the upholstered chair. His bloodred face and angry look made my heart skip a beat. Charles had been sitting on a kitchen chair inside the doorway, but now stood up. I scooted to the edge of my seat, ready to leap in front of Gramma to protect her from my father's rage.

"I never said you did."

"But you believe it."

"What I believe and what I expect from you are two different things."

With his hate-filled eyes firmly focused on my grandmother, Father's voice dropped to a quiet, menacing tone.

"Get your things, Laurel. We're leaving now."

"But Father, I—"

"I said get your things!" His roar threw me back against the chair. Mother shrank into the sofa, her face blanched and eyes closed tight. I now understood what Gramma had tried to explain to me. Father had Mother so emotionally beaten down she simply went into self-preservation mode whenever he raged. I had always protected myself by steering clear of Father as much as possible and by preparing for my future—attending and completing the design school—so one day I could get out from under his thumb. This time, I wouldn't steer clear.

"I'm not going home with you." I stood up, squared my shoulders, and lifted my chin, giving the impression of confidence. Inside, my heart thumped, threatening to burst from my chest. "I'm staying here."

"But Laurel, what about the art school? Your painting has been chosen for the spring show. What about graduation?" Mother's voice quivered as she twisted her hands in her lap.

"I'm going back to Philadelphia to finish the school year right after Christmas."

"If you don't come with us right now, you'll have no home to come to," Father said.

"I'll find a room at a boardinghouse. There's one near the school."

"Ha! You think you could afford to live in a fancy boardinghouse in that part of town? How will you pay for it?" I knew what he was about to say as soon as that repulsive sneer formed on his face. "Never mind. I know how you'll pay for it. As I suspected when you left in the dark of night."

"Don't you dare—"

"Selling yourself. But instead of giving it away like your Gramma, you make 'em pay."

This brought everyone still sitting to their feet. Charles charged at Father, knocking him into the sofa. Blood spurted from his nose where Charles's fist had landed. Mother shrieked and Helen got in front of Charles, pushing him away.

"You're a horrible man." I leaned over Father, our faces but inches away. "Don't you ever speak to me or Gramma or anyone else in this house that way again! You have no right."

"I have every right." His words came out muffled as he held a handkerchief up to his nose. It quickly saturated with blood. "No daughter of mine is going to act like her." He pointed at Gramma, who was still sitting like a marble statue. She hadn't moved or spoken during the melee, but her face had gone slack and her eyes narrowed. Her glare at Father was so cold it could freeze a burning log.

"Calvin, please." Mother's plea fell on deaf ears.

"I'll throw you over my shoulder and carry you out of here."

"Why? Why would you want me living under your roof if I'm nothing but a whore?"

"Laurel! Your language." Mother attempted to pull me away from Father, but I shrugged her hand off my arm.

"Calvin, it's time you and Susan left our home." Charles had composed himself enough to quietly request their departure.

"Your home? *Your* home?" Father shoved me out of the way and got to his feet, stuffing the bloody handkerchief in his trouser pocket. "This would have been my home if it weren't for John Hayward."

"I don't think now is the time to revisit history." This time, Helen spoke up, fighting to remain calm.

"Why isn't it, *sister*? Why don't you tell Laurel how you and your bastard brother stole my birthright?"

"That's enough." Charles grabbed Father by the arm and dragged him out of the room. Like a volcanic eruption, everyone spoke at once as Charles forced Father toward the door. Mother tugged on Father, begging him to leave. Helen pulled Charles's arm, hoping he'd release Father. I was shouting that he needed to go. No one wanted him here. Everyone was yelling and no one was listening. As Charles opened the front door, Gramma stood and somehow over the din, we all heard her speak.

"I never promised you this land," Gramma said to Father, unfurling her back until she stood tall as a soldier. "I told you years ago this land would belong to Robert and Helen."

"Daddy promised it to me," Father said.

"He had no right to do that. This was my land—always had been. Your daddy squandered everything he'd been given, every penny he made."

"But I was your firstborn."

"This house and this land were never going to belong to you or Sarah or Jeremy. Not after what the three of you did."

Father charged toward Gramma and my heart dropped to my feet. He was going to hurt her. Charles and Helen grabbed each of his arms and held him back. He was like a raging bull, fighting for freedom. In all the times he'd railed at me, I'd never seen him this angry.

"Calvin, stop this at once." Mother stepped between him and Gramma. Her fists dug into her hips and her eyes glared with anger. "You're acting like an imbecile." I stumbled back from the shock of seeing Mother standing up to him. When she wagged her finger at him like an old schoolmarm, Father seemed to recoil. "I've had about enough of your theatrics. Apologize to your mother and to Laurel. They don't deserve this behavior."

"Susan Whitman," Father seethed, hissing her name through clamped teeth. "Stay out of this or else."

"Or else what? You'll hit me? It wouldn't be the first time."

A collective gasp went up and I fell against the doorframe. I knew Father had always been patronizing and condescending toward Mother, even verbally abusive. But I had never known him to strike her. There had never been any visible scars or bruises. I was nauseous, knowing that she had kept this horrid secret from us children. All this time, I thought his harshest cruelty was reserved for me alone.

"Father," I said, keeping my voice and demeanor much calmer than the emotions roiling through my body, "it would be best if you left now."

He shook off Charles and Helen's restraining hands and straightened his jacket, casting a hateful glare at each of us.

"Sarah, Jeremy, and I—we told the truth on that stand." Father glared at Gramma. "And nothing but the truth."

"According to you." Gramma shuffled over to Father and lifted her chin, meeting him eye to eye. "How does it make you feel to know an innocent man spent five long years in prison?"

"I've slept soundly enough all these years."

"Get out of this house," Gramma seethed.

Father muffled a groan and slammed the door on his way out, leaving Mother to fall into my arms. I held her as she sobbed.

CHARLES DRAGGED AN OLD MATTRESS UP TO THE GIRLS' ROOM FOR them to sleep on, and Helen made up the bed with fresh linens for Mother and me. Neither one of us could sleep because of the ruckus earlier—Mother tossed and turned, and my eyelids refused to close. Dinner had been eaten in near silence, each of us deep in our own thoughts. Now that Cora and Belle were asleep and Mother and I were alone in bed, it seemed necessary to talk about it.

"It isn't fair," I murmured, as much to Mother as myself. "None of us deserved what happened today."

"Or what's happened before." Her quiet reply confirmed she was as wide awake as I.

"If you could leave, would you?"

"Leave your father?" The notion sounded surprising to her. "What would I do? Where would I go?"

"Aunt Edith's?"

"She lives in Harrisburg." She talked as if it were on the other side of the country. "Besides, she doesn't have room for the five of us."

"Four. I can live on my own."

"Oh, Laurel. A respectable young lady can't live on her own." She turned on her side, resting her head on her arm as she looked at me. Her eyes glowed brightly in the moonlight.

"Mother, it's 1877. Women work alongside men in the mills and factories. Many of them are the sole breadwinners for their families. I'm more than capable of supporting myself once I finish school."

"But a boardinghouse?" She said this as if I planned to move into a brothel. That's what Father thought I deserved.

"There are several very respectable, safe boardinghouses in the center of the city where unmarried, professional women live. Teachers and nurses and social workers."

"Don't you want to get married?"

"To whom? A man like Father? Live like you?" It was out of my mouth before I could stop it and I felt terrible as Mother's chin began to quiver. "I'm sorry, Mother. That was unfair and very unkind."

"It's true. We don't have an ideal marriage. In fact, most days I'm quite unhappy. But he provides for the family. We live in a nice home in a good neighborhood and we always have plenty to eat and warm clothes to wear. It could be worse."

"But Mother, did you ever have dreams beyond being a wife and mother?" I crawled onto my knees and gripped her shoulder in my hand, giving her a little shake as if to tear loose the aspirations she had long ago buried. "Something you wanted for yourself?"

"I enjoyed working as a milliner. And I've always loved flowers."

"Flowers? But Mother, everyone loves—"

"Growing them, cultivating unique varieties." Through the window, the moonlight illuminated her smile and glistening gaze. She sat up and tucked her long blond hair behind her ears, making her look like a young girl. "My grandfather had a greenhouse outside his home where he grew roses and gardenias and orchids. Oh, his orchids were magnificent."

"I never knew that."

"He died shortly after you were born and my uncle took over the greenhouse. I had always wanted to visit him, but it was a full day's ride and there never seemed to be time once you children came along."

"But Mother, now that we're mostly grown, you have time to do it. Build a small greenhouse in the backyard. Start your own flower garden."

"I don't remember all my grandfather taught me. It's been a long time."

"Join the horticulture society. Go to the new hall, the one they built for the Centennial Exposition. I'm sure someone could teach you."

She sat up, cupped her warm hands around my face, and laughed. "Oh Laurel, I've always loved your optimism. You have such a can-do spirit."

"But you *can do* this."

"I wouldn't have the time with taking care of the house and the meals and going to the market."

"Mother!"

"Laurel, you are so sweet to suggest it, but my life is taking care of my husband and family. It's what I was destined to do." As I pulled away, she tightened her hold on me. "But don't give up your dreams, dear. You have enormous talent and ambition."

"But I thought you wanted me to get married and have children."

"I just want you to be happy—whatever that means to you."

CHAPTER 37

Not long after, I fell into a deep sleep, dreaming strange, confusing dreams that disappeared the moment I opened my eyes. A loud, pounding sound reverberated from down below and as I awoke, I recognized it as someone knocking his fist against the front door. The thumping stopped and muffled voices filtered upstairs. Curiosity brought me to my feet and I scrambled downstairs as I tied my wrapper around my waist. Was Father back so early?

As I reached the bottom of the staircase, I drew up short. It wasn't Father, but a tall, dark-haired young man who reminded me of Cillian. When he turned around, I nearly fainted with joy. It was Cillian! Charles, Helen, Mother, and the girls were gathered 'round him as if he were an oddity at a circus, but I elbowed my way between them and threw my arms around his waist. His heart was thrumming wildly under my ear, and I delighted in his warm embrace.

"What are you doing here?" His mouth was drawn in a tight line and I realized I must look a fright, having just risen from bed. Though I'd braided my thick mass of hair the night before, wild, defiant curls haloed my face.

"Can I talk to ye a moment, Laurel?" He whispered it even though everyone could hear him.

"Yes, of course. Come in the parlor."

"Would your friend like some coffee, Laurel?" Mother asked with a note of hope in her voice.

"That would be most kind of ye, ma'am."

I grabbed Cillian's elbow and tugged him into the parlor, inviting him to sit beside me on the sofa.

"You're all out of breath. What's brought you here in such a rush?" I clasped my hands tightly in my lap, twisting and turning them until they were numb. Something was wrong.

"I got to ye as quick as I could. Had to borrow Geordie's horse. Couldn't get a train ticket, eh? The strike is over, but there's a mess to clean up."

"Cillian." I laid my hand on his bouncing knee to settle him. "Why are you here?"

"Right." He cleared his throat and smoothed his ruffled hair with his broad hand. "I saw Emily last week and she was telling me yer da was planning to come here and drag ye back. I came to warn ye."

I sagged with relief against the sofa back. What a dear friend was Cillian. He rode day and night to alert me to Father's arrival, only to get here too late. His brows were drawn together and his bright blue eyes had turned to gray. He was worried for me, and it made my heart swell. As I was about to explain, Mother arrived with two steaming mugs and a broad smile on her face. Cillian stood up and bowed slightly.

"Here you go." She handed a cup to each of us and then stepped back, fingering a loose strand behind her ear. "In all the hubbub, I didn't get a chance to introduce myself. I'm Laurel's mother. It is nice to finally meet you, Cillian."

"Her moth—well, yes ma'am, Mrs. Whitman, 'tis a delight to meet ye as well."

"Such a charming brogue." Mother giggled like a schoolgirl and my cheeks turned fiery hot with embarrassment.

"Aye, well, 'tis County Cork I hail from." Cillian was pouring on his Irish charm and I thought my mother would swoon. There was no question he was quite handsome with his dark, wavy hair, crystal blue eyes, and broad shoulders.

"How fascinating. I guess I should let the two of you visit."

"Thank you, Mother." My tone let her know we indeed wanted to be left alone, but she dawdled in the doorway, twisting a bit of hair around her finger.

"If there's anything else you need, let me know. Helen is fixing breakfast. You're welcome to join us, Cillian."

"Yes, ma'am. I'd be much obliged."

"I'll call for you when it's ready."

With one last twist of her hair, my mother finally left us alone. I dropped my face into my hands to hide my embarrassment.

"Yer ma is a very nice woman. I see where ye get it."

"My mother has a crush on you already."

"Most women do after they meet me." He took a sip from his cup, hiding his wry smile behind the rim.

He may have said it in jest, but I believed it was true.

"I'm sorry you came all this way, but my father and mother arrived yesterday."

"'Tis a pity I couldn't get here sooner to warn ye. Why aren't ye on the first train out of here? Emily said he would make sure ye came home."

"After the terrible things he said to Gramma and me, he was asked to leave last night. We had quite a row."

"Where is he now? Yer mother's still here."

"I'm not sure where he went last night. We haven't seen him yet this morning. He tried to make me leave with him, but I refused."

Cillian's head snapped back from his coffee cup as if he'd

been burned, and his eyes grew large. "I thought ye said ye were coming home. Ye promised." His worried expression and pleading tone made my heart rip in two. He had missed me.

"I will. I thought I would stay until after Christmas and then take a room at Mrs. Owen's Home for Proper Young Ladies. I sent her a letter yesterday inquiring about a room."

"Well, now, quite an impressive address y'are moving to."

"It's close to the design school. I know it will be costly, but I think I'll be able to manage on my mill wages—if they'll take me back—and then by summer, after I graduate, I'll be able to supplement my income with designing until I'm hired on full-time."

Cillian rested an elbow on his knee and rubbed his forehead between his long, thick fingers. "Would ye consider moving to Fishtown? I know where ye can get a room that won't cost ye a cent."

A warm blush crawled up my neck and settled in my cheeks. If Mother thought my living in a boardinghouse was inappropriate, what would she say about me living with Cillian?

"Mrs. Murphy has a spare room she'd like to rent out. She mentioned to me that if she could find a young lady to help with the children while she worked, she would offer the room for free."

I dragged my hand over the bumps and ridges of my braid, wondering at the letdown that made my shoulders sag. How silly of me to be disappointed he hadn't offered his own home.

"Free?"

"In exchange for watching the children."

"She has three, if I remember correctly?"

"Indeed. They're a bit rambunctious, but good kiddies over all."

"That would be perfect. I could go back to the mill part time and go to the academy on my days off, leaving my evenings free to watch the children. Unless she wanted me to watch them during the day, but either way, I—"

"Slow down, missy. Y'are getting winded. I'll talk to Mrs. Murphy as soon as I return."

"Cillian. Thank you." Without thinking, I threw my arms around him and planted a kiss on his check. When I attempted to pull back, his arms tightened around my back and his gaze locked on mine. My lungs seized up, unable to inflate as he looked at me with raw emotion playing in his eyes.

Just as his head tilted and his face drew closer to mine, Mother called from the kitchen, "Breakfast is ready." We both burst out in a nervous chuckle. His face was as red as the heat in mine.

"We probably shouldn't keep them waiting." Even as I said it, I wanted to rewind the clock a few seconds to that moment when he was about to kiss me. The feeling was strange and unexpected.

"Aye." He slowly loosened his hold on me, as reluctant as I was to separate. Cillian stood up and offered his hand to me, and at that moment, I remembered I was still dressed in my night clothes.

"Go ahead and have a seat." I pointed toward the bench where Cora and Belle had saved an empty space. "I'll get dressed and join you in a few minutes."

WITH BREAKFAST OVER AND NO SIGN OF FATHER, CILLIAN AND I wrapped up in our winter coats and walked down the lane toward the creek as I introduced him to the farm where my father had grown up. I pointed out the cheese-making shed and the outbuilding where Charles sheared the sheep. Uncle Robert's house stood across the fallow field, with smoke wafting from his chimney. I wondered if Father had created a ruckus at his house as well last night. As we passed the main barn, I looped my arm through Cillian's and led him inside to the small room which had been John Hayward's.

"This is where Gramma's husband, Helen's father, slept when he first came here from England."

The winter sun was peeking between the wall boards and Cillian shivered. "I wouldn't want to sleep in here this time of year."

"He didn't for long. That's how it all began."

As we continued down the lane toward the creek, I told him the story Gramma had told me about her life with my grandfather and with John Hayward.

"So yer granny's husband went to prison?"

"He was accused of stealing a horse and then not long after, the sheriff arrested him for beating Father with a shovel."

"Och, that must've been painful, eh?"

"I'm sure it was, but obviously, Father suffered no lasting effects."

Cillian took my hand and intertwined his fingers with mine. He'd held my hand before, but never so intimately. My stomach filled with butterfly wings and I lowered my chin to hide my smile. All this time, he had been my friend, but with him here, nearly kissing me this morning and now holding my hand, I wondered if perhaps it was something more. I'd heard it said that absence makes the heart grow fonder. Could that explain the warm jitters coursing through my veins?

"I've been doing some thinking about my future while ye've been gone, lass."

"Oh?" Those words, *my future,* created a frightful hole in my belly. Whatever it was he was about to say didn't involve me, and the disappointment burned.

"Aye, I've been thinking I could make something of my rotating ramp, sell it to a few more shipping companies, maybe even to the mill. It could come in quite handy in any industry."

"I agree."

"Mr. Schumer has ordered two more and he even said he'd lend me money if I needed it to make more, ye see."

"Cillian, that's wonderful."

"With enough money, I could move Ma and my sister's family out of that cramped house and buy one, big enough for all of us."

"Your mother would like that."

I swallowed the knot that had formed in my throat. Silly of me to hope he'd include me in his plans. I withdrew my hand from his and trotted down the lane to the creek, giving myself a moment to come to my senses.

"Isn't it lovely down here? It's so peaceful with the water flowing over the rocks and the birds singing. Cora and Belle and I walk down here sometimes."

"Aye, 'tis lovely. Quiet, eh?"

"Yes. Sometimes all you can hear is the wind blowing."

"My ma would like a place like this. Reminds me of Cork." Cillian picked up a stone and tossed it into the creek. It bounced and pinged off several rocks before it disappeared in the water. "Ye like it here, do ye?"

"It is beautiful. I can only imagine what it's like in the summertime with the flowers in bloom, the trees lush with leaves, and the corn growing tall." I followed his lead and threw a stone into the water, but it sank at once. "I do miss the city though. The streetcars and vendors, the energy and noise. It was difficult sleeping when I first arrived. The quiet kept me up."

Cillian chuckled and captured my hand in his, pulling me closer. "Well then, ye'll need a noisier place to live. Outside the city, but not far, eh?"

"Perhaps."

"There's a building boom west of Philadelphia. Big brick homes with wide verandas and gardens behind. The streetcar goes out there now."

"I saw it on our way out of the city. The houses are lovely."

He tugged me closer and his crystal gaze took my breath away. His top lip quivered as it stretched into a nervous smile.

"I was thinking one of those west side houses would be plenty big enough for Ma, my sister's family, me..." He blinked, keeping his lids lowered a second longer, and then he released the breath he was holding. "...and you."

"Me?" So I *was* part of his future. I had tried to ignore his declaration outside the train station as I fled to Maryland for reasons I still didn't understand, but I knew enough to understand something had changed. Maybe spending so much time with Gramma, hearing her reveal truths even when they were difficult to face, had forced me to see the truth about myself as well—that as afraid as I was to lose my independence, I couldn't deny how I felt for Cillian.

"I hear some of them have six bedrooms. Six! Can ye imagine that, Laurel?" He stepped back, dropping my hand, and threw his arms out wide. "It wouldn't be a farm like this, but you could have a kitchen garden out back to grow fresh vegetables. You could plant flowers. The children could play safely in the garden or go to the park that's being planned. Can you imagine the fresh air, away from the mills and factories, where our children can play without worry?"

"How many children are you thinking of?"

"Five, six...twelve. It doesn't matter." He gathered me in a bear hug and lifted me from the ground, spinning me around until I was dizzy.

"Would you like that, Laurel?"

When he placed me back on my feet, I saw two and three of him, my brain was so scrambled. As the spinning stopped, the romance of a marriage proposal faded while I stared at the button on his shirt and envisioned an enormous home with dozens of rooms to clean, a large family to feed, and me in the middle of it all. My hair would turn gray and I would be stooped over from years of hard work and childrearing. Cillian would go off to his big manufacturing plant in the city each day, dressed like a baron, and I'd be left at home in a well-worn cotton dress, ready to start my long day of cooking and cleaning. I'd have a baby on my hip and a wooden spoon in my hand as my mother-in-law criticized the porridge. My canvases would have turned yellow in the attic and the paints dried up right along with my dreams.

"Well? Would ye, lass?"

I tore my gaze from the button my eyes had been fixed upon and looked into his eyes, so hopeful and pleading.

"No."

CHAPTER 38

"No? Why the devil not?"

The deep crease between Cillian's brows told me he was hurt and furious. His eyes narrowed as he dug his fists into his hips. Great white clouds puffed from his nostrils, making him look like a raging bull. I giggled, which didn't help his mood.

"Ye dare to laugh at me, Laurel Rose Whitman?" he bellowed.

Watching his indignant rage made me laugh even more. His face had turned as red as an apple and his hair stood on end where he'd raked his hand through it. Folding in half, I held the stitch paining my side and continued to laugh as he ranted and stomped around.

"This is the thanks I get for riding all this way, nearly killing the horse to get here. I share my dreams with ye, offer ye a lovely home in which to live, and ye dare to laugh at me. Maybe I'd better rescind my hand if this is the way it's going to be."

"Ci-Cillian, I-I..." I tried my best to pull myself together, but it seemed the more he roared, the more I laughed. It was rather embarrassing.

"Have I ever laughed at yer dreams, eh? Have I? No. I'd suggest we live here, but my work will be in the city. I don't see much use for my ramp on a farm. Besides, if y'are going to laugh like a hyena every time I tell ye my plans, I'm not sure I'd want to marry ye. Ever think about that?"

My flood of laughter stopped as quickly as turning off a faucet. I blinked the mirth from my eyes and swiped the tears from my cheeks.

"Marry me?"

"Aye, ye raving ninny, what do ye think I've been talking about?"

Of course he had been talking about marriage, I knew that. When he had spoken of children, I knew he meant ours, but hearing the actual words from his lips brought me up short. Now I was the one to be angry.

"Why would I marry you?"

"Jesus, Mary, and Joseph," he muttered as he stomped down to the creek and picked up a large rock, slamming it into the water. The plume wetted the bottom of his trousers. "Ye are as hard-headed as this rock." He dropped his chin to his chest and shook his head.

"I guess what I mean is..." I joined him alongside the creek and tugged on his shoulder, forcing him to look at me. "*Why* do you want to marry me?"

He shook his head again. "Are ye daft, lass?"

He hadn't declared his feelings for me, and I had to know.

"Laurel!" Cora's panicked cry tore us from our pivotal moment and we turned to find her running down the lane, arms swinging like a windmill. "Laurel. Come quick. Gramma has fallen."

Lifting my skirt, I charged up the embankment with Cillian on my heels. We ran up the lane, following in Cora's wake. Gramma had been doing so well, growing stronger every day. Helen and I constantly urged her to use her cane, but she insisted her legs could hold her. I couldn't help but think Father's visit had something to do with this.

Surging toward the house, I grew winded and my boot came unlaced. Cillian came to my aid, encircling my waist with his strong arm and lifting me slightly, helping me to make it the last few yards. Mother met us at the back door as we rushed through. "She collapsed. In the kitchen. Hurry."

Gramma was lying on the kitchen floor with Cora and Belle kneeling beside her and Helen pressing a cold rag to her forehead.

"Help me get her into her bed." Charles directed the request at me, but Cillian shifted me behind him and knelt down beside Charles. The men carried Gramma to her room and delicately deposited her on the mattress. They then stepped back and let the women take over.

"Bring me a pail of cool water, Cora." With quiet, efficient calm, Helen directed Gramma's care. "And bring the headache powder. Tell Aunt Susan to get it. It's on the top shelf of the pantry." She glanced over her shoulder at me. "Laurel, help me tuck some of these pillows behind her. Get on the other side of the bed and we'll lift her."

"Let me do that, Mrs. Smith." I hadn't realized Cillian was still there, standing outside the doorway, watching. He stepped in front of Helen and ran his hands under Gramma's arms and around her back, lifting her while I stuffed a mound of pillows behind her head and shoulders. Her face was pale and her breathing shallow, but she let out a sigh of what might have been relief. Helen took over once again.

"Can you hear me, Mother? It's Helen."

Gramma grunted a reply.

"Are you hurt? Any pains? How's your head?" Helen asked her questions as she ran her hands over Gramma's body, gently squeezing and prodding, checking for broken bones or bruises. Gramma never flinched or indicated a pain. Her mouth hung open and her lids drooped, but she was awake and aware.

"Here you are, Mother." Cora set a bowl of water on the nightstand and Belle shadowed behind her.

"Thank you, girls. You've been a big help." Helen took the jar of white powder and glass of clear water Belle was holding. "Go on, now. Laurel and I will tend to Gramma."

Helen spooned the powder into the water, swirled it until the white flakes were mostly dissolved, and held it up to Gramma's mouth. I held a linen towel below her chin as Helen administered the medicine.

"Are you warm enough, Gramma?" I asked as I tucked the blanket over her shoulders. She replied with a grunt, which I took to mean yes. We stayed with her until her eyes closed and her breathing steadied. I pulled the draperies closed as I followed Helen out of her room, leaving it dark and cozy—a perfect cave in which to rest.

Cillian, Charles, and the children were seated at the kitchen table. My mother filled the kettle with water.

"She may have hit her head. I'm not sure," Helen said, fingering a loose strand behind her ear.

"Should I fetch Dr. Huber?" Charles asked.

"I don't know what he could do for her." Helen took a seat on the bench beside her husband and rested her head on his shoulder. "She's an old woman, and falls are to be expected."

Though there wasn't a sound among us, it was as if our hearts thumped as one with the realization that this fall would set back Gramma's recovery. She'd been sick only a few weeks ago with pneumonia, and now had fallen. At seventy-eight, Gramma had lived longer than most. An old woman's body could only handle so much before it gave out. I'd had so little time with her, and knowing that time might be growing short overwhelmed me. I rushed from the kitchen, grabbed my coat from the peg, and ran out the back door. The cold autumn air couldn't dry the tears streaming down my face. When I reached the fence that corralled the horses and cows, I rested my head against the top plank and sobbed.

"There, there, lass." Though I was unaware Cillian had followed me, it wasn't really a surprise when he gathered me in his arms and held my head against his chest. Loud, snotty sobs racked my body and I held on to Cillian for fear I'd collapse. He gathered me tighter to him and rested his cheek against the top of my head.

"Let it out, dearie. 'Tis a sad day."

His soothing words, like the cooing of a dove, were a balm to my broken heart. He eased the two of us to the ground, the grass crunching under us from the morning frost, and leaned his back against the fence post. Opening his coat, I slipped my arms around his waist and he cocooned me against the cold breeze, his strong arms holding me tight as I let the tears fall. He didn't rush me, didn't try to stop my sobs. He held me and murmured sweet words to comfort me.

"Oh, Cillian, I-I..." The clump in my throat and the tears that wouldn't stop made it hard to speak.

"No need to talk, lass."

There was so much I wanted to tell him, so much I wanted to share about my time with Gramma. But mostly, I wanted to apologize for the way I reacted to his unorthodox marriage proposal.

"Cillian," I croaked, forcing the clog out of my throat. I sat up and swiped the tears from my face. He handed me his handkerchief and I blew like a train whistle.

"Feel better?"

"Much." I blew again and looked down at the saturated cloth. "I think I better launder this before I give it back."

"Perhaps ye should." As Cillian chuckled, he ran a knuckle over my cheeks, catching the last of my tears.

"I'm sorry about earlier." I dabbed my eyes and tucked the

wet handkerchief in my pocket. "I shouldn't have laughed at you, or lost my temper."

"Ye weren't the only one to get angry. I'm not sure what happened."

"I'm not either. One minute you were talking about selling more rotating ramps and buying a bigger house, and the next you were talking about children."

"Perhaps I didn't give ye fair warning of my plans."

"Perhaps."

With nervous laughs between us, we rose up and brushed the grass from our damp backsides, neither of us looking at the other. Cillian rested his arms on the top rail of the fence and looked out across the field.

"'Tis beautiful country."

"Yes."

"Reminds me of Ireland." He laughed and turned around, resting his back against the fence. "And yer lovely painting."

"Do you think so?"

"Aye, I do. Are ye happy here, Laurel?" His smile faded along with his gaze. He played with a button on his coat, seeming afraid to hear my answer.

"It's...I do love it here...but—"

"So ye plan to stay?"

"Only until Gramma is better. Then I'll return to Philadelphia."

"And look for a place to stay at a boardinghouse? Or with Mrs. Murphy?"

"I'll decide on that later."

Earlier, down by the creek, he'd spoken of marriage, but hadn't officially asked me. If I were honest with myself, that's what I'd been angry about earlier. I'd always been so sure I didn't want to marry, determined to make it on my own. But when he held my hand and almost kissed me, the idea of love and marriage consumed my heart. Suddenly, a romantic proposal, down on one knee with a bouquet of lavender and a promise ring for my finger, filled my imagination. How silly. But then the fear of losing my dreams had confused me even more. Watching Helen's family come together in a tragedy, and Charles there to comfort her, made me realize *that* was that kind of love I wanted. Cillian had shown me that kind of love a few minutes ago.

I wrapped my coat around myself and looked out across the field at the chestnut horse, daughter of Ruby, nibbling at the frosty grass.

"I should sketch this scene, from this vista. It would make a lovely painting."

"Can ye turn it into wallpaper?"

"Horses? On wallpaper?" I whipped around to see if he'd been joking, but found him looking across the meadow, seriously considering his suggestion.

"Who in the world would want such a thing? In what room?"

"Perhaps some wealthy sot's hunting lodge?"

"A hunting lodge?"

"Or a weekend home? Perhaps Mr. Vanderbilt would like to decorate one of his smoking rooms with wallpaper that looks just like this meadow. Better you add some leaves to the trees."

We stood side by side, elbows resting on the fence, glancing at the beautiful field with its rolling hills and windswept grasses.

"Maybe I'll hang it in the dining room, to always remember this lovely place." He turned toward me, keeping one arm perched on the rail while he took my hand in his. "I'd like ye to sit beside me in that dining room, Laurel. Live yer life with me."

Cillian's thumb drew circles on the back of my hand and he watched its movement closely, afraid to look at my reaction.

"I don't have much to offer ye right now, but I'll make

something of myself, that's for sure. With my machines and yer artwork, we can build something together."

"You won't mind my working?"

"I figure ye don't see it as work, but a calling. Ye could no more set aside yer art as I could my tinkering."

"But what about the cooking, cleaning, raising the babies?"

"Aye, the babies we'll do together. The rest we'll share."

My heart swelled to bursting. He was offering me a future. Not one of homebound drudgery, but opportunity and freedom. He'd stand by me and support me, and most importantly, be my partner in everything. All my earlier protests faded away.

His lips spread into a mischievous grin and he pressed a tender kiss to the palm of my hand. "After I make my first million, we'll hire a staff to run the house."

"You're that confident you'll be dining at the Vanderbilts' table?"

"No, maybe not, but I plan for them to dine at ours."

I fell into his arms to the sound of our laughter and he kissed my forehead. For a moment, I'd forgotten my grandmother inside the house, possibly taking her last breath.

"We should go back inside," I said, but Cillian wasn't finished.

"Aye, we should, but first you have to answer my question."

"What question was that?"

"The one about marrying me."

I stepped out of his arms and brushed imaginary lint from my sleeve. After straightening the collar of my coat, I gave him a dubious look. I couldn't resist the opportunity to make him ask properly. I'd only be asked once, and I wanted it to be memorable.

"I don't remember you officially asking."

"Ah, but I did, lass."

"No, I believe you told me what you wanted, but I don't believe you *asked*."

Cillian threw back his head and fisted his hands on his hips, muttering something under his breath. He rubbed the back of his hand over the crease between his brows as I fought to control my laughter.

"Mother Mary, give me strength." He shook his head and his crystal blue eyes locked with mine. "Laurel Rose Whitman..." With a wry grin and a twinkle in his eye, he dropped to one knee and gathered my left hand in his. "Would you do me the distinct honor of becoming my wife? Share yer life with me, raise a family, and grow old together?"

I covered my mouth with my hand and fought back a giggle. I'd suddenly grown nervous. I'd never dreamed how exhilarating it would be to hear those words. I loved him, and he was asking me to marry him.

Cillian tossed my hand away.

"Och, I've had enough of yer laughing at me, ye brat."

"Don't be mad."

"Down on me knee..." He stood up and brushed the grass from his trousers. "...acting the fool."

"No, Cillian, you're not a fool. I'm laughing because—"

"Because I look like a fool. Admit it."

"No, really. I'm thrilled." I grabbed his hands before he could walk away and tugged him close, gathering them against my heart. I had to make him understand. "Yes. Yes, I'll marry you."

"I'm not sure I want to marry ye after all, ye squirrelly lass."

"Please, Cillian. I promise I only laughed because, well..." I tapped kisses across his knuckles and he finally softened. "I never thought of the two of us getting married, never thought of marrying at all. But after what you said by the creek and how kind you were earlier, holding me while I cried, I realized how dear you are to me. You respect my desire to have a career and are willing to be my partner in all aspects of our lives."

"Aye, and I meant it."

"So, if you'll still have me, it would bring me the greatest pleasure to become your wife."

As if on cue, the mockingbirds sitting in the leafless oak tree began singing a tune as Cillian wrapped his arms around me and kissed my lips. My heart fluttered and my knees grew weak, and suddenly I knew I'd made the right decision. I'd been held in Garin's strong arms after the church social and had felt nothing. I'd been nearly raped in a filthy travelers' inn and thought I'd never want another man to touch me. But now, as Cillian deepened his kiss, all my fears washed away, replaced by desire for my friend, who would soon become my husband.

CHAPTER 39

Tiny snowflakes dotted my cheeks, mixing with the tears I couldn't hold back. Wind whipped my coat, lifting it like an umbrella as I stood with Helen's and Robert's families alongside the pine casket. Gramma died the morning after she fell, slipping into a coma around midnight. She never uttered another word. Though I was incredibly sad our time together had been so short, I was thankful for the stories she had shared with me. I'd accomplished what I had set out to do—discover the grandmother from whom I had inherited so many traits.

Mother stood alongside me, holding my right hand, while Cillian stood on my left, holding the other. Last evening, my mother and I had sat alone in the parlor after everyone else had gone to bed and talked like never before. She told me about her love of poetry, and how she had three books full of prose she had written over the years. Most of them were written for my father. "Despite his awful temper and brutish ways, I truly love him, Laurel. He's not perfect, but he's been a good provider and most of the time a good husband to me."

I didn't argue with her or attempt to dissuade her feelings, choosing instead to hug my mother as a few errant tears escaped her eyes.

"Tomorrow after the funeral, I'm going back to Philadelphia. I've been away from the other children too long."

"What about Father?" I asked, running my fingertips over her damp cheeks.

"He left a note for me before he returned to Philadelphia. He hoped you'd change your mind and come home."

"I'm going back to Philadelphia next week, but I won't be returning home."

"Laurel, I don't feel good about you living in a boardinghouse. It's not right for a young girl your age. Not proper."

"I won't be staying in a boardinghouse. I'm moving in with Mrs. Murphy, Cillian's neighbor. She just had a baby and would like some help in exchange for free room and board."

"Cillian's neighbor?"

"Yes, and in the summer, once I've finished school and the art show, I'll find a job as a designer."

"Then will you move to the boardinghouse?"

"Perhaps. Or maybe by then, Cillian and I will be married."

"Married?" The surprise threw Mother against the sofa cushions. Her hand fluttered at her throat.

"He asked me the other day, after Gramma's fall."

"Why, he hasn't even asked for your father's blessing."

"Mother, please don't pretend that things are somehow different than they truly are. Father is no more interested in my happiness than that lamp."

"That's not true, Laurel."

"Besides, it's rather old-fashioned, don't you think?"

"No, I don't."

"Well, I do. I'm a grown woman, an adult, and my decision to marry Cillian is mine alone, not yours or Father's."

Mother's mouth flapped open, ready to spew out an

argument, but she seemed to think better of it. She twisted her hands in her lap and offered a tentative smile.

"Well, I guess I have a lot to learn about this new generation of young women, so strong and independent. You're right. Ultimately, it is your decision whether or not to marry. Cillian seems like a fine young man, hardworking and ambitious, even if he is Irish."

"Yes, he's Irish, but that doesn't matter to me, and it shouldn't matter to you."

"We've never had an Irishman in our family."

"There's a first time for everything."

GRAMMA WAS BURIED BESIDE JOHN HAYWARD ON THE BACK HILL. During the funeral service, I glanced at my mother, her face set like stone while she stared at the minister. She had said last night she liked Gramma and felt no ill will toward her. I wished Father could say the same.

When I turned to look at Cillian, I caught him watching me with a tender smile on his lips. He squeezed my hand, reassuring me he'd be by my side through all of life's ups and downs. We all bowed our heads for a final prayer of blessing on Gramma's soul and muttered our amens before we were excused. Cillian stood between Mother and me, offering an elbow to each of us. We walked solemnly toward the house.

My feet stumbled when I found Garin waiting at the bottom of the hill with the Moffitt twins standing beside him.

"What is it, lass?" Cillian stopped and glanced at me with concern. Mother continued down the hill toward the back of the house.

"I, um, there's someone I need to speak with." I turned and smiled at Cillian, patting his arm before pulling my hand away. He looked toward Garin and the twins and gave me a questioning gaze.

"Go on down to the house," I said. "I'll be right there."

"Are ye sure?"

"Yes. I won't be long."

Cillian slapped his hat back on his head and followed the others toward the back porch. Once he was through the door, I walked toward our guests, noticing Garin's expression was one of anger mixed with confusion.

"Hello, Garin, Samuel, Solomon. Thank you for coming to the funeral."

"Our condolences, Miss," Samuel or Solomon said with a tip of his chin.

"Who was that?" Garin got right to the heart of the matter, ignoring social graces and words of sympathy. "Is that the fellow you mentioned to me?"

"Cillian? Yes, he came a couple of days ago."

"You said he was just a friend."

"Well, yes, but—"

"Now, now, Garin. You promised to keep your anger in check," one of the twins said as he laid his hand on Garin's shoulder.

Garin tugged out of the twin's grip. "I'd say he's more than a friend."

"As a matter of fact—"

Garin took a long step toward me, closing the wide gap between us, and scowled down at me. "You let me make a fool of myself over you."

"I did no such thing." I crossed my arms and raised my chin, showing him he couldn't frighten me with his height and angry countenance.

"Schmidt, take it easy," one of the twins warned.

"I took you to the social, introduced you to everyone, and you let me."

"So? That's what you do when you bring a guest to an outing."

"Let me think you cared."

"Oh, no. Wait one minute." I pressed my palm to his chest, giving him a shove. Samuel or Solomon steadied him. "I did no such thing."

"Everything all right out here, lass?" Cillian stood on the top step of the porch, directing the question at me while his eyes bore into Garin.

"It's fine, Cillian. Garin was just leaving."

"I have no such intention," Garin said, narrowing his eyes. "It's not for you to decide."

"Let's go." Together, the twins attempted to pull Garin away, but he wouldn't be deterred. "Only your Uncle Charles can ask me to leave."

"I believe she just did." Cillian slowly descended the stairs and walked toward us. The last thing we needed was a fight. Cillian might be high spirited, but Garin was much taller and had at least thirty pounds more of bulk—and who knew if the twins would jump in to defend their friend.

"Just because I'm a woman doesn't mean I can't tell you to leave." I'd survived a brute in a tavern, hate-filled words from my father, and a long, arduous trip here mostly on my own. I wasn't about to allow a rude, arrogant young man tell me what I could and could not do. I wrapped my hands around the wooden rod used to hold up the sagging clothesline and held it in front of me like a spear. "Don't make me use this, Garin."

"I wouldn't test her, lad." Cillian stood beside me and I caught his wry grin through my periphery.

"Listen to her, man." Once again, the twins tried to haul him away.

"Crazy." Garin seethed as he fisted his hands at his side. "You're crazy, you know that?"

"Maybe I am."

Garin threw up his hands in frustration and turned on his heel. "Good luck to you." He tossed the comment over his shoulder to Cillian as he stomped across the yard with the twins in tow.

As soon as he rounded the house and out of our view, Cillian and I burst into a fit of laughter. I dropped the pole on the ground and fell into his outstretched arms.

"Remind me to always heed yer commands, lass. I wouldn't want to be on the wrong side of yer temper."

"Oh, I'll be sure to remind you." I hugged him close, savoring his strong arms wrapped tightly around me. "Thank you for letting me deal with Garin."

"Ye had the situation quite in hand. Y'are a strong woman."

"But that doesn't mean I don't need you, in other ways."

"'Tis good to know."

FRIENDS AND NEIGHBORS HAD LAID OUT A SPREAD OF FOOD IN THE kitchen and we all ate quietly, occasionally recalling a precious memory of Gramma. After the meal, Charles rigged up the wagon, offering a ride to the train station for Mother and Cillian, who would return to Philadelphia together. Though I was afraid it would be awkward with the two of them traveling as companions, Cillian assured me he looked forward to getting to know my mother better. It was an honor for him to deliver her safely back home.

Cillian and I stood at the back of Charles' wagon, saying our goodbyes.

"I'm sorry I'm hurrying off so soon after the funeral, lass."

"It's fine. You can't keep Mr. Schumer waiting much longer. He needs another rotating ramp for his shipping business."

"I'll meet ye at the station next Friday at three o'clock."

"I plan to be there."

"If y'are not, I'll come here and drag ye back to the city if need be."

"You won't have to. Don't worry."

Cillian glanced over each shoulder, making sure no one was watching before he kissed me briefly on the lips. A sweet quiver ran through my veins and suddenly I wished I was climbing on the wagon with him.

"Be well, my dear. I'll see ye next week." He tapped a quick kiss against my mouth again and scrambled into the back of the wagon as Charles snapped the whip against the mule's rump. I stood in the cold breeze, waving at Cillian and Mother as their wagon rolled down the lane and disappeared onto the main road.

THE NEXT MORNING ARRIVED LIKE ANY OTHER. THE SUN PEEKED between the blinds, Cora's elbow poked into my ribs, and Belle's leg draped across mine. I was trapped under the layers of quilts between the two little girls, smelling of lavender from last night's bath. In a few days, I would be on my way back to Philadelphia, and my heart ached at the thought of leaving them behind. I had grown fond of the whole family and couldn't imagine my life without them. But school, my career, and most especially Cillian were waiting for me back home. I had to return.

Once I wiggled out from under the covers without disturbing the sleeping cherubs, I found Helen waiting for me at the bottom of the stairs.

"I've found something you need to read," she said, not even giving me a chance to say good morning.

She grabbed my hand and dragged me past the kitchen table into Gramma's room. My heart leapt to my throat when I saw the empty bed, stripped bare to the mattress. Bending over in Gramma's closet, Helen emerged with a pile of books—her journals—and handed me the one on top. I took the leather-bound book, which seemed to buzz with life. It felt traitorous holding Gramma's journal, but she was gone and I couldn't help but wonder if she had purposely left them to us. Inside, we were sure to find the rest of the story she hadn't been able to relay.

"Of course, you're welcome to read all of them, but you should start with this one. I think you'll find some of the answers we've both been looking for."

Helen laid the pile of books on Gramma's bed and left the room, returning briefly to set a cup of coffee on the bedside table. The leather creaked as I pulled open the journal.

May 10, 1865

Today is our wedding anniversary. John and I would have been married twelve years. How sad to think of the time we lost. It's been five years since he's been gone and I still miss him each day.

While cleaning out my bureau drawers this morning, I found the document announcing John's prison release. It brought back memories of the few days I had with him before he died. He'd insisted he was guilty of the horse theft, but at the time I wouldn't believe it. The John I married would never have lied to me, but now I accept that perhaps he did. I'd kept him so high on a pedestal, I never considered he could fall from it. He was a sinner like the rest of us. He'd done something he shouldn't have, and he paid the ultimate price.

I struggle to find a way to make things right with Calvin. Perhaps I never will. He was so angry the day he came to speak with me about the farm. I know I hurt him and the other children when I told him they wouldn't inherit the property. Through his disappointment, his Whitman anger took over. Thank heavens Karl and Gunter came to my rescue and escorted him off the land. He said some hateful things I've yet to forgive. Maybe I'm incapable of forgiveness.For many years, I thought Norville had staged the horse stealing, and then I concluded Calvin had been the one to steal the horse and tie it to a tree in the woods. He'd hated John so, and I thought he'd done it to hurt the two of us. In my heart, I knew John wouldn't lie to me, but he did. It took me until recently to accept the truth.

I slammed the journal closed and squeezed the book between my hands. It wasn't Father's fault after all. No wonder he got so angry when he was here. He believed Gramma still blamed him. I tossed the book on the mattress, gathered the now empty mug in my hands, and went into the kitchen, where I found Helen looking through a box.

"What do you have there?" I asked as I refilled the mug.

"It's Mother's box of trinkets. I've found a hair ribbon I used to wear as a child and some baby shoes. I never realized how sentimental she was. Look, here's a locket."

Helen held up a rather long chain with an intricately scrolled locket on the end. She pried it open with her fingernail and held it up to the window.

"I believe this may be Mother and Father."

I joined her near the window and glanced at the portraits. The man's portrait was the same as the one that sat on Gramma's bureau and the woman could be none other than Gramma, but much younger.

"Look here, on the back. It's inscribed." Helen held it out for both of us to see. "From JH to MEH. May 10, 1853."

"He must have given it to her as a wedding gift."

"I've never seen this before." Helen engulfed the locket in her hand and held it to her breast.

"He loved her." I wrapped my arm around Helen's shoulder and pulled her to my side. "That you can be sure of."

"Yes." She swiped a tear from her cheek and dropped the locket in her dress pocket.

"What else is in the box?" I asked, leafing through the ribbons and jewelry Gramma had kept all those years. In the bottom of the box, I found an envelope with my name on it. "Helen, what's this?"

Helen took the envelope from my hand and studied it like a scientist. "It's not yellowed and old like the other papers in the box. It looks recent."

"There's only one way to find out."

I sat on the bench and slipped the crisp, creamy paper from its sleeve.

My dearest Laurel,

My time is short. With my recent illness, I figure my old body won't hold out much longer. I need to be sure I tell you everything —hence this letter. I'm sorry for the scribble. My hands are shaking and my eyesight is failing, so I know I won't have many more months.

Meeting you, spending time with you, coming to love you, dear granddaughter, has been one of my greatest joys. You are strong and wise and lovely. Continue to be so, but don't rely too heavily on your independence. It's a wonderful trait to have, but it can also keep you from experiencing great joy.

I should've married John the first time he asked me. For many years, I had to rely on my own strength and fortitude to get through each day. With little help from Gray, I raised three children and ran a successful farm. When John came along, I couldn't let go of my fierce pride. If only I had married him sooner. He gave me my precious Robert and Helen, stood by me through hard times, and protected me from public scorn. That scorn I brought on myself by being too stubborn to marry the greatest man I'd ever known. I often wonder how things would have turned out if we had married before Robert was born.

It's all written down in my journal, but suffice it to say, our lives would've been different if I'd followed my heart instead of my head. We wouldn't have been the subject of Norville's scorn or the neighbors' gossip. In turn, John might have won the horse at auction without any backlash. He may not have needed to beat Calvin if we had been married. The children wouldn't have had a reason to testify against him. I've blamed myself every day for not marrying John five years earlier.

You came to me to learn who you are, where you came from, and why your father treats you with such hatred. Now you know. He takes out my mistakes on you, punishes you for looking and acting like the mother who wronged him.

Anger is an unwelcome houseguest. It moves in to the private spaces of your heart, eats away at your soul, refusing to leave. Please don't mistake my words at your sudden and unexpected arrival. You've been the balm to the fury that had twisted my mind for so long. I'm an old woman who has finally faced up to her shortcomings.

Forgive your father, Laurel. Yes, he is cut from the same cloth as Gray Whitman, but he had some fine qualities until I made his life difficult by bringing on the embarrassment and ridicule. If only I had it to do over again.

Your father was so angry when he was here last night and rightly so. I wish I handled things better. I've written a letter to him, asking for his forgiveness. I've forgiven him for his part in John's prison sentence. In the letter, I told him I accepted the truth that John stole the horse and that he had testified because he had no other choice. It may be too late, but at least I can go to my grave with a clear conscience.

My greatest prayer is that you and your father reconcile your differences and he becomes the father I know he can be. Your short time here has brought me so much joy, and I wish only the best for your future.

With sincerest love,
Gramma

"She must have written this after Father left, before she fell." I handed the letter to Helen, who had patiently waited as I read it. "She said she wrote a letter to Father as well."

"Charles mailed it." Helen's eyes moved back and forth with

quick speed, absorbing the last words her mother had written. When she was finished, she dropped the letter on the table and dropped her head in her hands.

"So it's true. Daddy did steal the horse. I always thought he'd been framed. How different things would've been if they had only married right away."

"You can't be angry with your mother." I grabbed her wrists, forcing her to look at me. "She thought she was doing the right thing."

"Yet so much of this could have been avoided."

"Helen..."

"Don't worry. I'm not angry with Mother. How could I be? She raised Robert and me to be good people, and she looked out for our welfare by selling the farm to the two of us at a very reasonable price. She did that so there would be no chance it could be split between the five us—if her older children had contested her will."

"At least you know her marriage to your father—their relationship—was based on love."

"I've always known that." Helen refolded the letter, slipped it inside the envelope, and slid it across the table to me. "She would want you to marry Cillian and have a happy life with him."

I held the letter to my chest and smiled at Helen. "I plan on it."

CHAPTER 40

The train puffed great clouds of black smoke into the air as it chugged slowly past factories and warehouses where men were piling boxes into the backs of wagons. I shivered in sympathy with their hard work in the cold, December wind. The ground was blanketed with gray, dirty snow and the trees were barren of their leaves. No matter how bleak it appeared outside, my limbs were tingling with the anticipation of seeing Cillian waiting for me on the station platform. As promised, I had said my goodbyes to Helen and her family on Friday and boarded the eleven o'clock locomotive in North East.

It had been hard leaving Belle and Cora behind. They clung to my legs and sobbed into my skirt. Charles had to peel them away from me before I could climb onto the buckboard. Helen kept her tears at bay, but they teetered on her red rims, ready to fall.

"I'll come for a visit in the summer, after graduation," I said as I gave Helen a fierce hug.

"That would be nice."

"Maybe you and Charles and the girls could come to the art show."

"We've never been to the city."

"Then you must." With a final hug, I climbed to the bench and Charles snapped the whip against the mule's back. I turned and waved both my arms until my view of Helen and the girls disappeared behind a knoll. Though I'd only known my aunt—now my dear friend—for a little over a month, my heart ripped as if it had been a lifetime.

THE TRAIN PULLED INTO THE STATION AND STOPPED WITH A whoosh of steam beside the platform. I peered out the window, hoping to catch a glimpse of Cillian, but saw only a swarm of dark hats and coats huddled against the cold. Somewhere in the crowd, he was waiting.

Tucking my carpetbag against my midriff, I extended my hand to the porter, who assisted me down the metal steps. The winter breeze funneling through the parked trains nearly blew my bonnet from my head. I walked toward the staircase which led inside to the station, looking left and right for Cillian. He had said he would wait for me on the platform, so I leaned against a pillar out of the way of the people heading toward the station above. Somewhere in the mix would be Cillian, anxiously looking for me.

Five minutes later, after most of the crowd had dispersed, I still stood with my back against the pole. There was no sign of Cillian. Perhaps I had misunderstood and he was waiting for me in the station. I walked behind an elderly man who relied on his cane and a young man to lead him toward the staircase. Too jittery to move at such a snail's pace, I passed the two men and rushed up the steps. When I threw open the door, my lungs seized up.

Father.

My gaze darted around the station, hoping I'd see Cillian hurrying toward me, but he was nowhere to be found. The door slammed behind me, smacking my backside, and I stumbled forward. I squared my shoulders, released my breath, and approached Father with my chin held high.

"Father, what are you doing here?"

"I've come to collect you from the train station."

He was wearing his policeman's uniform with his cap tucked under his arm.

"Why? Where's Cillian? He was supposed to meet me."

"I told him not to bother."

"What did you do?" Frantic, I dropped my bag and rushed to Father, gripping his lapels in my fists. "Where is he? What did you—"

"Settle down now." He removed my hands from their iron grip and brushed at his coat until it was back in order. "I haven't done anything. I only asked him if he'd mind my meeting you instead."

"You...you what?" Something wasn't right about all this. Father's demeanor was calm and pleasant. He spoke to me as if he had forgotten our history, as if he'd never called me a slut or pushed me out into the cold. What game was he playing?

"Yes, when he stopped by the house the other night, I offered to pick you up so he wouldn't have to end his shift early to get you."

"What are you up to, Father? Cillian wouldn't stop by the house."

"He would if he was invited to do so."

"I don't believe you. What have you done with him? Is he in jail?"

Father threw back his head with a hearty laugh and took my carpetbag from where I'd dropped it beside me. "Come along, Laurel. We have a lot to talk about."

Father guided me to the waiting streetcar outside the

station, and I sat beside him on the bench for the long ride home as questions swirled through my mind. It wasn't like Father to be so jovial with me. I didn't believe I had ever heard him laugh at anything I said. His kindness in helping me to the streetcar was rather suspicious.

We rode in silence until we hopped off the car. He carried my carpetbag and held my arm as we walked toward home, and climbed our marble steps. I pulled free from his grasp and looked at the green door, frightened that if I walked through it, the old Father I knew so well would reemerge.

"Come inside. You'll catch your death."

When I stepped into the foyer, I was hit with the familiar smell of wood smoke, meat roasting, and lingering pipe tobacco. I was home. Tears stung my eyes when Emily called to me.

"Laurel?" She rushed down the stairs, sounding like a herd of wild buffalo, and gathered me in her arms. "You're back. Oh, how I've missed you." She kissed my cheek with a loud smack and held me at arm's length. "I want to hear everything."

"And I can't wait to tell you everything."

"Well, you will—wait, that is." Father separated the two of us and guided Emily toward the stairs. "Run along for a bit, Emily."

"But Father, I haven't seen Laurel forever and I want to talk to her."

"Later."

Father dismissed her with a wave of his hand and led me toward the sofa. Something was going on and my nerves tingled with fear. It was unlike Father to shoo Emily away.

"What is going on, Father? I demand you to tell me right this minute."

"As soon as your mother joins us." He walked into the dining room and shouted "Susan?" through the kitchen door.

Mother came, drying her hands on her apron. "Join us in the living room, please."

Once we were all settled—me on the sofa and Father and Mother sitting in armchairs, smiling broadly at me—Father began.

"I owe you an apology, Laurel."

"An apology?"

"For the way I acted the night you left."

"You mean the night you tossed me out the door."

"Yes...That was harsh of me, and I'm sorry."

"What about all the other times?" I didn't think the way I'd been treated my whole life could be forgotten with a simple apology.

"Now, Laurel. Give your father a chance to explain."

I folded my arms across my chest and leaned against the back of the sofa.

"I stopped over at Robert's place before I came back to Philadelphia. We had a long talk. There are some things you should know that I doubt my mother shared with you."

"Such as?"

"The real reason she cut Sarah, Jeremy, and me from her will. Of course, in the end it didn't matter because she split the farm in two and sold each half to Robert and Helen."

"She cut the three of you out because of your false testimony against John."

"John would've received far more years in jail for the shovel incident if I hadn't. The sheriff dropped the charges in exchange for our testimony."

"I can't listen to this." I marched toward the stairs but Father stepped in front of me.

"You must. John wasn't the prince she made him out to be."

"What do you mean?"

"He came to America to get away from a jail sentence hanging over his head. A fugitive from justice."

"How does Robert know this?"

"John told him. He sent a letter to Robert from prison."

"Let me see it."

I doubted there was such a letter and prepared to lay down my righteous indignation in a surge of angry words, but Father pulled a yellowed square from his pocket and handed it to me. I handled the paper gently, as if it were alive, and went back to the sofa, where I sat close to the lamp. The paper crackled as I slowly unfolded it.

"Robert said the letter was delivered to him by a fellow prisoner about three years after John had died. He asked that it not be given to Robert until after his death."

As soon as I glanced at the paper, I knew it was John's handwriting. The distinctive curls and loops could only have come from his hand.

January 3, 1858

Dear Robert, my son,

I asked Ebenezer to deliver this letter to you after my death, but not until you turned eighteenth. Then you would be old enough to understand.

I'm sorry for what I put you and your sister and your mother through these past years. The humiliation and embarrassment you endured by being the son of a convicted horse thief burns my soul. I would've given anything to spare you the trouble. But the truth of the matter is I deserved it.

That evening, when the sheriff came to question me about Norville's missing horse, I was sure he'd never be able to pin the crime on me. I'd done a good job of hiding the horse. My plan was to give it to a local farmer, someone who could never afford such a fine animal. It turned out to be an unwise course of action. Wasn't I shocked when it was tied to a tree four days later? I was never able to confirm it, but I believe Norville was the one who did it. He found my hiding place and moved the horse so the sheriff would be sure to arrest me. I lied to your mother, telling her I had returned the horse. I just couldn't let that scoundrel get away with his stunt. Wealthy, arrogant men like Norville Whitman shouldn't be allowed to trample over people like me.

Over the years, I've thought about telling your mother the truth, but I couldn't imagine breaking her heart in that way. She had a terrible life with her first husband and had all but lost trust in any man. Until the horse incident, I believe I had earned her trust and her love, which is something I never had before.

I grew up in a poor family, working from a young age on the estate of an earl, feeding and watering his horses. My father was a coal miner like most men in my village of Bury, and I swore I'd never work in the mines. I had hoped to become a groom on the estate, but was caught stealing coins from a wealthy merchant. I had done it to help feed our family, who were all but starving the winter after my father died, but the constable didn't have a shred of sympathy. It was a banner day when I saw Thaddeus Edwards' advertisement for a farmhand in Maryland. I corresponded with him while I awaited trial and hopped the first ship leaving England when I got the job.

Stealing the coins and the horse may have been done for good reasons, but they were crimes all the same. I'm telling you all this because I believe you inherited the sharp mind and good soul of your mother, and I urge you to never do anything dishonest or illegal. Whether you feel your actions are justified or not, it's not worth the pain and suffering you would put your family through. If anyone should treat you unfairly because of me, proudly renounce my name and prove to them you are nothing like me. Be your own man and don't let your father's history control your destiny.

I'd rather you not share this letter with your mother. Let her believe I acted honorably. I ask this because your mother is the dearest, finest woman I've ever known. She's had a rough life and I wouldn't want her to suffer any more than she already has. She *gave me a family when I was lonely and far from home. I cared for Calvin, Jeremy, and Sarah like they were my own children. Their testimony in court was all true. Find a way to help your mother to forgive them. My only regret is that Calvin hated me so. He, too, had suffered humiliation when his mother and I lived out of wedlock. That was too much for a young man to endure.*

The light is growing dim and my hand is stiff from the cold. Take care of your mother and sister. I'm sorry for the misery I've caused you, but hope you won't follow in my footsteps. Live a good life, proud that you're the son of Margaret Edwards Hayward.

All my love,

John Hayward, your father

With tender care, I refolded the letter and handed it back to Father. I was stunned beyond words.

"Well?" Father said, perched on the edge of his chair.

"He told Gramma the truth on his deathbed. He stole the horse and never returned it like he first told her."

"Mother told me in her letter. She was furious with all of us for testifying what we saw that day."

"He lied to her." I shook my head, bewildered and confused. Gramma had loved John and had such faith in him. "It was hard for her to accept he'd committed a crime."

"My mother never forgave any of us for our testimony in court—not until her recent letter."

"And what about you, Father? Have you forgiven her for how she treated you?"

Father shook his head and blew out a heavy breath. Once again I made to rise, to leave the room and the hateful tirade I knew was coming, but Father's words stopped me. "I have."

I sat back down heavily, shocked to see Father leaning his elbows on his knees with his head hung low.

"You heard what John said in the letter. It was hard on me— them not being married and all those years waiting for his trial.

You have no idea the comments and looks I received. The other children teased me at school when I was young. That's why I quit early. My mother didn't seem the least bit concerned that people were talking about them. It was awful."

"I'm sorry you went through that."

"Regardless, I shouldn't have taken it out on John, or Robert and Helen. The truth is, John was good to me, but between all the gossip and Norville poisoning my mind against him, I was full of rage I couldn't seem to control."

I was at a loss for words. My father, the man who had ranted and ridiculed me, always right and so stubborn, was sharing a hurt that still pained him. He had confessed he was human and had made a mistake. What could I say?

"The worst part is, all these years, I've taken it out on you, Laurel." He stood up and crossed the room to me. He wrapped his big hands around my shoulders and looked deep into my eyes. "I've been angry at my mother and I've punished you for it."

"Father, I—"

"I know it will take a while for you to forgive me, but I hope someday you will."

A loud knocking at the door saved me from thinking of the right words to say.

"That will be Cillian," Father said, giving my shoulders a squeeze. "Why don't you let him in? Invite him to supper?"

Another jolt rolled through me and I was paralyzed by it. I couldn't comprehend this new and improved Father. Not only had he apologized and opened up to me about his childhood, but he was inviting my fiancé—my *Irish* fiancé—to dinner. Would wonders ever cease?

CHAPTER 41

"Isn't this exciting, Cillian? Look at all the magnificent paintings and etchings."

"None as magnificent as *Nature's Awakening* by the fine young artist, Miss Laurel Rose Whitman." Cillian tapped a discrete kiss to my brow, causing my cheeks to grown warm. "Soon to be O'Brien," he whispered.

Heat flared in my chest and I was thankful only my face flamed red with joy while my neck and bosom were hidden behind the lace-adorned neckline of my new frock.

"You're too kind, sir." Curling my lips into a smile and tilting my chin proudly, I looped my arm through Cillian's and led him into the fine arts salon, where several of my classmates' works were on display. The room was crowded with patrons of the arts, wealthy men and their richly dressed wives, admiring the works of future teachers, illustrators, and designers. My own work would have been placed in this room if it weren't for Mr. Ferretti. Where in the world might he be? I'd expected to find him inside the gallery when I arrived.

"I haven't seen Mr. Ferretti this evening. Have you?"

"No, but he's sure to be here. He wouldn't miss this esteemed event, eh?"

"Surely not." As if summoned, Mr. Ferretti appeared, shoving and elbowing his way through the throng toward us.

"There you are, my dear." He pulled my arm from Cillian's and tugged me behind him, causing me to trip over my own feet. "You must hurry. Mr. Thomas Eakins himself has arrived and he's asking about the artist who created the pre-eminent work inside the gallery."

"Thomas Eakins?" My hand flew to my head for fear I'd lose the new bonnet Mother had sewn to match my dress. It wouldn't do at all for it to fall to the floor and be trampled by the masses. "But Mr. Ferretti, what should I say?"

He answered me over his shoulder as he dragged me through the crowd. "Simply agree with everything he says or suggests."

"But I—"

"Come along, Laurel. There's no time to waste."

Reaching the hallway that separated the four exhibit rooms, Mr. Ferretti pulled me around the corner and placed me directly in front of my painting. Keeping a hand on my shoulder—perhaps he feared I'd run away—he leaned toward a man of slight build with dark hair and a short beard. "Mr. Eakins, may I present Miss Laurel Whitman? She's my student who created this fine work of art."

Mr. Eakins turned and held out his hand to me, giving me a rather limp shake. "Miss Whitman, is it? I must say this is quite a fine piece of work for such a young artist."

"Thank you, Mr. Eakins." His palm was cold and damp as he continued to hold fast to my hand.

"If I didn't know better, I'd say you've been moonlighting classes at the Academy of the Fine Arts."

He was making me rather uncomfortable with his clammy

hand still claiming mine. If only I could retrieve my hand from his clutches without appearing rude.

"Please tell me you plan to continue your studies. Have you considered going to Paris?"

"No, sir."

"I highly recommend it. In fact, several female painters have pursued their art in Paris. You'd feel right at home."

"That's very kind of you, sir, but my pursuits are more of the industrial nature."

He dropped my hand—thank heavens—seeming put out by my career plans.

"I've been preparing for work as a textile designer, creating wallpaper, carpets, and such."

"I know what a textile designer does." He turned his gaze back to my triptych, perched his hand on his hip in a rather feminine manner, and blew out a deep breath. "Such a pity."

No longer interested in my pursuits, Mr. Eakins walked away in the direction of the fine arts room.

"I suppose I know where I stand," I said, turning to find Mr. Ferretti scurrying across the room to a plainly dressed man who had entered the gallery. I seemed to have a most uncanny way of making men run from me.

"Laurel, dear." My mother's voice drew my attention away from Mr. Ferretti's animated conversation. She was pushing through the people with Sampson, Emily, and Elvin following behind. My heart sank when Father didn't bring up the rear.

"Hello, Mother." I gave her a brief hug and turned to my siblings, who were lined up like birds on a branch, staring open-mouthed at my painting. "So, what do you think?"

"It's even better than I remember," Sampson said with awe in his voice.

"I love it, Laurel." Emily leapt into my arms and squeezed until I could no longer breathe. "I wish I had an ounce of your talent."

"You have other talents." She rolled her eyes, doubting my words. "It's true. Your embroidery and sewing skills are most impressive."

"Thank you." She blushed as a smile grew on her lips.

"I think Father will be quite amazed," Elvin said.

"Where is Father?" I held my breath for fear my mother would say he'd refused to come. Our relationship had improved vastly since my return, but I knew deep in his soul he thought my art studies had been a waste of time.

"He was paying the driver. He'll be along."

"A driver?"

"He wanted us to arrive in style." Mother giggled and pinched my ribs. She'd been so jovial of late, a most welcome sight. "There he is."

I glanced over her shoulder to find Father scowling as he pressed between the people clustered at the entryway. He seemed to have lost patience with those too wrapped up in conversation to move into the gallery. With a final push, he threaded between some gentlemen and brushed his lapel as if his coat had been soiled.

"I haven't seen such a ruckus since the centennial celebration," he grumbled. "Lucky I found the lot of you."

"Hello, Father."

"Laurel. Well?" His bushy brows arched and his lips pursed. "Where is it? Show me this masterpiece I've heard so much about."

"It's right there, dear." Mother stood behind Father, placed her hands on his shoulders, and turned him toward my painting.

Silently, he stared at the triptych. His brows remained arched, but his eyes grew wide with fascination. He took a step forward and his gaze trailed from left to right and back again, taking in each detail of the scene.

"Well?" My insides quivered as I stood beside him, waiting for his verdict. "What do you think?"

"I, um..." Father cleared his throat and turned to me. His eyes glistened with emotion. "I don't know much about art, Laurel."

"That's fine. You don't have to know anything about art. It's more the feeling it evokes."

"I'm not sure what I feel." He glanced back at the painting and rubbed his fingers over his forehead. "It reminds me of home, back in Zion." He stepped a little closer, seeming to concentrate on the barn. "We didn't have a peach orchard or sheep, but this barn." He reached out but stopped before touching the painting. "Quite amazing." Finally tearing his gaze from the canvases, he turned back to me. "You painted this before you went to Zion?"

"Yes. It was nearly finished when I left."

"Well, its likeness is quite remarkable."

Father said no more, simply gazed at the picture with myriad emotions playing on his face. Emily slipped her arm through his with Mother on his other side and my brothers standing nearby. My whole family stared in wonder. It was the greatest compliment I could have received.

THE ART EXHIBITION WAS COMING TO A CLOSE, WITH FEWER AND fewer people filling the hall. Cillian had a grand time talking with the artists and wealthy patrons, making sure to mention his fiancée had created the featured piece. He also took the opportunity to promote his rotating ramp, telling several men he was seeking investors in his burgeoning company. After seeing my family off, I found him speaking to three men all dressed in the finest wool coats with velvet lapels, discussing the various uses for his ramp.

"This machine will make work more efficient in every

industry. For example, Mr. Hires, perhaps a smaller, tabletop version of the machine would help in yer pharmacy or with the production of yer new root beer. I've heard the elixir was well received at the centennial exposition."

"Yes, quite," Mr. Hires said, scratching his chin in thought.

"Or ye, Mr. Reynolds, can ye imagine using my ramp to lift yer radiators and ranges? Those buggers are a might bit heavy for a man to carry."

"It is a problem." Mr. Reynolds glanced at the other gentlemen around him, who nodded in silent agreement.

I hated to interrupt, but the hall would soon be closing and I promised Father I wouldn't arrive home too late.

"Cillian?"

He turned toward me with a broad smile, melting my heart. Each day, I grew fonder of him, surprising myself at the depth of my feelings.

"Laurel, there ye be. May I introduce ye to these fine gentlemen?"

After brief introductions, the gentlemen left us, each asking to meet with Cillian soon about his invention.

"It seems you've had quite a successful evening."

"'Tis true. And what about ye? I've heard I'm not the only one who made the most of this evening."

"What do you mean?"

"Mr. Ferretti came buzzing by and said the First National Bank purchased yer painting. They plan to hang it in the lobby of their office there on Chestnut Street."

"No! You can't mean it." Bouncing on my toes, I gripped Cillian's arms for fear I'd topple over with joy. Could this night get any better?

"Aye, I do, lass. That's what he told me. I thought ye knew. I should've come looking for ye."

"That's fine. I was busy talking to so many people." My

hand fluttered to my bosom, overcome with joy. "Oh, Cillian, I'm thrilled."

"Ye should be, dearie. Yer painting is a marvel."

I didn't care what it looked like, whether or not it was proper. I threw myself into Cillian's arms and kissed him soundly. This surely would be one of the happiest days of my life. My family had attended the show and was quite pleased with my work, Cillian had made several contacts with the city's business moguls, and I'd sold my painting to a respectable establishment. How could it get any better?

"My dear, Miss Whitman." Mr. Ferretti rushed toward me, out of breath, perspiration glistening his brow. "I've been searching for you everywhere."

"Mr. Ferretti, Cillian just told me the good news."

"How did he know?" Mr. Ferretti's confusion led to my own.

"About my painting being sold to the bank," I said, restating the good news to which he surely was referring.

"Oh that, yes, I'm quite pleased. But no, my dear." He gripped my arm, giving it a shake. "Mr. McFadden wanted to meet you. He was quite taken with your painting. After I told him about your aspirations to be a designer, he was anxious to make your acquaintance."

My heart leapt to my throat. Elias McFadden had one of the largest textile mills in the city. "Where is he now? I'll be happy to speak with him."

"Unfortunately, he left, but he gave me his card to pass on to you and asked that you contact him at your earliest convenience. He's most interested in seeing your portfolio."

"Oh, Mr. Ferretti." I'd lost all sense of propriety and jumped into his arms, hugging him fearlessly around the neck. He laughed along with me and hugged me tight before setting me back on my feet.

"Now, listen to me, Laurel, dear. You must not dawdle. Go home, get a good night's sleep, and call on Mr. McFadden in the morning. He has quite a large operation and is keen to hire you on."

"I will, Mr. Ferretti." I grabbed Cillian by the hand. "Thank you, Mr. Ferretti." I dragged my fiancé out of the hall and onto the brick sidewalk, where we fell into each other's arms in a fit of laughter. We didn't care that we were attracting attention. This had been the greatest night, beyond our wildest dreams.

Pulling ourselves together, Cillian gripped my shoulders and bent down to meet my gaze. "Do ye see that, lass? Can ye imagine it? We're on our way. What a future we'll have."

"Yes, Cillian, dear. What a future we will have."

EPILOGUE

"My goodness, Laurel, would you stop fidgeting?"

"Mother, you've been fiddling with my hair long enough. It's fine."

"But this is your wedding day, dear."

I pivoted around on the vanity bench to face Mother, who stood behind me. Layers of satin swirled around my legs and I felt confined under their weight. I smiled up at her as she held a long hat pin in her quivering hand.

"I look fine, Mother. You've done a very nice job on my hair, and the placement of my bonnet is perfect."

"Let me secure your bonnet with this pin, dear, and we'll be all finished. It's rather breezy outside."

When I spun back around to face the mirror, I found a picture of the ideal bride. All Mother's fuss was worth it. I looked lovely, I had to admit. Today I would marry Cillian in a small ceremony at the Episcopal church, followed by cake and punch in the church hall. Together, Mother and Emily had sewn a lovely gown of burgundy taffeta with ivory lace and a hefty bustle—the latest fashion—creating a most fetching bridal gown.

Cillian planned to wear tails and top hat, which had been given to him by Mr. Schumer. The efficiency of the rotating ramp had brought so much more business to the shipyard that Mr. Schumer insisted on giving him the suit as a wedding gift, along with a hundred dollars to spend on a honeymoon. We were taking the train to New York City, where we would spend two nights at the Windsor Hotel and attend a performance at the Metropolitan Opera House. It was all rather glamorous, much more than I could have imagined. I assured Cillian I would have been satisfied with a trip to Atlantic City like most newly married couples, but he wanted us to honeymoon in style.

"Someday we'll be hobnobbing with the likes of the Vanderbilts, so we might as well get used to it now, eh?"

I had laughed at his silly notion and agreed to go along. I'd never been to New York and had heard it was quite impressive. Who was I to pass up an opportunity to hobnob with the Vanderbilts?

When we returned from our honeymoon, we would settle into the lovely apartment we'd found on Second Street, not far from the factory space Cillian had secured to manufacture his ramps. I planned to work from home, designing carpets for Mr. McFadden's textile mill, as well as teaching a class at the design school.

Satisfied all my preparations were complete, I stood up and brushed the wrinkles from my satin skirting. Adjusting the waistband, I startled when Emily stormed into the room.

"I saw Cillian and Mr. Schumer walking into the church." Emily skidded to a stop as her mouth dropped open. "Laurel, oh my. Aren't you lovely?"

"Thanks to your beautifully designed dress and bonnet."

"They are quite nice, aren't they?" Emily rearranged the netting on the bonnet so it highlighted my eyes. "Turn around. Let me look at you."

I giggled, feeling flushed, as Emily slowly took a loop around me, studying the beautiful gown she had created, but paying particular attention to the hat. She had recently decided to go into the millinery business.

"You've inspired me, Laurel. I, too, can have a career. One that uses my talents," she'd said. It was true that Emily had developed exceptional skills with a needle and thread. With her sense of style and Mother sharing her experience as a milliner herself, Emily was destined to make a name for herself in Philadelphia fashion.

When she finished her inspection, tears filled her eyes.

"Oh, Laurel, you are lovely. I hope someday I fall deeply in love and look as beautiful as you on my wedding day."

"What about Emmett Miller? He's sweet on you." I tickled beneath Emily's chin.

"That big oaf? I could never love him. Besides, if I'm going to start my millinery business, I'll need a man who respects and supports me. Like your Cillian."

"You have no problem accepting his gifts of candy and flowers." Mother pursed her lips as she admonished Emily. "If you're not careful, he'll get the wrong idea."

"I never asked for those things. I hardly speak to the man. Is it my fault he can't take a hint?"

"Emily Ann—"

Before Mother could scold Emily and put her in a foul mood, I wrapped my arm around my sister and led her toward the door. I kissed her lightly on the cheek as I tucked a loose strand behind her ear.

"Someday soon, you'll meet the perfect man for you, I promise. In the meantime, go find Father and let him know I'm ready."

As I reached for the doorknob, a loud knocking echoed through the room, and I found Father on the other side of the door. Dressed in a gray striped suit and a black vest with gold buttons, he looked as dapper as I'd ever seen him. Between his hands, he spun a shiny top hat.

"Well, it looks as though my ladies are ready. Laurel? Shall we?"

"Yes, Father. Is everyone here?"

"It looks as though they are. Your groom is waiting anxiously at the front of the church. If you don't hurry, he'll come looking for you."

"Well, we better get out there." As Mother went through the door, Sampson appeared and offered his arm to escort her down the aisle. Father kissed Mother quickly on the cheek as she disappeared around the corner.

"I'm next." Emily rushed out of the room, snatching up a nosegay of daisies on her way.

"Well, my dear. There's no turning back now." Father chuckled and extended his elbow for my hand. As we walked down the short hallway toward the sanctuary, I stopped before the heavy oak door. Emotions whirled inside me. I had so much to say.

"Father, wait, please."

"Not having second thoughts, are you?"

The pipe organ blared out the wedding march, so I knew I didn't have much time.

"I want to thank you for accepting Cillian, even welcoming him into our family."

"Why, I've come to recognize him as a fine young man— even if he is Irish." Father's chuckle couldn't hide the glassy reflection in his eyes. "He's a lucky man to have you."

"I know I've never said it, but thank you for throwing me out of the house that night."

"Not my finest moment, I might say."

"No, but because of it I found Gramma and Helen and Charles and Robert, Cora and Belle. For that, I thank you."

Father looked down and cleared his throat, swiping his

large hands over each eye. He coughed into his fist and then raised his chin, which quivered as he spoke. I'd never seen him so close to tears.

"I should thank you. If it weren't for you finding my mother and her settling things between us in her letter before she died, I would still be holding in all that resentment. I hope I can be a better father to you in the future."

"And I a better daughter."

We pulled each other into a warm embrace and suddenly jumped apart when the organist banged out the prelude with ferocity unlike anything I had ever heard.

"That's your cue." Father gathered my hand in his, pressing a kiss to the back of it. "Time to walk my little girl down the aisle."

The usher swung the door open and the congregation rose as I floated down the aisle, casting smiles at family and friends. Helen and Charles were in the fourth row, having a hard time keeping Cora and Belle from rushing forward to greet me. I smiled at Robert and his family, sitting in the pew in front of them. Aunt Sarah and Uncle Jeremy, Father's siblings, who I hadn't seen since I was a child, were seated with their families behind Mother, Sampson, and Elvin. Since Gramma's passing, all of Father's siblings—halves and wholes—had visited one another and were now keeping up regular correspondences.

Passing the last pew, I blew a kiss to Mother, who was furiously dabbing a lace handkerchief to her eyes. I had promised myself I wouldn't cry, but seeing Mother so overcome with emotion made my eyes sting. All these people who were here today were part of the story that led me to this moment. I was suddenly overwhelmed. Father stopped our march in front of the reverend and I turned to Cillian, standing tall and strong. His posture couldn't hide the emotion in his eyes.

The next few moments were a blur as the pastor welcomed everyone, Father handed me off to Cillian, and the ceremony began. I only absorbed a few words of the pastor's sermon as Cillian and I gazed deeply at one another. Until I had lowered my defenses and let him in, I never could have imagined the depth to which I could love him. He was my rock, my protector, and my biggest supporter.

The reverend was in for a surprise when it was time to recite our vows.

"Please repeat after me," he began. "I, Laurel Rose."

"I, Laurel Rose."

"Take thee, Cillian Aengus, to be my husband."

"Take thee, Cillian Aengus, to be my husband." I barely contained my glee at speaking that word for the first time.

"I promise to love, honor, cherish, and obey you all the days of my life."

"I promise to love, honor, and cherish you all the days of my life."

"I prom—" The reverend stopped and glared over his spectacles at me. I simply smiled back at him.

"Go ahead, Father," I whispered.

"Do as the lady says." Cillian smiled down at me and gave my hands a gentle squeeze. "We wouldn't want her to break her vows now, would we?"

The congregation erupted in laughter. Mother dragged her handkerchief across her brow and Father shook his head. Despite the flowers, the organ, the beautiful satin gown, and reception to follow, there would be very little about our marriage one could call traditional—and that suited the two of us just fine.

ACKNOWLEDGMENTS

The Truth of the Matter began on a snowy day ten years ago when I signed up for Ancestry.com. My kids were away at college, my husband was at work, and I had the house to myself. Right away, I was sucked down the rabbit hole of my family's history. For the next several weeks, I feverishly poured over every census report, death certificate, marriage license, and military record I could find until I stumbled onto something unusual and shocking that would become the inspiration for this novel.

I discovered that in the early 1800s, my great-great grandmother had been married with four children when her husband died. She then hired my future great-great grandfather as a farmhand soon after he arrived from England. They lived together unmarried and had two children until my great-great grandfather was convicted of stealing a horse, a high crime in 1848, and was sentenced to eight years in the Maryland State Penitentiary in Baltimore.

The story had so many holes that I could not have filled without the help of my sister, Pamela Howard—the true genealogist in the family. Pam gathered newspaper articles about his arrest and trial. She took me to the county courthouse to search wills and land records. We visited the Maryland State Archives where we discovered that our great-great grandfather hadn't returned home but had actually died in prison of enteritis—inflammation of the small intestine due to food or drink contamination. Pam's contribution to the research was invaluable, and I can't thank her enough. She also did a final read and edit of the manuscript before it went to print which I truly appreciate.

I also have to give a special thank you to Rebecca Faith Heyman for her developmental and line editing. She pushed me to bring the characters to life and make the story stronger.

Thank you to Susan Gottfriend for her eagle-eye proofreading.

Thank you to the talented Shona Andrew for creating a beautiful cover, which captured the essence of Laurel's story.

Thank you to my daughter, Liza Fleming, who beta-read the story in its early stages, and edited smaller parts of the book.

Thank you to my husband, Pat, my son, Tom, my daughter, Liza, and my son-in-law, Jose, for all of their love and support.

Most importantly, thank you to my great-great grandparents who loved and lived through difficult times. Without them, I wouldn't be here to tell their story.

ABOUT THE AUTHOR

Leigh Fleming is an award-winning author of romantic suspense, and has published contemporary romance. *The Truth of the Matter* is her first work of historical women's fiction.

Leigh lives in West Virginia with her husband and her deaf French bulldog. When not writing, she enjoys reading, travelling, scrapbooking, and spending time with friends.

Contact Leigh at
leigh@leighfleming.com
Website: http://www.leighfleming.com
Follow her:
http://www.facebook.com/leighhflemingauthor
http://www.twitter.com/leighhfleming1
http://www.instagram.com/lhfauthor

Made in the USA
Coppell, TX
06 July 2021

58623165R00203